MW01124629

The Death of Dahlgren Place

A Brooklyn Tale

Eliot Sefrin

iUniverse, Inc.
New York Bloomington

The Death of Dahlgren Place
A Brooklyn Tale

iUniverse books may be ordered through booksellers or by contacting:

iUniverse
1663 Liberty Drive
Bloomington, IN 47403
www.iuniverse.com
1-800-Authors (1-800-288-4677)

ISBN: 978-1-4401-2909-4 (sc)
ISBN: 978-1-4401-2910-0 (ebook)

Printed in the United States of America

iUniverse Rev. 5/28/2009

To Dara and Josh, who grew up hearing stories about growing up in Brooklyn.

Part 1

New cities have always replaced old cities, by periods. But today it is possible for the city of modern times, the happy city, the radiant city, to be born.

—LE CORBUSIER

Nothing is too good for the people of the Empire State.

—ROBERT MOSES

Chapter 1

The news arrived in a whisper. It was big news back then in Brooklyn, but you'd never have known it from the quiet way it landed on people's doorsteps. Hardly anyone noticed when the paperboy swung his shiny Schwinn onto Dahlgren Place, pulling copies of the *Bay Ridge Spectator* from his canvas saddlebag and flipping them casually onto front yards and stoops. He disappeared just as quickly, too, pedaling out of our cul-de-sac as if fleeing the scene of a crime. He might as well have been. The news he was delivering was that unnerving.

We had no idea anything unusual was going on. Why would we? At thirteen years old, my friends and I didn't pay much attention to stories in our neighborhood weekly. Besides, we were fully engaged in the king of Brooklyn street games, Ringalevio, in which opposing teams launched massive manhunts, imprisoning opponents in imaginary prisons before trading sides. The game had our undivided attention.

Others on our block, however, weren't immersed in such playful escape.

"Nathan," one of our neighbors, Mr. Sandusky, called to me. He was pacing the sidewalk, his doughy belly bulging against his white tank top and spilling over his waistband.

"NAY-THIN!" he bellowed.

That got my attention. I stopped running and looked up.

"Where's yer ol' man? He home yet?"

"Nah," I replied, breathless. "He should be home soon."

It was already close to 6 PM. I knew my father would be rounding the corner any minute. Most working men arrived back in Bay Ridge around that time, pouring out of the Fourth Avenue subway stops, where the BMT's R-line ran through downtown Brooklyn into Manhattan. Within half an hour, nearly every bar along the subway route would be three-deep with guys angling for elbow room. My father always came straight home, though. He never was much of a drinker. A little schnapps at our annual Family Circle meetings—that was about it.

"Well, make sure yer ol' man sees me right away," said Mr. Sandusky, a copy of the *Spectator* in hand. "There's somethin' important I gotta talk to him about."

"Sure thing," I promised.

Until that moment, the day had been entirely ordinary, thick with the smothering haze that blanketed Brooklyn all through the summer of 1959. With my friends and me starting high school in mere weeks, we were anxious to squeeze as much fun as possible into our waning time off. We'd begun the day with stickball at the P.S. 104 schoolyard, and had spent most of the afternoon flipping baseball cards in the cool, baroque lobby of Tommy Lowery's apartment building. After Ringalevio and a quick supper, we'd be heading to the garage rooftop of the Schmidts, two houses away, to catch the Tuesday night fireworks spectacular at Coney Island.

Or so we thought.

"Hey there, slugger," my father chirped, smiling broadly as he ambled up Dahlgren Place, toolbox in hand.

He was dressed as usual—in the tan Chinos and blue shirt worn by all the mechanics at the company he worked for. Stitched in white above his left breast pocket was the company's name, Mergenthaler Linotype of New York. Above the other pocket, in matching script, was my father's name, Arthur.

He was midway down the block when Mr. Sandusky intercepted him.

"Ya seen this week's *Spectator* yet, Artie?"

"Nah, what's up?" asked my father, setting down his toolbox. I edged closer to listen in.

"Read this, will ya?" Mr. Sandusky held up the paper. "It's about this bridge the city's supposedly gonna build."

"A *bridge*?"

"Yeah. Believe that? A goddamn bridge."

"Where?"

"Right here in Bay Ridge. 'Cross the Narrows."

Mr. Sandusky rapped the newspaper with the back of his hand and thrust it at my father, who accepted it curiously, his eyes narrowing as he began to read.

Splashed across the front page was an artist's rendering of an enormous bridge, arching rainbow-like across the narrow channel separating Brooklyn from Staten Island. Below it was a map detailing Brooklyn's westernmost quadrant and the section of Staten Island nearest the channel. A thick, dotted line spanned the waterway, connecting the two boroughs. An article about the proposed bridge consumed the entire page.

"This story says the bridge is pretty much a done deal," Mr. Sandusky said. "The money's in place. The state's signed off on it. All that's left is for the city to approve construction and get the necessary … whaddaya call 'em ?"

"Rights-of-way?"

"Yeah, that's it. All they gotta do is buy the land they need and start buildin'."

Our game of Ringalevio had come to an abrupt halt by now. Everyone gathered around the two men. I watched as my father read the story, deliberate and studious as always.

"Holy shit," he muttered.

It wasn't often that I heard him curse. I knew whatever he was reading had to be serious.

It was.

According to the *Spectator*, the city was indeed planning to build a huge suspension bridge between two projections of land occupied by Fort Hamilton in Brooklyn and Fort Wadsworth in Staten Island—a pair of defense fortifications that once guarded the main entryway to New York Harbor. The mile-wide tidal strait between the forts, linking Upper and Lower New York Bays, represented the thinnest passageway into the harbor, a bottleneck that shielded New York's most precious natural resource, its deepwater port, from fierce Atlantic storms. Known as the Narrows, it was considered the optimum location for the bridge, the article stated. We lived about a hundred yards from its shoreline.

"Jeez," my father said. "According to this, that bridge'll be right on top of us."

"Wait," Mr. Sandusky interrupted. "The bridge ain't even the *worst* of it."

"Whaddaya mean?"

"Check this out," our neighbor said, opening the newspaper to its centerfold. On it was another map, detailing a block-by-block section of Bay Ridge and the adjacent neighborhoods of Fort Hamilton and Sunset Park.

Mr. Sandusky and my father spread the newspaper across the trunk of our Plymouth and leaned in to study it. My friends and I drew in closer.

"See," said Mr. Sandusky, running a finger across the map. "The *real* problem ain't the bridge. It's the *road* that leads to the bridge."

My father studied the map, the impact of what he was reading becoming resoundingly clear in his expression.

"Holy shit," he muttered again.

And with good reason.

In order to provide access to the proposed bridge, the *Spectator* article said, engineers would have to build a lengthy approach and a pair of immense on-off ramps on the Brooklyn side of the Narrows. The impact of that on Bay Ridge, it was clear, would be profound. Planners would literally have to scythe their way through the neighborhood, clearing broad swaths of land and demolishing everything in their path. Telephone poles, utility lines, water mains, and other infrastructure would have to be relocated. Entire streets would have to be rerouted or eliminated. Dozens of stores and businesses along Seventh Avenue, the neighborhood's busiest commercial thoroughfare, would need to be leveled. Worst of all, nearly eight hundred private homes and several apartment buildings would have to be razed, and more than seven thousand residents relocated.

By the time the project was completed, in an estimated five years, Bay Ridge would be permanently transformed. The expressway, requiring twelve-foot-wide traffic lanes and equally wide shoulders, would literally slice the neighborhood in two. Traffic would pour through to the tune of thousands of vehicles a day. Elevated sections of the roadway would see traffic riding literally above the rooftops of the remaining dwellings. Other sections would run below existing streets, so that the only way to traverse the massive road would be through a series of overpasses.

"And this ain't no *ordinary* road we're talking about," Mr. Sandusky said. "Hell no. It's one of them *expressways* they're buildin' all over the country."

My father said nothing, his eyes flitting across the page.

"We're talkin' a *superhighway* here," Mr. Sandusky continued. "Two-hundred-feet wide. Trucks, tractor-trailers, buses, and other commercial traffic travelin' at high speed. Noise, exhaust fumes, congestion, the whole *magilla*."

Finished with the story, my father lowered the newspaper to his waist, as if it had grown too heavy to hold.

"They can't really be buildin' this road through Bay Ridge, can they?" he asked.

"Damned if I know," Mr. Sandusky said. "But according to this story, they sure as hell *are*."

"But what'll that mean for us?"

"It'll be like a knife," Mr. Sandusky said grimly. "A knife through the heart of Dahlgren Place."

My father, immersed in thought, again said nothing.

"If that road comes through here, Artie, we're *finished*," Mr. Sandusky said. "All of us. Bay Ridge. Dahlgren Place. Everything. We're dead and buried."

Suddenly, my father seemed ashen, his eyes dull, his curly black hair matted, as if the news had washed over him like a tidal surge. His gaze swung westward toward the Narrows, its waters sparkling in the late-afternoon sun as if surfaced with diamonds.

"Dad," I said, reaching for his arm.

But he was silent, unmoving. All he did was stare into the distance, as if trying to envision a sudden new course for our life—something that, until that very moment, had never so much as crossed his mind.

Chapter 2

It was to be a bridge like none other, planners said—an architectural masterpiece that would vault the entryway to New York Harbor, serving as a majestic gateway to America's greatest city. Taking a staggering three hundred and twenty million dollars to build, its description alone was couched in superlatives. It would be the world's longest suspended water crossing, the crown jewel of a public works program that had shaped New York City across half a century. Its beauty, city officials gushed, would be breathtaking, its lifespan nearly limitless. A soaring fusion of engineering and art, it would fire the imagination of New Yorkers, inspire visitors, and offer travelers a sweeping panorama of the booming metropolis—Upper and Lower New York Bays, the Statue of Liberty, the Manhattan skyline, the docks and piers of the world's mightiest port.

There'd be far more to the bridge, however, than simply its size and scope.

For one thing, officials said, a bridge across the Narrows would unify New York for the first time, connecting Staten Island at long last to the city's four other boroughs. That alone was significant. Then tied more closely to neighboring New Jersey than to the city of which it was a part, Staten Island was still largely a forgotten borough—isolated, sparsely populated, accessible only by ferry. And access was hardly easy. Ferries were often jam-packed with commuters. The city's aging fleet was prone to breakdowns. Ice and fog made harbor crossings time-consuming, even hazardous at times.

Those problems, planners reasoned, would be instantly remedied with the building of a Narrows bridge. Such a bridge, they said, would shorten the crossing between Brooklyn and Staten Island to several unimpeded minutes. Freed from its isolation, New York's forgotten borough would be opened to development at a critical time in the city's growth. Commerce would be stimulated, too. No longer would the delivery of goods to New York be hamstrung by a frustrating stop-and-go journey through Manhattan's traffic-clogged streets; a Narrows bridge would allow easy access to the city, generating millions of dollars in toll revenue to boot. Connected to existing bypass routes, it would facilitate travel from New York to points north, south and west, serving as an essential link in the East Coast interstate highway system. It would similarly link New York for the first time to mainland America, literally connecting the old world to the modern age.

But more than of that, advocates said, a Narrows bridge would stand as a *symbol*.

Not merely a proud addition to New York's wealth of bridges, it would be nothing less than a dramatic statement about the spirit of enterprise that was possible, more than anywhere, in America's greatest city. It would symbolize the dynamism that permeated postwar New York, a city of unbridled energy and audacious dreamers; a city asserting itself as the unquestioned global center of commerce, culture, finance and intellect; a city in which literally *nothing* was beyond the realm of possibility.

The bridge, at the same time, would make a resounding statement about America, as well. Buoyed still by its World War II victory, America was very much on the move in the 1950s—flexing its muscles, expanding its outreach, fulfilling its role as the most powerful nation on earth. Fueled by billions of dollars in federal funds, a vast network of superhighways was taking shape across the length and breadth of the country, transforming the very face of the nation's landscape. Freeways and interstates were radiating in all directions, connecting city to countryside, tying industrial America to the nation's rural heartland. Bridges and tunnels were spanning rivers and ravines. Highways were being built through valleys and forests, across desert and farmland, over and around mountain ranges. Expressways were being carved through the nation's expanding urban terrain. The past was fading. A bold new era of modernity was taking hold, a bright new future beckoning.

Highways and bridges were seen as doorways to that future, arteries through which the lifeblood of commerce, prosperity and growth would flow. Even more, they were seen as the physical expression of a proud, dynamic nation seeking to tame its wide open spaces—nothing less than a reflection of the prevailing American spirit: that of an optimistic, energetic people embracing the future, celebrating their innate wanderlust, expressing their love of freedom and the open road.

The bridge across the Narrows, advocates said, would serve to symbolize that spirit. Not only would it usher in an exciting new decade—the 1960s—it would remind the world that good old American ingenuity could surmount any obstacle, overcome any challenge, light the way for the rest of the world. The bridge would represent a rousing new pinnacle for technological achievement, a testament to how technology could serve, even grace, humanity—solve our problems, inspire us, move us forward.

Forever, planners asserted, the bridge would change New York in a profound and positive way. Forever, they said, it would serve the city and its people.

CHAPTER 3

The news about the impending bridge spread through Bay Ridge like an unchecked virus, shattering the neighborhood's usual sleepy, late-summer calm.

Within hours after the *Spectator* story broke, much of the neighborhood was in an uproar. People milled about on sidewalks and stoops, trying to make sense of the drama enveloping them. Shopkeepers stood outside their stores, comparing notes, wondering aloud if the crisis could be as dire as it seemed. On some streets, the mood bordered on outright panic. People's fears were compounded by skepticism, confusion, and outrage.

"I can't believe the city is just going to march in here, take our street, and force us to move," said Mrs. Pedersen, who'd drifted along with several neighbors into our cul-de-sac. "This can't be real. It can't be happening."

Nightfall had descended by now and Dahlgren Place was bathed in the amber glow of curbside lampposts. As usual, the street was swarming with activity. A group of girls took turns jumping rope and playing Potsy, a form of hopscotch. Down the block, kids played Kick the Can, shot cap guns, and spun hula hoops, still a year-old craze. On the edge of the cul-de-sac, smaller kids raced about, giggling and chasing fireflies through a thicket of spindly young trees. In the distance, the fireworks at Coney Island lit up the ink-black sky, amid faint crackling sounds and spent flares cascading to earth.

The fireworks were rendered inconsequential, however, by the matter at hand.

"Just like that they're gonna throw us outta our homes?" asked Mr. Sandusky, dragging on a half-smoked Chesterfield. "And for what? A *bridge*? Who the hell needs a bridge?"

"We sure don't," Mrs. Pedersen said.

Indeed, the whole idea seemed unfathomable. The mere *location* of Dahlgren Place had always provided a palpable sense that we were sheltered from the world at large, far from the sight line of city officials and, in many ways, virtually invisible. Few cars ever traversed our street. Outside of us, the only people who seemed to know it even existed were our mailman, our milk and soda deliverymen, the Dugan's Bakery man who went door-to-door selling pastries, a pair of Fuller Brush and *World Book Encyclopedia* salesmen, and the Good Humor and Bungalow Bar ice cream trucks, whose jingling bells drew hordes of kids on steamy summer nights.

Suddenly, though, our quiet, forgotten street seemed exceedingly visible—and just as vulnerable. Situated literally at the foot of the proposed bridge, Dahlgren Place lay directly in the path of the proposed expressway.

"This bridge'll destroy us." Mr. Sandusky flicked his cigarette to the ground and stamped it out.

"I don't know what we're gonna do," echoed another neighbor, Leo Banion. "What's gonna happen to us? Where're we gonna live?"

No one, it seemed, had a ready answer.

About a dozen adults, including my parents, were now huddled together, their faces contorted in the glow of the lampposts. My friends and I stood off to a side, mature enough to feel threatened, but sufficiently naïve to feel confident that somehow, someone would figure out a way to save the day.

"To be honest wit' you, I don't believe a word of it," barked Gus Pappas, who lived down the block. A burly, ruddy faced man who drove a delivery truck for Brooklyn's most popular bakery, Ebinger's, Mr. Pappas was accompanied by his dog, a lean young boxer that tugged on its leash.

"I been hearin' rumors 'bout a bridge for more'n twenty years," Mr. Pappas sniffed. "All they ever amount to is a lotta hot air."

"Really think so?" someone asked.

Mr. Pappas yanked on his dog's leash and the boxer let out a whine.

"Hell, yeah," he scowled. "Hot air's all it is. Face it—no one in Bay Ridge wants a bridge. People won't stand for it. Ain't a politician in Brooklyn who'll have the guts to support it. He'd have his ass handed to him on a platter."

Several people laughed, seeming momentarily relieved. Everyone wanted in the worst way to believe Mr. Pappas. And, in reality, they had every reason to do just that.

Rumors about a Narrows bridge, in fact, had rumbled through Bay Ridge for decades, surfacing as far back as a century earlier, when railroad officials had pushed for a freight tunnel that never left the drawing board. Other proposals—doomed by fiscal constraints, approval delays, conflicting political interests, two world wars, and stiff neighborhood opposition—had met a similar fate. The last serious proposal, thirty years earlier, had seen the city actually begin work on a twin-tube railway tunnel, only to see funding evaporate midway through the project. The only remaining evidence of the aborted tunnel was two abandoned, ninety-foot-deep holes near the Brooklyn shoreline, marked by a pair of rotting wooden palisades. Local residents had a derisive name for the tunnel shafts. They called them "Hylan's Holes," after John Hylan, New York's mayor at the time.

Given this history of failed attempts, most people in Bay Ridge had long since convinced themselves that any talk about a Narrows bridge was simply idle banter, nothing more than the wistful dream of city planners. And everyone had gone about their lives as if any such plan would never see the light of day.

Until now.

"I'm tellin' ya, most people want nuthin' to do wit' no bridge," Mr. Pappas reiterated. "Trust me. Even the military's against it. From what I hear, the Defense Department opposes any bridge seaward of the Brooklyn Navy Yard. They're afraid that if there's another war, the bridge could be blown up and our warships would be trapped in New York Harbor."

"I'm not so sure about that anymore," Mr. Sandusky demurred, and everyone looked his way.

Mr. Sandusky was well respected on Dahlgren Place—not as well respected as my father, perhaps, but someone whose opinion mattered. The owner of a TV repair shop, his was the only house on our block to have a rooftop antenna; the rest of us still had a pair of rabbit ears sitting atop our living room consoles. By our standards, Mr. Sandusky was nothing short of a visionary.

"I hear the military ain't as opposed to a bridge as they once were," he said. "From what I hear, they ain't that worried anymore about our ships being trapped in the navy yard. Now that we got missiles and atom bombs, ships don't matter as much as they did during World War II and Korea."

Even Mr. Pappas was quieted by that.

"In fact," Mr. Sandusky continued, "that's why the country's supposedly buildin' all these roads and bridges in the first place."

"Why's that?" someone asked.

"It's because in case of a nuclear attack, the government needs mass evacuation routes outta the city. A lot of the highways they're buildin', from what I hear, are really military routes."

None of us knew if he was right or not, but Mr. Sandusky's remarks sparked a private debate between me and my friends, a quirky collection of postwar street urchins.

"We'll be the first to get hit if the Russians drop the bomb," Vincent Pucci declared.

Contentious and irreverent, Vincent, known as Pooch, had a quick wit and an edgy, wise-guy persona. Savvy and tough, he was perfectly suited to flourish on Brooklyn's competitive street scene. He was also the best, if unlikeliest, friend I'd ever had—Italian, while I was Jewish; swaggering, while I was shy; a swift, muscular counterpoint to my bookish, slower-moving persona. Despite our differences, though, the two of us were nearly inseparable—except at school, where I was in the more advanced classes.

"Why'll we get hit first by the Russians?" Tommy Lowery asked.

"Brooklyn's part of New York, knucklehead," Pooch replied. "We got all these important companies here. The stock market. The Empire State Building. The Statue of Liberty. New York's like the freakin' capital of America."

"I dunno," demurred Lowery, a plodding, roly-poly kid garbed in a striped T-shirt, dungarees, and high-top Keds. Everyone called him Lumpy, after the pudgy character from the TV show *Leave it to Beaver*.

"My father says Washington DC will be the first place bombed," Lowery said.

Pooch squinted, as if mulling the possibility. He hitched up a pair of dungarees patched at the knees, then turned his belt buckle askew, in the affectation of a street hood.

"Whadda *you* think, Wolf?" he asked me.

He never called me by my given name—Nathan—always by my surname.

"Tell us. You're the one wit' the brains."

"I dunno. Lumpy could be right," I decided. "Washington's got the White House, Congress, the Pentagon. You knock those things out, kill the president, all the senators and the army brass, and who's gonna make decisions?"

Everyone pondered that for a moment.

"How 'bout the places where we got our naval bases?" offered Nick Pappas, whose father, Gus, was still insisting that the bridge story was simply a rumor. "The Russians could hit them or our missile silos first."

"And what about Pittsburgh, where our steel factories are?" Lumpy Lowery asked.

"All of them are targets, I guess," I said.

It certainly was something to think about, smack dab in the middle of the Cold War like we were.

"They're up there spying on us, ya' know," Pooch warned.

"Who is?"

"The Rushkies, knucklehead," he replied.

All of us gazed skyward, trying to catch a glimpse of an orbiting Sputnik, glowing ominously in the nighttime sky.

"Khrushchev will probably hit us everywhere at once," Pooch concluded. "Half our country will be wiped out. Then we'll wipe out the Russians. The only ones left will be some freakin' natives livin' somewhere in caves."

We stifled our laughter, given the serious nature of the adult conversation around us.

"I dunno," Mr. Sandusky said. "I know we never got a bridge in Bay Ridge all these years. But things … sure feel different this time."

I saw looks of concern creep across people's faces.

"Haven't ya seen all them boats anchored in the Narrows?" Mr. Sandusky asked.

"What about 'em?" someone inquired.

"I hear they're drillin' for somethin'. Testin' what's under the water."

"Probably seeking soil samples and taking soundings to determine the underwater topography," my father said. He knew about stuff like that.

"Whaddaya mean, Artie?" Leo Banion asked.

"That's part of the planning process," my father explained. "If they're gonna build a bridge, engineers need to know what things look like under the water, and what kind of surface they're dealing with."

"See—what did I tell ya?" Mr. Sandusky said, his viewpoint validated by my father's observation. "Would they be doin' all that if they weren't serious 'bout a bridge?"

No one uttered a word.

"And what about the planes?" Mr. Sandusky asked, even more ominously.

"*What* planes?"

"Haven't you seen 'em? All these small, single-engine jobs buzzin' around lately? I hear they're up there takin' aerial photos, so engineers can map the route for the expressway."

"Ah, nuthin' but rumors," Mr. Pappas scoffed.

"Maybe, maybe not," Mr. Sandusky said. "But I don't think this bridge talk's just a rumor this time. I think somethin's really gonna happen. We're gonna get a bridge in Bay Ridge, all right, and a lot of people are gonna get hurt … unless we figure out some way to stop it."

The adults stood around talking deep into the night. Most of them were still out on Dahlgren Place long after the ice cream trucks made their rounds and the street emptied of kids and the fireworks ended at Coney Island.

Despite all the talk, though, no one could really be sure where things were headed. No one could be sure what a bridge might mean for us, the neighborhood we called home, and the life we'd led on our quiet little street. No one could be sure about any of that anymore.

Chapter 4

We were ordinary. Even with the uncertainty swirling around Bay Ridge now, that was one thing we could all be certain about: Bay Ridge was as ordinary as the Narrows bridge would be spectacular. An inconspicuous speck on the sprawling landscape of Greater New York. A collective entity of people and places that paled in importance to the historic project on the drawing board of planners. Overshadowed, like Brooklyn itself, by the towering presence of Manhattan.

Absent New York's iconic landmarks, lacking the fame or social weight of the city's exclusive enclaves, our neighborhood, by most standards, was run of the mill—a community of Average Joes in a city run by Power Players, a quiet, provincial enclave woven into the patchwork of the seventy-odd neighborhoods that comprised postwar Brooklyn.

Like Bay Ridge, most of those neighborhoods had assumed their modern-day shape half a century earlier. It was then that sailboats, ferries, and newly opened East River bridges began allowing waves of working-class New Yorkers to escape their rundown Manhattan tenements and secure inexpensive housing in Brooklyn's expanding frontier. Buses, horse-drawn railroads, and trolleys soon provided greater access, with sections of Brooklyn becoming fashionable among affluent businessmen seeking an easy commute to jobs across the river.

Then came the subways.

The advent of subway service into Brooklyn's vast, undeveloped midsection fueled a 1920s housing boom unparalleled in New York's history. Large tracts of vacant land were swallowed up nearly overnight. Stores sprang up, along with schools, banks, hospitals, and places of worship. Roads and sewer lines were built. Municipal services were introduced. Before long, Brooklyn's population had swelled to more than two million, and the balance of New York's population had shifted forever. One in every three New Yorkers lived in Kings County now.

With a thick web of subway lines soon sprouting across the borough, Brooklyn's growth literally exploded, fed by successive waves of immigrants lured by jobs in the borough's factories, warehouses, and docks.

The Irish, escaping their famine-ravaged homeland, settled in Brooklyn's northwest quadrant. Jews, fleeing the dumbbell apartments and "lung blocks" of the Lower East Side, clustered in Williamsburg, Brownsville, Crown Heights, and Borough Park. Italians, in search of tree-filled neighborhoods reminiscent of Italy, formed enclaves in Gravesend, Greenpoint, and Gerritsen Beach. Germans, drawn to Brooklyn's busy breweries, settled in Bushwick and adjacent enclaves in the borough's eastern district. Scandinavians, lured by the city's thriving maritime trade, established homes near the waterfront. Others—Greeks, Poles, Ukrainians, Hungarians, Syrians, and Lebanese among them—soon followed.

And Brooklyn absorbed them all.

One by one, the borough's neighborhoods took shape—each a product of common roots, ethnicity, religion, language, race, and class. Many rose up around the water that surrounded Brooklyn on three sides. Red Hook was developed as a breakwater for ships docking at the city's bustling harbor. Gowanus was settled around an industrial canal. Other neighborhoods took shape as developers spread into Brooklyn's expansive southern tier. Second- and third-generation immigrants pushed into neighborhoods like Bensonhurst, Midwood, Flatbush, New Utrecht, and Marine Park. Still others followed. And soon, Brooklyn had become a patchwork of small neighborhood-towns—ethnic epicenters whose streetscapes often reflected old world hamlets. Each had its own distinct sights, sounds, cuisine, and character. Each had its own architecture and landmarks. Each had boundaries that were often only vaguely defined, but were well known by residents.

Bay Ridge was typical of those neighborhoods in every way.

Except for its location.

Originally called Yellow Hook because of its rich deposits of yellowish clay, the neighborhood's name was changed after a nineteenth-century yellow fever epidemic, its current name reflecting its two most prominent features: a steep, centuries-old glacial ridge that ran through parts of the community, and its location at the westernmost point in Brooklyn, near the surrounding New York Bay.

With its long stretch of shorefront and its panoramic view, Bay Ridge in its early days had served as an exclusive summer retreat for New York's elite. Elegant restaurants and fine shops lined its streets. Yacht races and polo matches drew crowds of wealthy denizens. High atop a bluff overlooking the Narrows, a string of fashionable villas, country estates, and luxury hotels sat fronted by lush green lawns, shade trees, tennis courts, swimming pools, and bathhouses. Adjacent to those dwellings was Fort Hamilton, whose buildings, barracks, and parade grounds were spread across a hundred and fifty acres.

But Bay Ridge, like other Brooklyn neighborhoods, had changed dramatically through the years. Open space, once plentiful, had long since been gobbled up, and nearly all the early estates had been subdivided into more affordable forms of housing. A parkway and seawall now separated the neighborhood from the Narrows. A string of modest homes and six-story brick apartment buildings occupied the high ground near Fort Hamilton, which was still in use as an army induction center.

The only constant amid all the change was the long stretch of shoreline that abutted the Narrows and gave Bay Ridge the distinct feel of the sea. The neighborhood, at its western perimeter—nearest New York Harbor and the Atlantic Ocean—still retained its original open, airy feel. The scent of salt, carried inland by bay breezes, was pervasive. Each day, a procession of oil tankers, freighters, barges, tugboats and ocean liners streamed past on their way to sea or to harbor berths in Brooklyn and Manhattan. Ferries and pleasure craft plied the channel. All along the shoreline, people picnicked, sunbathed, strolled, biked, and fished the foamy, white-capped waters.

Like its appearance, Bay Ridge's population had also changed over time, altered by decades of ethnic succession.

In its early years, emigrant Norwegians, Swedes, Danes, and Finns—many displaced by the collapse of the Scandinavian shipbuilding industry—were lured to the neighborhood because of its proximity to Brooklyn's teeming docks. The subway lines brought a potpourri of second- and third-generation Italians, Irish, Greeks, Lebanese, Russians, and Jews.

Despite this influx, however, Bay Ridge retained a distinct Scandinavian feel. Known by some as Little Norway, the neighborhood possessed the largest Scandinavian population in America outside of Minnesota. Eighth Avenue was known informally as Labskaus Boulevard, the Norwegian name for a hearty stew. Shops named Olsen's, Leske's, and Hinrichsen's dotted streets with names like Frederickson, Johannsen, and Bakke. Newsstands stocked Scandinavian newspapers. And every May 17, commemorating Norwegian independence from Sweden, thousands of people in colorful costumes marched in the largest annual *Syttende Mai* parade outside of Oslo, gathering to crown Miss Norway at a statue of explorer Leif Ericson.

By the 1950s, Bay Ridge, in many ways, was a metaphor for the typical middle-class Brooklyn neighborhood. Its people worked not in the spotlight of New York's glamour industries, but in the city's shadows and underbelly. Its men held jobs as cops and firemen, truck drivers and postal workers, deliverymen and mechanics, longshoremen and construction tradesmen. Its women, for the most part, were housewives. Those who worked outside the home did so part- or full-time in typical roles: as dressmakers, secretaries, nurses, teachers, or school aides. The vast majority remained home each day, tending to family and household.

Consistent with its blue-collar makeup, Bay Ridge was devoid of any distinct social hierarchy. Few families could be considered wealthy; most worked hard simply to make ends meet. Traditional values were the norm. People raised families, tended to their homes, and went quietly about their lives. Flags were hung on Memorial Day, Flag Day, and the Fourth of July. Homes and lawns glittered with garlands of holiday lights and colorful nativity scenes for weeks around Christmas. Modest houses of worship reflected the neighborhood's diverse ethnic mix.

Bay Ridge also *looked* like most Brooklyn neighborhoods. Anchored at the corners by drugstores, candy stores and stately looking banks, its main thoroughfare, Seventh Avenue, was lined with dozens of stores tucked into three-story walkups housing offices and apartments. Cars, delivery trucks, and buses wound their way along the avenue. Shoppers moved in and out of stores, and past fish, fruit and vegetable stands that jutted onto sidewalks tattooed with discarded chewing gum. Store windows were affixed with colorful decals: Ex-Lax, Coca-Cola, Salada Tea, Cat's Paw Heels, Optimo Cigars.

Those kinds of stores, in large part, gave Bay Ridge a familiar, down-home feel. Jonas Millinery sold spools of thread, yarn, and other sewing products. Kleinfeld's, a popular wedding outlet, catered to crowds of would-be brides. At Phelp's Pharmacy, pill bottles were stuffed into glass-fronted cabinets behind a high counter and massive cash register. At Hessemann's Grocery, men used long wooden poles to jostle dry goods stacked on ceiling-high shelves, and then caught and packed the groceries, tallying their prices on brown paper bags. At Caruso's Barber Shop, five chairs were busy with men getting haircuts and shaves. At Rose's Beauty Salon, women seated under bullet-shaped hair dryers leafed through magazines while awaiting manicures or appointments to have their hair pressed, curled, or dyed.

Similar stores stretched on for blocks.

At Holstein's Butcher Shop, its floor sprinkled with sawdust, sides of beef hung behind refrigerated cases stocked with cuts of meat and poultry. At Hinsch's Ice Cream Parlor, circular spinning stools stood on gleaming checkerboard tiles in front of a soda fountain and polished mirrors. At Norma's Bake Shop, white-aproned women, their hair bunned in nets, wrapped and boxed pastries. At Thumann's

Candy Store, vending machines stocked with Chicklets, Pez, Sen-Sen, mixed nuts, colored dots, and other penny candy fronted an entryway lined with newspaper racks.

The scene was much the same on the neighborhood's other major thoroughfare, Eighty-sixth Street, which ran beneath the elevated D-line—its service roads lined with restaurants and stores, the shadows cast by overhead railroad ties falling across the street as if through the slats of a giant Venetian blind.

But if its thriving shopping district housed Bay Ridge's *heart*, the neighborhood's *soul* resided on its narrow, leafy side streets. Atypical of the city's rigid, rectangular grid-like layout, many of those streets seemed to meander without rhyme or reason. Cul-de-sacs, curvilinear drives, and step-up streets bled into dead-ends, blind alleyways, and cross-streets lined with an eclectic mix of homes. Attached and semi-attached one- and two-family brick homes with peaked roofs, chimneys, and hand-carved archways stood alongside modest, closely spaced aluminum-sided homes. Arts-and-crafts dwellings abutted Greek revival homes. Waist-high wrought-iron gates fronted tidy, well-tended lawns. Stoops, sided by brick walls and balustrades, protruded onto sidewalks. Clotheslines were strung from bedroom windows to backyard trees. On some blocks, luxury apartment buildings with names like the Royal Poinciana and the Chatelaine were set behind rows of tall, well-trimmed hedges.

To those of us who lived there, though, there was more—*much more*—to Bay Ridge than its look, its location, or its population mix.

To us, Bay Ridge was familiar.

We knew the neighborhood inside out—its terrain and its landmarks, its sights and sounds, its boundaries and nuances. We knew where everything was and the quickest way to get there: fences we could climb; shortcuts we could traverse; pathways through backyards, over garage rooftops, and down alleyways.

It was self-contained.

Everything we needed—schools, stores, the library, the post office, the bus and subway stops—was there at our fingertips, able to be reached in minutes.

It was intimate.

We saw the same people all the time—shopping, tending to their homes, chatting with teachers at school. People routinely passed each other on sidewalks, waved from stoops, made small talk, kept an eye on each other's homes, minded each other's children, borrowed openly from one another. People knew their neighbors. Shopkeepers knew their customers by name, regularly extending credit, offering free candy to children.

It was communal.

Lives were out there for everyone to see. Windows were open. Doors were unlocked. People could see into other's homes, overhear conversations, and smell food cooking. On most summer nights, people sat street side, lounging on folding chairs, stoops, fire escapes, porches and rooftops—trying to escape the stifling heat.

It was vibrant.

Bay Ridge possessed a rhythm, a pulse as familiar as it was palpable. Traffic flowed along its streets. People moved in and out of its stores. Children played in its playgrounds and schoolyards. Groups of teenagers sang doo-wop on street corners and in apartment-building lobbies. Knots of people stood in front of appliance stores to catch glimpses of the television sets they'd soon be buying.

And it was manageable.

New York, even Brooklyn, was far too overwhelming to digest in its entirety. But Bay Ridge, orderly and self-contained, enabled us to experience city life in a bite-sized way. Within its borders we could experience the essence of small-town life in the largest city on earth. We could feel anchored amid the enormous web of neighborhoods that comprised New York's complex fabric. We could feel secure in the vast, shifting sea of people that defined America's greatest city. We could feel, for the most part, in control of our lives.

Above all else, though, Bay Ridge was *ours*—something we could identify with, something we could call our own. It was the one place on earth where we felt comfortable, rooted, connected to one another, whole. It was our *neighborhood*—something to cling to, cherish, and preserve. In many real ways, it was our world. In other ways, equally as real, it was *us*.

To lose it, most of us felt, would be like losing a part of who we were. In some ways, it would even be akin to dying.

Chapter 5

It didn't take long to discover that the story about the bridge was true. Early-morning telephone calls to the *Spectator* bore confirmation. Frantic calls to the office of Alan Sherman, who represented Bay Ridge on the City Council, further confirmed that not only was a Narrows bridge indeed in the final planning stages, but that the proposed approach to the bridge followed a path directly through the heart of Bay Ridge. Both bridge and expressway were merely awaiting formal city approval, Sherman's office said. And approval, as things stood now, seemed highly likely.

It was the worst possible news for most people in Bay Ridge, and neighborhood concern, tempered initially by doubt over the story's veracity, was quickly replaced by wholesale panic and a billowing rage. Almost immediately, what had begun as a series of impromptu street gatherings about the bridge morphed into a full-blown, organized rally to protest the city's plan.

The rally took place at P.S. 104, a thirty-year-old, red-brick elementary school several blocks from Dahlgren Place. About three hundred residents, including my parents, flooded the auditorium, where speakers waited onstage to address the overflow crowd.

"Let's take our seats so we can begin," Walter Staziak coughed into a microphone set center-stage on a tall wooden lectern. "We have a lot to discuss."

The restless audience came to order.

Well known throughout Bay Ridge, Staziak was president of the local chamber of commerce. His pharmacy, a neighborhood landmark for thirty-seven years, was located on Seventh Avenue, directly in the path of the proposed expressway, as were the stores of several other merchants seated onstage. Alongside them were Councilman Sherman and an associate of Michael Esposito, a state assemblyman said to be at a legislative session in Albany.

"I think we all agree that the bridge and its planned approach will prove catastrophic to Bay Ridge," Staziak began. "Homes and businesses will be demolished. Thousands of us will be forced to move. Property values will plunge. We'll face major traffic issues. Our entire way of life will be destroyed."

"Is this really gonna happen?" someone yelled from the crowd.

"I'm afraid it might—if we allow it," Staziak responded.

The audience buzzed.

"I don't see how the supposed benefits of this bridge will justify what would happen to Bay Ridge if it was built," Staziak continued. "A beautiful neighborhood will be destroyed and cruelty inflicted on its people, all in the name of progress. But this progress, in reality, is not progress at all—only change for the worse. Frankly, I question not only the *location* of this bridge, but the *need* for it at all."

"Yeah, why the hell do we need this bridge?" a man shouted, his gravelly voice bristling with contempt. "We need someone from the city to come here and explain why Bay Ridge has to pay such a heavy price for a project New York has done fine without for two hundred years."

The audience applauded.

"If they wanna build a bridge so bad," someone shouted, "let 'em find another neighborhood to sacrifice!"

Again, the audience applauded.

Staziak stepped aside, as Chester Jablonski, a local funeral director, ambled to the podium. Angular and taller than the squat Staziak, Jablonski twisted the microphone wire to accommodate his height.

"This project demonstrates a blatant disregard for everything we hold dear," he said. "These are our homes and our neighborhood we're talking about. It's everything that's important to us. We can't allow the city to take it! We can't stand still while monstrosities like this bridge are planned behind our backs!"

"You're goddamned right!" another man bellowed.

Nearly the entire audience swiveled in their seats as the man, whose name was Joey Palumbo, rose to speak. A retired longshoreman and ex-marine, Palumbo had lived in Bay Ridge forty-two years and was known for his no-nonsense language and fiery temper. He also, it was rumored, had ties to mob leader Albert Anastasia, whose brother Anthony purportedly controlled the Brooklyn docks.

"Damn this bridge and the people who planned it!" snarled Palumbo, his flattop needle-like, a *Semper Fi* tattoo on his chiseled forearm. "What gives the city the right to play God with people's lives?"

Riled by the rhetoric, the audience cheered.

"I resent being forced from my home," shouted Palumbo. "I resent that the city feels it can impose its will on us."

Whistles and hoots rang through the auditorium.

"You know what the city's gonna turn Bay Ridge into?" Palumbo asked. "They're gonna turn it into another Sunset Park!"

Immediately, the audience hushed.

"That's right," Palumbo repeated. "*Sunset Park*!"

Palumbo, it was clear, had hit a raw nerve. Any reference to Sunset Park had a somber impact on people from Bay Ridge. And with good reason.

LIKE OTHER NEIGHBORHOODS, Sunset Park was tucked into Brooklyn's quilt-like mosaic, mere blocks from Bay Ridge, literally bleeding into parts of the adjacent community. In some ways, however, it could easily have been a world away.

Named for a popular greensward near its East River border, Sunset Park had begun as a vibrant, working-class neighborhood whose growth had paralleled Brooklyn's evolution as a major maritime port.

Known for years as South Brooklyn, the neighborhood consisted mainly of factories, shipyards, warehouses, piers, and hundreds of machine shops, trucking firms, and other waterfront suppliers.

Its streets teemed each day with thousands of longshoremen, warehousemen, cargo handlers, truckers, and others tied to Brooklyn's bustling docks. It also served as the site of the Brooklyn Army Terminal, a processing center for troops and supplies during World War II, and Bush Terminal, a sprawling industrial complex of rail yards, storage facilities, wharves, and loft-style manufacturing spaces.

But that hardly defined everything Sunset Park was.

For years the neighborhood had also been home to thousands of northern and western European immigrants—a living, breathing community whose heart and soul resided on Third Avenue, a bustling commercial street similar to the main thoroughfares in Bay Ridge.

Then right before World War II, everything changed. It was then that the city unveiled plans to construct a massive highway to serve as an extension to the existing Brooklyn-Queens Expressway and form part of an enormous loop encircling four New York boroughs. Plans dictated the highway be built atop the pillars of an elevated subway line above Third Avenue.

Sunset Park residents pleaded with city officials to consider an alternate route, requesting the highway be built one block to the west. Not along Third Avenue, but closer to the waterfront. Not through the heart of the neighborhood, but through the industrial landscape of Bush Terminal.

They staged protest marches and demonstrations at City Hall and the state capitol in Albany. They waged an extensive media campaign. They fought for months to preserve the essence of their neighborhood: those homes and businesses in the roadway's path.

In the end, however, they lost.

Despite pleas from political allies, protracted public hearings, and an intense legal battle, the city prevailed: Interstate 278, better known as the Gowanus Expressway, was built.

The immense new roadway swooped down from an existing overpass and entered an enormous trench that was carved through the very center of Sunset Park. Streets were obliterated. Homes were leveled. Landmarks were demolished. More than a hundred stores were razed. Over three thousand families were relocated. And Sunset Park nearly died.

The construction of the Gowanus Expressway delivered a staggering blow to the neighborhood, tearing apart the very fabric of the lively, tight-knit community. Soon after it was built, the roadway was carrying thousands of vehicles a day, many of them trucks and diesel tractor-trailers. The steady stream of traffic brought the noxious odor of gasoline and exhaust fumes into homes. Apartments vibrated with noise spikes and blaring horns. Residents suffered nausea, headaches, and other ailments. Unable to sleep or even hear each other talk, many abandoned rooms nearest the congested expressway, moving their belongings to the rear of their apartments.

But that was only part of it.

Underneath the expressway, Third Avenue had been transformed from a quiet four-lane street into a major ten-lane thoroughfare. Impossible for residents to even cross safely, the street literally quaked with the steady, unrelenting rumble of overhead traffic. Water, formed by condensation, dripped from the concrete pillars supporting the roadway, collecting in festering pools. Debris from overhead traffic littered the ground. Even worse, the elevated roadway obliterated almost all sunlight, casting a permanent shadow across the street.

Robbed of its very sunlight, Third Avenue quickly lost its appeal. Hundreds of residents moved. Property values plummeted. Panic spread. Unable to generate enough business to survive, or even sell out, shopkeepers simply boarded up and left. As commercial life eroded, sideway security withered, and as crime soared, so did insurance premiums, driving many remaining businesses into bankruptcy. The once-vibrant street assumed a ghostly, uninviting feel.

And the blighting effect spread.

The Gowanus Expressway had created, in effect, an enormous wall between the industrial and residential sections of Sunset Park. Isolated physically, socially, and economically from the rest of the neighborhood, sections of the community deteriorated. Neglected by homeowners and landlords, buildings decayed. Homes were dumped at discount prices. Into the vacuum moved less-desirable newcomers. Vagrants took up quarters in vacated apartments and local parks. Drug addicts and derelicts occupied abandoned buildings.

Vandals roamed the neighborhood, smashing windows, destroying shrubbery, scrawling graffiti on walls and fences, urinating and smearing excrement in hallways and elevators.

Before long, Sunset Park had assumed the look of a neighborhood ravaged by a horrific disease. Rats picked through rubble in empty lots. Saloons, sex parlors, pawn shops, and check-cashing stores replaced restaurants, shops, theaters, and other businesses on Third Avenue. Shards of glass and bags of trash lay rotting near the ravaged hulks of dumped, stolen automobiles.

More important, Sunset Park, in a very real way, was considered dead to its remaining residents. The neighborhood had literally been disemboweled. It had lost its identity, its soul, everything that once made it unique and appealing. Its people had been uprooted, severed from their sense of place, disconnected from everything familiar and safe. Families had been split and friendships destroyed. An entire way of life had been lost.

It was obvious now that the Gowanus Expressway had been only part of a much larger plan—the next step being for the city to extend the road through Bay Ridge, enabling an eastern approach to the planned Narrows bridge. It was equally clear to most people that, if the city's plan was realized, Bay Ridge faced a fate similar to that of Sunset Park. Bay Ridge, too, most everyone felt, would be ruined. Bay Ridge, too, would be killed by the road.

JOEY PALUMBO CLIMBED atop his seat in the auditorium, craning his neck so he'd be visible to everyone.

"I'm tellin' ya, as God is my witness, I'm not gonna let what happened to Sunset Park happen to Bay Ridge!" he shouted.

The audience began to chant in unison, their collective voices rumbling through the auditorium and echoing through the hallways of P.S. 104.

"No Sunset Park!"

"No Sunset Park!"

"No Sunset Park!"

"We've got to fight this bridge plan with every ounce of strength we got," implored Walter Staziak, barely audible through the din. "Everything we own, everything we love, everything we fought for during the war, is at stake. Our homes. Our businesses. *Everything*!"

The audience let out a rousing cheer.

"We need to make everyone in Bay Ridge aware of what's going on," Staziak said. "We need to make *a lot* of noise. We need to tell the city, loud and clear, that we don't want an expressway rammed through our neighborhood, and we're not gonna let 'em take our homes!"

The cheer, this time, was deafening.

Then Staziak beckoned Alan Sherman to the microphone and the local councilman took center-stage.

Born and raised in the Jewish enclave of East New York, Alan Sherman had attended Brooklyn College and received a law degree from NYU, serving as a public defender in New York's criminal court system before beginning his political career by organizing the Flatbush Tenants Council, the largest tenants' advocacy organization in the state. Although his actions at the FTC had attracted favorable press, Sherman's greatest political asset was, perhaps, his sparkling, biscuit-colored eyes and sunny, disarming personality. Buoyant and blithe, he was widely seen as a Democratic up-and-comer, a smile rarely far from his lean, clean-shaven face.

Except for now.

"I agree with everything that's been said—and I want you to know you have my unqualified support," the councilman said grimly.

Then he gestured toward the rear of the auditorium, where Joey Palumbo remained perched atop his seat.

"I agree with you, too, Joey!" he beamed. "A bit less vocally, perhaps—but just as passionately."

The audience laughed nervously, then calmed.

"The plan for this bridge," Sherman resumed, "is clearly not in the best interests of Bay Ridge. We must stand together and deliver that message to the city."

The audience applauded politely.

"You know what *I* think we ought to do?" Joey Palumbo shouted. "I think we ought to kick their fat asses back to wherever the hell they come from."

The audience laughed again, more lustily this time.

Sherman calmly raised a hand.

"I understand your emotions, but there are more appropriate ways of expressing our feelings," he reasoned. "Let's pursue those avenues first."

Then he smiled and winked at Palumbo. "We'll revert to your suggestion, Joey, if nothing else works."

The audience seemed placated.

"The important thing to remember is that the more of us who speak, the more forceful our message will be," said Sherman, shifting his gaze toward the representative of Assemblyman Esposito, who nodded.

"They've got to hear what we're saying clear over to City Hall," Sherman said. "They've got to hear us in Albany and Washington, too. We need to make it resoundingly clear that the people of Bay Ridge want no part of this bridge or the disruption it'll bring to our lives."

The rally lasted four hours, adjourning with a collective vow to strongly oppose the city's plan. A meeting to develop a definitive protest strategy was scheduled for the following night at Sherman's office. Walter Staziak, Chester Jablonski, and several others were designated to spearhead the effort.

Then the audience dispersed, weary but determined to band together for the fight to save their neighborhood, their homes and, in some cases, their very lives.

Chapter 6

It was well past midnight when my parents trudged in from the P.S. 104 rally. My sister was chatting on the living room phone with a girlfriend. I was watching a rerun of *The Day the Earth Stood Still* on The Million Dollar Movie, heeding the chilling warning of the alien Klaatu and memorizing the only words that could save Planet Earth from destruction by the robot Gort:

"*Klaatu barada nikto! Klaatu barada nikto!*"

"What are you still doing awake?" my mother asked. "It's kinda late, don't you think?"

"Never mind that," my sister said, hanging up the phone. "What happened at the rally?"

"There was a meeting," my father replied calmly. "People expressed their opposition to the city's plan to build a bridge and expressway."

"So the whole thing is really true," my sister said. "I knew it. I just *knew*."

"The only thing that's true at this point is that the city has a plan," my father said. "But a lot of people are vowing to fight it."

"What do you mean *fight*?" I asked.

"I mean people will express their concerns to the officials in charge. Hopefully, they'll listen to the protests and discard their plan."

"What are the chances of that?"

"To be honest with you, we're not sure."

"But I don't want to move," my sister protested. "I can't believe the city's gonna make us leave this house, maybe leave Bay Ridge altogether."

At fourteen, my sister was a year older than me, the image of my mother at that age—auburn hair set shoulder-length in a flip, her cheeks angular and smooth. Unlike either of our parents, however, she was prone to melodrama, the spontaneous outbursts of a teenager.

"Let's not jump to conclusions," my father said. "Nothing's been decided yet. This could all just be a lot of nothing. Until we know for sure, we can't know *what* to think."

"I *already* know what to think," my sister said flatly.

"And what's that?"

"My life is ruined. I'll have to go to a new school. Make new friends. Start a whole new life."

"I think you're getting a little carried away, Beth," said my mother.

"Yeah," I chimed in.

"You shut up!" My sister glared at me. "*You* don't have to worry. You're just *starting* high school. I'm already in the middle of it. Moving would be worse for me than anyone."

"It would be bad for me, too," I said. "I love Bay Ridge, too. You're not the only one."

"Why don't *both* of you calm down," my father suggested. "Having to move would be hard on all of us. But there's no need to panic. Let's see what happens first with the anti-bridge protests."

He was good that way, my father: rational and calm no matter the circumstances. My mother was the same: reasoned and intelligent, and although more intuitive and emotional than my father, also rarely prone to outbursts.

My parents were right, I thought. There was nothing to get overly concerned about yet, no reason for hysteria. The two of them would deal with whatever crisis might be looming. Just like they always had, they'd figure out a way to make everything all right.

CHAPTER 7

They were barely in their teens when they met, a couple of kids from working-class enclaves drawn to a weekend dance at the Jewish Community House, a popular recreation center in a quiet Brooklyn neighborhood known as Bensonhurst.

It was 1936 then, and for the first time since they could remember, things were looking up. It would be five full years yet until the Great Depression would release its viselike grip on New York, but the monstrous cloud that had hovered over the city since the stock market crash seemed, at long last, to be lifting. The shantytowns along the East and Hudson Rivers were gone by then. So, too, were the relief lines on Broadway—the queues of gaunt, desperate men waiting for stale bread and scraps of food—and the legions of lost souls sleeping under blankets of newspapers in the empty water mains of Central Park.

New York was rising again.

New Deal money, funneled through a rash of federal agencies, was flowing virtually uncapped into the city. Thousands of WPA workers were building hospitals, schools, highways, bridges, and airports. Playgrounds were opening, along with beaches, zoos, marinas, and ball fields. Central Park, a shameful ruin for years, was being transformed into an oasis of gardens, shade trees, walkways, terraces, sculptures, and flowing fountains.

It was a time of renaissance. You could see it, feel it.

In midtown Manhattan, soaring, newly built spires—the Empire State Building, the Chrysler Building, Rockefeller Center—reached to the sky. In Queens, a desolate wasteland was being transformed into the site of the World's Fair, a dazzling vision of the future. All around the city, federally funded artists were painting murals on the walls and lobbies of buildings, as if the artwork itself could somehow ennoble the public realm, lift people from their despair, give them reason to hope.

Even the tired old neighborhoods of Brooklyn were being touched by the rebirth, with magnificent outdoor swimming pools opening almost weekly that summer to huge, excited crowds. No longer were blue-collar Brooklynites forced to flee the sweltering heat by dousing themselves in jets of water from uncapped fire hydrants, or swimming in waterways clogged with industrial waste. Now they could go to McCarren Park in Greenpoint, where a new open-air swimming complex featured spacious brick bathhouses, banks of glass-block windows, and decorative details inspired by Roman imperial architecture. They could go to the Sol Sussman Pool in Red Hook, climb the broad granite steps, walk through solid bronze doors, and swim in an Olympic-sized pool with filtered water and underwater lights. They could go to Sunset Pool, high above the Brooklyn docks, and lounge on a shaded rooftop terrace so close to Wall Street and dreams of wealth that they could almost reach across the river and claim them as their own.

To my parents, shaped and calloused solely by hard times, 1936 was a year of small but palpable miracles. It was a year to look ahead, to breathe, even to dream.

Then it got even better. Then they found each other.

THE GYM AT the JCH was pulsing that night with laughter and the swirl of young bodies. Music poured from a scratchy Victrola: Rodgers and Hart, Irving Berlin, and George and Ira Gershwin; the swing music of Goodman and Basie; songs from the new Lucky Strike *Hit Parade*; familiar old standards by the tunesmiths of Tin Pan Alley.

Tentative and awkward around girls, my father mingled with a group of boys on one side of the gym. Against the opposite wall, my mother sat with several girls on a row of bridge chairs. On the sneaker-scuffed basketball court between them, dozens of couples danced the Foxtrot, the Lindy Hop, the Shag.

My mother walked clear across the gym to meet him. Girls didn't do that much back then, but my mother was never shy. Something about my father caught her eye—his alert gaze and easy smile, she told us later—and she just decided to go meet him.

"You belong to the J?" she asked.

Startled, my father retreated instinctively, squaring the padded shoulders of his tobacco-colored blazer, tucking his arms in to hide the blazer's patched pockets. Speechless, his heart racing, he simply stood in place and drank in the sight before him.

My mother was beautiful back then, womanlike even at thirteen, looking all grown-up in lipstick and rouge. Her blue organdy dress, its hemline at mid-calf, had yellow polka-dots and a bow tied just beneath the neckline. Her skin was smooth and unblemished, fresh with the scent of Coty. Her reddish-brown hair, shoulder length and wavy, seemed iridescent in the overhead lights of the gym.

"I don't really belong ... I just play basketball here sometimes," my father stammered.

"How often you come?"

"Coupla times a year. You?"

"Me, too. Only to the dances, though."

"Where you from?"

"Thirteenth Avenue in Borough Park. What about you?"

"Grand and Humboldt streets. Williamsburg."

Trapped momentarily by awkward silence, the two glanced absently around the gym. The music was slower now. Lanny Ross was singing "Stay as Sweet as You Are."

"I'm Lillian," said my mother, extending a hand. "Lily Kramer."

"Artie Wolf," my father said.

"Well, Artie Wolf," my mother smiled, "wanna dance?"

Then, before he had a chance to utter a response, she took him by the hand and led him onto the floor. And, before long, they were dancing easily, laughing and chatting, lost in the moment, caught up in the music.

Fred Astaire was singing "Cheek to Cheek," the same way he was doing it on Broadway in *Top Hat*. Nelson Eddy and Jeanette MacDonald, America's singing sweethearts, were crooning, too. Then "Smoke Gets in Your Eyes," from the Broadway musical *Roberta*, came on. Then a Billie Holiday song and a Harold Arlen tune about having the world on a string. And, before long, someone was singing "Now's The Time to Fall in Love," the same way Eddie Cantor used to on his weekly radio show.

And my father gazed at my mother—radiant and smiling, innocent and young—and he was struck by the thought that, yes, what they were singing about might really be possible. Anything might be possible on a summer night like this. It might be possible, even, to fall in love.

And, quickly, they did.

On their first date, the following Sunday, they took a ferry ride, sailing from a dock in Sheepshead Bay across a broad, sun-drenched inlet to Breezy Point, at the western end of the Rockaway Peninsula. There, they spent the day gazing out past the breakers to the vast Atlantic horizon, wondering what the world was like on the other side of the ocean. They feasted on hot dogs, custard and cotton candy, and strolled down gas-lit, cobblestone streets lined with shorefront bungalows, tiny boutiques, and eateries. They talked endlessly. They laughed. And on the ferry ride home to Brooklyn, they kissed for the first time, the mist-like spray from the vessel's wake cool on their faces, the distant city skyline catching the shimmer of sunset across the waters of New York Bay.

It was right then and there, my mother told us later, that the two of them fell in love.

"*She* fell in love that day," my father would tease. "*I* still wasn't so sure."

"Oh, he was sure—don't kid yourself," my mother would say, casting a crooked gaze at him.

And my father couldn't help but smile.

Yes, he'd admit, already they were very much in love.

Chapter 8

Lying in bed after the P.S. 104 rally, I tossed in the darkness, trying to slip into sleep. Outside, the lights from the amusement rides at Coney Island cast their familiar band of clean white light across the nighttime horizon. In our backyard, the tall plants hugging our house rustled gently with a bay-borne breeze that rung a buoy somewhere off in the Narrows.

Sleep, however, was proving more elusive than usual.

Flooding my mind were thoughts about the crisis facing Bay Ridge—the bridge that could spell the end to our way of life; the expressway that could chew apart our familiar, beloved neighborhood; the unwelcome possibility of being forced unwillingly from our home.

I thought about what my father had said about angry residents fighting the city over the bridge plan. I still wasn't sure exactly what that meant. Would people actually be *fighting* on the streets? Would it be a *rumble*, like the pitched battles in the toughest neighborhoods of Brooklyn, where rowdy gangs fought one another with bats, chains, knives, and zip guns?

And who'd win a fight like that?

The city had a lot of tough cops, I was sure of that. They could probably even call in the army. But there were a lot of tough guys in Bay Ridge, too: construction workers, truck drivers, ex-GIs, longshoremen like Joey Palumbo. They'd put up a pretty good fight if it came to that, I was convinced. And what about the cops who *lived* in Bay Ridge? Whose side would they be on? If tested, where would their loyalties lie?

It was a lot for a thirteen-year-old to ponder.

But there was even more to wrestle with at the moment. Tucked securely beneath the bedcovers, my transistor radio was tuned to a broadcast of the Dodgers' game, still only half-complete, even past midnight, because of the West Coast time difference. I adjusted the tuner to pick up a clearer signal. Over the static, I could make out the voice of Dodger play-by-play man Vin Scully.

"The *Dah-jahs*," Scully said in his rich, syrupy tenor, "are trying to scratch their way out of a bases-loaded jam here in the fifth."

Scully sounded the same as always, painting vivid imagery with his words, building drama, allowing the crowd noise to augment the tension and emotion. But listening to a Dodgers' game now was nothing like listening to it when they'd played in Brooklyn. Nothing at all.

Back then, we'd lived so close to Ebbets Field that some nights I could see the arc lights of the cozy bandbox stadium brighten the nighttime sky; I could imagine hearing the crowd roar with each big hit. Now, the Dodgers were half a world away, far from sight, well out of earshot. It was hard for me to get my arms around.

The Dodgers should have never left Brooklyn, I thought. Ebbets Field shouldn't be lying abandoned on Bedford Avenue, reduced to a venue for high school games and demolition derbies, soon to be replaced by a bleak, city-run housing project. The Dodgers had no business playing in California. Their caps didn't even look right with an L.A. logo stitched to them instead of a *B* for Brooklyn. It wasn't fair that their home games started so late at night that all I could catch was the first few innings off some scratchy, faded radio signal.

I wasn't sure if I should even be a *fan* anymore.

Why should I? Most of my favorite players were either at the end of the line or already out of baseball. Pee Wee Reese, Jackie Robinson, and Gil Hodges had retired. Duke Snider and Carl Furillo were playing out the string. Don Newcombe had been traded to Cincinnati. Worst of all, Roy Campanella, the great catcher, was confined to a wheelchair, paralyzed after his horrific car crash on Long Island. The rest of the players had simply disappeared—evaporating into a swirling mix of betrayal and anger, disillusionment and hurt. They weren't around to root for anymore. You couldn't see them on the streets, like we once did, when many of them actually lived in Brooklyn, rented homes in Bay Ridge, took the subway to work like my father, ran local errands like the rest of us.

How could I root for them now? They were no longer around. No longer real. No longer mine.

But if I couldn't root for the Dodgers, who *could* I root for? The Giants had left for California, too, and New York, the capital of baseball all my life, suddenly had only one big league team—the Yankees. And no matter how great they were, I just couldn't bring myself to root for them. Not after they'd pummeled the Dodgers so mercilessly for so many years. Not after I'd grown up, like everyone else in Brooklyn, hating their guts.

Things sure weren't as clear-cut as they used to be.

I thought about that, too—wishing things were the way they'd once been, wishing that when you liked something, it could just stay the same, always. Never change unless you wanted it to.

But that wasn't possible. The Dodgers leaving Brooklyn had taught me that. And now the specter of a bridge and expressway seemed poised to drive the point home again.

"What's the score, slugger?" my father whispered, peeking in through a crack in my bedroom doorway.

Startled, I moved to click off my transistor, but quickly realized I didn't have to. He knew the radio was tuned to the ballgame—and it was all right. He was easy that way. He knew that if he were me, he'd be listening to the Dodger game, too. Just like me: Lost in thought. Lost in his fantasies. Lost in his dreams.

WE WERE ALIKE that way, my father and me. He was a dreamer once, too. Residing, at my age, in a world of grandiose plans and glittering possibilities. Convinced then, like I was now, that he'd somehow find a way to soar above his mundane surroundings. Certain, despite the Depression's harsh realities, that a boy from working-class Brooklyn could do big and important things with his life.

Inspired by the New Deal programs transforming New York, my father dreamed of building great public works projects like the ones lifting the city from its Depression-era malaise. He dreamed of building stately government buildings like the venerable landmarks—the Jefferson Building, the Arbuckle Building, the old Kings County Courthouse—that he saw in downtown Brooklyn. He dreamed of building Beaux Arts museums and tall-pillared libraries like the ones that graced Eastern Parkway; monuments like the Soldiers' and Sailors' Memorial Arch at Grand Army Plaza, with its carved spandrel figures and heroic bronze reliefs; majestic structures like Manhattan's Penn Station, modeled after the ancient Roman Baths of Carcalla, and Grand Central Station, its Park Avenue façade evoking the triumphal gateways of ancient Roman cities.

Those were the things that inspired a quiet, glowing hope in my father. Those were the things he dreamed about creating while growing up in the squalid tenements of Williamsburg. Tangible things. Lasting things. Meaningful things that would enrich people's lives and stand for something noble and important.

And he wouldn't have to go far to learn how to build them, either. That was what made the dream even more exciting, even more real. He'd learn everything he needed to know right there in Clinton Hill, minutes from where he lived. Right there in Brooklyn. Right there at another New York treasure. Right there at Pratt.

Founded half a century earlier by Brooklyn's richest man, Charles Pratt, The Pratt Institute was the leading college in America for urban design and architecture. My father longed to go there.

At Pratt, he reasoned, he'd study all the great architects. He'd study the giants who'd ushered in the Age of the American Skyscraper: William Le Baron Jenney, the father of them all; William Holabird, the founder of the Chicago School; and Cass Gilbert, who'd designed the Woolworth Building, New York's own gothic masterpiece. He'd study the works of Henry Hobson Jacobson, the first American who'd broken from European traditions, and the Bauhaus genius of Walter Gropius, who'd just fled Nazi Germany for sanctuary in Great Britain. He'd study America's most famous architect, Frank Lloyd Wright, of course, along with Louis Sullivan, the modernist who'd trained Wright, and Stanford White, whose Fifth Avenue mansions were the focal points of high society.

At Pratt, he'd study them all. And then, one day, maybe he, too, could build things like that: wondrous, inspiring things that would last for centuries and symbolize something noble; bold civic architecture that would remind the world that he'd left his mark and aspired for more than just an average Brooklyn life.

But dreams were worthless currency in 1930s Brooklyn. Even with the Depression winding down, blue-collar families like my father's remained in dire straits. College and its passage to a better life required a tariff few could afford. Most boys from Williamsburg attended high school a couple of years, at best, and then traded in their heady dreams for the stark necessity of a steady paycheck.

My father was no exception.

Pushed by his own father, a down-on-his-luck furrier, to learn a trade, he enrolled at Manual Training High School—a vocational school that specialized in carpentry, plumbing, masonry, and electrical work—dropping out in his sophomore year to help with the family's finances. Armed with the skills of an apprentice machinist, he landed an entry-level job mere blocks from Pratt, close enough to pass the college on his way to work each day, close enough to feel the things he wanted to do with his life slipping, like sand, through his fingers.

He was fifteen when his dream about becoming an architect ended. If there were to be any other big, bold dreams in his life, he'd have to stumble blindly upon them, somewhere along the way, and seize them if he could. Or watch as others—perhaps even me—lived big, bold dreams of their own.

"ANY SCORE?" HE repeated about the Dodger game on my transistor.

"Nothin' yet."

"Who they playin'?"

"Pittsburgh."

"Who's pitchin'?"

"Koufax."

"How's he doin'?"

"Six strikeouts, six walks in five innings. No one can touch his pitches, but most of the time he can't get the ball over the plate."

"Give him time," my father said. "Sometimes, even for the great ones, all it takes is time."

"Still think he'll be great?"

"Yep."

Young and wild, but potentially brilliant, Sandy Koufax was my father's favorite big-league ballplayer. It was easy enough to understand why. Even though Koufax now played three thousand miles away, a lasting connection to us remained. Like us, Koufax had been born and raised in Brooklyn, attending Lafayette High School, mere miles from where we lived. As a teenager, he'd also played basketball on the same court where my parents had met, at the JCH in Bensonhurst. And, like us, he was Jewish—almost unheard of for a major leaguer.

"Your Uncle Phil and I saw him pitch a couple of times at the Parade Grounds," my father said, referring to a complex of ballfields near Prospect Park, where big league scouts gathered regularly to watch the top ballplayers in New York.

"Uncle Phil said Koufax would be special the first time he saw him," my father said. "He said he could tell by the pop of Koufax's fastball in the catcher's mitt. Made a special sound, Uncle Phil said. Like a rifle shot."

I lowered the volume on my transistor, hoping my father would stay and chat about baseball. That's what we talked about most of the time. Family aside, baseball was our one common ground, our singular constant bond. Was it trivial? Maybe—but who cared? It gave us something to talk about, a reason to be together. What else could possibly matter?

"How did *you* feel when you first saw Koufax?" I asked.

"Well, I wasn't as sure about him as Uncle Phil," my father admitted. "But I sure was happy that a Jew from Brooklyn made it to the majors. It made *all* Jews look better, you know? Made us feel good about ourselves."

My father was quiet for a moment, and then cleared his throat. I knew he was thinking not about Sandy Koufax now, but about my Uncle Phil.

My mother's older brother, Uncle Phil and my father had always been close. They'd bowled together, gone to ballgames, played cards. When my parents got married, Uncle Phil was my father's best man. The two of them even waited out my sister's birth at Junior's, a popular Brooklyn restaurant. Then, because they figured it had brought them luck, they waited out *my* birth there, too.

But then Uncle Phil got sick—stomach cancer, it was—and, just like that, within months, he was gone. Dead at thirty-eight. The same age my father was now.

"Your Uncle Phil," my father said. "Now there was someone I wish you could've gotten to know."

He paused, as if groping to find his voice.

"No one," he said, "loved the Dodgers more than your Uncle Phil."

Then he edged into my bedroom and I shut off my radio. The ballgame didn't matter anymore. I was just happy my father and I could take a few minutes to talk. Not just about baseball. About anything.

HIGH SCHOOL OVER, his dream of attending Pratt gone, my father joined New York's manual workforce, the army of tradesmen and civil servants that comprised the city's huge blue-collar base. The company he went to work for, Mergenthaler Linotype, seemed typical of many manufacturing firms in Brooklyn, operating out of a block-long factory on Ryerson Street, a stone's throw from the Brooklyn Navy Yard. Mergenthaler Linotype, however, was anything but typical.

Founded fifty years earlier by a German-born clockmaker, the company manufactured clunky, cleverly designed mechanisms known as linotype machines. Linotype machines were far from beautiful—nothing like the architectural wonders my father had dreamed of building. Their utility, though, was beyond question.

Before the linotype's invention, printers had set type by manually picking up and positioning one letter at a time. Because the process was so laborious and time-consuming, the printing industry had been entrapped for centuries in a primitive-like state: Newspapers rarely contained more than several pages; books, periodicals, and other literature were beyond the reach of mass markets.

The linotype machine changed all that. With it, type could be set mechanically by depressing the keys of a ninety-character keyboard similar to that of a typewriter. The linotype machine enabled operators to assemble a row of metal matrices containing the imprints of letters, punctuation marks, and empty space bars. The machine then poured molten lead into the matrices, resulting in a line of type—only in reverse, so that it would read correctly when inked and transferred to paper. Using a complex configuration of conveyor belts, levers, assembly boxes, and flywheels, the machine then automatically repositioned the matrices after the lead was poured.

Regarded as the greatest advance in centuries, Mergenthaler's linotype revolutionized the printing industry. A skilled linotype operator could set type five times faster than a hand-typesetter could—a gain in efficiency that dramatically increased output and reduced the cost of printed material. Newspapers grew exponentially in size and variety. Books, magazines, and other periodicals reached unprecedented numbers of readers. Entire industries relying on printed information rose and flourished. And so did Mergenthaler Linotype.

By the time my father went to work there, in 1938, the company had produced most of the typesetting equipment used by printing operations worldwide—nearly thirty thousand linotype machines in all. Mergenthaler's customer base was diverse and worldwide. Business was booming.

But that changed, too.

Within three years of his arrival, Mergenthaler's focus shifted dramatically. So did my father's life.

World War II had fully engulfed America by then, and Brooklyn's workplaces were emptying by the day, with nearly every able-bodied man lining up to volunteer for armed service. Mergenthaler, like many factories, was converted to a defense facility and began producing armaments for the U.S. Navy. My father joined the Army Air Force and shipped out overseas. And my mother, fresh from high school, went to work at a company called Eberhard Faber, where she worked on an assembly line making pencils. And waited for the war to end, so she and my father could marry.

Like many couples then, they didn't wait quite that long.

Instead, on his first leave, in 1943, my father returned stateside and married my mother in a large, domed synagogue on Ocean Parkway, a broad, tree-lined avenue that reminded my mother of a boulevard she saw in a newsreel about Paris. She wanted to start their married life that way, she said. She wanted it to feel as much like a fairy tale as it possibly could in a world torn apart by war.

FOR A LONG while, their life together felt that way, too. Romantic. Ascending. Not quite like a fairy tale, but close enough. Not quite like Paris, but good enough for Brooklyn.

The war over, their long wait ended, my parents lived, contentedly for the most part, in a converted attic in Borough Park, while my father worked double shifts at Mergenthaler and my mother went searching for a house of their own.

Her search, quite by accident, led to Dahlgren Place.

Obscure enough to be unlisted even on New York's official records, Dahlgren Place was tucked into a quiet corner of Bay Ridge, swallowed up almost entirely by the crosshatch of thoroughfares around it. The entire street, in fact, was only five blocks long, terminating on one end at Seventh Avenue and dead-ending on its other end into a cul-de-sac on which five modest houses sat on high ground overlooking the Narrows. About a hundred yards behind them, through a tiny grove of trees, stood Fort Hamilton, close enough for residents to hear the daily blowing of reveille and taps.

Dahlgren Place was linked to the army fort by more than proximity, however. The street had actually been named in honor of John A. B. Dahlgren, an ordnance expert known for his invention of a massive, muzzle-loading cannon with explosive-proof walls at its breech. Able to pierce not only wooden vessels, but also ironclad ships and coastal fortifications, the Dahlgren gun had been an important weapon for the Union Navy during the Civil War. A pair of the bottle-shaped cannons, their muzzles long since plugged, still stood symbolic guard over the entryway to New York Harbor—positioned as if they were safeguarding Dahlgren Place, as well.

My mother instantly fell in love with the quiet little street. She fell even more in love with one of its houses.

Hidden almost entirely by a row of tall, unkempt hedges, the house was barely visible as my mother and a realtor looped their car around the cul-de-sac after making a wrong turn.

"What's that?" my mother asked, pointing to a rusting, tilted For Sale sign.

"I'm not sure," the realtor replied.

They found out, to their mutual delight, soon enough.

Behind the hedges, nearly obscured by overgrown vegetation, a small wood-framed house stood basking in the sunshine. The two-story arts-and-crafts dwelling was painted white with green trim. Belgian brick encircling the arched front doorway was echoed on dual chimneys and a curving walkway. Oriented to the south to make the most of daylight, the house seemed to emanate a warm, welcoming quality.

It was perfect, my mother thought. Not too big. Not too fancy. Just right.

"Why, this is a little jewel," she blurted unabashedly.

And, indeed, it was.

Built during Brooklyn's 1920s housing boom, the dwelling had been designed by the eccentric architect Clayton Smith, a disciple of Frank Lloyd Wright. Years ahead of his time, Smith had expressed his vision of residential architecture largely through Wright's concept of usonian dwellings—houses that were small and unpretentious, but resonated with a special interior quality, a personality, that evoked harmony, warmth, and a feeling of intimacy.

Scattered throughout Brooklyn, Smith's houses resonated with a unique signature. Only a thousand square feet in size, they were sensitively scaled—small enough to feel intimate but never claustrophobic; large enough to be livable but never too big to make inhabitants feel lost. Visual patterns provided connectedness. Light animated each space. Natural materials were used throughout.

The house on Dahlgren Place fit Smith's signature to a tee. Rooms flowed seamlessly from one to the other. Varied ceiling heights created a sense of openness. Built-in shelves provided display space and storage. Passageways enabled an unencumbered view from front to back. And details abounded throughout. In the living room, a coffered ceiling of hand-rubbed fir beams was set against white bead board. On either side of a fireplace mantel, display nooks were built into the walls. A rich wood pattern on the walls and wainscoting echoed the trim around windows inset with stained glass. In the kitchen, window seats built into a cheery breakfast nook enabled a view to the backyard. Even more appealing to my mother was an "away room"—a cozy little retreat separated from the adjacent living room by French doors, with bookshelves built into the walls and a desk nook tucked into a corner.

From the moment my mother entered the house, she felt the instant bond Clayton Smith had intended. There was just something about the house, she told us later, that made her feel comfortable and welcome. Houses could be like that, she said. They could embrace you, nurture you, make you feel at home.

The house on Dahlgren Place, my mother felt, was a house that was begging to be lived in. Smith himself had resided there nearly a decade before abandoning Brooklyn for Spain, where he'd lived with other American expatriates since the outset of World War II. The house had remained vacant all through the war, falling slowly into disrepair. Anxious to sell, Smith was offering it at nine thousand dollars, a hefty sum for my parents but, in many ways, a genuine bargain.

My mother saw that instantly. She saw the house for the gem it was. More than that, she saw it as a house into which she and my father could truly settle, a house into which they could pour whatever memories they'd accumulate across their lifetime together, a house they could make into a repository of everything the two of them held dear. Even the address, number eight Dahlgren Place, seemed right. Eight was a lucky number in the Jewish faith. It meant *chai*, or *life*.

"I think I found us a place to live," she gushed when my father trudged in from work that day.

He fell in love with it, too. "It does seem right for us, Lily," he said when he saw it the first time.

"This house has good bones," my mother said. "It has a heartbeat, arms we can nestle into."

She leaned in to kiss him on the cheek.

"Oh, Artie," she whispered. "It's a perfect place to raise a family, a place to build wonderful memories. Can't you feel it?"

Yes, my father agreed. He could feel it, too. The house made him feel it. So did the light in my mother's eyes, the way she looked when she spoke.

And why not believe it?

Things were finally looking up, weren't they? The Depression was behind them. The war was over. Their life together had begun. Everything they dreamed about as a couple was right there in front of them, there for the taking.

Why *not* believe?

Maybe the hard times really *were* over. Maybe it was their turn for a little time in the sun. Who knew? It could be true. You never could really count on it, of course. That was the scar left by the past two decades. You could never quite bring yourself to believe that good times would ever last. Life worked in unexpected ways, after all. You planned. And God—he just laughed.

Still, maybe. *Just maybe*.

"How are we gonna swing it, Lily?" my father asked. "Nine thousand bucks. That's a lot of money."

"I have an idea," my mother said.

Then, borrowing a thousand dollars from her parents and an identical sum from an uncle with a thriving Manhattan business, my parents took their biggest leap of faith ever. They bought the house on Dahlgren Place. And, to it, they staked their married dreams.

"THE PIRATES ARE getting better," my father said, standing at the foot of my bed.

"Think so?"

"Yeah. They got this new rightfielder, Roberto Clemente. Now, he's somethin' special. Great arm. Even better than Furillo's."

"Really?"

"Yep. He can hit, too."

"They got the best double-play combination in the league, with Groat and Mazeroski," I said. "And a good centerfielder in Bill Virdon. Solid up the middle."

"Solid pitching, too," my father added. "You watch. In another year or two they could go all the way—win the World Series."

"Beat the Yankees?"

"Why not? Anything's possible, you know. Every dog has his day. Even the Dodgers."

"What do you think about the team *they* have?"

"Heck, with the Dodgers' pitching, they could win it all *this* year."

In the stillness of my room, I could hear my father draw in a breath.

"Too bad we can't get to see 'em play anymore, huh?" he said, an uncommon heaviness in his voice.

He sounded that way whenever he talked about the Dodgers now. It was the same when he talked about Uncle Phil. Both losses, I knew, had cut deep. You could hear it in his voice. It was part of who he'd become.

"Yeah," I said. "It stinks not being able to see them."

He sighed again.

"To be honest with you, Nathan, I never thought they'd leave Brooklyn," he said. "I never thought the city would *let* 'em leave. Everyone figured Walter O'Malley was only bluffing."

"Bluffing?"

"Bluffing when he said he'd move the Dodgers to California. Everyone thought that as the team's owner, he was just putting pressure on the city. Ebbets Field was too old, too small for him. He wanted the city to build a new stadium."

"And he couldn't get 'em to?"

"Nah. The city wouldn't use public money to build O'Malley a ballpark that he alone would profit from."

"He was a greedy bastard," I said, trying to sound tough.

My father chuckled. "Well, a lot of people in Brooklyn think so. There's a riddle about him, you know."

"What's that?"

"If you found yourself in a room with Adolf Hitler, Josef Stalin, and Walter O'Malley, but you had only two bullets in your gun, who would you shoot?"

"What's the answer?"

"The answer is you'd shoot O'Malley twice."

My father laughed again. I did, too, feeling grown-up for understanding the humor, the betrayal Brooklynites felt over O'Malley's perceived villainy.

"Ah, but I don't know," my father said thoughtfully. "There's two sides to every story. Maybe, in the end, it was the city's fault as much as O'Malley's. Maybe O'Malley just saw an opportunity out West. Whatever the reason, it doesn't make any difference now. Either way, the Dodgers are gone."

My father sat at the edge of my bed, his weight tilting it toward him.

"It damn near broke our hearts to see 'em go." He shook his head. "Sure broke your Uncle Phil's heart, I'll tell you that."

He paused and pursed his lips, seeming about to cry. That was something I'd never seen. Like most men of his generation, my father was highly sentimental, but uncomfortable revealing what he felt. His emotions, I sensed, ran deep, but were tightly bound by traditional male shackles. For him to open up in any way, I knew, was special. Suddenly, I felt even more grown-up, grateful he had enough faith in me to think I was capable of understanding what he was saying, happy he was talking not just about baseball but about something he felt deeply—even if that something was connected to loss and pain.

"Well," he shrugged, "at least Brooklyn had a good run with the Dodgers. Too bad they had to leave. For a lot of years, though, it was good."

That much was true. It had been good in Brooklyn. Good in lots of ways. Good for a very long time.

IT WAS EASY for my parents to settle into the welcome arms of Number Eight Dahlgren Place, and the cozy little house quickly became the centerpiece of their life.

My mother's instincts had been right all along: the house, indeed, had very good bones. All it needed was a fresh new wardrobe and people living in it.

Soon it had both.

Within a year of moving in, the neglected gem had been transformed inside and out. The unkempt front hedges were trimmed and accented by plantings of azaleas, geraniums, and rhododendrons. A flagstone walkway and vine-covered arbor replaced the rutted stones out front. Fresh paint enlivened the interior and exterior. My mother added her own special touches, too. Nothing fancy, just nice: drapes, curtains, and slipcovers she'd sewn herself; odd pieces of furniture culled from garage sales and family members; promotional dinnerware proffered by gas stations and movie theaters; housewares purchased at Fortunoff's, a popular retail outlet in Brownsville, and E. J. Korvette's, a chain of discount department stores.

Like most couples just starting out, they didn't have much to speak of. But what they *had* meant far more than what they *didn't*: They had each other. They had their entire married life stretching out before them, bulging with promise. And soon they had a family: my sister, Beth, born in the summer of 1945, and me, sixteen months later—the two of us at the leading edge of a baby boom reshaping America to its core, ours the prototypical postwar Brooklyn family.

It was the best of all times in Brooklyn then, too. The Golden Age, people were calling it. A special place at a special time. No better place on earth to be.

It was hard to disagree.

Brooklyn was in its heyday—alive, full of itself, the arc of its trajectory at its very apex. The hardships wrought by two decades of war and economic misery had dissipated. People were fixing up their homes, buying furniture, appliances, TV sets, cars. The Dodgers, almost miraculously, were finally winning pennants. The beaches and boardwalks at Coney Island swelled with summertime crowds.

Restaurants were jammed with patrons. The streets and playgrounds teemed with a new generation of children. The sense of optimism was as palpable as the feeling of unbridled ascent.

And people were working.

Brooklyn's factories, warehouses, and shipyards were booming in those early postwar years. The nation's third largest urban center by then, Brooklyn was nothing less than a manufacturing powerhouse, a well-tuned engine helping to drive America's soaring economy. Its factories employed tens of thousands. Its identity as a maritime center was legendary. Its outreach spanned the globe. Its manufacturing heartland was an incubator for companies of virtually every kind.

And it looked every bit the part.

Gone by then was most evidence of Brooklyn's agrarian past—the orchards, truck farms, and dairy mills that marked the borough's early years. In their place stood a patchwork of densely populated residential neighborhoods and a sprawling industrial landscape centered along the borough's East River border with Manhattan. Docks, wharves, piers, and shipyards ran along miles of waterfront. Oil refineries, chemical plants, storage tanks, junkyards, and concrete coal bunkers lined canals traversed by drawbridges and railway trestles. Barges and tugboats plied commercial waterways. Acres of factories, warehouses, foundries, machine shops, and lumber yards stretched inland—bleeding, first, into gritty working-class enclaves and eventually into newer, upscale neighborhoods.

And Brooklyn's output was nothing short of staggering.

While never dominated by a single industry—like Detroit with autos or Pittsburgh with steel—Brooklyn made a lot of almost everything. Its largest industry, sugar refining, produced half the sugar and molasses consumed in America, much of it at the Domino Sugar plant on the East River. American Manufacturing Company was the nation's largest producer of rope and bagging, Gair Manufacturing was the country's largest supplier of cardboard boxes, Eberhard Faber was the world's largest pencil manufacturer, and Astral Oil Works was world renowned for its kerosene. In Williamsburg, Pfizer Inc. produced the penicillin that many people credited with helping win World War II. Nearby, Brillo manufactured its soap pads, Drake baked its pastries, Fox's U-Bet made its chocolate syrup, Squibb Pharmaceutical produced textile dyes, and dozens of breweries accounted for much of America's beer consumption.

Surrounding these large enterprises were hundreds of smaller firms catering to the industries that defined postwar New York. Textile suppliers, button companies, sewing machinery dealers, and thread manufacturers serviced the city's apparel trade. Paper mills and printing plants fed Manhattan's advertising and publishing industries. Dry goods merchants, jewelry suppliers, and manufacturers of shoes and hats supplied the city's retail trade. Processing plants produced pigments, flavors, extracts, and oils for the food and beverage industry, along with consumables ranging from baked goods and chewing gum to cigarettes and cigars. Other factories produced cement, glass, porcelain china, flour, soap, paint, tin cans, and furniture.

All of this evoked an image shaped as much by fact as legend.

Brooklyn was one of those rare locations that existed not solely as a place name, but as a state of mind. Its most famous icons—the Brooklyn Bridge, the Dodgers, Coney Island, the navy yard—were instantly identifiable. Its unique, almost mythic status was firmly established in the public culture. It was universally seen for what it largely was: big-shouldered, combative, resilient, cocky, street smart. You could knock it on its ass, but you could never keep it down. You could throw roadblocks in its path, but overcoming them was a routine fact of life. You could laugh at it, but that was all right—it was equally capable of laughing at itself.

It was vastly different, too, than any of New York's other boroughs—especially Manhattan. If Manhattan represented America's cultural and intellectual capital, Brooklyn symbolized the nation's fierce, beating heart. If Manhattan stood for ambition, enterprise, and wealth, Brooklyn epitomized boundless energy, hard-boiled attitude, and muscle. If Manhattan evoked images of suited, briefcase-carrying businessmen heading to work in giant office towers, Brooklyn evoked images of an army of men in overalls and work boots, grimy and sweat-stained, nodding off on the subway as they headed home from work at night.

My father was one of those men: working day in and day out, and accepting all the overtime he could possibly handle. Trying to work hard, raise a family, and do the right thing. Never whining or causing a fuss. Staying busy all the time.

That part was easy. Mergenthaler Linotype was busy, too.

Demand for typesetting was at an all-time high in postwar New York, with paper and ink swallowed up by speedy new presses that roared day and night. Linotype machines were the mainstay of most printing operations serving the city's financial, advertising, and legal professions. Wall Street and Madison Avenue owed their very existence to the machines. So did the multitude of print shops serving bulk mailers, restaurants, retail firms, and other businesses in the city.

Then there were the newspapers. New York had no fewer than a dozen dailies then, and Mergenthaler linotype machines could be found in the composing rooms of all of them. Type at the city's three tabloids—the *Daily News*, the *New York Post*, and the *Daily Mirror*—was set on Mergenthaler machines. So was the type at the major broadsheets—the *New York Times*, the *Herald Tribune*, the *Journal American*, the *World-Telegram and Sun,* the *Wall Street Journal*, and Brooklyn's own *Daily Eagle*.

Mergenthaler also produced linotype machines in sixteen foreign languages, for newspapers like the Yiddish *Jewish Daily Forward,* the Italian *Il Progresso Italo-Americano,* the *Polish Daily Zgoda,* the *Berlingske Tidende,* and others aimed at New York's unique ethnic polyglot. Scores of neighborhood and special-interest periodicals like the *Amsterdam News* and the Communist *Daily Worker* also utilized the company's machines.

By 1959, my father had been employed at Mergenthaler for eighteen years, counting his prewar time, and had helped build countless linotypes. A master machinist, he'd also helped implement key improvements and was considered one of Mergenthaler's finest mechanics—meticulous, respected, resourceful, and relied upon for his expertise. There were few machine-related challenges he couldn't meet. We used to joke that he could fix literally anything, using little more than a screwdriver and masking tape. If he couldn't find a tool to do a job, he produced his own, fashioning handmade contraptions in a workshop he built in our cellar. A perfectionist who always went the extra mile, he took tremendous pride in his work.

"Don't do the job at all," he'd say, "if you can't do it right."

It was a cliché, of course. Old school. Ingrained in many men of that generation. But my father believed it. And, for ninety dollars a week plus overtime, he lived it every day of his life.

HE STOOD IN the doorway of my bedroom, a silhouette in the muted light of our hallway. It was just the two of us now, awake at nearly 1 AM. My mother and sister had long been asleep. I listened to him carefully, wanting to understand everything he said.

"When the Dodgers left town," he said, "people in Brooklyn were bitter, depressed. They didn't have as much to look forward to anymore, or even to talk about. You know, even when there was nothing else to say to each other, people could talk about the Dodgers. On the streets, on subways, in stores …"

"Like you and I always did, right?"

"Right. When the Dodgers left Brooklyn, though, they took that with them. They robbed people of the ability to make ordinary, everyday conversation. Understand? When the Dodgers moved, we lost a connection we'd always had, something that brought us together. It was like we'd become … almost strangers. Like we'd lost not only the team, but each other, too."

He looked at me and smiled.

"Can you understand that?"

I told him I could. But, in truth, it would take me years.

It would take me years to understand how the Dodgers had been the backbone of my father's Brooklyn, something to rally around, a unifying force that made Brooklyn, the quintessential loser borough, feel like a winner. It would take years to understand how the Dodgers, with their diverse ethnic mix, were a truer reflection of New York, more a mirror of democracy at work, than any other team in town; how, like Brooklyn itself, they were, to their fans, all about fortitude, perseverance, the ability to cling to a dream. "Wait till next year" was the borough's mantra then. Hang in there. Keep playing.

Keep rooting. Keep hoping. One of these years something good will happen. One of these years you'll have your day in the sun.

It would take me years to fully understand that. And to understand how, when the Dodgers left, they took not just a big part of Brooklyn's self-image, but its vitality, its swagger, its confidence; how, when they left, it signaled the end to a way of life for people like my father, the beginning of the end of the Brooklyn they'd always known.

I'd come to see that eventually. To truly understand it, however, I'd have to live through a similar loss. I didn't know it at the moment, but it was coming straight for me—coming with the Narrows bridge.

"Brooklyn'll never be the same now that the Dodgers are gone," my father sighed. "It'll never really be *Brooklyn* again."

My father would never be quite the same, either. He could never think about the Dodgers without remembering about what they took from Brooklyn when they left, without remembering the things he no longer had. He couldn't think about the Dodgers, either, without also thinking about my Uncle Phil.

He rose from the edge of my bed. "Whaddaya say you get some sleep now, slugger?"

"All right."

I pulled my transistor out and placed it on my nightstand. My father turned to leave, but then came back and kissed me on the forehead.

"Good night," he said, easing away.

"Dad?"

Now just a shadow in the half-open door, he peeked over his shoulder.

"Yeah?" he said.

"The bridge…"

"What about it?"

"What do you think's gonna happen to Dahlgren Place … to us?"

"To be honest with you, son, I really don't know."

"Will we really be forced to move?"

"I can't answer that yet. All I can say for sure is that I think the city's in for a helluva fight."

"A lot of people are angry?"

"That's for sure. Frightened, too."

"Are you?"

"What?"

"Angry?"

"A bit, I suppose."

"Frightened?"

"That, too, I guess. A little."

"But I don't want to have to move."

"None of us do, Nathan. Moving may be something we have to face, though. Things change. That's one thing you can always count on. It's tough to accept, but change is part of life."

"But we'll be all right, won't we? I mean, as a *family*?"

"We'll be fine," he said. "No matter what, we'll be okay."

"How do you know?"

"Because things have a way of working out most of the time, no matter how tough they get. They just do. Sometimes you just have to give 'em time."

"You mean, like Sandy Koufax?" I joked.

"Yeah," my father laughed, "just like Sandy Koufax."

He pulled away again, and then stopped a final time.

"Hey, I got an idea," he said. "Don't think about having to leave Dahlgren Place for now. Think about school. Think about being a kid. Think about baseball."

I promised him I would and soon slipped into sleep, hoping he was right. I didn't want to see another part of Brooklyn pulled from my father's grasp. I didn't want to see a bridge over the Narrows or an expressway through Bay Ridge break his heart like the Dodgers once did. I didn't want to see it break anyone's heart.

Chapter 9

With the battle lines drawn, bridge opponents squared off against city officials in a confrontation dubbed by the press as the Battle of Bay Ridge.

It was a battle that bore no resemblance to my adolescent vision of a violent clash between police and the neighborhood's toughest fighters. In contrast, the confrontation more closely resembled a divisive political campaign—a war of words marked by demonstrations, legal actions, and behind-the-scenes maneuvering. In some ways, however, it was even more ferocious than the gang-like rumble I'd imagined. It was certainly more sustained. The battle, in fact, would rage on for months.

Within days of the P.S. 104 rally, an organization calling itself the Committee to Save Bay Ridge emerged to spearhead opposition to the Narrows bridge proposal. Support poured in from throughout the neighborhood. Block associations mobilized. Civic groups sprang into action. Organizers went door to door soliciting backing. And the movement grew more militant by the day.

The Sunday after the *Spectator* story broke, John Paul Jones Park, a grassy tract overlooking the Narrows, became the site of a large-scale rally. Gathering under a bright, cloudless sky, protestors closed ranks near the Dover Monument, a tall granite obelisk fronted by several Dahlgren cannons and naval war plaques.

A cloth banner, held aloft by metal poles, flapped in the gusts.

"SAVE OUR NEIGHBORHOOD!" it read.

"We cannot allow the city's bridge plan to go forward," Councilman Alan Sherman shouted into a megaphone, his usual sunny demeanor masked by a look of steely determination.

"Look around you." He gestured down the steep incline toward the Narrows, then inland toward a string of umber brick apartment buildings at the mouth of Seventh Avenue, which emptied into the park. From the high ground at the monument, the Narrows stretched ribbon-like for miles, its sunlit waters sparkling as if capped by crystals of ice. Barges hauling railroad freight cars steamed up-channel. Sailboats and cabin cruisers crisscrossed the waterway, past anchored freighters and passenger liners. Ferries edged into slips in Staten Island and Brooklyn, discharging passengers and cars.

"What we have in Bay Ridge," Councilman Sherman said, "is very special. But all of it—everything you see today—will be gone if the city has its way. Our shoreline will be stripped of its beauty. The bridge and expressway will spell the end of Bay Ridge as we know and love it."

Sherman continued for several minutes, followed by others who echoed his plea. Then the protestors marched toward the center of Bay Ridge, following the shoreline before turning onto Seventh Avenue and making their way along the path of the planned expressway. Marchers, walking several abreast, linked arms in a show of unity. Veterans groups and others with common identity marched in semi-organized formations. Cardboard signs, held aloft by broomsticks, conveyed messages scrawled in crayon and paint.

"Don't Take Our Homes!" they read.

"No Expressway Through Our Neighborhood!"

"Halt Heartbreak Highway!"

Walking the fifteen-block length of Seventh Avenue, the marchers passed the dozens of stores targeted for demolition by the expressway plan: Phelps Pharmacy, a Bay Ridge landmark for thirty-plus years; Buster's Men's Shop, where my father had his work clothes dry cleaned; Miller's Appetizing, where we bought our bagels and cold cuts; Hessemann's Grocery, where Wilmer Hessemann, the owner, sometimes gave Pooch and me a nickel apiece for sweeping the sidewalk in front of his store.

The march wound along the avenue for the better part of an hour. Past the Jablonski Funeral Chapel and Boschwitz Jewelers and the Life Insurance Offices of Roger and Henry Kekich and the dental office of Dr. Ruben Shapiro. Past Andresen's Famous Chocolates and Thumann's Candy Store. Past Daley's Hardware Store, Richard's TV repair shop, a Robert Hall clothing store, a pizza parlor, a Chinese laundry, a Chevrolet dealership, Thom McCann and Miles shoe stores, and a Bohack's supermarket.

"Not another Sunset Park!" the protestors chanted.

"Not another Sunset Park!"

"Not another Sunset Park!"

Cheering the marchers were hundreds of onlookers, many of whom unfurled signs and bed sheets from second-story windows. Strung across the thoroughfare, a massive banner read "Save Bay Ridge!"

In the minds of protestors, nothing short of that was the goal. It was life or death for the neighborhood. If the city's plan was defeated, Bay Ridge would survive intact; life would go on as before. If the plan was approved, Bay Ridge as it had existed for decades would die as surely as someone shot through the heart.

They would not let that happen, protestors vowed. They'd do everything in their power to save Bay Ridge, or die themselves trying.

Chapter 10

Standing at our kitchen counter, my mother, silent and withdrawn, chopped a slab of calf's liver in a circular wooden bowl, gazing out our backyard window as if studying something off on the horizon. Her thoughts seemed equally distant.

"You all right, Lily?" my father asked.

"Yes. Fine."

But when she turned to join us for supper, her face was ashen, as if the tumult in Bay Ridge had sparked a fear that was far more unsettling than she was letting on, far more disturbing than simply the destructive specter of the bridge and expressway.

She set the bowl of chopped liver on the table.

"We need to play an active role in the anti-bridge protests," she said. "What we have here, our life on Dahlgren Place, is far too precious to allow the city to take without a fight."

She glanced at my father, then at my sister and me. "Don't you agree?"

"Yeah, I do," my father said, his tone assured but lacking my mother's intense conviction.

"Artie?"

"Yes," my father repeated. "We have to fight."

We helped ourselves to the liver, then to the rest of supper: pot roast, mashed potatoes, peas and carrots, rye bread, Coca-Cola.

My mother, however, barely touched her food.

"I hope you don't mind if I get heavily involved in the protests," she said.

"We won't mind at all," my father replied. "We'll all get involved to whatever degree we can."

"Good," my mother said. "We need to do whatever we can. There's a lot at stake. We need to fight as hard as humanly possible to save our home."

Then she drifted into thought, somewhere far from all of us, alone again with her troubling, deep-seated fear.

SHE MOVED THROUGH a different world than that of my father—with a different personality, different sensibilities, a different way of seeing the things around us. Her life had been different than my father's, too. Intertwined with his from the moment they'd met, but different from his, in some ways, as night from day.

My mother's parents, for one thing, had money. Not a lot. But enough so that she'd been able to avoid the hardscrabble childhood my father had endured in Depression-era Williamsburg. Enough so that her own father—a Russian-born tailor—could afford a decent apartment in the more-upscale Borough Park section. Enough so that, unlike my father, she'd never really felt *poor*.

Unlike my father, my mother had also made it all the way through high school, graduating with honors and going to work as secretary to the president of Eberhard Faber, where her well-paid position afforded her access to the high-level operations of one of Brooklyn's top employers. And unlike my father, who was forced to abandon his childhood dream of becoming an architect, my mother was able to live her long-held dream of being a housewife and mother—fully comfortable in that role, never once regretting her decision to abandon career for family, never feeling compromised or cheated in any way.

Her daily life was very different than my father's, too. While he worked full time in the heart of industrial Brooklyn, she worked part time at home, typing envelopes for a mail-order firm on a rickety, old typewriter she'd set up in the tiny retreat off our living room. The piecework helped. At a nickel an envelope, my mother could work four to five hours at a clip and earn fifteen dollars. Between her and my father, we usually had enough money to make ends meet.

Mostly, though, my mother did what many women in postwar Brooklyn did. She shopped and cooked and cleaned. She washed and ironed. She managed our family's finances. She kept our home.

"Homes are very special things," she'd often say. "They're more than just a shelter, you know. The things we cherish the most—everything that's most important to us—are right inside our walls. A home should reflect that. It should be cared for. It should be a place to spend time in, celebrate happy occasions, build memories. It should be just as important to us as the people we love."

My mother treated our house as if she believed that through and through. It meant everything to her, that house. It was part of her, a reflection of all she held dear. And she immersed herself in it in every conceivable way, filling it with sunlight and color, photos and memorabilia, music and the books she read in every spare moment she could carve from her busy days.

The shelves in her retreat were lined with those books: novels by all the top writers—Ayn Rand, James Jones, J. D. Salinger, Herman Wouk, Hemingway, Steinbeck, Cheever, Bellow; poetry by Sandburg, Frost, and T.S. Eliot; biographies of every public figure from Dwight Eisenhower to J. Edgar Hoover; plays by Tennessee Williams, Arthur Miller, and Lorraine Hansberry.

The house was filled with her music, too. A bit of everything. Jazz. Blues. Ragtime. Big band. But mostly opera, the music she loved most of all, the music she surrounded herself with.

Opera was as much a part of my mother's life as our family and our house. Sometimes on summer nights, she and my father would take the A Train to Lewisohn Stadium, a sprawling amphitheater on the City College campus in Harlem, where they'd sit in the concrete bleachers while Arthur Rubenstein, Robert Merrill, Beverly Sills, George Gershwin, and other leading artists performed in the city's annual Concerts Under the Stars.

Most of the time, though, she listened to her opera at home. For their tenth anniversary, my father surprised her with a mahogany-veneered Philco console that housed a pie-sized TV screen, radio, and Victrola. That was all she needed. Maybe they couldn't afford to attend the opera in Manhattan, or even at the Brooklyn Academy of Music, but that didn't stop my mother from listening to the weekly Texaco-sponsored radio broadcasts from the Met, or to the stack of seventy-eights piled atop the console. She listened while cleaning, cooking, reading, typing her envelopes. Almost always, it seemed, our house was filled with my mother's music. Almost always, she moved about humming an aria, happy in the space she'd created, surrounded by the things she loved, at peace inside the walls of our home.

She was even more at peace, however, in our backyard. In the space where she kept our garden.

Backyard gardens were common then in Brooklyn. One of our neighbors, Mrs. Pedersen, grew lettuce, spinach, basil, and other herbs in a narrow patch of land alongside her house. Another neighbor, Mr. Mancini, raised tomatoes, cucumbers, and peppers in a garden of twisting vines. A fig tree, wrapped in tar paper for protection from the harsh New York winters, was set at the rear of Mr. Pappas' house, behind which wreathes of grapevines clung to tall wooden arbors.

"Between all of us," Mrs. Pedersen once boasted, "we can grow everything we'd ever need."

That was probably true. But my mother didn't grow vegetables or tend formal flowerbeds as other gardeners in Bay Ridge did. Instead, she preferred the native plants found in woodlands and meadows, alongside streams and country roads.

Instead, she grew wildflowers.

My mother loved wildflowers, she said, because they made her feel as close to nature as was possible in bustling, overbuilt Brooklyn. She loved them because they bloomed in all the different seasons and so could surround us with color almost year-round. She loved them because they let her bring the outdoors into our home.

Her garden was a lush, overflowing paradise of plants, perennials, and flowering shrubs. Bright yellow sunflowers opened like full moons. Bluebonnets, buttercups, violets, and African daisies bloomed in warm weather. Tall jewelweed hugged the rear of our house, where a cobblestone path wound through beds of geraniums, forsythias, morning glories, and rhododendrons. A shed my father built served as a repository for watering cans, concrete urns, clay pots, and gardening tools. A tiny weeping willow swayed with the gentlest of breezes, making it seem as if the entire garden were always moving, breathing, alive.

But my mother did more than simply grow wildflowers. She *studied* them. And she passed much of what she knew on to us.

"Without plants, none of us could exist," she told me one day when I was about six. "Plants provide food, clothing and medicines. In fact, the very air we breathe—our oxygen—comes from plants."

"I knew that already," I said proudly. "I learned it in school."

"Ah, but did you know that many wildflowers have been around since the days of the dinosaurs, and some were once thought to have magical properties?"

That I *didn't* know.

"Did you know that different kinds of wildflowers grow in different areas, and that there are thousands of species in our part of the country alone?"

That I didn't know, either.

"And did you know that wild-growing plants have been used for centuries to cure illness, and by Indians for soap and war paint?"

By now, she had my complete attention.

And so she walked me around her garden and fed my interest.

She explained how wildflowers originated from spores blown about by the wind, and how many of them had traveled to North America as weeds in the seed sacks of colonists. She explained how wildflowers were equipped to grow in nature, but how, because they were stationary, were dependent for survival on pollination and fertilization by insects and birds attracted to their color, shape, and scent.

"See that?" she said, pointing at butterflies and bees moving through the flower petals, and at colonies of ants laboring in the soil. "The garden is a world unto itself, and insects and birds help keep it alive."

But I was interested in other facets of the garden, and she told me about those, as well.

She told me how colonists had used the down from milkweed seeds as stuffing for pillows, and how they'd spun it into thread; how American Indians brewed tea from snakeroot and used wildflowers as cures for snake bites and various ailments; how plants like marsh marigold, purple coneflower, bloodroot, and dame's rocket had gotten their exotic names; how Pilgrims struck by the mayflower's beauty named it after their ship; how black-eyed Susans and sweet Williams were named for legendary lovers; how Viper's Bugloss drew its name from its resemblance to a snake.

She also told me how certain wildflowers had long and fascinating histories, often shrouded in the folklore, legend, and romance of other civilizations—and how some had been used to ward off evil spirits during religious ceremonies in the days of witch doctors and black magic.

"Doctors still use wildflowers in the practice of medicine," she said. "But not all these plants are good. Some are poisonous and must be avoided at all costs. Then there are plants I call thugs."

"What are thugs?"

"They're plants that grow very quickly and try to take over a garden by killing other plants. Some can destroy entire forests and farms."

"Will they take over our garden?"

"No, I won't allow them to. But that's why we must know what we're doing at all times and grow these plants with extreme care. And with love."

And that's what my mother did.

She spent hours nurturing her wildflowers and teaching us about them. Each spring, we bought seed packets from the Brooklyn Botanical Garden, planted them, and watched them grow. We placed amaryllis bulbs in pots and saw them sprout into exotic red flowers on tall, straight stems. We replanted wildflowers in wooden barrels and hanging baskets around the backyard, and in vases inside our house.

Sometimes, at the height of their colors, my mother would pick African daisies and tie them into braids for my sister's hair, or give kids on Dahlgren Place bouquets for their teachers. When I was in elementary school, and I'd see those flowers in vases on my teacher's desk, I'd imagine that part of my mother was right there in the classroom, watching over me. And I'd think that as long she shared her flowers with us like that, she could never truly be far away.

I'd often think about her digging through the rich, dark soil of our backyard, humming arias, the sunlight gleaming in her hair. And I'd think it was only fitting that her nickname was that of a flower. It was only right that people called her Lily.

"WE CAN'T ALLOW the city to take our house, Artie," I overheard her tell my father again later that night. "You understand that, don't you?"

"Yes."

"You know how frightening that thought is to me, right?"

"I do."

"Please help."

"I will," my father pledged. "We'll fight the bridge every way possible."

"Good," I heard her say, her voice trailing off. "We must do everything we can to hold onto this house. There's too much to lose, Artie. Much too much to lose."

Chapter 11

My mother was right. There *was* a lot at stake, a lot to fight for, a lot to lose. Not just for my parents and the growing legion of anti-bridge protestors. Not just for me and my sister and my friends. There was a lot to lose for most kids growing up in postwar Brooklyn—where the world, at last, was at peace and the borough seemed in bloom and our parents were busy working and we were free to immerse ourselves in the comforting magic of childhood.

And play.

Play came easy in quiet, middle-class neighborhoods like 1950s Bay Ridge. All forms of play. It didn't matter what day of the week it was, or what time. All you had to do was walk outside. Anywhere you looked you could find another kid; anywhere you turned you could find something to play. No parents, no umpires, no uniforms, no organized leagues, no manicured fields—you just chose up sides and played. Wherever you could. All day and into the night.

We played stickball, punchball, boxball and stoopball with pink rubber balls called spaldeens. We played cowboys and Indians, shooting cap guns and mimicking Roy Rogers, Gene Autry, Hopalong Cassidy, and the Lone Ranger. We played war games, pretending we were American GIs engaged in life-and-death firefights with German and Japanese enemies. We staged mock roller derbies and tag-team wrestling matches, pitting nasty villains like the Masked Marvel and Killer Kowalski against acrobatic heroes like Antonino

Rocca and the Flying Frenchman, Édouard Carpentier. We played Ringalevio and other age-old street games, too: Skelly, where bottle caps weighted with melted wax were used to score points on a chalk-drawn grid; Territory, where penknives were thrust into a dirt patch to establish turf supremacy; and Johnny on the Pony, where we leapt onto the backs of our opponents until the entire row of kids, swaying under the weight, collapsed in a giant, laughing heap.

Then there were the fads—all of them eagerly embraced, all of them part of our daily routine as they swept across America.

We wore coonskin caps, twirled hula hoops, spun yo-yos, shot marbles, played jacks. We fashioned scooters from two-by-fours, wooden milk crates and steel roller skates, and rode bikes with playing cards clothes-pinned to the spokes and thwacking like the engine of a motorcycle. We applied cockamamie decals to our forearms and hands, built model planes, tinkered with chemistry and Erector sets, and collected stamps, coins, and comic books. We flipped and traded baseball cards, clung to the annual World Series updates on the P.A. system at school, and talked sports incessantly, rattling off the names of every player in the eight-team National and American Leagues, arguing endlessly about which New York centerfielder—Mantle, Mays, or Snider—was really the best.

In many ways, Bay Ridge itself—its architecture and terrain—was our playground. We played hide-and-seek in the courtyards, alcoves, stairwells, and lobbies of apartment buildings. We scaled garage rooftops, explored alleyways, and raced through backyards and driveways. We played in schoolyards and parks, on stoops and sidewalks, on streets and in yards.

At Owl's Head Park, the site of a former industrialist's estate, we belly-flopped on Flexible Flyers down steep hills in the winter, and played softball with hard white balls called clinchers in summer and spring. At John Paul Jones Park, we climbed atop gun emplacements that once protected the entrance to New York Harbor. At the Denyse Wharf, a Colonial-era ferry slip, we flew kites and imagined what it was like when the British landed there for the Battle of Long Island. From Old Glory Lookout, on the Narrows shoreline, we fished and watched tankers, cargo vessels, and passenger ships streaming in and out of New York Harbor, wondering what it would be like to stow away and sail to some exotic land far from Brooklyn.

Mostly, though, we played on Dahlgren Place.

Dahlgren Place was far different than most Brooklyn's streets—and not just because we lived on it. Its proximity to the Narrows made it almost unique, for one thing. So did its shape. On the vast majority of Brooklyn's streets, laid out in a rigid gridiron, traffic continuously interrupted games, forcing kids into hurried bursts of play between passing vehicles. Because Dahlgren Place terminated at a cul-de-sac, however, our play was generally unimpeded. Games could unwind at their own pace. The danger of losing a ball—or even a playmate—to a passing car was non-existent.

The street's curving contours were also tailor-made for games like punchball and stickball. Home plate was a manhole cover in the center of the cul-de-sac. First base was a Johnny pump, second was another manhole cover down the street, and third was a lamppost. Foul lines were marked by telephone poles on either side of the street. If you hit a fly ball past the fire alarm box on the corner, it was an automatic home run. Other landmarks were designated for singles, doubles, and triples. An outfielder usually stood guard near the storm sewer at the end of the street to prevent balls from dropping through the metal grate into the smelly muck below. Breaking a window was an automatic out.

But Dahlgren Place was more than simply our playground. It was also our *sanctuary*, a tiny village unto itself, a safe and familiar stage on which we could act out the roles we played as we moved through childhood. We knew its rhythms and heartbeat, its place marks and idiosyncrasies, its sights, sounds, and smells. We knew the real estate defined by its homes, sidewalks, curbs, and stoops better than any other place on earth. We knew where the asphalt, warped by sunlight and frost, humped in a way that would send balls bounding askew, resulting in "hindus" or "do-overs." We knew where tree roots poked through cracks in the sidewalk, making it risky to run or ride a bike. We knew how the street looked when lazy afternoons melted into twilight, and the cul-de-sac was filled with the aroma of supper, and our fathers arrived from work, and our mothers called us in for the night.

On Dahlgren Place, we measured our achievements, calibrated our growing maturity, discovered our limitations, forged our first friendships, welcomed the arrival of siblings, and sought comfort during setbacks, illness, and grief. On Dahlgren Place, we hit our first home runs, learned to ride two-wheelers, celebrated holidays with neighbors, and mastered the geography of our world. On Dahlgren Place, we won, lost, laughed, cried, fought, aspired, and began the long, unsteady journey through the rest of our lives.

No other place was quite the same. We could go around the corner or over to a park or down to the schoolyard and still be connected to Bay Ridge. We could walk to the stores on Seventh Avenue and still be *in the neighborhood.* But nothing was the same as being on *our street*; nothing was like being on Dahlgren Place. Wherever we went, once we turned the corner and walked onto it, we knew we were on familiar turf, knew we were safe, knew we were home.

And all of it was comforting.

There was a predictable choreography to the way we lived back then, routines as reassuring as childhood itself. Each day, our fathers woke before dawn and left for work before we even saw them. Each day, our mothers packed our lunches, shopped for groceries, cooked supper, and cared for our homes. Each day, we walked to school past familiar homes and shade trees that formed a lush, green canopy over the streets. At school, we lined up in size places and sat in alphabetical order and pledged allegiance to the flag and obeyed hall monitors and lived in fear of getting a Referral Card or, even worse, a notation on our Permanent Record. In class, we diagrammed sentences and practiced our penmanship and wrestled with fractions and anxiously awaited gym class, where we warmed up with jumping jacks and then played dodgeball and kickball. Every Wednesday—dressed in red, white and blue—we attended school assemblies, where we sat through films about the evils of juvenile delinquency, or lectures on dental hygiene, or concerts by an out-of-tune ensemble. Once a week we had fire drills, grabbing our coats and marching in pairs to the street, where we awaited the all-clear. Sometimes we practiced air-raid drills, wondering if the flimsy wooden desks we huddled beneath would really protect us from an atomic blast.

Even the worst of our Cold War fears, however, were merely fleeting—dissipating with the 3 PM dismissal bell, when we hustled home, gobbled down a snack and raced outside to play until nightfall.

After which our routine continued.

Each evening, we ate precisely at 6 PM. Each night, we finished our homework and watched our tiny, black-and-white TVs, the medium shaping our views of the world. We received our news from Huntley and Brinkley, Walter Cronkite and Edward R. Murrow. We were entertained with variety shows hosted by Ed Sullivan and Steve Allen, and by the comedians—Milton Berle, Jack Benny, Red Skelton, Groucho Marx and Lucille Ball—that our parents found so funny. We watched Saturday morning shows like *Fury* and *Sky King*; cartoons like *Mighty Mouse, Popeye* and *Looney Tunes*; children's shows like *Howdy Doody* and *The Merry Mailman;* westerns like *Gunsmoke*, *Paladin,* and *The Cisco Kid*; adventure series like *Lassie*, *Zorro*, *Superman*, *Sea Hunt,* and *Ramar of the Jungle*; sci-fi fantasies like *The Twilight Zone*; wacky comedy series like *Abbott and Costello*, *The Three Stooges,* and *Our Little Rascals*; and sit-coms like *Father Knows Best, The Adventures* of *Ozzie and Harriet, Leave it to Beaver,* and *The Honeymooners.*

All through childhood, this same routine persisted, mirrored by nearly everyone we knew, part of the weekly rhythm of Bay Ridge and neighborhoods like it.

On and on it went.

Tuesday nights, my father anchored the Mergenthaler Linotype bowling team at the Freddie Fitzsimmons Lanes near Ebbets Field. Wednesday nights, my mother played mahjong with her Bay Ridge friends. Friday nights, my parents played canasta with couples from the Knights of Pythias, my father's fraternal lodge. Sunday mornings, my father played handball at the Seaside Courts in Coney Island, a mecca for the top one-wall players in New York. Sunday afternoons we'd visit my grandparents or other relatives in Brooklyn.

Even our eating habits followed a familiar pattern: Meat meals four nights a week. "Dairy" on Thursdays. Eating out on weekends. And always the same food at the same restaurants: Chinese food at the New Toyson Restaurant on Coney Island Avenue; Italian meals at

Gragnano's on McDonald Avenue; deli at Adelman's on Thirteenth Avenue; kosher specialties at Juniors on Flatbush Avenue; shore dinners in the noisy circus atmosphere of Lundy's in Sheepshead Bay.

That's what we did. That's how we lived. Behind closed doors, other families may have been struggling, falling apart, battling illness, despair, even each other. But we were lucky. We weren't forced to confront those realities. In contrast, our life seemed simple, unfettered, flowing across the fifties like a gentle stream through a quiet forest.

Not that it was easy. The daily grind took its toll. Brooklyn's factories, docks, and other workplaces could be unforgiving. Accidents and illnesses were commonplace. Labor conflicts were frequent and often bitter. And making ends meet was hard. Like us, most people we knew struggled financially, living paycheck to paycheck, always one step away from outright disaster. There were never any savings to speak of, nothing to weather a storm. And always this vague, unspoken fear, borne of hard times: fear of getting fired or too sick to work, fear of missing a paycheck, fear of losing everything we had.

Nor was postwar Brooklyn a nirvana—the innocent, sanitized fairyland some make it out to be. Sections were dirty and crumbling. Factories threw off blankets of sludge and smog. Some neighborhoods were breeding grounds for social tension, discontent, and crime. Ethnic factions shunned and battled one another. Epithets like mick, wop, spic, polack, kike, and nigger were part of the daily parlance.

The times were far from perfect, too. The Civil Rights movement, casting a glare on the ugliness of racism, was bubbling to a head in the Deep South. The stench of McCarthyism and the Communist witch hunts pervaded government, businesses, the arts, even our schools. The Cold War had us frightened of the blinding light and billowing mushroom cloud everyone thought was imminent.

But, somehow, in the midst of all this, we were happy. Somehow, the world we lived in—our Brooklyn—seemed safe, secure, insulated, idyllic even.

Was it really that way? Who knows? Maybe, insulated by childhood and protected by our parents, we kids were just living in a dream. Maybe we were simply too naïve, or too blind, to see troubling changes creeping across Brooklyn and our city. Maybe time and wishful thinking have blurred the memory of things we'd rather forget.

But growing up in postwar Brooklyn really did seem to be a time of simple, innocent pleasures. I knew that most families in Bay Ridge didn't have much to show for their hard work, but somehow I believed that most were just like ours: intact, loving, bonded to each other, secure in the womb of neighborhood and friends.

It was utterly naïve, of course, but, in my innocence, I believed that most kids in Brooklyn lived the same life I did—caught in the innocent glow of childhood, captive to the same comforting routines, just happy being kids. I was certain most of them awoke each morning to parents who loved them, to lives awash with discovery and adventure. I was certain they went to bed each night secretly listening to Dodger games, wondering what it would be like to play in the big leagues, dreaming about heroic exploits, fantasizing about girls, and falling asleep, finally, to the rustle of shade trees and adult laughter mixed with the muted sounds of television shows from the living room.

I really thought it was that way for everyone in Brooklyn. Just like it was for us across the fourteen years we'd lived on Dahlgren Place. In a house we knew as well as we knew each other. In a neighborhood we thought of as home. On a street we felt was ours.

It was easy to believe it would never end.

That was naïve, too, I know. But it was entirely possible to feel that way. After all, we *wanted* to believe it—*needed* to. We needed to believe that things could remain that innocent and simple. We needed to believe that nothing about our life in Brooklyn would ever really change.

CHAPTER 12

The next big anti-bridge rally took place at Alexander Hamilton High, the school I was about to enter as a freshman. There, more than a thousand anxious, angry protestors flooded the auditorium to hear from Attorney Stephen Calico, who'd been summoned to answer questions about the crisis facing Bay Ridge.

Boyish and smartly clad in blue slacks, a matching blazer and an open-collar shirt, Calico stood onstage in the cavernous school auditorium, poised behind a microphone supported by an adjustable metal pole. Next to him was Walter Staziak, the pharmacist heading the Committee to Save Bay Ridge.

Staziak introduced Calico as a man who had cut his teeth as an assistant to the city's Corporation Counsel, representing the mayor's office in real estate litigation. More recently, he'd founded a firm that provided *pro bono* legal representation for Navy Yard workers suffering from health problems related to asbestos exposure. His practice also represented homeowners in condemnation cases tied to the city's expanding efforts at urban renewal.

Staziak then asked Calico to explain, in legal terms, exactly what was occurring.

"You are being subjected to what's known as 'eminent domain'," Calico began.

The audience was attentive. And in way over their heads.

"Eminent domain?" Staziak asked. "Can you explain that in layman's language? I'm sure most people here have no idea what it is."

"Eminent domain," Calico said, "is the right of federal, state or local governments to acquire private property without the voluntary consent of the owner."

"Just like that?" Staziak queried. "You're telling us that the city can just barge in on the whim of some bureaucrat, seize our homes, and put us on the street?"

Calico was momentarily quieted.

Staziak went on. "You mean everything we've worked for, everything we've built, people's lives and dreams, can be bulldozed anytime the government sees fit?"

"I'm afraid so … yes," Calico replied.

The crowd buzzed.

"I didn't know they did those kinds of things in *my* America," a voice rang from the back. It was Joey Palumbo, the bull-necked former dockworker with the hair-trigger temper. "It sure don't sound American to me."

Calico cleared his throat and leaned into the microphone.

"Actually," he said, "it's as American as the constitution itself."

"And how's that?" Palumbo asked.

"Ownership of private property is as much a basic American right as freedom of speech or religion," Calico said. "But the Fifth Amendment—in something called the 'takings clause'—gives governments the power to seize private property."

"You mean we can be forced to surrender our property to the government, even if we don't want to?" Staziak queried.

"Actually, it's not that cut and dried," Calico explained. "There are several conditions that must exist for governments to exercise eminent domain."

"Conditions?"

"Yes. Restrictions that our founding fathers placed on government."

"What *kind* of restrictions?"

"Well, for one thing, any land that's seized must be used for a legitimate public purpose. Projects like roads, bridges, schools, subways, and public buildings all qualify because, in the government's view, they're in the broad public interest. In addition, no private property can be taken without fair and just compensation to the property owner. Landowners also have the protection of due process—adequate notice of the taking and a chance to contest it."

"I never heard of this before," Staziak said.

"Well, it's not common knowledge," Calico replied. "But, in truth, eminent domain has been around for centuries. Its origins actually date to feudal times in England, when the king was considered eminent and all land was his domain. Back then, the crown could freely seize any property it wanted, for any reason, and force the owner out."

"Well, Bay Ridge ain't part of England no more," Palumbo called out, "and there ain't no kings or crowns in Brooklyn. Maybe we ought to remind the city of that."

The audience stirred amid laughter and small talk.

"That's true," Calico smiled. "There are no kings in America, but the concept of sovereign power over property *did* carry over to this country. As I said, our nation's founders, while recognizing that governments would have legitimate needs for private property, wisely sought to protect property owners from abuse by eminent domain. That's why governments are limited in using the power."

"But is the power really necessary?" Staziak asked.

"As a matter of fact, it is," Calico said. "Governments need to have the right to control their destiny for the common good. They have tools for doing this—building codes, zoning laws and the like. Eminent domain is one of those tools. It may seem harsh, but it serves an important function."

"And what's that?"

"In reality, eminent domain is necessary for society to function," Calico explained. "How could public projects possibly be built if the government couldn't obtain the land to build them? Look at the 1800s, when the government granted the power to expand railroads westward, and then funded the purchase of easements across land owned by farmers and ranchers. That's just one example."

Calico told the audience that, in fact, one of the most controversial cases of eminent domain had just been resolved in, of all places, Los Angeles, where hundreds of impoverished Mexican-Americans had lost a bitter, eight-year fight over the city's right to seize private property in nearby Chavez Ravine, where the Dodgers wanted to build a new stadium.

"Walter O'Malley isn't hated only in Brooklyn," Calico joked. "Chicanos in L.A. aren't too thrilled with him, either."

Only a few people chuckled.

"My point," the attorney resumed, "is that eminent domain is nothing new. It's quite common, and it happens all across America."

The audience grew silent now.

"But what about ... individual rights?" Walter Staziak stammered. "What about the freedom we have to determine our own destiny?"

"The government's power, I'm afraid, supersedes that of the individual," Calico said.

"What about taking the city to court—fighting it legally?" Staziak asked.

"To be perfectly blunt, the legal process is pretty much rigged against you," Calico explained.

"Rigged?"

"Yes. You might win a challenge, but you'd have to prove that the taking of your property is either not for a necessary public use or that the city failed to follow the proper procedures—in other words, defeat the government on a legal technicality. That's extremely difficult."

"Are you saying there's no way to fight this?" Staziak asked.

"No. What I'm saying is that successful challenges to the government's right to take property for a public works project are rare, and they usually only delay seizures rather than prevent them," Calico said. "All any lawyer can do for you, in truth, is to help get a fair financial settlement for your property, not prevent the government's right to take it."

"So you're tellin' us we got no choice?" Joey Palumbo growled. "You're tellin' us that if we don't leave our homes, the city will put us out on the street?"

"Hopefully, it won't come to that," Councilman Sherman interrupted, striding to the microphone. "Hopefully, we can fight the city and win."

"You're goddamned right we can fight!" Palumbo yelled.

"When I say *fight*, I mean we can present unified, vocal opposition to the authorization of eminent domain in Bay Ridge," Sherman said evenly. "We can organize, go to the newspapers, rally people to our side, and take our voices to City Hall."

"Will the city really listen to people like us?" a woman asked. "I mean, most of us don't know much about how government works. How are we supposed to deal with the men who are part of this system, powerful men who run the city?"

"You people are voters, aren't you?" Sherman asked.

His question was greeted with silence.

"Well, *aren't you*?"

"Yes," the woman answered.

"Well, the men you'll be dealing with are politicians—remember that. And politicians listen to voters."

"But will they listen to *us*?" she continued

"There's only one way to find out," Sherman said.

"Are you saying we actually have a chance to get the city to back down, change its mind about the bridge and expressway?" Staziak asked.

Calico jumped back in. "It's unlikely, as I said, but it's possible. Highway battles are usually fought against tremendous odds, and can get highly emotional. They can take decades to be resolved, too. But … sometimes homeowners prevail."

"Hear that?" Joey Palumbo shouted. "We can win if we stick together and fight!"

Palumbo's rousing remark set the audience to prolonged chatter, broken only by Staziak's voice, amplified by the microphone.

"I understand the city is close to making a decision, but the bridge plan still hasn't been officially approved yet," Staziak said. "Isn't that right?"

"That's correct," Councilman Sherman nodded.

"Who makes that decision?"

"The New York City Board of Estimate," Sherman replied. "They're responsible for all budget and land-use decisions. They also have control over condemnation proceedings and have the final say on projects like this."

The Board of Estimate, Sherman informed the audience, consisted of eight members: the mayor, the city's comptroller, the president of the City Council, and the five borough presidents.

But despite its sweeping powers, Sherman noted, the board was not responsible for the final decision on precisely where the expressway was to be located. That decision, he said, was one man's alone.

"*One* man?" Staziak was incredulous.

Sherman and Calico nodded.

"And who's that?"

"That man," Sherman said, "is none other than … Robert Moses."

And, with that, a hush descended that was so quiet, the mere sound of Sherman clearing his throat in the microphone reverberated like a shot from one of the Dahlgren cannons standing vigil over our street.

Chapter 13

There was more to lose in the Battle of Bay Ridge, we feared, than simply our neighborhood and street, more to forfeit than merely a sense of permanence borne of wishful thinking and our almost dreamlike innocence. There was more to our childhood, too, than the welcome embrace of Dahlgren Place, with its family and friends, familiar landmarks, and comforting routines.

There was the broader world around us. There was Brooklyn.

Brooklyn was as much a part of our lives as anything we did or felt, ingrained in the way we saw ourselves and the world, conjoined to us in almost every way. And we were part of Brooklyn, too—absorbed in it completely, moving through it freely from an early age on.

By the time we were twelve, we were permitted to leave the sheltered confines of Bay Ridge, unaccompanied by adults, and venture across the sprawling landscape that traced the Narrows shoreline southward, past quiet beachfront and bayside neighborhoods, and then veered north toward Brooklyn's industrial heartland and inland into the heart of the borough—a dense stratum of streets, homes, apartment buildings, church steeples, rooftop water towers, and elevated subway lines.

Childhood sojourns like that were common then. Postwar Brooklyn, for the most part, was benign, safe to explore. We could journey almost anywhere we wanted, as long as we returned by nightfall and were smart enough to avoid the sacred turf of street gangs like the Fort Greene Chaplains, the Bishops, the Stompers, and the Phantom Lords. Those guys you didn't want to mess around with. Even Pooch, tough and street-smart as he was, wanted no part of them.

Our forays into Brooklyn generally carried little risk, however—and just as little hassle. Public transportation could take us virtually anywhere we wanted for a ten-cent fare and a series of free transfers. The city's subway, bus and trolley routes were simple enough to master.

And so we began to explore. Starting, as most kids did, with Coney Island.

Coney Island was all that the masses from Brooklyn had for summertime entertainment back then. Modern theme parks had yet to emerge. Few people from neighborhoods like Bay Ridge could afford travel to trendy vacation spots. The beaches and parks of Long Island were similarly out of the reach of anyone who couldn't drive. Coney Island, though, was only a short hop away. Four stops on the BMT R-line with a transfer to the Sea Beach Express and, in minutes, we could be at sun-splashed Surf and Stillwell avenues, surrounded by the sights, sounds and scents of summer: fresh salt air, the ocean surf, a smorgasbord of food, a cacophony of music, the roar of rides, the joyous screams of riders.

We bucked the crowds at Nathan's Famous, gorging on hot dogs, hamburgers, ripple-cut fries, corn on the cob, and orangeade. We wandered streets lined with freak shows, fortune tellers, and other carnival-like attractions. We strolled the boardwalk, feasting on popcorn, custard, knishes, salt water toffee, and cotton candy. We played skeeball, Fascination, and other games at Fabers Sportsland and similar arcades. We rode the Cyclone, Wonder Wheel, Thunderbolt, Parachute Jump, bumper cars, and other popular rides. We staked our claim to the beach with blankets secured at the corners by sneakers and transistor radios, then explored the sand and jetties for crabs, starfish and shells, before plunging into the bracing Atlantic. Sometimes we'd camp all night on the beach, sleeping near entire families huddled on blankets, the amusement rides still, the sky aglow with stars, the dark ocean stretching to the farthest corners of the earth.

Coney Island was just the beginning, though. Our journeys outside Bay Ridge exposed us to many of Brooklyn's other moving parts—landmarks we stumbled upon, hot spots we heard about from other kids, other neighborhoods.

And, especially, the movies.

The movie houses that dotted Brooklyn were in their heyday back then, popular epicenters of social life. Cable television, movie rentals and multiplex cinemas were still years away. Suburban drive-ins were tantalizing, but solely the province of teenagers with access to cars. In contrast, small, independent movie theaters were virtually everywhere.

In Bay Ridge, the Loews Alpine, Stanley, and RKO Dyker theaters were within easy walking distance. Minutes away by subway or bus were the Avalon and Kingsway theaters on Kings Highway, the Claridge on Avenue P, the Mayfair on Avenue U, the Walker on Eighteenth Avenue, and more obscure theaters like the Jewel, the Granada, the Rugby, the Astor, and the Marboro. All were air-conditioned, accessible, and cheap. All provided a dark, satisfying escape for the lines of kids that began at the box office and wound their way around the corner when a top-flight feature opened.

Even more enticing than the neighborhood theaters, though, were the stately, ornate movie palaces on Flatbush Avenue, Brooklyn's largest commercial thoroughfare. There, we could take our choice among a string of theaters stretching for blocks: the Albemarle, the Rialto, the RKO Kenmore, the Beverly, and the crown jewel of them all, the thirty-five-hundred-seat Loews Kings, where many Brooklyn high schools held their commencement exercises.

Majestic and elegant, the Flatbush Avenue movie palaces were built during the Great Depression, when scenic effects ranged beyond stage and screen, and theaters enabled moviegoers to lose themselves in rich, escapist fantasies. Dark and cavernous, they reflected a stately opulence. Glittering chandeliers hung from gilded, vaulted ceilings over plush, reclining orchestra seats. Curving marble staircases with brass handrails led to double and triple balconies. Velvet stanchions marked holding lines. Lobby fountains flanked by massive columns flowed into fully stocked fish ponds.

Not yet ready for the wave of introspective, socially conscious films still to come, we immersed ourselves in horror movies like *Frankenstein, Dracula,* and *The Wolf Man;* monster movies like *Godzilla* and *Rodan*; sci-fi flicks like *The Blob* and *War of the Worlds*, and low-budget B-movies that offered scintillating images of lush, big-breasted women.

Rock 'n' roll films with Elvis Presley and Ricky Nelson were popular with older kids; so was the beach-blanket series with Frankie Avalon and Annette Funicello. For us, cops-and-robbers and cowboy movies more than filled the bill. So did the Johnny Weissmuller *Tarzan* series; comedies with Abbott and Costello, Martin and Lewis, and The Three Stooges, and adventure films like *The Time Machine, Around the World in Eighty Days,* and *Twenty Thousand Leagues Under the Sea.*

Going to the Flatbush Avenue movies, like going to Coney Island, was an all-day affair. Shows ran continuously from noon to midnight. For a quarter you could see two full-length features, a dozen cartoons, a newsreel, and coming attractions. You could giggle and toss popcorn kernels across rows of seats. You could mock the ushers and matrons padding up and down the aisles. You could gawk at the teenagers making out in the balconies. You could sit in a plush seat and escape into everything Hollywood was offering, then emerge onto sunlit sidewalks swarming with kids heading for Jahn's Ice Cream Parlor or the Hamburger Host or automats like Horn & Hardot, Garfields, and Dubrows.

But even Flatbush Avenue only *hinted* at what was out there to see. Driven by a growing desire to broaden our scope and relish in our escapes from parental oversight, our journeys grew more ambitious over time.

We roller-skated at the Park Circle Rink, renting high-top skates and circling varnished hardwood to the strains of pipe-organ music and raucous, gleeful shouts. We went swimming at the St. George Hotel, where an enormous salt-water pool, its glass-lined ceiling dazzling with lights, was surrounded by carvings of dolphins and mermaids swimming in a sea of foaming waves. We rode the Bay-

Ridge-St. George Ferry to Staten Island, gaping at the Statue of Liberty, the ghostlike ruins of Ellis Island, and the craggy contours of the Brooklyn and Manhattan waterfronts. We rode the R-line through dark, serpentine tunnels into Manhattan, emerging onto streets where wispy sewer gas was blown about by fleets of yellow taxis, and enormous towers soared to the sky. More than once we traveled all the way to the Bronx, where we stood transfixed before the imposing edifice of Yankee Stadium, the surrounding neighborhood far more forbidding than Crown Heights, where Ebbets Field stood tucked amid familiar streets.

Mostly, though, we stayed in Brooklyn.

By then we all had bikes—large Schwinn or Ross two-wheelers and, some of us, sleek English racers replete with hand brakes and four-speed gearshifts. And on some weekends, we rode them for hours at a time, exploring Brooklyn's immense geography.

We biked Eastern Parkway to the famed Institute Triangle Complex—the Brooklyn Museum and Central Library, the Osborne and Botanic Gardens—then stood beneath the imposing Civil War monument at Grand Army Plaza, pretending we were victorious liberators being serenaded by grateful Parisian women at the *Arc de Triomphe*. We biked along the Promenade, a mile-long esplanade that cantilevered the East River docks and offered stunning vistas of the Statue of Liberty and the Wall Street skyline. We biked to Bedford Avenue and explored the Georgian buildings and sunken gardens of Brooklyn College. We biked into Prospect Park, losing ourselves in that vast, pastoral wonderland, gliding along winding paths past enormous shade trees, rock formations, rolling meadows, and placid lakes.

Sometimes we biked along the open expanse of the Belt Parkway, following the shoreline to Manhattan Beach and Sheepshead Bay. Other times we rode the six-mile path along Ocean Parkway; past elegant supper clubs and luxury apartment buildings; past people strolling the broad, sumptuous boulevard; past streets with names like Church and Ditmas Avenues, and Clarendon, Albemarle, Farragut and Cortelyou Roads; past the synagogue where my parents were married, its stone stairway crowded with worshippers waiting to hear Pierre Pinchik and other famous cantors, as if their hymns could purge the pain wrought by the revelations of Nazi Germany.

Mostly, though, there was little pain on our journeys through Brooklyn—only the gift of freedom and escape, a series of eye-opening revelations, a growing sense of wonder and surprise.

Brooklyn, we discovered, was far more than the sum of its world-famous icons, its image and identity, its reputation for folklore, legend and mystique. For one thing, it was immense beyond our wildest imaginations. A huge and sweeping mosaic. Cosmopolitan yet parochial. A patchwork of distinct neighborhoods tied together by a common thread. Stunning in its complexity, yet containing a common culture, language, and view of the world. It was also, we discovered, rich with contradiction, a jarring mix of the elegant and ordinary.

We biked into fashionable neighborhoods where tranquil streets were lined with richly furnished brownstones, picturesque row houses and stately, historic dwellings. We rode past opulent mansions with expansive porches, rooftop gardens and hand-carved, ornamented facades; past exclusive manor homes, their interiors flush with parquet floors, stained-glass windows, wood-paneled fireplaces and crystal chandeliers; past villas and carriage homes whose rooflines were punctuated by towers, chimneys, dormer windows, and gables.

We biked, too, past the grungy and mundane: past overgrown lots and fleabag hotels, rundown tenements and littered streets, garish billboards and thoroughfares lined with butcher shops, delis, bakeries, pizza parlors, candy stores, and other retail outlets. We biked in the shadows of the elevated BMT-Culver line, sitting atop rusted iron pillars that ran the length of McDonald Avenue. We biked past the empty skeletons of former factories, through neighborhoods that seemed tired and worn, past junkyards and auto repair shops, past overgrown cemeteries and reeking trash cans, past homes not of the wealthy and privileged, but of the city's blue-collar working stock, people who Brooklyn grew up around.

People like us.

That's what made it feel so comfortable, so safe. Everywhere, were homes like ours. Everywhere, were people like us.

Many neighborhoods we biked through looked and felt strikingly like Bay Ridge: orderly, well kept, fanning out around small, self-contained shopping districts. Long stretches of six-story, fire-escaped apartment buildings stood near bus and subway stops. Narrow one-way streets were lined with wood-framed and aluminum-sided houses, rows of attached two-family townhomes, and modest bungalows of sandstone and terra cotta. Religious statues stood in front yards. Garments hung on clotheslines strung to poles set in fenced-in backyards. Rose bushes spilled over garden gates. Ivy tendrils drooped from window boxes. Towering maple, oak and sycamores formed lush canopies over side streets. Red-brick schools surrounded by chain-link fences stood alongside synagogues, yeshivas and churches.

Because of this, Brooklyn felt familiar—oddly like *home*—wherever we biked. Devoid of Manhattan's pretense and glitz, it was quieter, more down to earth than the borough we called "the city." Absent Manhattan's soaring, vertical skyline, it seemed spacious, even airy, in most places. Unlike in Manhattan, you never felt overwhelmed or trapped. From almost anywhere, you could see the horizon. From almost anywhere, you could see the sky. And breathe.

Brooklyn was also far more diverse than we'd ever dreamed possible. Bustling. Vital. Dynamic. A great bubbling cauldron of people and personalities. The epitome of New York's alloy of race, class, religion, ideology, lifestyle, and identity. Everyone different, yet somehow melded into a common identifiable entity. Everyone co-existing within the borough's tightly packed geography. Connected by virtue of the place they called home. Bound by the common pressures of trying to make it in a chaotic, competitive city. Rubbing shoulders while moving through simple daily acts. Coping with the same struggles, relishing the same triumphs, reaching for the same dreams.

I'd never feel quite the same way anywhere else. None of us would. We'd never feel the same commonality, the same connectedness, the same feeling of being anchored to something that would be part of us forever.

We'd never feel the same way we did when we were kids in Brooklyn: safe and secure in the cocoon of our neighborhood. Surrounded by people who lived, laughed, cried, celebrated, mourned, and struggled along with us. Bit players in the daily intercourse of New York. Part of a cycle that was repetitive and comforting and familiar. Living together through the seasons of our lives. Bathed for all time in Brooklyn's eternal, shining light.

Chapter 14

It was easy to understand the uneasy hush that enveloped the Hamilton High auditorium at the mere mention of Robert Moses' name. Everyone at the anti-bridge rally knew who he was. Moses, by then, had long since cemented his reputation in the collective mind of New Yorkers. No public figure, in fact, had ever had a greater impact on the physical geography—the very look and feel—of New York. No government official had ever cast as giant a shadow over the city's political landscape, or had a greater impact on its daily life.

"So, it's *Robert Moses* who's behind the bridge, huh?" Joey Palumbo barked. "Well, we all know who that is, don't we?"

"Yeah," someone shouted. "He's the guy who built the Gowanus Expressway and killed Sunset Park."

"You got that right!" Palumbo roared.

"He's the bastard who threw fourteen-hundred families outta their homes to build the Cross Bronx Expressway," another man said.

"Yep," Palumbo exclaimed. "He coulda saved hundreds of them homes, too. But he wouldn't move the road a block outta the way 'cause of some real estate cronies he was helpin' out."

The audience stirred with random chatter.

"Moses is also the sonovabitch who drove the Dodgers outta town," someone else chimed in, echoing the popular belief that the team had abandoned Brooklyn only after Moses refused to offer Walter O'Malley a suitable alternative to the aging Ebbets Field.

"You got it now!" Palumbo growled.

The audience simmered again. Yes—everyone was well aware who Robert Moses was. Even if they knew only part of the story. Even if their opinions had been shaped by rumor, innuendo, and half-truths. Even if they were blinded by their growing hysteria, ruled by their growing fear.

But who Robert Moses *really* was hardly mattered at the moment. What mattered was that if Moses was behind the plan to build the Narrows bridge, then anyone who stood in his way was in for a hell of a fight. For the protestors gathered in the Hamilton High auditorium, Robert Moses wasn't simply an empty-suited city official armed with a plan. He was the fiercest adversary any of them could have imagined. He was, in many ways, their worst possible nightmare.

MORE THAN ANY other single individual, Robert Moses had made modern-day New York all that it was. In some ways, it was said, he'd almost singlehandedly rescued the city from ruin. In other ways, critics argued, he was bringing it to the brink of despair. Either way, his impact on New York was indisputable, his story inseparable from that of the city itself.

Before his rise to power in the 1920s, America's greatest city was being literally strangled by its own traffic. Its century-old street grid, built for horses and horse-drawn railroads, was being overwhelmed by the growing number of trolleys and cars. Travel through Manhattan, in particular, was nightmarish. The borough's highway loop, built in bits and pieces, was wholly inadequate. There were numerous river-to-river thoroughfares but no viable north-south avenues. Traffic crawled along narrow, unpaved streets. Tiny, antiquated drawbridges were crammed with vehicles. With only the Bronx connected to mainland America, not a single vehicular link existed between New York's central island and the rest of the nation. Separated by waterways, the boroughs themselves were unconnected.

To make matters worse, the dilemma seemed insoluble. Dozens of plans to build highways, bridges, and tunnels had been scuttled, victimized by exorbitant costs, engineering limitations, petty self-interests, and bureaucratic red tape.

Robert Moses changed all that.

An idealistic dreamer in his early years, Moses believed that New York, for all its grandeur, was in dire peril. Crowded and inaccessible, he saw the city as a wilderness of stone and steel, ill-equipped to function in the modern age. At the same time, he saw beyond New York's clutter and shortcomings, envisioning the city and its surrounding region as an immense canvas on which he could create a dazzling new vision for urban America.

And that's precisely what he did.

During an unprecedented, four-decade-long reign as the city's top planner, Moses breathed life into ideas that, until then, had been nearly unthinkable, masterminding public works projects that dwarfed any ever built in America. Literally dismantling and remaking the city, Moses created a New York that was nothing less than the model metropolis of twentieth century America, the unchallenged center of American life. He revitalized the city, modernized it, and created attractions that drew worldwide attention. He built airports, dams, piers, marinas, and promenades. He built schools, libraries, hospitals, sewage disposal plants, playgrounds, parks, and public housing projects. He built the United Nations building, Lincoln Center, the New York Coliseum, and other landmark structures.

But even those projects paled in comparison to the roads Robert Moses built. During a career that spanned the administrations of five mayors and six governors, Moses conceived and constructed a network of highways and river crossings whose scope was unparalleled. Considered the greatest feat of urban construction in history, Moses' transportation template—encompassing hundreds of miles of parkways, expressways, causeways, and traffic interchanges, along with dozens of bridges and tunnels—literally redefined New York, enabling unprecedented access to the city, creating bypass routes around it, transforming New York into the beating heart of a region whose growth was exploding.

Built largely in a frenzied two-decade period after World War II, Moses' roads became forever ingrained in the daily parlance of New Yorkers. Circumventing Manhattan, Moses built the Harlem River Drive and the East and West Side Highways. Around and through Brooklyn, Queens and the Bronx, he built the Major Deegan, Bruckner and Cross-Bronx Expressways, the Belt and Grand Central Parkways, and the Van Wyck, Gowanus and Brooklyn-Queens Expressways. Heading north, out of the city, he built the Henry Hudson, Saw Mill, Bronx River, Hutchinson River, and Taconic State Parkways. He also built most of the bridges and tunnels that wove together what he called the loose strands and frayed edges of New York's arterial tapestry.

And all that's to say nothing about what Moses did on Long Island.

Little more than an undeveloped wilderness when he began his career, Moses transformed Long Island into a landscape of roads that were nothing less than masterpieces of modern engineering. Conceived for scenic pleasure drives rather than utility, Moses' Long Island roads were breathtaking works of art that literally emanated sunlight and color. Flanked by verdant parkland, the roads followed the natural contours of the land, curving through meadows and around the bends of rivers and streams. Commercial traffic was banned. Speed limits were set at forty-five miles per hour. Virtually no aesthetic detail was ignored.

On Moses' Long Island roads, light poles and barrier posts, hewn from logs, were stained to match nature. Signs were mounted on rustic wooden standards. Granite-faced overpasses arched gracefully across the parkways. Maintenance buildings and roadside gas stations were fashioned of stone, slate and copper. Promenades and bicycle paths meandered through landscaped spaces bursting with azaleas and dogwoods.

But what Moses built on Long Island was more than simply a network of beautiful roads. Long before anyone, in fact, Moses had envisioned Long Island not simply as a potential suburban outpost, but as a recreational playground for New Yorkers. And he'd transformed that vision into a stunning reality. Moses snapped up shoreline properties and built beaches and recreation areas. He acquired barren tracts of woodland and built state parks, complete with boathouses and bridle paths, picnic groves and hiking trails, skating rinks and campgrounds. Then he connected his roads to the beaches and parks, opening those natural wonders to the masses.

Suddenly, thanks to Robert Moses, New Yorkers were no longer trapped in their cramped, stifling apartments, unable to escape the hubbub of city life. They no longer had to rely on rail lines or ferries, or endure hours of traffic, in their quest for fresh air and nature. All they had to do was hop in a car and head out on Robert Moses' beautiful parkways to Robert Moses' pristine beaches and verdant parks. All of it was mere miles away, all of it within easy reach.

Even more impressive than the projects themselves was *how* Moses built them. On Long Island's exclusive North Shore, he'd carved his roads across private estates and hunting preserves owned by powerful land barons. On the South Shore, he'd built them over the objections of reclusive fishermen who zealously protected every inch of shorefront property. In mid-island, he'd gobbled up nearly forgotten city-owned watersheds and huge tracts from farmers whose families had owned the land for generations. In each case, he'd moved figurative mountains in his quest to build, cleverly outsmarting opponents, cutting deals with local politicians, defeating powerful attorneys in court, acquiring rights-of-way through skillful negotiations and land-swapping deals, seizing and condemning properties at will.

And yet even that paled by comparison to the way Moses had built within the city limits of New York itself.

Moses' urban roads were nothing like his Long Island parkways. Unlike those roads—restricted to private cars and slow-moving pleasure drives—Moses' city roads featured neither amenities nor charm. The era of the richly landscaped parkway had ended with World War II. Tied to modern guidelines for federal funding, Moses' city roads were high-speed expressways aimed at expanding America's highway infrastructure, designed for commercial traffic and a new generation of fast-moving cars.

And New York was hardly open country—nothing like the undeveloped, sparsely populated areas on the city's outskirts. No, to build his city roads, Moses had to carve his way, inch by inch, through New York's dense, existing infrastructure. Rights-of-way were wrested from powerful real estate interests—banks, utilities, corporations, even the Catholic Church. Private homes, apartment buildings, factories, businesses, and other structures were demolished in droves. Hundreds of thousands of people were relocated. Subway and sewer lines were rerouted. Roads were lifted over the tops of streets onto huge elevated structures. In some cases, entire city blocks were rearranged, with existing structures hoisted from their foundations and relocated to other sites, set on different angles, or supported while construction proceeded underneath.

Moses' monumental achievements had earned him a status that was nearly exalted. To many New Yorkers, he was seen as a modern-day hero, a miracle worker possessed of almost mythic qualities. His ideas served as a model for other American cities. Urban planners studied at his feet. Children chanted his name as he presided over the opening of playgrounds. Heralded for his achievements, idealized by an adoring press, he was hailed as "Public Friend Number One," a visionary who, in the field of urban planning, ranked alongside geniuses like Mozart, Einstein, and da Vinci. He was Big Bob: The Master Builder who conceived projects thought unimaginable. Big Bob: The genius who solved engineering challenges thought insoluble. Big Bob: A public champion leading New York to new heights of greatness. Big Bob: The Man Who Got Things Done.

A bridge across the Narrows was to be the crowning glory of Robert Moses' career, a final monument to his achievements. Moses called the project "the bridge of his dreams"—the most expensive, most ambitious, most important piece of arterial roadway ever conceived. He'd waited decades to build it. He'd calculated the optimum location for the crossing and determined that his proposed approach would be less costly and less disruptive than any alternative. He'd completed the feasibility studies, procured the funds, and surmounted nearly all the obstacles.

Sure, he'd have to carve his way through the heart of Bay Ridge, thrusting a massive ribbon of concrete across the neighborhood's densely populated landscape. Sure, he'd have to move hundreds of homes and businesses out of the way. But all that, Moses reasoned, was a small price to pay for progress, insignificant when measured against everything to be achieved.

To Moses, the end justified the means. People may be hurt, he understood, but that was inevitable. After all, he was fond of saying, you couldn't hack your way through a crowded metropolis without using a meat cleaver. You couldn't rebuild a city without moving people any more than you could make an omelet without breaking an egg.

JOEY PALUMBO ROSE from his seat and strode to the front of the Hamilton High auditorium, mounting the stage. Councilman Alan Sherman, Stephen Calico, Walter Staziak, and the others stepped aside as the gruff ex-marine grabbed the microphone, all but strangling it in his grasp.

"So now we know who's behind this bridge—the great and powerful *Robert Moses*," Palumbo snarled. "The guy who's knockin' down half the city to build his projects. The guy who's puttin' thousands of people outta their homes."

He leaned forward, scanning the audience.

"This is the sonovabitch who likes roads and bridges more than he likes Brooklyn," Palumbo said. "This is the guy who thinks his pretty new beaches on Long Island are better than the beach at Coney Island. This is the guy who doesn't give a good goddamn 'bout workin' stiffs like us."

The audience murmured in agreement—for that was surely the consensus then in blue-collar Brooklyn. Robert Moses, the legendary Master Builder, had come to be seen by most Brooklynites as The Enemy. His once-gleaming image had become tarnished through the years. The very qualities that made him so successful had also done him in. He was seen as ruthless, arrogant, unyielding, insensitive to the needs of average New Yorkers—corrupted by the power he arbitrarily wielded. His methods had become a lighting rod for controversy. His name alone was anathema.

"I don't give a damn who's makin' these decisions—Robert Moses or the good Lord himself," Joey Palumbo said. "What the city's plannin' to do to Bay Ridge is wrong!"

The audience applauded.

"Now, I ain't no legal expert, like Mr. Calico here, and I don't know nothin' about *eminent domain* or any of that other mumbo jumbo," Palumbo said. "But we're talkin' about our homes, our neighborhood, our lives. Everything we've worked for, everything we got in this world."

Palumbo stared out defiantly.

"I can't speak for all of you," he told the hushed assemblage, "but there's too much at stake to just bow our heads and walk away. I'm gonna fight the city tooth and nail over this. My home ain't for sale—and I'll be goddamned if I'm gonna allow anyone to take it!"

Several men rose from their seats.

"We're with you!" one shouted.

"Yeah!" another said. "Let's fight the bastards!"

"You're goddamned right that's what we'll do," Palumbo vowed. "I swear to you: I'll lie down and let the city's bulldozers roll over me before I'm pried outta my home. If they want to evict me, they'll have to carry me out, kickin' and screamin'."

And, with that, the audience let out a rousing cheer, as if to tell city officials, in no uncertain terms, where the lines for the Battle of Bay Ridge had been drawn.

Chapter 15

Even amid the growing tumult, things seemed fairly normal around our house that evening. Back from the protest rally, my mother busied herself in her garden, pruning and watering her wildflowers, while my sister went upstairs to listen to her forty-fives and my father retreated to his cellar workshop.

The evening didn't feel normal to me, however. Restless, unnerved by the rhetoric at the Hamilton High School meeting, I drifted downstairs, where my father was rebuilding a linotype machine for a local print shop. He always kept busy that way. When he wasn't working at Mergenthaler, he was usually immersed in a stream of projects around the house, or on side jobs like the one he was tackling now, trying to earn a couple of extra bucks. He was like a lot of fathers that way. Worked hard. Never complained about it. Just got up the next day, and the next, and did it again.

"Hey slugger," he said, glancing up. "How you doin'?"

"Okay."

And I was at the moment.

I liked hanging around the tiny workshop my father had tucked into a corner of our cellar. I liked being around him when he worked, listening to him explain how his clunky linotype machines operated. And I liked nosing around his workshop, a cool, quiet sanctuary even in the blistering heat of summer.

Illuminated by a single lightbulb, the workshop was cluttered with tools and flushed with the scent of hot lead, grease, and printer's ink. Partially built linotype assemblages lay strewn atop a workbench, along with coffee cans, milk bottles, and cigar boxes overflowing with nuts, bolts, washers, and screws. Grimy work shirts hung from a nail in the cinder block foundation. Wooden shelves were stocked with canned goods, blankets, flashlights, a first-aid kit, radio, and other Cold War-related necessities.

Stuffed similarly into the nooks and crannies of the workshop were the byproducts of my father's trade. Old newspapers stood in tall, dusty stacks. Posters and playbills were taped to walls. Rickety bookcases overflowed with back issues of *Life, Look*, *Colliers,* and the *Saturday Evening Post*, along with hardcover books, paperbacks and catalogues produced by Mergenthaler customers. My father, as far as I knew, never read any of them. He simply liked having them around—a form of reassurance, I suppose, that his work, often mundane and grueling, helped produce something substantive, something meaningful to the people who bought them.

He was connected even more that way to newspapers. And those he *did* read.

"Best bargain in New York," he'd say. "Think about it, Nathan, for a coupla cents you can learn what's happening in the world. You can follow your favorite team or comic strip. Businesses can advertise. People can be entertained. Tell me, where else you gonna get all that for only a nickel?"

It was oversimplified, of course, blindly unsophisticated, like many things back then. Most newspapers in the 1950s were hardly beacons of journalism. My father, however, made it a point to see beyond their flaws. He forgave the lapdog journalists and the gossip mavens and the seedy editors who feasted on violence, sensationalism, sex, and cheap entertainment. He forgave the tabloids and scandal sheets for their shallowness and excess; forgave the prestigious papers for their arrogance and bias, for the way they pandered to advertisers and purported to be champions of the people but were usually gutless mouthpieces for government. Instead, he chose to see newspapers as an ideal. He saw them as watchdogs and beacons. Essential to freedom of expression and the public's right to know. Essential to the preservation of liberty itself.

"You know, the first thing dictators do when they take over a country is seize control of the newspapers," he'd say. "Think about that. You control newspapers, you control people's minds. Even Thomas Jefferson said it'd be better to have newspapers without government than government without newspapers."

Right or wrong, he believed that. He wanted to. I'm sure he needed to.

It made him feel good, he said, to see the army of straphangers on the subway every day, reading newspapers whose type was set by Mergenthaler linotypes. It made him feel good to see me reading the *Daily News* and the *New York Post*, digesting everything Jimmy Cannon, Dick Young, Roger Kahn and all the other big-time columnists wrote about things that were important to me. It made him feel that, through his work, he was somehow helping connect all of us, in some small way, to our world—even to each other.

Sometimes after supper, we'd walk to Seventh Avenue, where groups of men milled about in front of Thumann's Candy Store, awaiting the arrival of the evening papers. My father got a kick out of seeing that: the men standing in the glow of long-armed, chocolate-colored lampposts, chatting about business, politics, and sports; the delivery trucks sweeping past on their way to other newsstands; the newspapers, bundled in twine, tossed to the sidewalk, cut apart and gobbled up in minutes.

No, he hadn't become an architect—hadn't lived the grandiose dream he'd harbored as a boy. But he didn't harbor regrets either, becoming sour like some men do. Instead, he'd worked honestly and hard, and his work had become worthwhile in a way he could touch and feel, a surprise of sorts that he'd never envisioned when he'd first set out.

I was happy for him that way. I hoped that one day I'd grow to feel the same about my own work.

"Are you sorry?" I'd asked him just that summer.

"Sorry 'bout what?"

"You know—about not becoming an architect. That was your dream when you were a boy, wasn't it?"

"Yep."

"But you had to give it up, didn't you?"

He looked up from the machine he was working on.

"We were in a Depression," he said matter-of-factly. "Times were tough. My family needed help. A lot of boys like me quit school to go to work. Those were things we had to do. No one made a big deal out of it. We just did it."

"But do you regret it?"

He seemed more pensive now.

"Maybe a bit—sometimes. Everyone has regrets. They're part of life. But hopefully they're small ones."

Then he smiled.

"As far as dreams go—they're for kids like you, slugger. To tell you the truth, I don't have much time for 'em anymore. I'm too busy trying to make a buck."

He looked at me earnestly. "But *you* be sure you make the time," he said. "Part of the reason I work so hard is so that you can dream big. Understand?"

"Yes."

He went back to work.

"Thanks for asking, Nathan, but I'm okay," he said. "I really am. You know, it's a funny thing about regrets. For every one you have, there's a surprise or two that comes along, something you never imagined. If you're lucky, the surprises make up for the regrets."

"Surprises?"

"Sure," he smiled. "Things you never saw comin'."

"Like what?"

"Things like your mother," he smiled. "Things like you."

I poked around my father's workbench for awhile and found a lead slug produced once by one of his linotypes. I picked it up and ran my fingers across the Braille-like letters: N A H T A N. My name spelled in reverse.

"Remember when I made that?" he asked. "You had to be, what, seven or eight years old?"

“Probably,” I said, recalling when he gave me the slug—and how, when I applied it to an inkpad and pressed it to paper, I discovered that my name would print perfectly, exactly like in a newspaper.

“Boy, you sure loved that thing.” My father laughed. “We’d find your name printed all over the house—on pads, your mother’s typing paper, you name it.”

“Sometimes on the kitchen counter and my bedroom wall.”

“Yeah. That, too.”

Then he pulled a soiled rag from his back pocket.

“Listen, I’m just about finished here,” he said, wiping his hands. “Whaddaya say we have a little catch?”

I jumped at the chance. It wasn’t often, with his busy schedule, that he had the time. But there were few things I liked more. I raced upstairs and grabbed my glove, a Rawlings, four-finger Duke Snider model we’d bought the previous summer at Davegas, a sporting goods store on Kings Highway.

“Let’s take a peek at that,” my father said, and I tossed him the mitt.

“Still a little stiff.” He nodded toward a tin of Neatsfoot oil. “Hand me that.”

He squirted the lubricant onto my glove, working it deep into the leather, then punched the pocket to shape it before tucking his fingers halfway into the mitt.

“Jeez, you’re probably outgrowing this already,” he laughed.

He was right. The glove, not even a year old, was already feeling snug. It was far too small for my father’s hands—yet another byproduct of his work.

Swollen and heavy calloused, my father’s hands had been damaged by years of manual labor—his fingertips burned and discolored by hot lead and printer’s ink, his fingernails embedded with grime and worn to the nub, his right pinky, mangled in a jobsite accident, bent permanently to a side.

“Promise me you won’t ever let your hands look like this,” he said, shaking his head.

“Why not? What’s wrong with them?”

“They’re the hands of a working stiff, slugger. Understand? Not a man who’s gone very far in life. They’re a reminder of how hard I’ve gotta work.”

"What's wrong with working hard?"

"Nothing. It's just that I want things to be easier for you, Nathan. I want you to work hard, but in a different way. Learning a trade was okay when I was your age. But you can learn to work with your head instead of your hands. And you can go a lot further than I did."

He pulled his hand from my glove.

"Then," he smiled, "you won't have hands that look like they were caught in a meat grinder."

I wanted to tell him to stop—that he didn't have to apologize for hands that put food on our table, clothing on our backs. But I didn't know how. Words to express thoughts like that were years away, well beyond my teenaged grasp. My father was the same. I knew he felt things, felt them deeply, but couldn't bring himself to express those feelings in words—didn't know how, wasn't sure if it was all right. And so they remained unspoken.

"Understand what I'm trying to tell you?" was all he said.

I nodded.

"Good."

Then, from a shelf, he pulled out his own glove, a ragged three-fingered mitt, its binding knotted and frayed, its pocket paper thin.

"Now, let's get outside," he said, "before we lose whatever sunlight's left."

FOR NEARLY AN hour, we played catch in our cul-de-sac, using a grass-stained baseball we'd shagged during batting practice one day at Ebbets Field.

My father, a pretty fair ballplayer in his day, one-handed my throws and returned them effortlessly, his tosses stinging as they smacked into my glove. I tried to mimic his smooth, gliding movements, fielding his throws with one hand, wondering if my return tosses had enough zip to smart his calloused hands. There was no evidence they did. My father deftly caught everything I threw and tossed the ball back just as easily. I trapped his throws in the web of my glove so they wouldn't hurt.

"Want something different?" he asked.

"Okay."

He threw me some fly balls, showing me how to use my gloved hand to shield my eyes from the glare of the sun without losing sight of the ball. Then he tossed me some grounders, each one gaining speed as it spun across the asphalt pavement.

"Glide to the ball," he advised, showing me how to shift my weight and move laterally, without tripping over my own feet.

"Over the top," he said when I tossed him the ball sidearm. "It's better to throw from behind your ear. You get more accuracy and speed."

I followed his advice, imagining each throw beating a speeding runner to first. Then he squatted into a catcher's crouch and I tried to pitch, mimicking the windup and delivery of my favorite pitchers.

I couldn't imitate Sandy Koufax, of course, or Yankees' ace Whitey Ford, or even Johnny Podres, hero of the Fifty-five Series clincher. They were southpaws and I threw right-handed. But I could closely mimic the sweeping windup of the Dodgers' flamethrower Don Newcombe, and the high leg kick of Billy Loes, and the surly demeanor of Early Wynn, anchor of the Chicago White Sox' staff.

My father caught my pitches and flipped the ball back, smiling as I tried to snap off curveballs that barely veered off course.

"It's okay to imitate players, but try to be yourself," he said. "Do what comes naturally. Everyone's got their own way of doing things. Find yours."

Then he rose from his crouch and we soft-tossed back and forth.

"It's tough not having a team to root for anymore, huh?" he said.

"Yeah."

"Well, you'll find yourself a new team eventually."

"How do you know?"

"That's the way it works, Nathan. That's the beauty of baseball. There's always new players to root for, new teams. Even when your favorite players leave, the game goes on."

We talked for a while about all the great young players coming up from the minors, and all the ones entering the majors now that baseball had opened to minorities. We talked about Mays and Clemente, Hank Aaron, Frank Robinson and the other top players still in their prime. I asked what happened when players got old.

"Their skills start to fade," my father explained. "They're still very good players, much better than average people, just not as sharp as major leaguers need to be. You reach a certain age, things change."

"What age?"

"It's different for everyone. Some players age faster than others. Depends what kind of shape they're in. Their bodies change. Their reflexes slow. They're not quite as strong. They can't run as fast or throw as hard. Their eyesight changes a little."

My father laughed. "I know it's hard for you understand, but it gets tougher to move around when you get older, trust me. Time's a thief, slugger. It steals your skills. All it takes is a split second of timing. That's the difference between being able to hit a major league fastball and striking out."

"How old are players when they're in their prime?"

"I'd say anywhere from twenty-three to maybe thirty-two. After that, they usually tail off."

Based on that, I knew my father was well past his prime. At thirteen, though, I figured I still had plenty of years to go. I felt good about that.

We tossed the ball back and forth in silence for awhile, the only sound the thwack of horsehide on leather, like a heartbeat steady and strong. Off beyond the Narrows, the sun set in a dull orange glow, my father's shadow stretching long and angular as he moved in the gathering twilight. He smiled at me as if he, too, knew the moment was special—the entire world in a calm balance, quiet and at peace, untroubled and intact, the tumult in Bay Ridge as distant as the setting sun.

I wanted it to stay that way, a perfect snapshot from my childhood.

I wanted to be standing forever on Dahlgren Place, just like that, tossing a baseball back and forth with my father, the sunlight waning, summer in the air, my mind full of all the things my life could possibly be, pretending that nothing about who we were and how we lived could ever possibly change.

Chapter 16

But pretending was impossible. The proposed bridge and expressway, looming overhead like a double-edged sword, were unavoidable realities. There was no hiding from them, no escape. That much was evident as summer wound to a close and the anti-bridge campaign grew even more intense.

Nearly all of Bay Ridge was engaged now in the fight. Weekly demonstrations were scheduled like clockwork. Children distributed leaflets. Volunteers stood at storefronts and on street corners, collecting signatures on petitions. Rally notices were posted on telephone poles and streetlights. Theaters screened protest schedules in lieu of local ads and movie trailers.

Financial backing poured in, as well. Bake auctions, penny sales, car washes, and "blighted block" parties served as fundraisers. Private donations fed a community war chest earmarked for legal and other expenses. Shopkeepers contributed portions of their weekly proceeds to the cause.

Local businessmen, some with perceived clout, also aimed a steady barrage of anti-bridge correspondence at city and state officials. Letters to the editor and "Stop the Expressway" ads ran regularly in key newspapers. Civic organizations throughout Brooklyn lent their name to the protests. Sympathizers from all over the city flocked to local rallies.

"This is the way average people get things done," Truman Cushman told protest leaders at the office of Councilman Alan Sherman, where protest strategy sessions were conducted three nights a week.

Typical of the tenants' and labor union activists drawn as advisors to the protest movement, Cushman was the former head of the United Electrical Workers, and had once led workers in a major strike at the American Safety Razor Company, when the union fought the company's planned relocation from Brooklyn to Virginia. Cushman had all but disappeared when the anti-Communist purge of the 1950s decimated the ranks of organized labor in New York. He'd re-emerged, however, as an unpaid advisor for various activists' groups, and only recently had helped a coalition of Bronx housewives organize a boycott to force meat wholesalers to lower their prices.

"Protest movements usually succeed only when people have money or are well connected to politicians and the press," said Cushman, his eyes aglow with the excitement of yet another cause to back.

"Well, we have neither money nor connections," Walter Staziak replied. "People in Bay Ridge are just ordinary folks. We don't have much in the way of political clout."

"That's why it's essential we band together," Cushman said. "Individually, we don't amount to much. Collectively, though, we have a voice—a powerful voice that demands to be heard."

Cushman assisted protest leaders in modeling the anti-bridge campaign after a labor movement. Block captains were designated for nearly all local streets, so that residents would know who to turn to for information and advice. Second-line cadres were selected so that backups would always be available. People were assigned tasks based on their experience and expertise. Protestors were schooled on ways to conduct themselves during demonstrations, even in potential confrontations with police.

And the training was paying dividends.

By the end of summer, mere weeks after it had kicked off, the anti-bridge campaign was rolling along like a well-oiled machine. No longer was Bay Ridge gripped solely by its initial state of panic and shock. The prevailing mood, instead, was one of fierce determination. Protest leaders seemed organized and in control. Hopes ran high that city officials might actually yield to neighborhood demands. People were optimistic that the bridge plan could be defeated. They were confident that, with persistence and time, even Robert Moses might back down and change his mind.

BUT WHILE SPIRITS rose on the streets, they were dampened behind closed doors, where protest leaders were exposed to the long odds they faced in winning their fight against the city.

"I don't want to lead you down a road paved with false hope," Councilman Alan Sherman said at a meeting a month into the campaign. "I want you to understand exactly what we're up against."

Sherman, by now, appeared dour and drawn, as if he understood all too well what was at stake. While his home didn't lie in the path of the proposed expressway, his political future was clearly in danger of demolition. Public officials in New York generally didn't forge successful careers by openly opposing Robert Moses like he was.

Sunlight streamed through the councilman's office windows, which opened to a block-long stretch of Seventh Avenue two stories below. Except for protest banners and rally posters, there were few signs the thoroughfare was in imminent danger. Shoppers meandered in and out of stores. Traffic wound its way along the avenue, its asphalt worn enough to reveal old steel trolley tracks and patches of cobblestone.

"I'm afraid the crisis we're facing is far more dire than we initially thought," said Sherman, sitting at a conference table of protest leaders.

"Why?" queried Walter Staziak. "We've been feeling things are going fairly well, that we're doing everything necessary to fight the bridge."

"That's very true," Sherman said. "But I'm afraid this project has a tremendous amount of momentum. To be perfectly blunt, I'm not sure there's any way we can stop it."

"Are you serious?"

"Sadly—yes." Sherman then introduced a man seated at the far end of the table. The man's name, he said, was Bradley Jacobs.

Handicapped by a birth defect that had stunted the growth of his right hand, Jacobs, nevertheless, cut an imposing figure. A towering man, he all but obliterated the sunlight when he rose from his seat, extending a beefy left hand to the men closest to him and an introductory nod to the others. Jacobs' movements also mirrored a pent-up energy. His eyes darted inquisitively around the table, as if he were taking a measure of everyone. Then he sat again, drumming the conference table with his good left hand.

"Mr. Jacobs's insights make him a valuable ally," Sherman said.

Indeed, Jacobs brought a unique perspective to the anti-bridge battle. For the past dozen years, he'd battled Robert Moses over several of the master builder's proposed projects. And, more than once, he'd actually prevailed.

"Councilman Sherman is correct," Jacobs began. "Difficult as it may be to accept, it's highly unlikely that the Narrows bridge project can be stopped."

"We don't understand," said Walter Staziak. "Is a bridge really necessary, given the heartache that'll result in Bay Ridge? Why can't the city just leave things as they are?"

"Leaving things as they are, I'm afraid, is no longer possible," Jacobs intoned. "The situation, from the city's perspective, has been status quo for far too long. The issue of a Narrows bridge has been coming to a head for years. Its time, many officials believe, is *now*."

"Are you saying that the bridge is a foregone conclusion—that there's no way we can fight it?" Chester Jablonski inquired.

"I'm not saying you can't *fight* it," Jacobs replied. "What I am saying is that the forces you're up against are extremely powerful."

"What forces are you talking about?"

"Well," Jacobs said, "let's just start with Robert Moses."

THE FACT THAT Robert Moses had accomplished all he had in New York had, in many ways, been nothing short of miraculous—a product not only of audacious dreams and towering intellect, but of boundless energy, unmatched political savvy and raw, unadulterated power. It was a power that had been accumulated across decades in public office, a power Moses wielded like no city official before or since, a power that was still at its very height.

Arguably the most influential public official in New York's history, Robert Moses occupied no less than a dozen municipal posts simultaneously. As New York's construction coordinator, he had a free hand over the design and location of every public construction project in the city. The Planning Commission, on which he held a seat, reviewed the merits of projects he alone conceived. The public agency he'd created, the Triborough Bridge & Tunnel Authority, functioned with powers tantamount to those of an autonomous sovereign state. A brilliantly structured hybrid of public and private power, the TBTA financed its projects using no public money, but rather funds issued through the sale of bonds to private investors. It had the power to seize land, undertake projects without the formality of public hearings, award contracts without competitive bidding, and seal its records, rendering them off-limits to public scrutiny.

Moses presided over this empire like an all-powerful ruler, immune from the normal restrictions imposed on government agencies, free of public or political pressures, insulated by a loyal inner circle, wielding his power with a combination of ingenuity, cunning and ferocious intensity.

New York's master builder, it was said, was tantamount to an indomitable force of nature: dynamic and enterprising, his ego as immense as his imagination, his will savage and unyielding. A man of boundless energy, he worked literally round the clock, obsessed with the projects he conceived, hungering to attain immortality from rebuilding New York.

A master of behind-the-scenes maneuvering, Moses could pick his way like no one else through the maze of laws that governed the city. Tied to city, state and federal officials at the highest levels, he could tap funding streams, win approvals and obtain rights-of-way like no one alive. A problem-solver without peer, he could marshal whatever forces were needed to get the job done. A master propagandist, he could crush, discredit, or torment opponents on a whim. Arrogant and imperious, he possessed an aura of fearlessness and infallibility, as if he were above either governance or rules. Few politicians, bureaucrats, government agencies or special interest groups dared challenge his power. Accomplished engineers blindly did his bidding. Oblivious to the possibility of being wrong, nothing could dissuade him from pursuing his ideas. To Robert Moses, there were no barriers. Literally no obstacle stood in his way.

Despite his unrivaled power, Moses had faced stiff opposition to several of his projects. His proposal for a Battery Bridge between Brooklyn and Manhattan had been defeated by opponents, who'd believed the project would mar the beauty of the New York skyline. Another plan, to build an elevated expressway across Manhattan, had been halted by architectural historians who'd argued that irreplaceable buildings would be destroyed by the roadway.

Moses' most bitter defeat, however, had come several miles from Bay Ridge, in Brooklyn Heights, where residents had blocked his plan to construct the Brooklyn-Queens Expressway through the heart of the historic neighborhood, and had forced the roadway to be built instead under a mile-long pedestrian promenade overhanging the Brooklyn waterfront. That defeat had not only preserved the unique character of the Heights, it had led to the creation of the nation's first Landmarks Preservation Commission, which fought to protect historic sections of New York from indiscriminate development.

Bradley Jacobs had been at the center of each of those battles. He'd been drawn to the Bay Ridge campaign as a favor to Councilman Sherman.

"You have very little chance of convincing Moses that the Narrows bridge project is unfeasible," Jacobs said. "That's an argument you'll never win."

"Why not?" Walter Staziak said.

"It's simple. Moses is too stubborn to back down. He's too egotistical to admit he might actually be wrong."

"How can we get him, then, to change his mind?"

"The only conceivable way is to mobilize public sentiment against the project. Fight fire with fire. Make an awful lot of noise."

"Aren't we already doing that?" Staziak asked.

"Yes—and you need to continue. The real objective, though, is not simply to make noise, but to get people with influence behind you, win support in the *right* places."

"But how do we do that?" Chester Jablonski inquired. "Moses has most government officials, as well as the press, in his back pocket."

"It's a big challenge," Jacobs sighed. "No question about it."

Protest leaders paused, as if to gather their thoughts.

"I understand Moses is obsessed with these projects," Staziak finally said. "But is he really the only say? Doesn't he answer to other public officials?"

Sherman snickered. "He's not accountable to *anyone*, really," the councilman said.

Again, there was a pause, pregnant this time with disbelief.

"In many ways, that's true," Jacobs continued. "The power in New York, in reality, doesn't reside with elected officials. Robert Moses is the final authority. With the power he has, Macy's could literally condemn Gimbels if Moses gave the word."

"You mean he's virtually *unopposed*?" Staziak stammered. "His motives and tactics aren't even questioned?"

Jacobs and Sherman exchanged glances and smiled wryly.

"I'll let you in a little secret," Sherman said. "Politicians may fear, even loathe, Moses. They may not always agree with him, either. But he's a perfect hatchet man for them, someone to hide behind. If the public likes what Moses is doing, then everyone's a hero. If people get upset, politicians can simply point the finger of blame at Moses. It's a game that works for everyone."

"And Moses plays the game better than anyone," Jacobs asserted. "Hell, he's been using the same tactics for forty years."

"What he really is," Sherman said, "is a *doer*. Robert Moses will do whatever he needs to do to get the job done. He knows how the system works because he helped create it. He can ram programs through the approval process, bend the rules, invent new rules as he goes along."

"But mostly," Jacobs said, "he understands patronage."

Sherman laughed, as if he knew only too well.

"Robert Moses is the maestro of the New York political stage," Jacobs continued. "He doles out political favors like he's handing out Thanksgiving turkeys to the poor. Everyone who matters, he's got in his hip pocket. He knows the right buttons to push, how to call in favors, how to bring pressure from labor unions, politicians, banks."

"What about the *law*?" Staziak asked.

"That doesn't matter," Sherman said. "Moses is insulated from the law by his power. Legalities aren't as important to him as convincing the public that he's right. He not only has the weight of his power behind him, but the weight of public opinion. Remember—he's had forty years of public adulation. His legend has been accepted as fact. Even now, few people dispute the way he gets things done."

"Doesn't he have to listen to the citizens footing the bill for his projects?" Staziak asked.

"Moses finds ways to obtain funds that have nothing to do with public tax dollars," Jacobs said. "He's also immune to politics in the same way most officials are beholden to it. Since he's been appointed—not elected—to public office, he doesn't need voter approval for the things he does."

"To be perfectly blunt," Sherman said, "he doesn't even *care* what voters think. To Moses, the public is nothing more than a great, amorphous mass. He feels he knows better than anyone what's good for New York. He has only one way of dealing with protestors. Essentially, he ignores them."

Jacobs laughed. "To Moses, the surest recipe for inaction is to listen to voices other than his own."

"But what about something called a democracy?" Staziak asked. "Isn't Moses undermining the democratic process? Isn't this a country where the voice of the people counts?"

"In truth," Jacobs replied, "the people have no real voice in determining the city's future when it comes to public works."

"What?"

Jacobs studied the men around him.

"What we have here," he said, "is almost tantamount to an autocracy. Sure, Moses is ignoring the wishes of the public. In many ways, he's literally *suspending* democracy. Clearly, he feels that's the only way his projects will ever get built."

"And he may be right," Sherman sighed.

The protest leaders stared at the councilman, groping for an explanation.

"Think about it," Sherman continued. "Great public works projects have almost always been associated with totalitarian regimes. Caesar built Rome. Genghis Khan built the roads of Asia. The pharaohs built the pyramids. Hitler built the Autobahn. In order to build these kinds of dramatic public projects you need enough power to be able to ignore the wishes of the people. You don't have to convince anybody. You don't have to argue your point of view. All you need is a single person with the vision to build. That's what we have in New York. Robert Moses is using his powers ruthlessly, like a dictator."

"But Moses is *not* building in a totalitarian regime, Staziak argued. "He's building in *America*. He needs permission from public officials beholden to voters. And those voters have a right to speak."

"No one denies that," Jacobs said. "You have the right to speak—and you *must* speak."

"But will we be heard?"

"I told you the only way. And that's to beat Moses at his own game. Oppose his power with power of your own."

"But are we *big* enough?"

"To be brutally frank," Jacobs said, "probably not."

"You mean the people of Bay Ridge, even acting collectively, may not be powerful enough to defeat *one* man?"

Jacobs hesitated, stealing a glance at Sherman, who nodded at the attorney to continue.

"I'm afraid what you're really fighting," Jacobs said, "is far more powerful than any singular person or government agency, way beyond New York and the Narrows bridge project."

Jacobs drummed a pencil on the conference table, measuring his words.

"What you're facing, in truth," he said, "is a *machine*."

"A machine?" Chester Jablonski said.

"Yes. A highway lobby with unimagined outreach, a powerful engine that's literally changing the face of America."

Everyone fell silent, listening raptly as Jacobs explained.

"This is a lobby that's been chomping at the bit for decades to build the roads it wants," the attorney said. "It waited through a Depression and a war. And now it's hell-bent on making up for lost time."

The protest leaders seemed perplexed.

"Just look around," Jacobs elaborated. "Roads are *everything* these days. Highways, bridges, tunnels—you name it. The entire country is being made over to accommodate the car. New York is no exception. The city is being dismantled, transformed, rebuilt for the Age of the Automobile. It's a fact of life we all have to face."

"But why *now*?" Staziak asked. "Why the sudden urgency, if things have been status quo for so long? Why the rush to build when so many people are being hurt by it?"

"In a word—money," Jacobs replied. "Big money."

The protest leaders seemed at a loss.

"Just think about it," Jacobs said. "Large-scale public works projects like the Narrows bridge are worth millions to a lot of people: lucrative construction contracts for developers; legal fees for attorneys; huge premiums for insurance companies; profits for investors; thousands of jobs for labor unions with big-time political clout."

"And that's just the start," Sherman added. "There's a tidal wave of special interests involved, too: auto makers, oil companies, steel mills, rubber plants, hotel chains, real estate interests, manufacturers of asphalt, gravel, cement, equipment, lumber, tools, lighting, signage, landscaping—literally anything connected to the bridge and road."

"And," said Jacobs, "all of it seeps back into government. Everyone in the food chain stands to benefit: state licensing bureaus; city agencies; politicians; public works officials; anyone who sets official policy—congressmen, senators, governors, mayors, you name it."

Jacobs let his words sink in. "Do you understand now what I'm saying when I use the word *machine*?"

No one uttered a word.

"The truth is, when push comes to shove, there are very few elected officials who'll try to stop the Narrows bridge project," Jacobs continued. “They may hint at or even pledge their support, but that’s likely just a smokescreen. In reality, almost every politician has a vested interest in seeing the project through. They’re supporting it behind the scenes. As I said, Robert Moses is just the front man.”

Silence, like a shroud, hung over the conference room.

“What you’re saying, in effect, is that our battle is really hopeless,” Staziak said. “That, regardless of how hard we fight, the power brokers will get to build their bridge and expressway, and we’ll lose our neighborhood?”

“All I’m saying,” Jacobs said, “is that it’ll be a very difficult to win.”

Everyone there could see that now. It was obvious to bridge opponents that they were fighting not just Robert Moses, but a bureaucracy that seemed poised and ready to swallow all of them—and the entire neighborhood—whole.

Chapter 17

The long odds against winning their fight did little to dissuade bridge opponents from continuing to take to the streets. A second march along Seventh Avenue drew an avalanche of chanting, sign-carrying protestors. Nighttime rallies, conducted to the ominous glow of torchlight, saw effigies of Robert Moses hoisted onto lampposts and set ablaze.

"We will not let one man dictate how we're gonna live our lives," shouted Joey Palumbo, who'd emerged as leader of an ultra-militant protest faction.

"If we allow him to, Robert Moses will steal everything that's important to us," Palumbo declared.

The crackling flames of a burning Moses effigy cast angry shadows on the faces of protestors who lined the street.

"We can't let him steal our neighborhood!" Palumbo shook his fist.

"No way!" the protestors shouted.

"We can't let him take our homes!"

"No way!"

"We can't let him destroy our lives!"

"No way! No way!"

Equally strident, though more passive, forms of protest had also taken shape by now.

Only days earlier, it had been learned that the Archdiocese of Brooklyn, in lockstep with the city's plan, had agreed that one of Bay

Ridge's most established places of worship, All Saints Episcopal Church, would be sold to the city and demolished to make way for the planned expressway. The parish, the Archdiocese had decided, would be combined with another nearby church.

The center of religious life for four hundred parishioners, All Saints Episcopal Church was the least grandiose of Bay Ridge's six churches—a tiny wooden structure fronted by large oak doors and a prominent steeple. The church, however, had a long and eventful history. Known as the Church of the Generals, it had served as the house of worship where Stonewall Jackson, when stationed at Fort Hamilton, had been baptized in the nineteenth century. Confederate General Robert E. Lee had also done service as a vestryman there before the Civil War.

Now the hundred-and-fifty-year-old house landmark was making news in a far different way. Shocked at the plan to demolish the church, parishioners were petitioning Archdiocese officials to spare the structure. Led by their mild-mannered sixty-year-old pastor, Monsignor Terrence Dougherty, church members publicly condemned the decision. Then, defying Archdiocese officials, Monsignor Dougherty vowed to keep the church open at all costs.

At daily services, he led parishioners in prayer that the church be spared. During sermons, he asked God for the wisdom and strength to deal with the crisis.

"I pray that God has not abandoned us," Monsignor Dougherty said from his pulpit.

"Amen," parishioners responded in unison.

"I pray that he saves the church we cherish and the homes we love."

"Amen."

"I pray that we are able to carry our fight to the only end that's just."

"Amen."

All throughout Bay Ridge, it seemed, people were offering similar prayers. Either God would help them defeat the city, they vowed, or they'd do whatever was needed to win the battle on their own.

Chapter 18

It was about then that the anti-bridge campaign took a more personal turn. My mother was summoned to the office of Councilman Alan Sherman.

"Hello, Mrs. Wolf," Sherman greeted her as she entered the smoke-filled conference room at the councilman's office.

"Call me Lily, please."

"Certainly," Sherman smiled.

Seated around the conference table were half a dozen block captains, most of whom my mother knew from rallies she'd attended. Also present was anti-Moses attorney Bradley Jacobs.

Cradling a telephone receiver between a shoulder and an ear, Jacobs extended his good left arm and swallowed my mother's hand in his. The others nodded in greeting.

"We called you here to solicit your support," Sherman began.

"Support?"

"Yes. We'd like you to play more of a role in our protests."

"What kind of role?" my mother queried. She'd already attended virtually every public demonstration in support of the protest movement.

"We're looking for a block captain," Sherman said, "on Dahlgren Place."

Taken aback, my mother offered no reply.

"You're aware, aren't you, that Dahlgren Place is earmarked for demolition to make way for the expressway?" Sherman asked.

"Yes."

"Well, it's also one of several streets that still needs a block captain. People mentioned you as a possibility."

Sherman stared earnestly at my mother. Jacobs glanced up from his phone and winked.

"Oh, I don't know …" my mother demurred. "I'm not sure I'm qualified to assume that kind of responsibility. Why me?"

"People know and respect you, Lily," Sherman said. "They're aware you've been active in protest rallies. They know your house is in the path of the expressway and that you care a great deal about living in Bay Ridge."

"That much is certainly true."

"Well, people thought you might have the motivation to assist us even more than you have."

My mother hesitated and then asked, "What would I have to do?"

"I'm not going to lie to you—it's hard work," Sherman responded. "You'd be required to attend organizational meetings and rallies, of course. You'd work with us to develop strategies for fighting the bridge. You'd serve as liaison between us and the people of Dahlgren Place."

"Liaison?"

"In other words, you'd serve as their representative. Answer questions. Keep them abreast of developments. Help lead."

"I'm hardly a leader," my mother said.

"Don't underestimate your abilities, Lily," Jacobs interjected, hanging up the phone. "You may surprise yourself."

Unaccustomed to such compliments, especially from accomplished men such as Jacobs, my mother felt blood rush to her face. She absentmindedly brushed a cheek, as if to stop the facial flushing.

"You shouldn't be so modest," said Jacobs, reading her astutely. "You shouldn't be embarrassed because people think highly of you."

"But I'm only a housewife."

"A very smart and committed one, from what we hear," Jacobs said.

"Yes, and on top of everything," Sherman smiled, "we hear you can type."

"Yes," my mother said, smiling now, too. "That I can do."

"Well, at the very least we need lots of things typed," Sherman said. "Petitions. Correspondence. Copy for newspaper ads."

He glanced at the others, then at my mother. "So what do you say?"

Jacobs nodded encouragingly and my mother diverted her gaze, strangely reluctant to make eye contact with the attorney, whose presence seemed to overwhelm the room. And her.

"Can I give it some thought?" she asked.

"Not really," Sherman replied. "We need an answer now."

"Then, all right," my mother said without further hesitation. "I'll do what I can."

"Good," Sherman said, smiling again. "Now have a seat."

And just like that, my mother was smack in the middle of the Battle of Bay Ridge, wrapped up as tightly in the fight as she'd ever been in anything.

And so were we.

Chapter 19

Aside from pressing on with public protests, bridge opponents worked feverishly behind the scenes as well, pushing to garner support from would-be political allies. As part of that effort, protest leaders began shepherding city and state officials through Bay Ridge so government leaders could more clearly gauge the destructive impact the proposed expressway would have on the neighborhood.

"Neighborhoods like Bay Ridge are the heart and soul of New York," Councilman Alan Sherman said on a walking tour with City Comptroller William Marshall, who held a vote on the bridge plan, and State Assemblyman Michael Esposito, who represented a dozen Brooklyn neighborhoods in the New York State Legislature.

"New York is the great city it is because of vibrant neighborhoods like this," Sherman said. "They're a resource the city can't afford to lose."

Sherman escorted Esposito, Marshall and several aides down Gatling Place and Ninety-second Street, two of the thoroughfares earmarked for demolition.

The group chatted as they walked along sidewalks lined with overhanging shade trees and cars parked curbside. The entrances to some homes were draped in black mourning crepe. NOT FOR SALE signs were posted defiantly in many front yards.

"By building expressways like the one being planned, you're destroying vital parts of New York," said Sherman, ushering the officials through a vest-pocket park, where old men played checkers and several mothers sat crocheting, their infants asleep in carriages and strollers.

"I think we all recognize the value of neighborhoods like Bay Ridge," Marshall admitted. "But the future vitality of New York lies in enabling people to commute to businesses and resources. The city desperately needs the Narrows bridge. Where would you like us to build it?"

"Anywhere but Bay Ridge," Sherman replied.

"But there might not be a viable alternative," Marshall said.

"That would be most unfortunate," Sherman countered. "It'd be nothing less than a death blow to thousands of people."

"Perhaps," Marshall said. "But New York is changing. If the city doesn't build new bridges and roads, it may not survive."

"And what about the survival of Bay Ridge?" Sherman asked. "Don't people here have the right to survive, too? Don't they have the right to continue to live the peaceful, productive lives they've lived until now?"

"Of course they do," Assemblyman Esposito offered. "But progress often comes at a price. Sometimes people get hurt. I know it's difficult, but consider the benefits of expressways like the one being proposed."

"I've heard about those supposed benefits," Sherman said. "I've heard about how these expressways can connect us. But, in truth, they're doing even more to *divide* us. They're dispossessing tens of thousands of people. They're eradicating irreplaceable landmarks. They're taking the sidewalks away from people and turning our streets over to cars."

The group continued down Gatling Place. In several yards, people tended to flowers and hedges. Kids roller-skated, biked, and romped in the street.

"You say these expressways are helping cities survive," Sherman argued. "But we disagree. We see them chewing cities up, isolating residents, amputating people from their roots. We see them drawing businesses out of the city, sucking the life from downtowns, dividing cities by income and race."

The group crossed Seventh Avenue and walked several blocks along the busy thoroughfare, concluding their tour at Sherman's office.

"It's a crime—the kind of urban planning that's in vogue now," Sherman said.

"How so?" Esposito asked.

"Our cities are being designed by planners who seemingly hate everything traditional cities stand for," Sherman replied. "They hate noise and congestion. They find vitality and street life repelling."

He gestured toward Seventh Avenue, alive with traffic and pedestrians.

"Cities are *supposed* to be cramped and chaotic," Sherman said. "Instead, all we hear about is this notion of a 'radiant city,' this ivory-tower idea that we should cleanse cities of chaos and clutter—that we should eradicate traditional neighborhoods and build pristine, streamlined cities with endless rows of concrete-and-glass towers, all linked by these 'magic motorways' flowing across the landscape."

"Is that what you see happening?" Esposito asked.

"Yes, and I challenge the thinking behind it. Right now, I see pedestrians becoming secondary to drivers. I see homes and architectural treasures being demolished to make way for a tidal wave of public works projects. I see mammoth roads defacing our landscape. I see mass transit being starved as we pour all our resources into highways."

Sherman nodded to several passersby edging their way into Thumann's Candy Store, where customers sat at the soda fountain, and shelves filled with comic books, candy bars, and school supplies lined the walls.

"New York's future," the councilman said, "depends less on high-rise slabs and superhighways than in preserving what made this city great in the first place. Streets that are full of life. Blocks that are serendipitous and spontaneous. Neighborhoods with resources that are reachable by foot. Communities with a heart and soul."

Sherman shook his head in dismay as Marshall and Esposito each smiled vaguely, as if something they'd seen sparked a fond remembrance.

"We all grew up in neighborhoods like Bay Ridge, didn't we?" Sherman asked, and both politicians nodded.

"So you understand what we're fighting to preserve, don't you? You understand what we'd be losing?"

Neither Marshall nor Esposito said a word. It was clear from their expressions, however, that, deep down, both politicians understood exactly what Sherman was saying. Even if their hands were tied, and all they could offer in response was thoughtful silence.

"All we're doing these days is *building*," Sherman said. "When traffic increases, we build another road, which only creates more congestion. One day we won't know where the city begins and ends. All we'll have is this endless landscape of expressways, shopping malls, tract homes and parking lots—all of it accessible only by car. A vast, anonymous megalopolis that stretches forever."

"I'm not sure we have a choice," Marshall said.

"Of course we do," Sherman replied. "We can make a decision to avoid where all this is headed."

Marshall and Esposito eyed the councilman contemplatively.

"One day, gentlemen, we'll regret our decisions," Sherman said. "We'll miss the way of life we're losing. People will yearn to live in places like Bay Ridge—compact, intimate neighborhoods where they can walk, meet people they know, feel safe and connected. They'll yearn for the closeness, the coherence."

Marshall and Esposito offered only far-off gazes.

"You'll see," Sherman said. "If places like Bay Ridge disappear, a way of life will disappear along with them. Sure, we'll have our cars, but we'll be slaves to them. We'll need them to go anywhere. We'll drive faster and go further but we'll see and feel less. We'll question whether our mobility is worth the traffic jams. We'll lose the ability to walk places. We'll lose the connections we've always valued."

The men shook hands and moved toward their car.

"Gentlemen, I ask—no, I *beg*—for your support," Sherman said. "Help us preserve this beautiful neighborhood. Help us save Bay Ridge."

Esposito and Marshall seemed genuinely engaged, even moved. They remained decidedly noncommittal, however, ending the tour with expressions of empathy but leaving Bay Ridge with nothing even resembling an assurance of support.

OTHER POLITICIANS WERE playing it equally as coy. Most appeared sympathetic over the plight of Bay Ridge and its middle-class constituency, but remained wary of alienating government officials who backed the bridge plan. Torn between these conflicting interests, all fell short of offering their outright support for the beleaguered neighborhood.

One such politician was Brooklyn Borough President John Shea, who protest leaders had lobbied for weeks simply to secure a meeting. Winning Shea's support was critical to the anti-bridge campaign. For one thing, his office was involved in all decisions involving zoning and land use in Brooklyn. Equally important, Shea was a member of the Board of Estimate, charged with voting on the bridge plan.

"If nothing else, you need to meet with Shea and plead your case," Bradley Jacobs advised protest leaders. "You've got nothing to lose and everything to gain by meeting with him."

"We understand, but he's been hard to nail down," Walter Staziak said wryly. "He's playing hard to get."

"He'll meet with you," Jacobs said. "He's a politician, remember? They'll usually give you at least the courtesy of a meeting."

"What can we expect?" Councilman Sherman queried.

"Well, he'll *appear* sympathetic—that you can count on," Jacobs replied. "Voters in Democratic strongholds like Bay Ridge are too important to be blatantly slighted. Shea will probably tell you he understands how you feel and that he'll consider those feelings in any decisions he makes."

"But what about his *vote*?"

"That's another story."

The protest leaders seemed perplexed. My mother, present at the strategy session, listened in curious silence.

"What I mean is that when it comes to politicians like Shea, you never know what's real and what's a mirage," Jacobs said. "His apparent sympathy for your cause will likely evaporate behind closed doors."

"But why *wouldn't* he support us?"

"Because Shea is facing enormous pressure to get the bridge approved. As I've said, there are a lot of special interests pushing for this project."

Jacobs shuffled some paperwork, using his stunted right arm to steady the papers as he edged them into an orderly stack.

"The *real* pressure on Shea isn't coming only from special interests, though," he explained. "It's coming from Washington and Albany."

Again, the protest leaders seemed confused. It was difficult to grasp—how the federal and state governments worked in tandem.

"What you need to understand," Jacobs said, "is that there's a lot at stake *beyond* just this project."

"It's an issue of funding," Sherman elaborated. "Federal and state funds are a big piece of the financial pie on projects like this. If the Board of Estimate kayos the plan, Washington and Albany won't be happy."

"So?" someone asked.

"So if they're not happy," Jacobs said, "the city stands to lose government funding not only for this project, but for other public works projects in the future—projects that everyone may actually want. That's the way the game is played. City officials are not likely to let that potential funding disappear, so they have almost no choice but to approve the bridge plan."

"Including John Shea?"

"I'm afraid so."

"Even if we tell him there are thousands of people who don't want it?"

"The impact of that, I'm afraid, is likely to be minimal," said Jacobs, glancing around the conference table and then fixing his gaze on my mother, who dropped her eyes and wondered, fleetingly, if Jacobs' apparent interest in her went deeper than simply her involvement in the anti-bridge campaign.

"Well, we've got to at least try," she blurted, surprising even herself with her spontaneity. "We've got to do whatever it takes to get a meeting with Shea."

"Lily's right," Sherman said. "We've got to go to him and plead our case."

Jacobs smiled at my mother and nodded. "I admire your spunk."

And my mother, once again, felt herself blush.

Chapter 20

Even with the anti-bridge campaign proceeding at full bore, life in Bay Ridge settled into something resembling normalcy as autumn took hold.

The Dodgers, as my father had presaged, had made it to the World Series, their pitching anchored by Sandy Koufax, who'd emerged, per my father's other prediction, as the premier hurler in baseball. But with the Dodgers playing now in California and the White Sox—not the Yankees—as that year's opponent, the series lost almost all its impact in Brooklyn. There were no updates on the P.A. system at school, no reason to smuggle transistor radios into our desks, no racing through the streets with reports of a Dodger victory. Besides, the series was being played at odd hours to accommodate the Central and Pacific time zones. Hardly anyone in Brooklyn watched—or professed to care.

Instead, we moved through other autumn rituals.

With families back from summer vacation and local beaches emptied, the playgrounds, schoolyards, and streets were teeming again with kids. Games turned from softball and stickball to touch football and basketball. Acorns lay like stones on sidewalks colored with Halloween pastels. Leaves fluttered from trees and were burned curbside, the pungent smoke mingling with salty bay breezes.

And school, once again, was underway.

By the end of October, I'd settled into my freshman routine at Hamilton High School, a fortress-like structure situated on the steep bluff overlooking the Narrows.

Like other New York City high schools—with names like Lincoln, Madison, Jefferson, and Tilden—Hamilton High was named for a historical figure, in this case founding father Alexander Hamilton. Populated by a dedicated group of teachers, it was considered one of the finest high schools in Brooklyn. And that was saying a lot. New York City schools were considered the crown jewels of America's public education system at the time, and Brooklyn had been dubbed by some educators as "the Fertile Crescent," for its strong educational emphasis and enormous pool of bright students, bred and motivated to succeed.

School was something to be taken seriously. Unlike our parents', our futures were tied closely to the notion that we'd graduate high school and continue our education, likely at one of the city's four public colleges—Brooklyn College, CCNY, Queens College or Hunter—where the benefits of a free, top-flight education required nothing more than good grades: an eighty-five high school average for boys, a ninety average for girls.

Our parents pushed us hard to get those grades. We could have it better than they did, they told us. We could climb higher. We could have it all.

And who were we to argue? We weren't like the past two generations, after all. Not like our grandparents—fresh off the boat, hamstrung by language and a grade-school education, struggling for a simple foothold in America. And not like our parents, either—saddled by the Great Depression and World War II, clinging to their generation's values of self-discipline, frugality, and sacrifice.

No. We were unencumbered by those limitations. The "old ways" had faded by the time we reached high school. The thick foreign accents were gone, the rough immigrant edges worn smooth. We were fully assimilated, no longer bound to the ethnic enclaves and old-world restrictions. We could go to the city's first-class high schools, attend its colleges, and ascend. The rewards of hard work and study, we were told, were limitless. We could rise as high as our talents would allow, become whatever we set our minds to. Anything was possible. Nothing was standing in our way. And we believed that. Our entire generation did.

And so my sister and I immersed ourselves in school, the distraction of classes diverting our attention, often for days at a time, from the anti-bridge campaign. The protest movement was being waged as intensely as ever, however.

Especially by my mother.

MY MOTHER THREW herself body and soul into her role as Dahlgren Place block captain, working virtually every waking moment on the anti-bridge campaign, eschewing her generation's other defining quality—blind obedience to authority—and seemingly as obsessed with the protest movement as Robert Moses was said to be with rebuilding New York.

Her gardening by now had all but ceased, except for securing her wildflower plantings, far earlier than usual, for the onset of winter. Her other beloved pastimes—reading and music—had slipped from her daily routine, as well. Unread books sat stacked on a shelf in her retreat; albums rested in piles atop the Philco in our living room. Absent of the arias she usually listened to while doing housework, our house seemed oddly quiet. In many ways, it were as if the flow of energy usually contained inside our home was now elsewhere, creating a strange sort of vacuum within our walls.

Not to imply, however, that the vacuum was in any way inert.

My mother, it seemed now, literally raced through her days. Alternating between housework, shopping and cooking, she worked the telephone for hours—sometimes from our house, but mostly from Councilman Sherman's office—doggedly attempting to solicit support for the protest campaign. After supper, she retreated to her work space and labored well into the night, typing letters, petitions, and fliers. Once a week, she created a newsletter informing local residents about developments in the protest campaign, hand-delivering her typewritten copy to one of my father's linotype customers, who printed the materials for a nominal charge. Two nights a week, abandoning her mahjong and card games, she attended protest strategy sessions. All hours of the day and night she fielded calls from neighbors, offering reassurance, answering questions, rallying support, fighting to keep people from falling victim to the encroaching sense of hopelessness that enveloped many parts of Bay Ridge.

"Why bother fighting?" I overheard Mrs. Pedersen declare one night at a gathering in our cul-de-sac. "We might as well take whatever we can get from the city and just leave."

"We can't allow ourselves to feel that way," my mother argued.

"Why not? The city'll do whatever it wants to with Bay Ridge."

"Not if we stand together and fight, it won't."

"You're only kidding yourself, Lily," Mr. Sandusky scoffed. "People like us can't fight City Hall. We're powerless. We don't have a snowball's chance in hell of getting the city to change its mind."

"Yes, we do," my mother insisted. "We can't give in to despair. Please. We can't allow ourselves to be bullied by the city's power."

The others gathered around her, as if they, too, wanted to believe.

"We've to keep believing we can win this fight," she said. "We can't lose hope. Once we lose that, we're completely lost."

I'd never seen this side of my mother before, never realized such a steely determination resided behind her normally calm demeanor. Until now, there'd never been the slightest hint that such an iron will was so thoroughly ingrained in her makeup. I'm not sure that even my father knew it was there.

But now he did. All of us did.

The anti-bridge campaign had brought a whole new side of my mother to the surface. Suddenly, I saw her in a stunning new light—not merely as my *mother*, but as someone who'd been thrust by circumstances into a role that had instantly redefined who she was, compelling her to operate at a level far beyond anything required in her day-to-day persona as a housewife. For the first time, I saw her as a fighter: tough, focused, capable of being a leader, a role model, even a hero. Far different than the usual heroes I worshipped—ballplayers, comic book characters, soldiers, and G-men—but equally powerful, equally adept.

I wondered if there'd be times in my own life when I'd be like that—compelled to abandon the shadows of who I appeared to be and emerge as someone heroic. I wondered, if push ever came to shove, whether I'd have the conviction, the intelligence, the courage I was seeing now in my mother.

At the same time, though, there was something troubling, even vaguely frightening, about what had arisen within her. It was as if the specter of the expressway, the fact that we could be evicted from our home, had awakened something powerful within her, something fueled by more than merely insult, anger, or fear. Something far deeper, I sensed, was driving my mother now. What it was, I couldn't be sure. I wondered if I'd ever find out. I wondered if I really wanted to.

Chapter 21

Having finally procured a meeting with John Shea one week later, protest leaders were ushered into the borough president's office on the top floor of Borough Hall, where they waited anxiously for Shea to arrive back from a meeting in Manhattan.

Their anxiety was evident. Walter Staziak, lighting one cigarette after the next, paced the office. Chester Jablonski shifted restlessly in the chair in front of Shea's massive desk. Councilman Sherman occupied himself by examining a wall plastered with photos of Shea in the company of celebrities and public officials, including several with Robert Moses. My mother, there to take notes, stared out a bank of windows opening to the East River waterfront.

The city hummed with its usual activity. On the Manhattan side of the river, traffic wound along the East Side Highway, moving through the shadows of office buildings that gleamed in the sun. On the Brooklyn shoreline, the Domino Sugar refinery belched clouds of smoke that wafted over the circular storage tanks of the Brooklyn Union Gas Company and then past The Watchtower, the stolid gray headquarters of Jehovah's Witnesses. Out on the river, barges and tourist vessels sailed in and out of New York Harbor.

"Sorry we're late," John Shea puffed, entering the office along with Deputy Borough President Patrick Brennan, chief liaison between Shea and the people of Brooklyn.

Shea settled into a leather swivel chair. Brennan, arms crossed, stood like a bodyguard at Shea's side. The protest leaders each took seats.

"How're you doin'?" Shea asked in an accent that was Brooklyn through and through.

"Well, to be honest, we've been better," Sherman joked nervously.

"So I hear," the borough president said, smiling wanly.

A longtime fixture in New York politics, John Shea had been raised in Crown Heights, a central Brooklyn enclave of Irish, Italians, and Jews. One of eleven children, he'd never been formally educated past the fifth grade, instead working in his father's office supply business while being schooled on the streets of turn-of-the-century Brooklyn, where survival hinged on being as quick with your hands as you were with your wits.

Shea had been both.

Learning to box at an early age, he'd become a popular semi-pro at local fight clubs. Then, his boxing career thwarted by an injury, Shea had focused on helping build his father's business into the most successful of its kind in New York. Access to top executives at leading companies had helped him nurture his political aspirations, and he'd parlayed those connections into a career as Brooklyn borough president, a post he'd held for eighteen years.

At sixty-two, Shea was far heavier than in his fighting days, with fleshy features, a shock of white hair, and wire-rim glasses that he wore halfway down his nose. Despite his girth, however, he retained the persona of the resourceful, street-smart scuffler, shifty and fast on his feet.

As he joked and made small talk, his eyes moved across his visitors, as if he were sizing up each one. His eyebrows arched in curiosity at the sight of my mother, although he seemed to dismiss her presence as trivial, focusing squarely on Sherman.

"The four of us are here on behalf of Bay Ridge," the councilman said. "And we're here, sir, to enlist your support."

Shea nodded, and then glanced down to examine a food stain on his tie.

"Surely, you're aware of our neighborhood's opposition to the bridge being planned across the Narrows," Sherman said.

"I'm well aware," replied Shea, seeming distracted by the tie stain.

"Our position, of course," Sherman continued, "is that if the bridge and expressway are built, they'll destroy significant portions of Bay Ridge and disrupt thousands of lives."

Shea dipped a handkerchief into a half-filled water glass and rubbed the moist cloth on his tie, leaving a large blotch over the stain.

"Well," he said without looking up, "the city has concluded that a Narrows bridge is needed on a number of important levels."

"We're not questioning *the need* for the bridge, sir," Sherman contended. "We're only hopeful that the city can find another place to build it."

Shea glanced up at the protest leaders and half-smiled.

"I'm afraid the city has concluded that there *is* no other place to build it," he said evenly. "It's not an issue of politics as much as it is of geography. Because of its proximity to the Narrows, Bay Ridge has been deemed the best location. An enormous amount of study has gone into this plan, you know. It's a project of huge scope, not something the city is taking lightly."

"We understand the project's magnitude, and we're sure it's not being taken lightly, but … have other potential locations been considered?"

"They have."

"And I presume they've been rejected?"

"Yes. They were deemed unfeasible for a variety of reasons."

"But there are thousands of people in Bay Ridge who'll be hurt by this," Walter Staziak blurted. "Homes will be destroyed. Families will have to relocate. Businesses that have served Brooklyn for decades will be forced to close."

"That's unfortunate" Shea replied. "But try to understand. I'm obligated to do what's best for Brooklyn as a whole—not simply for one neighborhood."

"And what do you believe is best for Brooklyn?"

"What's best for Brooklyn is for me to consider the matter from all sides and vote my conscience."

"Can we count on you to consider *our* side, as well?" Chester Jablonski asked.

"You certainly can," Shea said.

"Can we count on you to vote the project down?" Jablonski said.

"I'm afraid I can't commit to that."

"Is there anything you *can* commit to?"

"Yes," Shea replied. "I can commit that I will not vote for any resolution seeking to authorize the acquisition or condemnation of Bay Ridge properties until the matter has been given the utmost consideration. And I will not allow the city to put the interests of a bridge before the interests of taxpaying homeowners. Human values are more important than any public works project."

Shea glanced again at his tie, rubbing a thumb over the stain.

"I'll commit to something else, too," he said. "I'll pledge to you that I won't vote to approve the expressway plan as it currently stands until all proposed *alternative routes* have been given careful consideration."

The protestor leaders glanced at one another, as if suddenly aware that a door had just been left slightly ajar.

"Are there other options on the table?" Sherman queried. "Is the city considering possible alternative routes?"

Shea glanced at Brennan, still holding his bodyguard-like pose.

"Not that I'm aware of," Brennan replied.

"*Really*?" Shea said, winking at the protestors.

Sherman jumped at the opening. "Exactly what type of alternatives are you talking about?"

"Perhaps," said Shea, "something that wouldn't halt the bridge and expressway altogether, but would alter its route to lessen its impact on Bay Ridge."

"Alter its route?"

"Yes. Divert the path of the expressway so that the fewest possible homes and businesses would be affected."

Again, Shea winked.

By now, the protest leaders were fully aware of where the crafty old politician was leading them.

"Well, what if we present the city with other options?" Sherman asked. "What if we work with professional engineers to develop a viable alternative to the existing expressway route? Is it possible the city might consider such an alternative?"

Shea smiled slyly.

"Why, I suppose that's entirely possible," he replied. "Wouldn't you agree, Pat?"

"Absolutely," the deputy borough president said.

"Then that's exactly what we'll do," Sherman concluded.

And the protest leaders left Shea's office and returned to Bay Ridge, awash for the first time in weeks with a genuine glimmer of hope.

Chapter 22

Hope, however, had a flip side. Even with the anti-bridge campaign looking up for the moment, the demands of the movement were exacting a price—not only on the collective psyche of Bay Ridge, but inside our household, as well.

With my mother thoroughly immersed in the protest movement, family life for her had become in many ways a mere afterthought. Nights found her buried with work related to the anti-bridge campaign. Almost daily now, she reported to the office of Councilman Sherman to work the phones, type correspondence and participate in protest strategy sessions, often involving Bradley Jacobs, the anti-Moses attorney about whom, despite herself, she felt a fascination.

A well-off bachelor with ruggedly handsome features, Jacobs possessed qualities my mother admired—energy, intelligence, biting wit, and conviction that matched her own. He was also consistently flattering, often complimenting my mother about skills that were obscured for the most part in her role as a housewife. Though unwilling to take the relationship even to the point of flirtation, my mother nevertheless basked in the attention.

And it was something my father clearly sensed—and resented. For the first time ever, I sensed a palpable tension between my parents, a small but growing tear in the fabric of a marriage that had always been steadfast, persevering through the daily trials of family, finances, and work.

Not anymore. Now it was as if a chasm separating my parents was growing by the day—along with a prickly, unspoken anger. Conversations, once relaxed and matter-of-fact, were now formal, almost curt. Suppers—hastily prepared tuna casseroles, even TV dinners in lieu of our normal meat meals—were rushed. Their time together was virtually non-existent. Begging off on the basis of work demands or fatigue, my father had become increasingly indifferent to the anti-bridge campaign, seeming almost resigned to the prospects of eviction. Rarely did he attend rallies or other anti-bridge activities. Rarely did he even ask about the protest movement. Most nights he watched TV, alone and silent, drifting off to sleep long before my mother completed her work.

It was, as much as anything, a clash of temperaments. My mother, by nature more spontaneous and emotional, seemed annoyed over my father's lack of commitment to the protest movement. My father, more analytical and laid back, seemed equally disturbed over the depth of my mother's involvement at the expense our family. More than once he made subtle, cutting references to the amount of time she spent working alongside Jacobs, never implying anything truly out of line, but suggesting that my mother clearly didn't mind the attorney's constant attention.

Then one night all of it boiled to a head. My father was watching an episode of *The Honeymooners*. My mother, walking toward her retreat with a stack of work, glared at him as he sat chuckling at the antics of Jackie Gleason and Art Carney.

"You know, I don't understand how you can just sit there and laugh at a time like this," she said.

"Why not?" he said, eyes still on the TV. "It's funny."

My mother seemed overwrought, frustrated by her lack of free time and inability to focus on household chores and part-time work, which had led to a pinch in the family finances.

"I feel like I'm in this fight all alone, Artie," she said. "Am I the only one who loves our house enough to fight for it? Am I the only one who's willing to lay it on the line to preserve the life we have?"

He looked up. "No, Lily. I love our house, too. I think you know that."

"Then please tell me: why aren't you more vocal in fighting what the city's forcing on us? Why are you just sitting on your hands?"

"Sitting on my hands? Oh, is *that* what I'm doing?"

"In a way, yes."

"Jeez," my father said. "And here I thought I was busy *working* all day. Busting my ass so we can hold our family together. Just taking it easy for a couple of hours at night so I can get up and do it again tomorrow. Well … silly me."

He seemed worn out, too, just as on edge as my mother.

"I'll tell you what, Lily, why don't *you* tell *me* why I'm not more vocal? Then tell me when I even have a *chance* to fight. It's not like I've got a lot of free time on my hands, you know. My boss won't give me time off to attend protest rallies. And, to tell you the truth, at the end of the day I'm pretty damn worn out."

There was a long, gnawing silence.

"Maybe being worn out," my mother suggested, "is just an excuse."

"Oh? An excuse for *what*?"

"Maybe it's an excuse for your willingness to simply accept what people in authority say you have to accept, Artie. Maybe it's an excuse for not being more willing to make noise in order to get the things you want."

The silence, this time, was even more cutting. It was clear my parents each sensed they were skating on thin ice.

"Frankly, it's the same quality," my mother said, "that held you back from going further than you could've at Mergenthaler."

"Oh, so it's *that* again, Lily, huh?"

That again.

My mother's insistence that my father could have advanced further at his job had he been more assertive, more confident about his skills and value.

That again.

My mother's belief that he ought to fight harder for things he deserved—that, despite his many virtues, he was too passive, too willing to accept whatever was handed to him.

That view, in truth, had come between them before, although never seriously enough to cause a genuine rift. But, nevertheless, it had been present for years, lurking just beneath the surface of an otherwise placid marriage. And now the hubbub over the bridge—and their differing reactions—was bringing it to a head again.

"Face it, Artie, you could've *run* Mergenthaler," my mother said. "You're smarter than any manager they have. You know more about the machines and the business than anyone. You just don't give yourself the credit you deserve. You just don't push hard enough."

"Thanks for the compliment—but don't be absurd," my father countered. "How's a guy with two years of high school supposed to advance at a company like Mergenthaler? Management's for guys with business backgrounds, college degrees."

"Yeah, and for years they'd come to you every time they'd have a problem to solve, didn't they? They'd come to you for advice that went far beyond what they'd expect from just a mechanic. Didn't they?"

"Yeah, they'd *come*, Lily. Past tense. They sure don't come anymore."

"That's a whole other story."

"Maybe. But what's your point?"

"My point is that your dropping out of high school is irrelevant to your lack of advancement. You had to help your family financially. That's the reason you left school. Your family couldn't have survived without the money you made, pure and simple. A lot of boys like you had to sacrifice their education, sometimes their future, to help out that way. That doesn't make you unqualified. All it makes you is a good son."

"None of that matters, Lily. The fact is, the die was cast once I dropped out of school."

"I don't believe that, Artie. It's all in your mind. I think you should've pushed harder. Sometimes you've got to push for what you want instead of expecting people to give it to you simply because you're terrific."

"You mean push for everything—like *you* do?"

"Maybe."

"Well, maybe it's not in my nature to push like that."

"And maybe it *should* be. It's the only way to get what you want in this world."

Again, there was an icy, edgy silence.

"We're different in that way, Lily. Just face it."

"Yeah, I suppose we are."

Another pregnant pause.

"Besides," my father said, "there was a whole other reason I didn't go further at Mergenthaler. You know that, and so do I."

To that, my mother had no retort. Because she, more than anyone, knew it was true. Passivity and a lack of confidence weren't the reasons my father hadn't climbed the ladder at his company. There was another reason. Something more specific and dramatic.

A strike.

THE STRIKE AT Mergenthaler Linotype erupted soon after my father returned to work there, shortly after World War II.

In many ways, it was inevitable.

Organized labor was at the height of its power in New York then, an army of municipal workers, manual laborers, and craftsmen whose impact was enormous. Celebrated as modern-day heroes, brimming with confidence and clout, blue-collar workers were fresh off their wartime triumph over a powerful Axis enemy. Having built New York from the ground up, they were raising it on their backs now to new heights as a working-class bastion. Outspoken and militant, unions controlled the city's workplace. Labor rallies were staged regularly at Madison Square Garden and Union Square. Contract negotiations were contentious. Rhetoric was rough and tumble.

But organized labor, for all its swagger, was facing grave threats. Wages and benefits were under attack from both management and government. Automation was sweeping through the workplace. Threats of corporate relocation loomed. Newly adopted Taft-Hartley laws were shifting the balance of power toward employers.

And New York was wracked, as never before, by labor strife.

Job actions shut down the city's docks, newspapers, office buildings, and transit system. Walkouts were staged by teamsters, meat packers, ironworkers, carpenters, and other craft unions. Crippling national strikes were waged by steel and copper workers, telegraph operators, and railway employees. Worst of all was a midwinter strike by tugboat workers that threatened the very survival of the city. Freight in and out of New York was halted. Fuel deliveries were suspended. Temperatures plunged in buildings, homes, hospitals, and hotels. Schools, libraries, theaters, restaurants, and museums were shuttered. Police stood guard at municipal offices and subway stations. The city, quiet and still, assumed a surreal, other-worldly quality—its lights dimmed, its residents forced indoors, its engine of commerce at a standstill.

In the midst of this turmoil, Mergenthaler Linotype was rocked by a strike of its own.

Typical of the many New York manufacturing firms that employed skilled manual workers, Mergenthaler was heavily dependent on machinists, tool-and-die makers, lathe operators, and mechanics like my father. Management, nevertheless, had adopted a rigid anti-union stance. And one day the union struck.

The strike, even by New York standards, was bitter and divisive. Strikers taunted management personnel and others as they crossed picket lines. Bricks were hurled through windows. Strikers blockaded the factory entrance by lying on the sidewalk until they were charged by club-wielding police. Fights broke out. Dozens were arrested.

Despite his youth and relative lack of education, my father had already been pegged by management as a rising star—hard-working, bright, already making key contributions to the company's mechanical procedures.

But when the strike began, my father, at the age of twenty-four, faced a gut-wrenching choice: join the job action and support his co-workers or cross the picket line and remain in management's good graces. Protect the union's interests or protect his own. Protect the men he worked with or protect his career.

In truth, my father had a difficult time justifying the strike, believing privately that the union's demands were excessive, that its staunch militancy would damage workers long-term. Still, these were men he clocked in and out with each day. Men he ate lunch with and bowled with. Men who were his friends.

Reluctantly, he decided to back the strike. It was a decision he'd live with the rest of his life.

The strike lasted more than a hundred days, through skirmishes and testy negotiations. Arbitrators were brought in. Other unions joined the dispute. A top company manager suffered a fatal heart attack. Wanting to avoid the picket lines, but unable to stay unemployed, my father took a job loading trucks.

When the strike was finally settled, he returned to Mergenthaler. Only he was never viewed by management through the same set of eyes. While still respected, his stature had been diminished. His advice was unsolicited. He was shunned by supervisors, passed over for promotions. His career, for all intents and purposes, had hit a wall. It would never advance beyond its current status of journeyman. He'd forever be just a common mechanic. A man whose position belied his true aptitude. A man, as he said to me, who'd never gone very far in life.

HE WALKED TO the television set and clicked it off, then turned toward my mother, who was still standing there in the living room, a pile of paperwork in hand.

"You know the reason I never advanced at Mergenthaler, Lily," I heard my father say. "It wasn't because I was unwilling to fight for what I believed in. It was because when I *did* decide to take a stand, I made a mistake. I was young and innocent, loyal to a fault. I chose the wrong fight … and picked the wrong side."

The two of them stood in silence, as if picking their way carefully through a dense thicket of emotion.

"To be perfectly honest with you," my father said, "I'm not sure fighting with the city will do us any good in this case, either. I think the city's made up its mind about what it's gonna do. Sometimes you just have to accept what's inevitable, what's out of your control."

"*Nothing* is inevitable, Artie," my mother argued. "What happens to people is a direct result of the actions they take. Sometimes you've got to fight like hell to hold onto something you cherish."

"And sometimes," he said, "you have to know when fighting is fruitless and you just have to move on with your life."

There was another lengthy silence, but it felt different now. Their fight, it seemed, was waning. The edge was off, the anger subsiding. Each seemed reconciled to the way things were. Each seemed to sense they'd have to handle the situation their own way. They'd have to live with their actions—and, more importantly, with each other—if they were to move past this.

"You know, when you think about it, I've been fighting all my life," my father said. "I fought to help my family get by when I was a boy. I fought four years in the war. I've fought for twenty-plus years to make a living."

She said nothing.

"Maybe I'm just tired of fighting," he said, his voice breaking slightly. "Maybe all I want now is just a little peace."

Silence again.

"Okay, Artie," my mother conceded, her voice softer now, as well. "But I'm not ready to quit yet. I hope you understand. I have a reason for the way I'm acting, too. There's a reason I'm fighting so hard to save our house. If anyone knows that, it's you."

My father paused, treading carefully again.

"What's happening in Bay Ridge," he said, "has nothing to do with that."

"*Doesn't it*?"

"No, Lily. What you're talking about is ancient history. It happened in another time, another place."

"Maybe so," my mother said, "but what happened back then is very real to me. I live with it every day. There's a fear deep inside me, Artie, a fear that's been part of me for years. It's something I never thought I'd have to confront. But now the bridge has awakened it … it's made it more real than ever."

She paused, as if groping for a distant memory.

"I've got to fight to keep what happened to my family from happening to us," she said. "I've just got to."

Then the two of them lapsed again into silence and I retreated to the sanctuary of my room, also fearful in an unfamiliar new way. Frightened of the corrosive effect of the events in Bay Ridge on my parents, of the way painful wounds were being reopened. Frightened to see scars on them I'd never seen, things they carried inside that shaped who they were as people, not just parents.

I felt bad for my father, for the way his career had collapsed because of well-meaning decisions he'd been forced to make. Most of all I wondered again what was driving my mother. I wondered what was buried so painfully in her past that she'd do literally anything to keep the emotions it evoked from being rekindled. I wondered what was haunting her so, making her fight to save our home as fiercely as if fighting for her very life.

Chapter 23

It didn't take long to find out. The following evening after supper, my mother moved almost trancelike through her cleanup chores, quiet and contemplative, wrapping leftovers in wax paper, washing and drying the dishes. My father, equally silent, stacked plates in the cabinet over the kitchen sink. The two of them, focused entirely inward, had barely exchanged a word our entire meal.

"I think it's important that you children know something," my mother finally said, summoning my sister and me to the kitchen. She looked drained and fragile, as if the slightest nudge would send her hurtling off an emotional precipice.

"I want the two of you to know," she said, "that there's a reason I'm fighting so hard to save our home."

"I *already* know," my sister interrupted. "You love living on Dahlgren Place. This is your dream house."

"That's true," my mother nodded. "But there's more to it than that."

"Lily," my father said. "I'm not sure this is really necessary."

"Oh, but it is, Artie," she replied, calm but resolute. "Both of them are old enough now to understand."

"Understand *what*?" my sister probed.

My mother beckoned us to the table, where all of us, except my father, took a seat. Her eyes widened as if opening to an approaching threat.

"Before they came to Brooklyn," she started, "your grandparents—my parents—lived in Russia."

"We already know that," I said.

"Yes, Nathan, but there are things … you *don't* know."

My father looked away. Vaguely fearful, I wondered where this was headed.

"Your grandparents," my mother resumed, "lived in a village called Kishinev."

"Kish-in-ev," I said, struggling with the pronunciation.

"Yes. Many Jews lived there. There were Jewish schools and several synagogues. Jews held good jobs and they owned many businesses. As a young man, your grandfather managed a button factory that *his* father owned. They were very successful. Nearly a hundred people worked there."

My mother's eyes narrowed.

"But one day," she said, "there was … an incident."

"An *incident*?" I asked.

"Yes. In 1905, on the eve of the Orthodox Christian Easter, a Christian boy was found dead. Although it was obvious the boy had died accidentally, the newspapers claimed he was murdered—by Jews."

"By *Jews*?" my sister said. "Why?"

"The newspapers in Kishinev were published by a group called The Black Hundred. It was an organization devoted to the Russian czar. Many people were involved: government officials, clergymen, merchants, landowners. *Why* did they lie? Simple—they hated Jews."

"But why?" my sister persisted.

My mother shrugged. "Who knows why people hate, Beth?" She sighed. "Anger, jealously, misunderstanding, prejudice—does it really matter? What matters is that Jews have been hated for centuries in some countries. And in Russia, at the turn of the century, the hatred ran deep."

I tried to grasp what she was saying. As a Jew, I'd never felt that kind of hatred in Brooklyn—not really. There were plenty of Jews in Bay Ridge—plenty of other nationalities and religions, too. Maybe I was naïve, but people seemed to get along most of the time. Sure, some kids poked fun at Jews, but they poked fun at other ethnicities, too. No one was immune. Getting ribbed about your religion or nationality was a give-and-take sort of thing, part of growing up on the streets of New York.

I realized soon enough, though, that things were different in czarist Russia.

"After the news about the dead boy got out, something horrible happened," my mother said. "Something called a *pogrom*."

"What's a pogrom?" my sister asked.

"It's a Yiddish word," my mother explained. "It's an organized riot directed against an ethnic or religious group. In Kishinev, it was a riot against the Jews."

"A riot?"

"Yes. It started over the dead boy. The newspapers said he was killed by Jews. They said it was a case of blood libel."

She was speaking gravely, using words unfamiliar to Beth and me.

"Blood libel is an accusation that Jews use human blood, particularly the blood of Christian children, in religious ceremonies," my mother said. "In Kishinev, they claimed the boy was murdered so that Jews could use his blood in the preparation of matzo."

"How would they make matzo using *blood*?" Beth asked.

"It doesn't really matter," my mother replied. "It's ludicrous, of course. They only needed an excuse for what happened next."

"What happened?"

She glanced at my father, who stood silently, his back to us, staring out our backyard window.

"When the riot started," my mother said, "mobs of men arrived on Kishinev's main shopping street. They carried weapons—shovels, axes, crowbars, gasoline."

She paused, as if to gather herself. Now I was really frightened. So was Beth. You could see it in her features, seeming to melt before our eyes.

"At first, the mobs went after all the Jewish shops," my mother said. "One by one, they were ransacked, looted, burned, and the Jewish merchants were herded into the center of town. Some were knifed or shot on the spot."

"Oh my God," my sister gasped.

My mother stared at us and shook her head knowingly.

"But that was only the *beginning*," she continued. "Soon, the rioting spread. Jewish schools were vandalized. Synagogues were desecrated. Cemetery stones were toppled. Graves were dug up and corpses hung from trees."

My sister and I were dumbstruck. I'd heard about things like this, atrocities and mass killings in Eastern Europe, South America, and Nazi Germany. I just never knew any such horror had hit this close to home, that they'd been part of our family's past.

"Soon the killing *really* started," my mother said. "Innocent, defenseless people, including children, were attacked. Men were beaten, shot, stoned, and stabbed right in front of their families. People were burned alive inside their homes. The streets were littered with corpses."

My sister gasped, twirling her hair anxiously.

"How long did the rioting last?" I asked.

"Three days. And each day it got worse."

"Worse?"

"Yes. Each day, the violence grew more unspeakable. Men, claiming they weren't Jewish, were forced to remove their pants and reveal if they'd been circumcised. If they were, they were killed or mutilated."

"Mutilated?" I said.

"Their penises were cut off, Nathan."

I heard my sister gasp, as if someone had struck her in the stomach. I recoiled from a powerful kinesthetic twinge.

"Women," my mother said, "were raped. One pregnant woman had her uterus cut open and was forced to watch as her unborn infant was slaughtered."

My father turned away from the window and toward my mother. "Lily," he implored. "Enough. Please …"

But my mother held up her hand, as if she wanted—no, *needed*—to let it all out.

"I must …" she said. And my father backed away

"Didn't anyone try to stop it?" Beth asked.

"Yes. People petitioned the Russian government. Our president, Teddy Roosevelt, issued an appeal to the Russian czar, demanding the violence be stopped. Supposedly, though, orders were given to the rioters *not* to stop. Many people believe the pogroms were actually supported, and maybe even organized, by the *Okhranka*, the Russian secret police."

"Were they?" I asked.

"Who really knows? All we know is that the Russian government did nothing to stop the violence. Most citizens were silent. Few rioters were ever punished."

"What about the Jews?" I asked. "Didn't they fight back?"

"Some did." My mother sighed. "Some armed themselves and resisted. But most, unfortunately, didn't."

"You mean, they just *died*, without fighting back?"

I couldn't fathom how anyone could simply allow themselves and their families to be attacked without resisting.

"Yes," my mother said solemnly.

"But *why*?"

"That's something for people far wiser than me to answer," she replied. "It's something that may never be understood."

"I would've fought those bastards," I declared. "I would've killed every goddamned one of them."

"That's easy for you to say, Nathan, sitting here fifty years later in the safety of Brooklyn. It's another thing, though, when you're confronted by a mob, when there's a gun at your head. You'd probably act very differently then."

Maybe she was right, I thought. How could you ever really know how you'd act if you'd never been in a situation like that? My bravado melted.

"But there's *more*," my mother went on.

"Lily," my father implored again. "Please. I think that's enough."

He nodded toward my sister, shivering now, clearly on the brink of tears.

"No," my mother resisted. "I know it hurts, Artie. But they need to know."

"Know *what*?" I asked.

"Know … what happened to my father."

My mother paused to gather herself again. She drew in a deep breath.

"When the rioters arrived at your grandfather's factory," she said, "they broke in and demanded to know if your grandfather or any of his workers were Jewish."

"What did he say?"

"He lied. He tried to spare the lives of his Jewish workers. He admitted *he* was a Jew, but told the rioters his workers were all Russian Christians."

"Did they believe him?"

"No. They knew he was lying. But as a 'reward' for his loyalty and courage, they decided to make an example of him. They decided that only your grandfather, no one else, would be punished for the crime of being a Jew."

My mother looked up, her eyes flitting between Beth and me, welling with tears.

"Your grandfather," she said, "was attacked."

"*Attacked*?"

"Yes—without mercy. Four of them beat him with a club. Over and over they hit him, on his body, his arms, his face. They tore clumps of hair from his head. And then, as if that weren't enough, they made him strip and stand naked and bleeding in front of his workers while the rioters taunted him."

"Lily," my father pleaded. "For God's sake … enough."

"Then," my mother said, without missing a beat, "they lifted your grandfather up, and threw him from a window. *Threw him!*"

She paused as her story sunk in. Then she resumed in a whisper. "Three stories, my father fell. Landing on his back. Breaking his spine."

My sister was weeping now, tears streaming down her cheeks. My father placed an arm around her, his own face creased with tears. I shivered uncontrollably, torn to pieces by rage and fear.

"Your grandfather," my mother said, "was saved only because several workers were brave enough to beg for his life. It's a miracle he survived at all."

My mother looked away, her shoulders heaving slightly. My sister struggled to compose herself. I felt as if I'd been rendered immobile, my extremities turned to stone.

"After the Kishinev pogrom, two million Jews fled Russia for America, England, and Israel, leaving most of their possessions behind," my mother said. "Thousands of them, forced to start their lives over, came to Brooklyn. Your grandparents were among them."

"How … did you find this out?" my sister asked through her sobs.

"Your grandmother told me."

"How old were you?"

"I was twelve, not even your age."

"And *grandpa*?"

"He's never said a word about it … and I've never asked."

I thought about my grandfather, then seventy-five, stooped and gray, barely able to walk, yet able to hold a steady job as a tailor. I thought about the way he'd smile and mumble something in Yiddish, then pull a Hershey Bar from his jacket pocket and slip it into my hand. I tried to imagine the humiliation he must have felt in Kishinev—being forced to disrobe in front of his employees, being thrown from a window and left for dead. I tried to understand how, forced to carry that memory inside him all these years, he was capable of even the faintest smile. And I felt a jumble of emotions I'd never felt before—a fury mixed with sorrow and pity, bitterness and shame.

"Your father is angry at me for sharing this story with you," my mother said, glancing at him. "And maybe I *shouldn't* have. Maybe it was wrong of me not to protect you from the truth."

My father turned away, silent again.

"But please just know, children—I told you not to hurt you. I'd rather die myself than do that. I told you only to help you understand why I'm fighting so hard to stay in our home." She looked at us earnestly.

"Please understand. America is not Russia. Brooklyn is not Kishinev. No mobs are going to attack us simply because we're Jews. But, you see, Jews throughout history have been victims of religious hatred, forced from their homes, exiled, dispersed. It's part of who we are as a people. And ever since I learned what happened to your grandfather, I've vowed that I'd never be put out of my home on the whim of a government bureaucrat—or even in the face of a mob. Ever since I was your age, I've vowed that I'd never allow myself or my family to be hurt the way my father was."

My mother shifted uneasily in her seat, seemingly ready to crack into tiny pieces.

"And now …" she sniffed, "my greatest fear has become a reality with this bridge. Now we're being forced from *our* home, told by the government we must leave against our will."

She stood up, ready to take her leave, as if she'd taken her explanation as far as she could.

"I think we need to make a statement to the city, if only for our own sake," she said. "We may lose our home, but we won't lose it without making our feelings known. We won't lose it because we simply gave in. We won't lose it … without a fight."

Then she excused herself, entering her retreat and closing the two French doors behind her. And soon we could hear the rhythmic cadence of her typewriter clattering away as she resumed typing the correspondence she hoped would save our home. Then, just as abruptly, the typing stopped and all we could hear was the sound of my mother's sobs, heavy and anguished, pouring from her like a cloudburst, as if nothing could ever make them stop.

Chapter 24

Down in our cellar, my father worked on one of his linotype machines, meticulously reassembling a flywheel mechanism he'd taken apart to repair a malfunction. Upstairs in her retreat, my mother worked busily on the anti-bridge campaign. Even in our tiny house, the distance between them could well have been miles. Lost somewhere inside themselves, bound by their emotions, they hadn't spoken to one another for nearly the entire week since my mother related the story about Kishinev. They'd barely uttered a word to my sister or me, either.

"Are things gonna be all right?" I asked, poking around the cellar workshop while my father worked from underneath the machine.

"Hand me a screwdriver, will ya?" he grunted, nodding at a workbench.

"Which one?"

"The Phillips-head. The one with the cross at the tip."

I found the screwdriver he wanted and handed it to him, watching as he tried to position the errant flywheel so he could connect it to a wayward conveyor belt.

"Gotta stretch this." He grunted again as he tugged on the belt, droplets of oil leaking onto his forehead.

He worked hard, his arms straining, rivulets of sweat pouring into his eyes. As I watched I understood why he always said he wanted me to work one day with my head instead of my hands. It was the mantra of every well-meaning father from that era. Sparing me the rigors of manual labor would be his way of validating that he'd gotten his message across, that he'd done his job, protected me from the grueling physical work he'd been forced to endure.

I loved him for that—the same way I loved my mother, in a very different way, for exposing us to the pain she and her family had experienced. Both of them, I knew, had our best interests at heart. Both were acting out of love. Both were trying to protect us, just in very different ways.

My father tightened several screws, then used a wrench to turn a large bolt, grunting, pushing against the flywheel to secure the connection. Then he pulled himself to his feet, wiping the grime from his face.

"That oughtta do it," he said, depressing a lever and watching as the linotype machine started with a metallic clunk.

"Done," he smiled, inspecting the machine. "Sounds like it's happy, huh?"

"Yeah," I agreed, thinking that the linotype, if it felt anything at all, was a lot happier than my father probably was just then. A lot happier than any of us were.

"Now, what were you saying?" he asked.

"I was asking if you think things'll be all right."

"Whaddaya mean?"

"Between you and mom. Are things gonna go back to the way they were?"

"How do you mean? How were they?"

"A lot more peaceful, for one thing. The two of you hardly ever fought. You always got along before this whole thing with the bridge came along."

My father dipped his fingertips into a jar of cleaning gunk, rubbing his hands together before wiping them dry with a rag.

"Your mother and I will be fine."

"How do you know?" I wanted reassurance. I'd never seen my parents steeped in such prolonged, festering anger. I'd never seen a gulf so wide between them.

"I know," he said, "because your mother and I will find a way to figure this out."

"But how can you be sure?"

"Things don't always go smoothly between married people, Nathan. Even couples who love each other have differences. But if you work at it, eventually things'll work out."

"What do you mean by *work at it*?"

"You talk. You listen. You try to see things through the other one's eyes. Accept your differences. Get past the bad stuff. Remember why you're together."

"So—are you and mom *working at it*?"

"That," he smiled, "is none of your business."

Then he paused again, deep in thought.

"To tell you the truth, Nathan—no, we really haven't been."

Then another pause.

"But maybe," he said, "it's finally time we tried."

He shut down the linotype, and the clunky machine churned to a halt.

"You'd feel better if your mother and I ironed out our differences, wouldn't you?"

"Yeah."

"It's kind of scary for you now?"

"Uh-huh."

"I guess that's understandable."

We walked to the base of the stairway and he flicked the cellar lights off.

"Well," he said, "maybe it's time I tried to fix something more important than a linotype machine."

And later that night he slipped outside, returning from our backyard with a bouquet of my mother's wildflowers, colorful and blooming on their long green stems.

I was watching TV in the living room, but I saw him knock on the doors to my mother's retreat, then enter and offer her the bouquet. I saw her clutch it and put it to her face, then smile, her eyes happy and aglow. Then he smiled, too, mouthing something only they could hear. Then she nodded and the two of them moved toward each other, tentatively at first, then with certainty, and joined in a long and loving embrace.

Chapter 25

By now, protest leaders had shifted their attention almost entirely to developing a viable alternative to the city's expressway plan. Brooklyn Borough President John Shea, after all, had steered them in that direction. It was only prudent, they reasoned, to follow his lead and propose an option that would be acceptable to the city, yet minimize the impact of the expressway on Bay Ridge.

Two such plans, in fact, had been developed over the past several weeks. One called for a bridge to be built two miles north, linking Brooklyn to New Jersey via an expressway that would bypass Bay Ridge entirely. The second proposal, considered far more viable, called for a rerouting of the Brooklyn approach to the existing bridge plan, swinging the proposed expressway two blocks north. This modification, engineers asserted, would save nine hundred families and nearly fifty businesses from having to relocate, since the expressway would pass primarily through the outer fringes of Owl's Head Park, precluding a far deeper cut through Bay Ridge.

"I think we may actually have something here," Walter Staziak gushed as he studied the plan in Councilman Alan Sherman's office. "We just might be in business with this."

"It's not a *perfect* solution," Sherman concurred, "but, by God, it's a lot less destructive to Bay Ridge than the city's current plan."

Protest leaders hovered over the drawing, reviewing it in detail.

"Just as important, this alternative makes a statement," Sherman said. "It reflects our willingness to offer a compromise that's satisfactory to both the city and the neighborhood. It demonstrates that we accept the city's need for a bridge and that we're not motivated purely by narrow self-interests—that all we're trying to do is preserve as much of Bay Ridge as possible."

"You see any major downside to this?" Sherman asked the civil engineer who'd drafted the plan, a studious, balding man named Maxwell Perry. A principal at a firm that, years earlier, had designed several of Robert Moses' groundbreaking Long Island roads, Perry, like attorney Bradley Jacobs, was intimately familiar with the Master Builder's thinking and had volunteered to assist with the anti-bridge campaign.

"There's no distinct downside that we can see," Perry stated definitively. "This alternative would compromise neither the grade nor the traffic pattern for the expressway. Just as importantly, the difference in cost compared to the city's current plan, we think, would be negligible."

The protest leaders studied Perry's plan further.

"Jeez, I think it's brilliant," said Sherman, reaching to pump Perry's hand.

"I agree," Staziak added. "But, remember, it's *our* plan—not Robert Moses'. The biggest obstacle in getting it approved could be that *we* devised it, not *him*."

Perry nodded knowingly.

"How likely is Moses to truly consider this?" Sherman queried.

"You never know with Moses," Perry replied. "He's as stubborn as he's brilliant. Once his mind is set, there's usually nothing that can change it. Then again, every so often, he surprises you and is willing to compromise."

"Maybe if we approach Moses directly with our plan—*reason* with him—he'll recognize that the alternative we've developed is feasible," Staziak suggested. "He'll still get the bridge and expressway he wants, but we'll get to keep more of our neighborhood intact."

"As I said," Perry shrugged, "it's not likely, but you never know."

"Well, we really have no choice but to give it a shot," Sherman said. "I think we've reached a point of desperation."

Everyone agreed. They had no choice but to go directly to Moses. And, surely, their prevailing emotion now was one of desperation.

A WEEK LATER, Sherman and Perry were sitting in the office of the city's chief engineer, along with representatives from the City Parks Department and the State Department of Public Works. Present as well was Patrick Brennan, John Shea's top lieutenant.

Sherman and Perry took turns explaining the details of the alternative expressway plan. The officials listened attentively and asked a series of questions that Perry answered adroitly.

"I agree that this proposed alternative has merit," admitted the city's chief engineer, Clifford Scott. "I'd say that it's at least worthy of consideration."

"Do you see any major drawbacks?" Sherman asked.

Scott sat silent, contemplating. "Not really."

Sherman turned to Patrick Brennan. "What do *you* think?"

"I think it behooves me to bring it to the borough president's attention," Shea's deputy replied. "If it's feasible in the view of our engineering staff, I'm sure Mr. Shea, as he pledged, will give it consideration."

"*Serious* consideration?" Sherman pressed.

"I anticipate he'll consider it quite seriously," Brennan replied.

"And how do you think he'll respond?"

"He'll be gratified you followed his advice and developed this alternative."

"But will he support it? Will he argue its merits to the Board of Estimate?"

"That, I can't tell you."

"What about Mr. Moses?" Sherman asked, turning to Scott. "You've got his ear, don't you?"

Scott smiled, as if struck by some unspoken irony. "I'm sure Mr. Moses will review it, as well."

"How soon will he get to see it?" Sherman said.

"There'll be a copy on his desk immediately following this meeting."

"That's the best you can tell us?"

"That's *all* we can tell you," Scott replied. "Mr. Moses will review the plan, and our office will be in touch. You and us both will just have to wait and see."

Chapter 26

The wait was short—and the city's response crushing. Within twenty-four hours of their meeting in the city, protest leaders were informed their proposal for an alternate expressway route had been rejected outright. For one thing, they were told, Robert Moses himself had given it the thumbs down, ruling the plan unduly costly. Equally damaging, the proposal had failed to win the backing of John Shea, who was apparently poised now to vote approval of Moses' existing blueprint.

Shea's decision, in particular, was tantamount to a kiss of death. In a very real sense, the borough president had been protestors' only real hope for defeating the city's existing plan. Like bridge opponents, after all, he had deep Brooklyn roots and had at least seemed sympathetic with their pleas to preserve Bay Ridge. He was also the only public official who'd suggested that an alternate expressway route might actually fly with city planners.

But any possibility of Shea's support had apparently evaporated now—and, with it, any remaining hope. With Shea's inevitable backing, a Board of Estimate vote to approve the city's existing plan was all but assured.

Protestors had nowhere left to turn. All possible means of voicing their dissent, other than the impending public hearing, had been exhausted. There was no political ground support in sight, no strings to pull or favors to call in. They'd lobbied every Board of Estimate member to no avail. Efforts to reach Robert Moses directly were proving fruitless. Even John Shea had suddenly become virtually invisible. Calls to him went unanswered. Letters, telegrams, even appeals dispatched via messenger, drew no response.

"I think we're screwed," Councilman Sherman told protest leaders gathered in his office. "The only plan the city will consider is the one Robert Moses wants."

"This is bullshit!" Walter Staziak said. "Our alternative wasn't rejected because it lacked merit. It was killed because Robert Moses felt like killing it."

"Maybe so." Sherman sighed. "But the result's the same."

"But our route made more sense," Staziak said. "It was more viable—better for everyone."

"My God," Chester Jablonski said, "what's gonna happen now?"

His question met silence. The protest leaders seemed crestfallen. Some buried their faces in their hands. Others stared blankly out the window.

"I don't understand," Staziak muttered. "All the rallies we mounted, the support we attracted, everything we've fought for—has it amounted to *nothing*?"

Again, there was silence—only the faint sound of traffic winding its way along Seventh Avenue, a thoroughfare that would literally vanish, along with hundreds of homes and businesses, with construction of the expressway.

"It makes no sense … " Staziak lamented.

"Actually, it makes *perfect* sense," Jablonski said bitterly. "Let's face it—no one gives a shit. No one in government listens to people like us. Who the hell are we? We're expendable, meaningless, in the way. An obstacle that gets moved … or gets trampled."

My mother, seated alongside Sherman and the others, felt the same way—steamrolled; an overwhelming sense that we were powerless, insignificant, inanimate, almost, to city officials; our destiny entirely in their hands.

"Chet's right, it's a losing battle," said Vern Bateman, owner of a local insurance firm. "Our hands are tied. They're gonna ram this expressway down our throats—and that's that. There's nothing left to do but pack up and get out."

"Bastards," someone mumbled. "Goddamned fuckin' bureaucrats!"

For several minutes no one spoke, the silence broken only by the drone of outside traffic—and then by a rap on the door. Sherman rose to open it. In the open doorway, to everyone's surprise, stood none other than Deputy Borough President Patrick Brennan.

"You got some pair of balls showing your face here," Staziak blurted. "You guys are stabbing us in the back. You're killing Bay Ridge and everyone in it."

"May I come in?" Brennan inquired sheepishly.

Sherman nodded and stepped aside. Brennan approached the conference table.

"I feel our office owes you an explanation," he said.

"Frankly, you owe us a helluva lot more than that," Staziak responded. "What your office is doing to Bay Ridge is a crime, and it won't be forgotten. I swear to God—you and your boss will hear that loud and clear in the next election."

Brennan winced. "I understand."

"*Do* you?"

"Yes, and I can assure you Borough President Shea understands, as well."

"Well, he sure has a strange way of showing it," Staziak said. "I thought it was his job to represent the interests of Brooklyn, not just genuflect to Robert Moses."

"Mr. Shea *is* representing the interests of Brooklyn," Brennan replied.

"Really? Well, what's more important than the lives of thousands of working people in Bay Ridge?"

"The future of New York is more important."

"Is that what we're *really* talking about here?"

"Yes. It may be difficult for you to recognize, but the truth is the city desperately needs the Narrows bridge—and the expressway leading to it."

"Bullshit," Staziak muttered. "New York needs this bridge only because there are bigger issues at stake: money, politics, power."

"I can assure you the bridge is needed for reasons that transcend those," Brennan said.

"Even if it kills our neighborhood?"

"Regrettably, a major portion of Bay Ridge will be impacted," Brennan said. "But not the entire neighborhood. Bay Ridge will be changed. But the neighborhood as a whole, I can assure you, will survive."

"You're certainly full of assurances, aren't you?" Chester Jablonski said. "How about the assurance your boss gave us that he'd give our alternative route careful consideration? He led us to believe he'd support the plan if it was found viable."

"And he honored that pledge," Brennan responded. "He studied the proposal carefully."

"And?" Jablonski asked.

"And he concluded it was unfeasible."

"*Why*?"

"He was advised as such by his engineering staff."

"But even the city's engineers felt our plan had merit," Sherman argued.

"Upon closer reflection, they apparently had a change of heart."

"Of course they did," Staziak said. "They changed their minds when Robert Moses told them to. We know that—and so do you. Why pull punches? We all know who wields the power in New York. Everyone does the bidding of King Moses."

Brennan dropped his gaze. "I won't dispute Mr. Moses' impact on these matters," he admitted.

"Do you dispute our view that some of his ideas are horribly flawed, and that some of his methods are arbitrary and unfair?" Sherman asked.

"I won't dispute that, either," Brennan said. "Trust me—many people in city government are aware that Robert Moses has flaws that rival his talent."

"Yeah," Sherman said. "For one thing, he's deaf and blind. Deaf to the ideas of others and blind to anything he himself hasn't conceived."

"In many ways, that's true," Brennan agreed. "Moses possesses genius—no doubt about it. But that genius often prevents him from understanding the impact his projects have on average people."

"Yeah," Staziak said, "he's supposed to be a champion of the people, but in reality *little people* don't mean a damn to him. He tramples average people in order to get things done. All that matters are his projects."

Brennan nodded as if he understood all too well. "Can I speak off the record?"

"Certainly, if you can be more candid," Sherman replied.

The others nodded their approval.

"What we're witnessing here," Brennan began, "is a classic example of top-down planning."

"Top-down?" Sherman asked,

"Yes. The reality is, Moses and his engineers essentially see the city from above, as a physical tapestry—a network of roads, waterways, and structures. People figure into that viewpoint only vaguely."

"Well, that's a problem right there," Staziak declared.

"Exactly," Brennan replied. "The problem is that, from up above, people and neighborhoods *disappear*. When you plan that way, you never get to walk the streets and feel the pulse of neighborhoods like Bay Ridge. You plan from ivory towers instead of from street corners and sidewalks."

"That's why planners don't understand why neighborhoods are so important to the people who live in them, why they're essential to the vibrancy of a city," Sherman said.

"But let's face it," Staziak contended. "It's not about neighborhoods anymore. It's all about the *car* these days, isn't it?"

"In many ways, that's true," Brennan sighed. "Robert Moses is a product of the Automobile Age. He believes the car is an invention that ranks right up there with fire, the sail, and the wheel. He sees New York through the eyes of someone who drives, not as someone who lives here and walks the streets."

"So *cars* are more important now than *people*?" Jablonski said.

"In a sense, that's true," Brennan said. "The city's emphasis now is on building roads. There's a battle going on to determine the fate of New York—a tug of war between the city block and the highway, the traditional neighborhood and the suburb, the pedestrian and the car."

"It's a battle being fought by foot soldiers like us, on the streets of neighborhoods like Bay Ridge," Sherman said. "It's a battle that's tearing New York apart."

"And it's a battle that the car is winning," Staziak lamented. "These days, the car is *king*. And it's open season on neighborhoods like Bay Ridge."

Once again, the group lapsed into silence.

"Well, we think the city should value people more than cars," Sherman said. "We think the experience of ordinary citizens should hold more weight than the so-called expertise of planners. Something important about New York is being destroyed with all these roads. We're sacrificing how livable our neighborhoods are when we build around the needs of cars instead of people."

Brennan glanced about, as if to assure himself no eavesdroppers were present.

"To be perfectly honest, I question what's going on, too," he admitted. "A lot of people do. At some point you wonder if all the construction we're undertaking has a real *purpose*, or if we're just building for the sake of building."

"That's our feeling," Sherman said. "Robert Moses is rebuilding New York in a way that's never been done before on this scale. But he's not necessarily rebuilding it for the better. What he's doing, instead, is slashing and bulldozing his way through established, vibrant neighborhoods—uprooting thousands of people, destroying everything they hold dear. The very fabric of the city's tapestry is being torn apart."

"I understand." Brennan sighed. "Your pain is very real. And it's shared by others, too. The road-building taking place these days may have profound benefits, but it's leaving a legacy of upheaval, chaos, and loss all across America."

"You mean Bay Ridge isn't alone?" Sherman asked.

"Hardly," Brennan asserted. "The reality is that we're currently in the midst of an era of dispossession unlike anything America has seen since the days of the Wild West. Roads are killing towns. Urban renewal is eviscerating neighborhoods. Businesses are being closed, private property seized, social bonds destroyed. Tens of thousands of people are being uprooted, stripped of their sense of place, their quality of life. In New York alone, half a million people have been displaced by the expressways we've built."

"Are these roads really necessary?" Staziak asked.

"That's debatable," Brennan replied. "But for the people being affected, they're nothing more than a brutal assault on their way of life."

"And there's nothing that can be done about it?" Staziak wondered. "We allow engineers to design our cities? We allow the highway lobby to run roughshod over our lives? And we have to just sit here and *take it*?"

Brennan looked sincerely moved but offered only a sigh.

"Do you have any idea," Jablonski said, "about the devastating impact this project will have on Bay Ridge?"

"I do," Brennan said.

"I mean, thousands of people will lose everything. The sense of displacement they'll feel will last their entire lives. For some people, this project will be a death sentence."

"I understand."

"And you're telling us that *doesn't matter* to the city?"

"Of course, it matters, but …"

"But it's the price of *progress*, right?"

"In many ways, yes."

"And there's a greater good that'll be achieved?"

"That's the hope," Brennan said.

"So the city lives—but Bay Ridge dies. New York moves on, but we fall by the wayside, right?"

"I'm sorry," Brennan whispered.

"Do we have any further recourse?" Sherman asked.

"Your only recourse now," Brennan replied, "is to plead your case at the public hearing. Tell the Board of Estimate what you think. Tell them what the bridge will mean to Bay Bridge and its people."

"Plead our case—or plead for our lives?" Staziak asked. "Reason or beg?"

"Whatever works," Brennan said. "The reality is you're at the board's mercy now. The public hearing is your only chance."

Chapter 27

Summer arrived far too soon for Bay Ridge in 1960, a year that made it seem as if we'd crossed some kind of unseen threshold into an uncertain new realm. We were on the shakiest of ground now. The public hearing, after months of dreaded anticipation, was mere days away. So much about our lives seemed up in the air. So many things seemed about to be pulled from our grasp.

"Our immediate future, in many ways, is in the city's hands now," said my father, gazing across the boardwalk at Coney Island, where the arcades were stirring to life and the sprawling white beach was peppered with eager sunbathers. "I don't feel like we're in control of our own lives anymore."

He was fresh from a steamy respite at Staunch's Bathhouse after a round of handball at the nearby Seaside Courts. The two of us were quaffing down orangeades before heading for home.

"You know, I still can't believe the 1950s are really over," my father mused. "It's strange to even say the words *nineteen-sixty*. It feels like we've left the past behind and suddenly … we're somewhere in the *future*."

He was right. It really felt that way.

The future, we could sense, was all over us—like it or not. The 1950s were gone for good; so was the decade's pervasive sense of innocence and stability. Staring us in the face was a whole new decade, along with the palpable sense that things were on the precipice of dramatic change. Nothing seemed solid anymore. Nothing seemed assured.

All this, in many ways, was epitomized by the specter of the bridge.

If constructed, the Narrows bridge would stand as the physical embodiment of everything that was changing in our world. It would symbolize an entire new era for Brooklyn—the end of a comfortable and familiar way of life, the start of something disquieting and uncertain.

"Things are different, Nathan," my father said, squinting into the sunlight and staring out at an ocean that seemed unfittingly calm. "It's a whole new world out there."

Perhaps.

At the moment, though, it was also the start of summer. And, despite the uncertainties we faced, that was something to be thoroughly embraced.

I'd done well my freshman year at Hamilton High—a 94 average, good enough to qualify for any of the city's public colleges and more than satisfactory to my parents. Now, freed from the drudgery of classes and homework, I relished the thought of two-plus months of sleeping late, playing ball in the streets and schoolyards, and spending languid, sun-filled days at the Brighton Beach Cabana Club, where we'd been members for years, joining legions of other Jewish families who spent their summers either at local pool clubs or at the hotels and bungalow colonies of the Catskills.

Located off the boardwalk at Brighton Beach, the BBCC was jammed-packed and raucous all summer long. Children splashed about in a huge T-shaped swimming pool with diving boards and a twisting, cascading waterfall at one end. Around the pool, people sunned themselves on chaise lounges, surrounded by cabanas, locker rooms, and umbrella-covered tables, where men played pinochle and cribbage, and women kibitzed over mahjong tiles.

The BBCC was where I'd spend much of that summer. There, it seemed as if any threat to Bay Ridge was as distant as the ocean horizon. There, for the time being, I could pretend it was summer as usual.

SUMMER KICKED OFF as usual on Dahlgren Place, too—with a Fourth of July block party in our cul-de-sac, the festivities unwinding as if the impending threat of the bridge was merely a figment of our collective imagination.

Music blared from transistor radios. Tables overflowed with food that mirrored the street's diverse ethnicity: bowls of Scandinavian rice pudding; pans of Swedish meatballs; platters of kielbasa, Italian sausage, and pickled herring; trays of Norwegian *fyrstekake* and Danish *helenesnitter*.

And the street scene was as lively as ever.

Kids raced about and skated. A large group played Red Light/ Green Light. My sister and several other girls giggled through a game of A, My Name Is, swinging their legs over a bouncing spaldeen as they recited names starting with each letter in the alphabet. Mr. Mangini, an elderly neighbor, strummed his mandolin, singing about happy times in the Old Country. Leo Banion played his concertina.

"How long have we been having these block parties?" asked Gus Pappas, pouring his homemade *ouzo* from a milk bottle into plastic drinking cups.

"I don't know," said Mrs. Schmidt, a heavyset woman toting a tray of strudel. "I've been living here twenty years and we've had one every year."

"Well, we better make this the best one yet," Leo Banion chimed in. "If that bridge gets built, it'll be the last one we ever have."

"Don't say that!" Mrs. Schmidt scolded. "Please. It hurts too much to even think about it. These block parties are part of what makes Dahlgren Place such a special place. They're part of why we love living here."

"That and our neighbors," Mrs. Pedersen said and smiled.

The two women hugged.

"Don't make this party feel like a good-bye," Mrs. Schmidt said.

"We've gotta face reality," Mr. Pappas intoned.

"Maybe so. But we don't have to face it today. Let's just have fun."

"And pretend?"

"Yes. Let's pretend."

"That's right," said my mother, setting out a tray of stuffed cabbage. "We've got to keep our spirits up. We've got to keep believing that we'll win our fight and things'll be all right."

"Lily's right," Mrs. Pedersen said. "We've got to have hope that—somehow, some way—our street will be saved."

And so our block party wound on.

Mr. Mangini strummed his mandolin and the adults drank Mr. Pappas' *ouzo* and ate each other's food and laughed and sang and told the same stories they'd been telling for years. A few of us played stoopball at Mr. Sandusky's house. The Good Humor man made his rounds, along with a truck that offered a swinging ride called the Half Moon. At Fort Hamilton, the bugler blew a solemn rendition of taps.

And Dahlgren Place felt as sheltered and intact as ever.

It was easy at that moment to believe that 1960 would be just another year, that this would be just another summer. It was easy to pretend that the games we played and the block parties we had and the way we lived would last nothing short of forever.

BUT CELEBRATIONS DIDN'T last long in Bay Ridge that year. Three days after our block party, nearly two thousand neighborhood residents gathered at a block-long staging area on Seventh Avenue. And soon after, a procession of chartered school buses wound its way through Brooklyn for the journey to City Hall.

The public hearing before the New York City Board of Estimate would be the day of reckoning—the final chance to dissuade city officials from approving appropriations for the bridge. If voted down, the project would be shelved, perhaps indefinitely. If approved, it would be forwarded to the city's Planning Commission for action, commencing with the immediate condemnation of homes. Either way, the uncertainty that had enveloped Bay Ridge for ten full months would end once and for all with a decisive rap of the mayor's gavel. The public hearing would instantly and irrevocably seal the neighborhood's fate.

Most of the people on the buses that day were housewives and children, including my mother and me. The vast majority of the neighborhood's men, my father among them, could ill afford to miss a day's pay or, even worse, lose their job because they took time off to stage a protest. They'd join us at the end of the workday, for a hearing that everyone knew would be vocal and emotional, and stretch well into the night.

When the buses arrived in Manhattan, two hours before the start of the 1 PM hearing, everyone disembarked and began marching along the sidewalk in front of City Hall. Many people toted signs. Some women wheeled baby carriages or held the hands of their young children. I walked alongside my mother, her expression grim and determined.

"Save our neighborhood!" people chanted.

"No bridge for Bay Ridge!"

"Spare our homes!"

The chants seemed to be swallowed up by the clamor of passing traffic and the stoic office towers on Lower Broadway. I found myself wondering if our voices could ever be truly heard amid the hubbub and motion of the city.

"Do we really have a chance of winning?" I asked my mother.

"We'll never know unless we fight," she said. "Fighting for what you believe in, Nathan, is always worth a try."

We marched for about an hour, after which we were ushered through the wrought-iron gates encircling City Hall and then herded into a long hallway outside the City Council chambers. The hallway, lined with paintings of historic figures and public officials, could barely contain the crowd. Benches were jammed, mostly with elderly women. Children ran and slid across the polished tile floors. Babies fussed and cried.

And we waited for more than two hours.

"You think they even realize we're here?" someone asked.

"Oh, they *realize* all right," said Betty Jablonski, the wife of protest leader Chester Jablonski. "What they're demonstrating is who's in charge. They'll meet when they're good and ready—not a minute before."

"Keeping us waiting is a ploy," someone else said. "They want to wear us down. Maybe they think if they keep us waiting long enough we'll just go away."

"Yeah—*disappear*," Betty Jablonski said. "That's what they want. Then they could build their bridge to their heart's content."

"Well, they can kiss my red-white-and-blue ass first," bellowed Joey Palumbo. "I ain't goin' nowhere!"

And neither did anyone—despite an interminable wait that ended when the doors to the council chamber swung open to finally allow everyone in.

The chamber was as imposing as the specter of the hearing itself, resembling a courtroom in which we'd be put to trial. Rows of shiny wooden benches lined either side of a carpeted aisle that split the chamber in two. Overhead, a gleaming chandelier sparkled. Up front, a massive wooden desk sat atop a riser that spanned nearly the entire width of the chamber. Carved into a wall behind it were images depicting the founding of New York City, along with the city's official seal. A pair of American flags flanked the desk, in front of which a flimsy microphone stood mounted on a metal pole.

This would not be a typical day in the council chamber, where the machinery of city government generally ground along with little fanfare and few witnesses. In contrast, the chamber literally overflowed now with people, some standing three deep at the rear and spilling into the hallway outside. Reporters and photographers jockeyed for position. The murmur of anticipation filled the room.

And we waited, just like that, for nearly another hour.

"What the hell is going on?" Joey Palumbo roared at one point. "Is *anyone* gonna come out and hear what we have to say?"

Palumbo was shushed by a uniformed City Hall worker who emerged from a door at the front of the chamber and announced that board members were engaged in a closed-door executive conference. The conference, he assured us, was purely procedural—nothing out of the ordinary.

"That's where they *really* make their decisions," someone said. "That's where Robert Moses tells them how to vote."

"Think so?"

"Hell, yeah. They *know* how they're gonna vote before they even start the hearing. That's what their caucus is for. The hearing is only for show."

"So why even bother to come?"

"It's the only way to let 'em know how we feel."

"I just want to look Robert Moses in the eye and tell him what I think of him and his goddamned bridge," Joey Palumbo chimed in.

Others felt the same.

That was the reason most of them were there. If nothing else, the hearing would be a unique opportunity to confront Moses and present the case for saving their homes. It would be their singular chance to demand the Master Builder defend his plan and answer their questions.

"If they're gonna throw us out of our homes," Joey Palumbo said, "I at least want the satisfaction of tellin' 'em what I think."

No sooner had he finished speaking than the door at the front of the chamber swung open and the board members filed in, chatting as casually as if they were out for a night on the town. A nervous hush settled over the chamber. Everyone's eyes were trained on the city officials as they assumed their places at the council desk. People seemed transfixed. It was, I knew, an imposing lineup.

"There's the mayor," whispered my mother, pointing to a short, balding man with a high-domed head, a jowly chin, and half-moon glasses.

I was in awe. I'd never been that close to the mayor before, never seen him live. Until that moment, he'd been almost a mystical figure to me, like a ballplayer or comic strip character. But he was real, all right—tinier and more leaden in complexion than his photos suggested—but as real as the hearing itself.

The mayor took his place at the center of the council desk. Flanking him were City Comptroller William Marshall, Corporation Counsel James Pierce, and the five borough presidents, including John Shea. All of them settled into high-backed leather chairs behind bronze nameplates set alongside pitchers of water and a string of tabletop microphones. Tucked into an alcove at the end of the desk, a stenographer prepared to record the hearing's minutes.

Then Robert Moses emerged from the caucus room, surrounded by a phalanx of assistants. Instantly, the audience stirred, their attention fixed on the Master Builder, who strode confidently up the steps, assuming a position directly behind the mayor.

For the past year, I'd harbored private images of Moses, the same way I had for all the heroic figures of my childhood. I'd imagined him worshipping at a statue of Mercury, overseer of highways, his personal messenger to the Gods. I'd imagined him sequestered in his office on Randall's Island, surrounded by photos of the public monuments he'd built, plotting new projects on a wall-sized map of New York. I'd imagined him at the controls of an enormous bulldozer, snarling at critics, laughing as he reduced entire city blocks to rubble. I'd imagined him surrounded by imperial trappings: chefs and waiters serving lavish receptions he'd ordered up, a fleet of limousines and yachts at his beck and call.

And now, taking his place at the hearing, he looked every bit as I'd imagined. Standing stoically, arms folded across his chest, jaw jutted outward, Moses stared stone-like at the audience, his posture magisterial, almost predatory.

To me, it was obvious from his very pose that *he*—not the mayor or any other city official—was in charge here. It was equally obvious that he'd be more than merely difficult to budge. To me, Robert Moses looked every bit as imposing as the Colossus of Rhodes, impossible to defeat or placate, powerful enough to bend even Mother Nature to his will.

Clifford Scott, the city's chief engineer, opened several cylindrical containers and withdrew a series of maps and drawings, which were spread out before the board members. And with a crack that reverberated through the chamber, the mayor rapped his gavel on a sturdy wooden block.

The public hearing into Bay Ridge's fate had begun.

CHAPTER 28

It was a grueling, nightmarish spectacle that unfolded in the City Council chamber, a harrowing ordeal that taxed both the imagination and the heart.

Lasting fourteen hours in all, the public hearing on the Narrows bridge droned on through the afternoon, then wound deep into the night and wee hours of the following morning—raucous, confrontational, charged with emotion.

And ruled by rigid governmental procedures.

One by one, the people of Bay Ridge were summoned to the front of the chamber, asked to state their names and places of residence, and granted a maximum of three minutes to address the Board of Estimate.

And one by one, they did.

Some, propelled by sheer resolve, strode confidently to the microphone and addressed board members calmly, reading from notes or speaking off the cuff, their voices strong and reasoned. Others, barely ambulatory, were assisted to the front of the chamber, where they rambled, at times incoherently, their voices quavering, their bodies trembling. People cried and begged for mercy. Parents pleaded on behalf of their children. Shopkeepers asked that their businesses be spared. Retirees argued they'd have nowhere to go if the city seized their homes.

And, in virtually every instance, the speakers were politely ignored.

City officials seemed highly practiced in their lack of response. As people offered their statements, not a single board member so much as issued a response, posed a question, or demonstrated even the slightest bit of interest. Instead, they chatted among themselves, as if the audience were invisible and the microphone mute. Each time a speaker concluded, the mayor offered a curt thank you and summoned the next speaker. The three-minute time limit was strictly enforced, marked by a crack of the mayor's gavel. Occasionally, a mayoral nod would summon a pair of cops who'd escort speakers back to their seat or, in some cases, out of the chamber entirely.

Still, people came forward to plead their case.

"It took my family four decades to build our pharmacy," rasped Walter Staziak. "Our business is our life. We've been there through thick and thin for the people of Bay Ridge, and we depend on them for our survival. The evictions you're planning will destroy everything we've worked for. I beg you not to let that happen."

"Thank you," the mayor said. "Next!"

"You are tearing our neighborhood apart in the name of so-called progress," insurance man Vern Bateman said. "If you proceed with your plan, a neighborhood that pulses with life will be reduced to rubble. People will be uprooted. Lives will be destroyed."

"Thank you," the mayor said. "Next!"

"Many people here today have no place to go if they're forced from their homes," said Betty Jablonski, pointing to a row of elderly residents.

Her statement had no discernible effect. No one's did. Board members busied themselves with paperwork and small talk, checked their wristwatches, and fidgeted in their seats. John Shea, shifting his posture uncomfortably, looked everywhere but at the audience. Robert Moses, arms crossed, stood statue-like behind the mayor.

"Look at these people!" Betty Jablonski beseeched. "For God's sake, will you at least *look* at the people who've come to pour their hearts out to you?"

Startled, board members glanced up.

"These people are old and frightened," Mrs. Jablonski said. "Most have lived their entire life in Bay Ridge. They're close to stores and loved ones. They can't afford the cost of moving. If you force them from their homes you might as well be handing them a death sentence. I swear to you, people will die if this bridge is built. They'll lose the will to live."

"Thank you," the mayor said. "Next!"

And Mrs. Jablonski, nudged along by a cop, drifted back into the audience and took her seat. Near her, several people wept.

ON AND ON the hearing continued, hour after hour, speaker after speaker. Through it all, Board of Estimate members seemed unaffected. Robert Moses, in particular, remained expressionless and aloof. Occasionally, he shook his head from side to side, smirking wryly. Periodically, he whispered in the mayor's ear or paced about impatiently, conversing with board members.

"Why don't you tell *us* what you're telling *them*, Mr. Moses?" Joey Palumbo bellowed at one point. "Why are your comments such a deep, dark secret?"

Moses ignored him, continuing to talk with his chief engineer.

"You can't stand being at this hearing, can you?" someone shouted. "Why don't you admit it—you can't stand *us*!"

Moses barely flinched.

"If this is city government at work, all I can say is that it's nothing but a goddamned charade," someone else spoke out.

"Excuse me?" said the mayor, looking up.

"This is not Nazi Germany, Mr. Mayor," the man said. "This is a democracy. This is *America!*"

The audience erupted in cheers. Board members halted their conversations. The stenographer glanced up, the twisting spool of paper collecting at her feet.

"In America, people have a right to speak their mind," the man challenged. "The public should have a voice."

"The public *has* a voice," the mayor retorted. "That's why we conduct hearings like this—so all of you can be heard."

"Then why isn't anyone *listening*?" Betty Jablonski asked. "No one on the board has heard a word we've said. You're ignoring us instead of engaging us. You're slapping us in the face."

"How are we doing that?" the mayor asked.

"By belittling us, making us feel as if what we're fighting for is unimportant, meaningless. This board is doing little more than quieting the voices you tell us we have. You're basically saying our voices don't matter."

"I assure you, we *are* listening," the mayor said.

"Then why won't someone at least give us the courtesy of looking at us when we speak? At least give us the *appearance* that you care."

The audience applauded roundly, until the mayor's gavel, crashing repeatedly, brought the chamber to silence.

"Let me reiterate—we *do* care about what you're saying," the mayor said, his face pinched as if in pain. "We understand your plight and we *sympathize*. We're not the unthinking, unfeeling municipal machine you're painting us out to be. We're not so heartless that we don't care."

"You coulda fooled us!" Joey Palumbo roared.

The mayor banged his gavel again.

"Those types of comments," he said, "will not be tolerated."

The audience grew still.

"Now, who's next?" the mayor inquired.

And, with that, my mother abruptly rose, slid down the aisle of people alongside us, and strode to the front of the chamber. It startled me. I'd had no idea she'd intended to speak. My sister slipped her hand into that of my father, who'd arrived moments earlier. Excited and fearful, I shrunk into my seat and watched.

"Your name?" the mayor inquired.

"Lillian Wolf."

"Address?"

"Eight Dahlgren Place. Bay Ridge."

The mayor gestured for my mother to proceed.

"Mr. Mayor, members of the board—I ask that you please try to understand what you're witnessing here today," she began.

The mayor eyes narrowed slightly, as if she'd somehow managed to capture his interest.

"What you're seeing," she said, "is the fear of people threatened with being displaced, separated from a place they call *home*."

Board members remained silent, but attentive. I craned my neck to see. All I could glimpse, though, were the backs of people's heads and the faces of board members staring stoically at my mother.

"We need you to understand why what we're trying to save is so important to us," she continued. "These are our *homes* we're fighting for. Understand? They're our *homes*."

"I think we understand that," the mayor said.

"Do you, Mr. Mayor? Do you *really*? Because if you understood, you wouldn't be surprised by the outpouring here. If you understood, you'd recognize that our homes are not simply bricks and mortar to us. They're much more."

I watched as people edged forward, listening intently.

"Our homes, sir, are *who we are*," my mother told the board. "They're full of the sights, sounds, smells, and feelings of our lives. They're where we've raised families, held celebrations, mourned losses. They're where we find shelter, sustenance, comfort, contentment, and peace. They're where we store our memories, live our dreams, gather the strength to face our lives, experience quiet, everyday moments that mean the world to us."

The chamber was utterly still now, the silence broken only by an occasional cough.

"We care deeply about our homes," my mother said. "We're part of them—conjoined to them. Our most powerful emotions flow through them."

A spattering of applause fluttered through the audience. My mother paused until it quieted.

"We're connected that same way to Bay Ridge," she continued. "To us, Bay Ridge is not simply a place on a map. It's our *world*. It gives us a sense of identity and place. We're drawn together by our neighborhood and the interlocking lives we lead."

My mother spoke resolutely, her voice carrying easily to the rear of the chamber.

"Bay Ridge connects us, draws us together, make us whole. If you knew Bay Ridge like we do, you'd understand what we're trying so desperately to protect. People put down roots in neighborhoods like ours. When you tear the roots out from under them, it's wrenching. When you take their homes, they're lost."

The audience applauded politely. My father's eyes brightened. My sister smiled. I felt a surge of pride over my mother's eloquence and courage, her character and substance, the passion she harbored for our neighborhood and our home. I wanted to stand up and shout out that she was my mother, so that everyone there would know that she and I, too, were connected.

But, like everyone else, I remained quiet.

"You're hearing today from people who desperately want you to understand their feelings," she continued. "You paint us out as self-centered, narrow-minded obstructionists, fighting to preserve the status quo. But all we are, really, are average, law-abiding, hard-working people who are *hurting*—people who are fighting for everything that's safe and familiar, fighting to preserve a sense of who we are and to save something we love."

The mayor nodded.

"All we ask is that you understand those feelings before making a decision," my mother concluded. "Understand why this means so much to us."

The mayor nodded again. Then he thanked my mother and requested a recess.

And, with that, the board members retreated to their caucus room and my mother returned to her seat to wait, like everyone else, for the hearing to resume. All the while people stopped by to thank her for what she'd said. All the while she clung to my father's hand, as if the two of them would never again let each other go.

UNCROSSING HIS ARMS and taking the podium, Robert Moses riffled through a sheath of papers. Then, gazing down at the audience, he began reciting a prepared statement.

"The Narrows bridge—"

"Make him tell us his name, Mr. Mayor," Joey Palumbo interrupted.

The audience stirred. Several people chuckled.

"All of us had to tell the board who *we* are," Palumbo insisted. "*He* should have to do the same."

"Make him say his name!" the audience chanted. "Make him say his name! Make him say his name!"

Flustered, the mayor sought out Moses with his eyes, sheepishly imploring him, with raised eyebrows, to comply. Moses merely pulled his head back, thrust out his chin and stood in defiant silence. He seemed implacable, indifferent to the chants filling the chamber.

"Make him say his name! Make him say his name!"

But the chants had no effect. The Master Builder merely smiled and stared impassively at the audience. Then, glancing at the mayor, he muttered, "Now, what are you going to do about this?"

The mayor seemed momentarily frozen. Wordlessly, he shrunk in his chair, his head barely visible over the council desk. Finally, he sputtered, "Now, all of you … know exactly who this is."

"No, we don't," Joey Palumbo declared. "Make him say his name, like the rest of us had to."

Moses smirked.

"The same rules that govern us should apply to him," someone else said. "Is he above the rules?"

"No," the mayor said, regaining his composure. "But *I'll* tell you who he is. His name … is Robert Moses."

Hoots and catcalls filled the chamber, evoking a toothy grin from Moses.

"Okay, we know his name," Joey Palumbo said. "Now make him tell us his address."

The audience again began to chant. "Make him tell us his address! Make him tell us his address!"

The mayor's gavel crashed down sharply.

"This is not necessary!" he fumed. "All of you know exactly who this is. His name, once again, is Robert Moses and he lives … across the street from me."

Then, glaring at the audience, he ordered, "Now, let's proceed."

The audience gradually calmed. Moses' eyes fell back to his notes.

"The project we're here to consider is an undertaking New York desperately needs," he began, his arms moving in grand, sweeping gestures. "It's the most ambitious piece of arterial construction in New York's history, and will change the course of the city's future."

Several people hooted, but Moses didn't so much as raise his eyes.

"This is an undertaking the city not only needs, but one the public should appreciate," he continued. "It will be the backbone of commerce for centuries, long after any protests about its worthiness have faded."

The hoots intensified, drowning out Moses in mid-sentence.

The outburst was met by repeated cracks from the mayor's gavel. "We need order!" he shouted, rising. "All of you have had an opportunity to speak. Now it's Mr. Moses' turn. If you can't remain quiet, I'll be forced to clear the chamber!"

When the audience calmed, the mayor sat back down.

Eschewing his prepared text, Moses stared contemptuously at the audience. He shook his head, as if in pity.

"All you people mention is what's *bad* about what we're planning," he said. "You criticize blindly, twist the truth."

"No, Mr. Moses," someone shouted. "It's *you* who's twisting the truth."

"Am I?" Moses asked. "The truth is that highways are needed by the residents of Greater New York. Like it or not, cars have become the lifeblood of this region, and highways are the arteries needed to pump that blood. The city is growing. The suburbs are opening to development. Without new roads, New York will die. We need this bridge to assure the city's survival. Future generations will be grateful we built it. They'll consider it a godsend."

"Ain't nobody in Bay Ridge gonna consider it a godsend," Joey Palumbo shouted. "To us, the bridge is a *curse*—nothing but another goddamned monument to yourself!"

The mayor rapped his gavel. "I will not stand for comments like that," he warned.

"I've lived in Bay Ridge forty-two years" Joey Palumbo snarled. "It's fine the way it is. Why can't you just leave it the hell alone?"

"Because everything changes with time," Moses said.

"But it's not changing for the *better*," Palumbo said.

"That's a matter of opinion."

"Well, why don't you let the people who live there make that decision?"

"The job of government is to make those decisions *for* the people," Moses said. "The people don't know what's good for the city. All the people care about is what's good for themselves."

"And *you*?" Palumbo asked.

"I speak for the City of New York."

"Oh—and how's that? You don't represent the people. You've never even been elected to public office. Who are you to make these decisions single-handedly? Who are you to ignore the wishes of people who vote?"

"The fact that I've never been elected is exactly *why* I'm in the best position to protect the public's interest," Moses said. "My interests lie in what's best for New York, pure and simple—not in trying to please voters. There are times when public officials have to decide what's right for the greater good, even if there's dissent. This is one of those times."

"Even if neighborhoods get destroyed?" Palumbo asked.

"Sometimes that happens."

"Even if people get hurt?"

"Sometimes that happens, too."

Moses' glare sharpened. "You people allow shortsightedness to stand in the way of progress. All you do is look *behind*, cling to the status quo. I'm looking *ahead* for decades. Why can't you see past your own narrow self-interests and recognize what's best for the city—a bridge that will usher New York into the next century?"

"Maybe so." Betty Jablonski stood again. "But look what'll be destroyed in the process. A living, breathing neighborhood of hard-working, law-abiding citizens simply trying to live their lives. Neighborhoods like Bay Ridge are what make New York great. When you destroy them, you're destroying the very city you're trying to protect."

"Tell me, then—" the mayor jumped in. "What do you suggest we do?"

"Build the bridge somewhere else!" Joey Palumbo shouted.

"That's out of the question," the mayor said. "Where are we supposed to build a bridge over the Narrows, except between Brooklyn and Staten Island? And where are we supposed to build the road to get traffic to the bridge, except through Bay Ridge?"

"Then don't build the bridge at all!" Palumbo shouted.

"That, too, is out of the question."

"Well, then why won't you consider the alternative route we've proposed?" Walter Staziak challenged. "Our plan was drafted by professional engineers. From every possible standpoint, it's technically feasible. Why won't the board even consider it?"

"The route we've selected," the mayor retorted, "has been judged to be the best route possible. It was based on years of planning."

"Well, we think it was based on nothing more than a whim," Staziak replied, "and the only reason you won't alter it is because Mr. Moses is stubborn."

The mayor slammed his gavel down, but to no apparent effect. The audience grew increasingly edgy. A row of cops at the front of the chamber edged forward, as if expecting trouble.

"Your plans are developed in secrecy, Mr. Moses, so you can spring them on the public," Staziak railed. "To support your views, you bring in so-called expert opinions. But those opinions are controlled by you. You're listening only to the voice inside your head. Instead, you should be listening to the voices of the people."

"Your arguments, in my view, are overblown," Moses retorted. "People will be inconvenienced, but they'll survive."

"Inconvenienced? You call getting evicted an inconvenience?"

"Whatever you call it, the fact is your pain will subside with time. Ultimately, you'll move on with your lives."

"And what about those of us who don't—or can't?"

"Their distress is unfortunate, but, frankly, it's the price of progress—a small price to pay, I might add, for the benefits the city will derive."

Moses leaned forward, as if trying to get closer to the crowd.

"We are rebuilding New York," he said, "not tearing it down. Progress often involves temporary hardships. That's nothing new. People have protested progress for centuries. If our leaders listened to those voices, there'd be no highways or bridges, no public works projects at all. Our society would still be in the Stone Age."

"Bullshit," Palumbo shouted. "Let's face it—you're nothin' but a goddamn dictator! You're playin' with peoples' lives and you don't give a damn!"

The audience rose as one and burst into applause. And with that, it was clear, Moses had simply had enough. He snatched his papers, whirled around, and exited the council chamber, followed like the Pied Piper by his inner circle of assistants. Their exit was accompanied by a chorus of jeers.

FROM THAT POINT on, the hearing seemed to dissolve into a proceeding with neither form nor substance, defined more by formality than meaning. Seemingly drained of all emotion, the audience sat listlessly as board members retreated to caucus for one final time.

Their vote came shortly before 4 AM.

"Mr. Pettibone?" the mayor called.

"Aye!" said Robert Pettibone, Manhattan borough president.

"You're killing us!" someone shouted. "You're destroying our lives!"

The mayor's gavel slammed against its wooden block. The cops standing before the council desk tensed again.

"Mr. Clark?" the mayor called out.

"Aye!" said Bronx Borough President Henry Clark.

"Why are you doing this to us?" someone shouted, catcalls resounding throughout the chamber. "All so a bunch of greedy bastards can make a buck?"

The mayor rapped his gavel again. Unable to quiet the clamor, the vote proceeded, nevertheless.

"Mr. Noonan?"

"Aye!" said Edward Noonan, borough president of Queens.

"Please don't let this happen!" an elderly woman shrieked. "Dear God, don't put us out of our homes! Please. Please!"

The mayor hammered his gavel and called the remaining board members.

"Mr. Cunningham."

"Aye!" said Thomas Cunningham, borough president of Staten Island.

The jeers grew louder.

"Mr. Marshall."

"Aye!" said Comptroller William Marshall, his voice nearly inaudible over the din.

"Why don't you just admit it?" someone shouted. "Robert Moses runs this city. All of you simply march to his commands."

The mayor ignored the comment, moving forward with his roll call.

"Mr. Shea."

Brooklyn Borough President John Shea blinked and paused. "Aye!" he finally said.

"You, Mr. Shea, have stabbed Bay Ridge in the back—and we will never forget it," Walter Staziak shouted.

Shea stared straight ahead, stone-faced.

"People have a word for what's happened here," Staziak exclaimed. "It's called *blackmail!* Politics as usual in New York!"

The mayor slammed his gavel, motioning for the cops to move on Staziak, whom the audience cheered roundly as he was escorted from the chamber.

"A farce!" he stammered. "This hearing is nothing but a farce!"

Then, leaping from his seat, Joey Palumbo rushed the council desk, tearing the roll of paper from the stenographer's machine and swinging it wildly overhead, letting its loose end trail like the tail of a kite.

"I guess this meeting never happened … because now there ain't no minutes of it, are there?" he shouted.

Then he tore the minutes to shreds, tossing them overhead, the audience stunned into silence as they watched the pieces flutter like confetti to the floor.

The mayor, his face beet-red, signaled for the cops.

"You, sir, are out of order!" he bellowed, as a pair of officers weighed into Palumbo, wrestling him to the floor. Other cops flooded the chamber, forming a cordon between the council desk and the angry audience.

Repeatedly, the mayor smacked his gavel. Children burst into tears. Reporters raced to file their stories. Photographers' flashbulbs popped in bursts of light. An elderly woman collapsed in a heap, and several people rushed to her side.

"This fight ain't over!" vowed Palumbo, squirming as cops carried him from the chamber. "Believe me, this ain't gonna end today!"

But it *was* all over now.

The mayor's final affirmative vote made the Board of Estimate's decision unanimous. The Narrows bridge would be built. The homes and businesses in the expressway's path would be acquired by the city, condemned, and demolished. Construction would begin immediately. Dahlgren Place and nearly thirty other streets in Bay Ridge would be bulldozed. Our neighborhood—our world—would never be the same.

The board members adjourned to their caucus room. The audience, a weary, shattered brigade, filed outside, emptying onto the sidewalk before City Hall. Then, slowly, they moved toward the school buses idling curbside.

"I don't know what we're gonna do," Gus Pappas said to my father. "You?"

"I don't think anyone knows," my father said, his voice barely a whisper. "Right now, all we want to do is go home and get some sleep. Maybe all this'll make more sense in the morning."

"Don't bet on it," Pappas grumbled.

The ride to Bay Ridge was eerily silent. All you could hear was the engine straining as the school bus climbed the ramp to the Manhattan Bridge and exited onto Brooklyn's deserted streets. Occasionally, you could hear someone sob, but most of us just sat numbly in our seats, staring out at the dark, quiet city. I sat next to my father, his eyes narrow, his jaw set tight. In front of us, my mother and sister leaned against each other, as if to keep themselves upright.

I was unable to comprehend it all fully, but was certain something seminal had just altered our lives. It felt as though something important had been severed, part of us abandoned and set adrift; as though we'd lost not just our home and each other, but were somehow also losing our way.

I wondered if I'd feel like that always, or if the feeling would be fleeting, part of a larger, undetermined journey that would still manage, as my father always said it would, to turn out all right. I wondered what would happen to Bay Ridge, to Brooklyn, to the life we'd always known, to us. I wondered if the wounds my parents had incurred would ever truly heal, or if the two of them, like so many others in Bay Ridge, would be damaged in a way that even time could never make right.

Part 2

Why should New York be loved as a city? It is never the same city for a dozen years altogether. A man born forty years ago finds nothing, absolutely nothing, of the New York he knew. If he chances to stumble upon a few old houses not yet leveled, he is fortunate. But the landmarks, the objects which marked the city to him, as a city, are gone.

—HARPER'S MONTHLY, 1856

There is a time for departure even when there's no certain place to go.

—TENNESSEE WILLIAMS, 1953

Chapter 29

The city moved ahead swiftly from there, and within days of the public hearing the wheels were already in motion for the demolition of homes, mass eviction of Bay Ridge residents, and construction of the Narrows bridge.

No obstacles stood any longer in the way. The caustic public discourse, at least from the city's perspective, had ended with the Board of Estimate vote. The political machinations were over. Every legal mandate had been met. A last-ditch effort to block the project failed when Circuit Court Judge Franklin Wilson, a City Hall crony, rejected arguments that the condemnation proceedings were illegal. City officials were free to exercise their power of eminent domain and proceed according to plan.

And that's exactly what they did.

Quickly on the heels of the Circuit Court decision, Brooklyn Supreme Court Judge Malcolm Josephson signed the first acquisition papers ordering four hundred families from their homes. The very next day, a blizzard of notices arrived in mailboxes, informing recipients that their homes stood in the right-of-way of the planned expressway, and that the city intended to acquire and condemn the properties. Notices taped to the lobby walls of apartment buildings similarly informed tenants that, with demolition set to begin in ninety days, they needed to find new living quarters immediately. People were also notified that "tenant relocation operations" were underway, and that they could contact the New York City Relocation Bureau, if they desired, for assistance in finding a new residence.

The eviction notices hit hard, conveying a painful certainty about the fate thousands of us now faced. It was *real*—seeing the words EVICTION and CONDEMNATION in black and white. There was no longer room for pretense or denial, or hope for some miraculous, last-minute reprieve.

"This can't *really* be happening, can it?" Gus Pappas asked incredulously, as he gathered with neighbors in our cul-de-sac. "Just like that, they're gonna put us out of our homes? All we get is a letter in the mail?"

"How could the city do this?" asked Mrs. Pedersen, her voice cracking. "What happens now? What do we do?"

For several days, we were simply left to wonder, until finally, we were summoned to another meeting in Hamilton High's auditorium. There, hundreds of bewildered, fearful residents were introduced by Councilman Sherman to Harlan Fitzhugh, chief of the city's Relocation Bureau, and Joseph Short, a real estate executive commissioned to assist with relocation.

"Please know that it's the city's aim to be of maximum assistance to all of you," Fitzhugh pledged. "We sympathize with the difficulties you're facing, and we'll cooperate in every way possible to avoid undue hardship. It's our intent not to begin construction until everyone facing eviction has been appropriately relocated."

"What do you mean by appropriately relocated?" inquired Sherman, still licking his wounds from the bitter defeat at the public hearing, his political future as tenuous as the streets of Bay Ridge.

"We mean that anyone forced from their home will be provided an opportunity for relocation to living quarters at least equivalent to what they currently occupy," Fitzhugh responded.

"Are you just going to throw people out of their homes?"

"Absolutely not," Fitzhugh replied. "No one will be evicted until they're relocated. No one will be denied assistance. We'll bend over backward to accommodate your needs. Everyone will be treated humanely and considerately."

The two officials then detailed plans for the mass relocation.

"You can seek new living quarters on your own, of course, but anyone who wishes to can work with the Relocation Bureau," Joseph Short, the realtor, stated. "You'll be provided with a list of sanitary, safe, and affordable housing alternatives from which to choose. You'll also be provided with financial assistance for relocation, as well as fair compensation for your homes."

"What type of compensation?" Sherman inquired.

"That'll be negotiated individually," Fitzhugh replied. "A city representative will be visiting each of you shortly to discuss that."

Fitzhugh explained that buyout prices for homes would start at six thousand dollars, and average thirteen thousand dollars.

"Thirteen thousand?" someone yelped. "Some of our homes are worth a lot more than that!"

"That's only an *average*," Fitzhugh elaborated. "The city will offer fair market value. Homeowners will also be eligible for up to two thousand dollars for the difference in price between their old and new homes. Another thousand dollars will be available for relocating within a designated time frame."

"What about moving expenses?"

"Those will be paid at the rate of a hundred dollars a room."

The audience, growing increasingly agitated, was full of questions.

"Does the city really think that by throwing us a few dollars it'll compensate us fairly for being forced to leave homes that we've lived in for years—homes we love?" someone asked.

Fitzhugh coughed nervously into his fist.

"There are also provisions for the remission of two months rent in cases where the city acquires property and allows occupants to remain until their homes are razed," he said, dodging the question.

"You mean we'll be allowed to live in our *own* homes—if we pay rent—until the city tears our homes down and throws us out?" someone asked.

"That's correct," Fitzhugh responded sheepishly.

"Wow!" someone joined in the sarcasm. "How *generous* of the city to do that!"

The meeting went on like that for roughly an hour, at which point Fitzhugh and Short, growing visibly more uncomfortable, excused themselves and headed for the exit. Additional meetings, they said, would be scheduled as needed. In the meantime, they advised people to await private meetings with city representatives. Then they departed to a rousing chorus of catcalls. Most of the audience remained to hear more.

"I think I'm more confused now than I was before," Mr. Sandusky told my parents. "All this *eminent domain* stuff—I don't think anyone really understands how it works."

My father shook his head. He wasn't sure, either.

Then Sherman introduced Stephen Calico, the attorney who'd been present at earlier meetings. Calico again explained how the government had the right to seize homes and businesses for legitimate public use, and how the condemning agency, in this case the Triborough Bridge and Tunnel Authority, would likely proceed.

"Essentially," Calico said, "the TBTA will be buying your house from you, and then condemning it and tearing it down."

"How does that work?" Councilman Sherman asked.

"Under eminent domain, governments are required to make every reasonable effort to obtain property by negotiating a voluntary agreement with the owner, based on what's called 'fair and just compensation,' rather than by forcing people to sell through a court proceeding," Calico explained. "All of you will be visited by a city-retained real estate appraiser who'll assess how much your property is worth."

The audience buzzed. Sherman calmed them with assurances that everyone's questions would be answered in time.

"After your appraisal, the city will make a written offer to purchase your property, along with a summary of the appraisal upon which the offer is based," Calico continued.

The questions came fast and furious. Calico fielded them all.

"What if we don't want to sell?"

"You have no choice."

"Do we have to allow the appraiser onto our property?"

"Legally, you're obligated to. It's also important that you be present during the appraiser's visit."

"Why?"

"You need to ensure that your property is thoroughly inspected, and that the appraiser is aware of anything that could positively affect the property's value. Don't forget, you want to get the best offer possible."

"Exactly what's considered 'fair and just compensation'?"

"That's difficult to determine. Under the law, victims of eminent domain must be provided with compensation for the property itself, for any improvements to the property, and for business good will. 'Just compensation' is generally determined to be the fair market value of each item as of a particular date."

"What you do mean by fair market value?"

"That's defined as the probable price a property would sell for in a competitive, open market, where the buyer and seller are well-informed, acting in their best interests, under no obligation to buy or sell, and provided with adequate time to consider the sale."

"Who determines that value?"

"That's what the appraiser is supposed to do. Remember, however, that real estate appraisal is not an exact science. Appraisers can have different opinions about what a property is worth. *Your* opinion can be quite different from the appraiser's, too. And it may be different by thousands of dollars."

"So, what if we don't agree with the price we're offered?"

"Once the offer is made, you can either accept it or refuse it and challenge the city's 'right to take.' Property owners have the right to make a claim for greater compensation. In other words, you have the right to either legally fight the city's offer or make a counteroffer and negotiate for a higher price. If you still don't accept the offered amount, the government may initiate an appropriation action in court."

"What happens then?"

"You fight it out and a jury decides. But I've got one important piece of advice to offer with regard to that."

"What's that?"

"Never accept their first offer."

"Why?"

"Because the entire appraisal process is little more than a game."

"A *game*?"

"Sure. Remember, the appraisers work for the city and do the city's bidding. In other words, they're automatically *biased*. They're not out to really give you a fair price. They're trying to save the city money. They know where their bread is buttered—where their next appraisal job is coming from. You can bet they'll low-ball you on their appraisals, try to acquire your property for a bargain-basement price."

"But I thought compensation is supposed to be just, and based on fair market value."

"Yes, but the reality is that eminent domain transactions *distort* the real estate market because you have to sell under less-than-ideal conditions. Condemning agencies know that. They'll always try to acquire property for a fraction of what it's worth in a voluntary transaction on the open market. Sometimes they offer settlements that are even below their own appraisals. They'll squeeze you until you crack. They won't move off an offer until they're faced with a lawsuit and trial date."

"And then?"

"Then they'll make a more reasonable, last-second offer because they recognize they may well lose in court."

"Does that ever happen? Do they ever lose?"

"Yes. There've been cases where property and business owners, by contesting a condemning agency's offer, have received higher compensation than the amount of the offer. In general, though, the city will bank on the belief that most people don't have the money or the will to fight for better valuation. They figure you'll just give up—sell your property at the bottom of the market, take the loss, and leave."

Fear and bewilderment seemed to render the audience mute.

"How soon do we have to be out of our homes?" someone finally asked.

"What did the vacate notices say?" Calico responded.

"Ninety days."

"That's a typical request."

"You mean if we're not out by then, they just throw us out?"

"They have that right, yes. But, in reality, the ninety-day deadline is just a legal necessity. In all honesty, it's meaningless."

"You mean we should ignore it?"

"That's exactly what I mean," Calico said. "Look—the city wants you out as soon as possible, but in truth, no one really expects you to sell your home and be gone in three months. They'll tell you that's the timetable, even threaten you, but realistically they're planning on the process taking far longer."

"How long?"

"I'd say six months for some of you, but as long as eighteen months for others, depending on where you live. Think about it: the city is only now in the process of acquiring rights-of-way for the expressway. Actual construction is still months away. And there'll be plenty of time, even once construction starts, for you to move. But, in the meantime, no one's really throwing you out on the street—no matter how many times they threaten you."

Dozens of other questions followed: Questions about legalities, litigation expenses and government obligations; questions about partial takings, compensation for business losses, leaseholder rights, and the value of property improvements. Calico patiently answered them all. In the end, though, one question continued to arise repeatedly.

"How do we know if we're getting a fair offer for our homes and businesses?"

"You *don't* really," Calico answered. "In truth, there's no such thing as a 'just price' for a home. How do you compensate someone who doesn't want to move in the first place? How do you make someone 'whole' when it comes to the loss of friends and neighbors, a view they love, memories they have? How do you compensate a business for the value of its good name, the customers it'll lose, the good will it has created? How can anyone compensate you for the heartache and uncertainty you'll be forced to endure?"

"They can't!" someone shouted.

"Exactly," Calico said. "No one, I'm afraid, can ever put an adequate price on that."

CHAPTER 30

We sat glumly through suppers the next few nights, the wounds wrought by the public hearing deep and painful, exacerbated by the realization that we'd struggled fruitlessly for months to prevent the uncertain future we now faced.

"What are we going to do?" my sister asked.

"We're not really sure," my father replied. "I imagine things'll be up in the air until we sort through our options."

"That's all you can say?"

"We have no other answers now. There's nothing else I *can* say."

Saying little was also certainly the case for my mother, who'd hardly uttered a word since the public hearing—the toll of our ordeal evident in her movements, tentative and labored, and her features, colorless and drawn. Lacking any appetite, she stood at the kitchen sink scrubbing a pot, the hot water steaming as it hissed from the tap.

"But do we really have to *move*?" asked my sister, picking at her food.

"The city is forcing us to," my father said. "They have that power."

"But it's not fair."

"Maybe not. It's something we have to deal with, though. We have no choice."

"We can't fight them anymore?"

"The fight's over, Beth. The city won."

"I can't believe it," my sister said, growing more agitated. "I can't believe this is really happening."

She threw her fork down, pushed her plate to the center of the table, and cradled her head in her arms. In seconds, she was sobbing.

My sister generally didn't inspire much sympathy from me, but I felt bad for her now, sorry that her life was seemingly in utter ruin, that she felt her world was collapsing so completely.

It was a world, my sister's, that was very different than mine. Parallel but entirely separate. Close enough to touch and feel, but very much its own.

My world was the playground, the schoolyard, and the street. Beth's was a world of music, shopping, and endless chatter on the telephone. She took tap lessons twice a week at an Arthur Murray dance studio on Bay Parkway. She shopped for horsehair crinolines, poodle skirts, nylon sweaters, cardigans, and discount dresses at Rothsteins on Thirteenth Avenue and at A&S and Loehmann's in downtown Brooklyn. She spun 45-rpm singles, watched *American Bandstand*, and listened to an endless stream of songs on WMCA and WABC, New York's most popular AM radio channels. When girlfriends came over, they all retreated behind closed doors to do what most girls did then—apply makeup, practice dances, and whisper about make-out parties in dimly lit basements in Bay Ridge, at frat houses near Brooklyn College, or on a stretch of nearby shoreline known as Plum Beach. On Friday nights—dressed in jeans, wool socks, and penny loafers, her hair in a headband—she roamed Flatbush Avenue with mobs of other kids, usually ending up at Jahn's Ice Cream Parlor, where lines of teens stood waiting on the sidewalk for a table.

It was only rarely that our parallel worlds overlapped.

Once, when I was eleven, I went with Beth to the Brooklyn Army Terminal, where we stood amid a horde of cameramen, army brass, music executives, and fans waiting to catch a glimpse of America's favorite GI, Elvis Presley, arriving on a troop train from Texas before shipping out to Germany. That was fun.

Another time, we went to one of the "Swingin' Soirees" hosted by disc jockeys Alan Freed and Murray "The K" Kaufman at the Brooklyn Paramount, where we waited for hours in the freezing cold for tickets to one of the all-day rock 'n' roll extravaganzas that ran over Christmas break. That was more than worth the wait.

Outside the Paramount, police on horseback kept the surging crowds contained behind barricades near the glittering marquee of the art-deco theater. Inside, every seat in the orchestra and balconies was packed. Girls shrieked. Kids stood and sang in the aisles. Dancers sashayed across the giant stage. And one famous act after another performed their greatest hits.

That day we saw The Drifters, The Miracles, Frankie Avalon, Fabian, The Shirelles, The Everly Brothers, Neil Sedaka, and Del Shannon—all in one six-hour show. It was unforgettable, electric. And I was as certain as I could possibly be that we were standing at the very center of the universe, convinced that nothing even remotely like this was going on anywhere else in America, certain beyond a shadow of a doubt that Brooklyn was not only the capital of rock 'n' roll, but the capital of the whole wide world, as special a place as I could possibly be in.

And I was happy that day that Beth was my sister, that I was part of her world—a world that she now felt was crumbling at her feet.

"Can't we at least stay in Bay Ridge?" she pleaded, her cheeks streaked with mascara. "We could find another place nearby. Another house. An apartment. Anything."

"Yes, that's possible," my father said. "We'll have to see what's available once we start looking."

"But what if we can't find anything in Bay Ridge?"

"Then we'll have to look somewhere else."

"But *where*?"

"At this point, we just don't know."

"You mean, we may have to leave Brooklyn altogether?"

"That's possible."

"That would be a nightmare," Beth said, exhaling. "My whole life's in Brooklyn."

"Well, wherever we move, we wouldn't be far."

"*Anywhere* is too far."

"We'd only be, at most, a car ride away. We can come back anytime we want."

"We'll *never* come back, I know it. Once we leave, we'll be gone for good."

"Well," said my mother, abruptly swirling about, "then … maybe we will."

Her comment took us by surprise.

"What?" my sister gasped.

"I said, then maybe we'll just leave Brooklyn," my mother repeated.

Wiping her hands on her apron, she approached the kitchen table.

"There's something I think it's time we finally recognized," she said, wearily but with a sense of clarity she'd apparently achieved through her days of silent contemplation. "I fought very hard to stay in this house, and the fight took a lot out of me. It took a lot out of *all* of us."

My father nodded.

"But the fight's over now," my mother continued. "We have to face reality, be strong. Life moves on. We have no choice but to move on, too."

She moved toward Beth and placed both palms on my sister's cheeks. Beth was calmer now, as if my mother's strength was enabling her to discover an inner resolve of her own.

"I know this is very difficult for you, sweetheart," my mother said calmly. "But you'll be okay. We *all* will. We've built many happy memories on Dahlgren Place. We'll build more happy memories wherever we go. Even if it's someplace other than Brooklyn."

Then I saw her smile for the first time in days. It was weak, weary, almost forced, but it was a smile, nonetheless.

"Who knows?" she said. "Maybe we'll discover a whole new life. Maybe everything in the end will work out for the better."

My sister sniffled. My father smiled. I nodded. My mother was right. It might not be easy, but we'd find a way to move on. Even though the only life we'd ever known as a family was coming to a close, our lives wouldn't end. We'd survive. We'd find a new reality, a new life. And we'd be okay.

"Dahlgren Place, as wonderful as it's been, isn't the only place on earth, after all," my mother said. "We'll be all right wherever we go. We'll be fine as long as we have each other."

Chapter 31

We were visited shortly after that by the city representatives. There were two of them. One was Harlan Fitzhugh, the official who'd addressed residents about relocation assistance. The other man was unfamiliar. Each carried black attaché cases and wore beige seersucker suits over wrinkled white shirts and thin black ties. They politely removed their fedoras when my mother greeted them at the door.

"Mrs. Wolf?" Fitzhugh said.

"Yes."

"My name is Harlan Fitzhugh." He offered my mother a business card from between fingertips clubbed from heavy smoking. "You might remember me from the other night."

My mother nodded.

"This is Wendell Rogers." Fitzhugh gestured to his companion, a chubby, florid-cheeked man who forced a weak smile. "I'm head of the city's Relocation Bureau. Mr. Rogers is with the Triborough Bridge and Tunnel Authority. May we come in?"

My mother showed them to the kitchen, offering each a beverage. Fitzhugh accepted a glass of seltzer; Rogers opted for a coke. They thanked my mother and took seats at our kitchen table. Sunlight poured in from windows at the rear of the house, drawing attention to my mother's wildflowers, which were in full bloom—a splash of yellows, blues, magentas, and whites.

"Nice garden," Rogers said.

My mother shot him an icy glare and Rogers shrunk in his seat.

Fitzhugh took a healthy gulp of seltzer. "As I'm sure you know, Mrs. Wolf, the city has the right to exercise the power of eminent domain to acquire land for public use."

"Yes, we're well aware," she said.

"You're also aware, I'm sure, that your home lies in the path of the planned expressway leading to a new bridge over the Narrows."

"We're aware of that, too."

"We're here to inform you that the city is doing everything in its power to offer fair compensation to everyone whose properties are being acquired for the purposes of construction."

"We've never been interested in the city's money," my mother said. "All we've ever wanted is to remain in our home."

Fitzhugh drew a weary breath, as if he'd heard the sentiment before.

"Yes, but remaining in your home is not an option," he replied. "I'm sure you recognize that. I hope you also recognize that not only will the city compensate you fairly for your home, but we'll do everything possible to help you relocate to comparable living quarters."

Rogers eyed my mother warily, using his palms to smooth the checkered oil cloth covering our kitchen table. Fitzhugh opened his attaché case and withdrew a slip of paper, using his forefinger to mark his place.

"Let's see—condemnation proceedings on Dahlgren Place are scheduled to begin in ninety days," he said.

Rogers shifted his gaze to the backyard when my mother glanced his way.

"We're being given *three months* to find a new place to live?" she asked.

"That's the timetable."

"But how's that possible? How can we be out of here—lock, stock, and barrel—in such a short period of time? We haven't even begun yet to look for another place to live."

Fitzhugh's expression suggested he'd heard that sentiment before, too, although the need to vacate quickly wasn't as much his problem as it was ours. He pulled another paper from his briefcase and slid it across the table.

"This," he said, "will require your signature."

"What is it?"

The document, Fitzhugh explained, was a binding contract, stipulating the date for our family's move and the price the city was willing to pay for our house.

"Eleven thousand dollars?" my mother asked.

"That's the amount being offered for *all* the homes on Dahlgren Place," Rogers said.

"Regardless of their size and condition?"

"Yes."

"Regardless of their age or any improvements that have been made?"

"Uh-huh."

"Well," my mother said, remembering Stephen Calico's advice about first offers and bogus three-month moving deadlines, "that doesn't seem fair. The city's own appraiser was here just last week."

"And?"

"He set our home's value at fourteen-five. And frankly, we were expecting even more. Our home is certainly worth it."

Fitzhugh studied his paperwork.

"Fourteen-five?" he said. "I don't see that figure on anything I have."

"Perhaps there was an error in communication," my mother said.

"Nope," Fitzhugh insisted. "The number we're offering is eleven thousand. That may not be fair in your eyes, Mrs. Wolf, but that's what the city is prepared to pay."

"It's fair market value," Rogers opined.

"Actually, it's far *below* what we could get if the city wasn't building a bridge," my mother said resolutely. "Two years ago, people down the street sold a house that was nowhere as nice as ours for sixteen thousand dollars. Sixteen-two, to be exact."

"Unfortunately, this is not two years ago," Fitzhugh retorted. "Things have changed."

"Well, maybe they have." She rose from her chair and slid the unsigned contract across the table toward Fitzhugh. "But other things *haven't* changed. And one of them is the value we place on our home."

Fitzhugh and Rogers eyed her cautiously.

"If you're telling us we have to leave our home, that's something I suppose we have to grudgingly accept," my mother said. "But the least the city can do is compensate us fairly for what we're being forced to abandon. We won't sell ourselves short. We won't sell our home for a penny less than it's worth."

Then she showed the two men to the door.

"Please don't come back," she said, "unless you're prepared to raise your offer."

Then she closed the door, sunk into a kitchen chair, and wept.

CHAPTER 32

Minutes later, our doorbell chimed again and my mother rose to greet an elderly woman perched on our stoop. It was our next-door neighbor, Eva Knudsen.

A seventy-two-year-old widow of Norwegian descent, Mrs. Knudsen had resided next door for the entire fourteen years we'd lived Dahlgren Place. She'd lived in her house thirty-nine years in all.

"May I please come in?" she inquired tentatively.

"Of course," said my mother, ushering her into our living room.

It was the first time I could recall Mrs. Knudsen stepping foot in our house. For the most part, she kept to herself. Sometimes, I'd see her padding along the sidewalk on weekly shopping excursions, head bowed, a black shawl covering her head, the wheels on her metal shopping cart squeaking as she towed it behind her. The only other times our paths crossed were early some mornings, as I was leaving for school. Then, she'd be down on her hands and knees, scrubbing her stoop and walkway with a hand brush, steam from the hot water in her pail rising wisplike in the crisp morning air. For years, Mrs. Knudsen had followed that routine, common among first-generation immigrants who'd brought the practice to Brooklyn from the Old Country.

As the crisis in Bay Ridge heightened, however, Mrs. Knudsen had become less and less visible, having retreated almost completely into her house, a white cottage with overhanging gables, a sharply pitched roof, and—pasted to the front window—a decal of a gold star superimposed over a blue star.

"What's that star?" I'd asked my father one day, when I was about eight.

"It means Mrs. Knudsen is a Gold Star Mother."

"Does that mean she's a *very good* mother?"

My father laughed. "No, it means she's the mother of a soldier who died in the war."

Then he got serious.

"Mrs. Knudsen received that star from the Defense Department," he said, "when her son Robbie was killed."

I was anxious to know more. Having been raised on a slew of action comics and war movies, I was fascinated, like most kids my age, by the topic of war. I wanted to know all about heroes so that one day I could become one, too.

"How did he die?" I asked.

"He was killed," my father replied, "in the Battle of the Bulge."

Now I was even more curious.

"Was that worse than what you fought in?"

"A lot worse," my father said. "Many people think it was the worst battle ever fought by American troops."

Like most veterans, my father never spoke much about World War II, except to say how good it felt to return home, put the war behind him, and start truly living again. Some things I was aware of, however. I knew that he'd served as a navigator in the U.S. Tenth Air Force, helping airlift supplies from northern India over "The Hump," a treacherous route through the Himalaya Mountains, to aid Chinese guerrillas fighting the Japanese. I knew that the lumbering, big-bellied transport planes he'd flown in had been attacked repeatedly by nimble enemy fighters and buffeted by unpredictable gusts as they flew their moonlit missions over the snow-capped mountain crests. I knew that the missions had led to a ground assault that had opened the Burma Road, an overland route critical to the Allied campaign against Japan. I knew that the efforts of brave, resourceful soldiers like my father, average men from places like Brooklyn, had helped win the war.

"But what I went through," he said then, "was no big deal. It was certainly nothing like the Battle of the Bulge."

IT WAS EARLY in 1945, my father told me, when Robbie Knudsen died. The Germans, by then, were desperate. The Luftwaffe had been broken. German armies on both the eastern and western fronts were reeling. A push through the rugged Ardenne Mountains would be their final major offensive. Aimed at splitting the Allied line in two, the German objective was to capture the Belgian port of Antwerp, then proceed into the industrial heart of the fatherland. Once there, they'd encircle the Allies, forcing a favorable peace treaty.

The German assault, my father explained, began with an artillery barrage against Allied soldiers, who soon faced an advance by armored troops. Fierce battles were fought in towns with names like Bastogne, Flamierge, Pettit-Coo, and Arloncourt.

"But bad as it was, the *fighting* wasn't the worst of it," my father said.

The Battle of the Bulge, he explained, was fought in conditions intolerable even for battled-hardened soldiers. It was the dead of winter, and a series of snowstorms had engulfed the mountains. With aircraft grounded and roads buried under mounds of snow, the movement of troops, supplies, and equipment was nearly impossible. Ammunition, fuel, food, and supplies were scarce. Most Allied medical personnel had been killed or captured. Trucks idled in place to prevent fuel lines from freezing. Soldiers urinated on rifles and handguns so that the weapons would function in the frigid temperatures. Short of blankets, unable to dig into the frozen ground, they huddled together for warmth, donning overcoats belonging to dead buddies. Still, they bravely held on, surviving repeated attacks.

Robbie Knudsen's infantry unit, my father said, was encircled by enemy forces who pounded the GIs with mortar barrages and tank artillery shells. Seeking shelter behind a stand of trees, the undermanned unit found itself pinned down by automatic and small-arms fire.

"Robbie was a corporal," my father told me. "A small kid. Not much bigger than you are, Nathan. But, obviously, very brave."

"What happened?"

"Two of his buddies went down, wounded by the German machine gun emplacement. He decided to try and bring them back."

My father told me how Robbie Knudsen had left the safety of cover and waded through waist-high snowdrifts, firing on the dug-in Germans while advancing to rescue the wounded soldiers.

"He pulled one of them to cover," my father said. "Then he went back for the other one."

Blown over by the impact of enemy fire, Robbie Knudsen crawled through the snow, sheltering the wounded soldier's body with his own. Then, lobbing a hand grenade, he destroyed the machine-gun nest. On his return to cover with his wounded comrade, he was killed by a single rifle shot. The two rescued soldiers survived.

"The Allies suffered nearly eighty-one thousand casualties in the Battle of the Bulge," my father said. "Ten thousand American soldiers died. It was the largest land battle in the history of the U.S. Army. And we won it, thanks to soldiers like Robbie Knudsen."

"He was a hero?"

"Yes. There's talk he may even be nominated for the Congressional Medal of Honor."

"What's that?"

"It's the highest honor the military can give."

"But he's dead."

"They can award it posthumously. That means after someone's dead. They award it to the soldier's family, in his memory."

I thought about that, trying to take it all in.

"Mrs. Knudsen must be very proud," I said.

"I'm sure she is," my father agreed.

"I think she's just *sad*," said my mother, who'd walked in on our conversation. "Very sad … and all alone."

To that, too, I could attest.

I'd discovered it quite by accident, not long after the talk with my father, when Pooch, a couple of other kids, and I were returning from a touch football game around the corner. We'd taken a shortcut, traversing a garage roof and traipsing through Mrs. Knudsen's backyard when we found ourselves in the alleyway beside her house.

Pooch heard the sound first, wafting from an open window.

"Holy shit," he said, stopping dead in his tracks. "Hear that?"

Then all of us did. It was the sound of Mrs. Knudsen's voice, starting off as little more than a whisper, then becoming more amplified.

"Why did you leave me?"

Then we heard her say it again. And again.

"Why did you leave me? Tell me, Fredrik, why did you leave me alone like this?"

"Who's she talking to?" asked Tommy Lowery—well aware, like the rest of us, that Mrs. Knudsen lived alone.

Pooch peeked.

"You ain't gonna believe this," he whispered, pulling back quickly. "She's talkin' to *pictures*. She's talkin' to *herself!*"

By now, Mrs. Knudsen had begun to weep, struggling through sobs as she addressed a pair of photos atop an old Dumont console.

"You shouldn't have done that to me," she said. "You shouldn't have."

We could barely make out her words as we hugged the outside wall of her house.

"You promised we'd grow old together, Fredrik. You told me we'd be there for one another, all our lives. You said you'd never leave me alone. You … promised."

She let out a wail, like that of a wounded puppy.

"And you, dear Robbie," she said. "My dear, sweet boy. Why did you have to leave so soon? Why? Dear God, you barely had a chance to live."

We retreated, moving furtively away, realizing to our discomfort that we had no place being there, no right invading Mrs. Knudsen's privacy like that.

"Tell me," she implored. "What am I going to do now that both of you are gone? What's to become of my life?"

Then she broke down completely, her sobs audible clear into the alleyway.

“Let’s get the hell outta here,” Pooch exclaimed, and we broke rank, racing toward our cul-de-sac and out of earshot.

I never told anyone about what we’d witnessed that day. Neither did Mrs. Knudsen ever hint that she knew we’d eavesdropped. In fact, the very next morning I ran into her on my way to school. As usual, she was scrubbing her stoop.

“Good morning, dear,” she said.

“Good morning, Mrs. Knudsen,” I replied, diverting my gaze.

Then she smiled, as if she had hardly a care in the world. And I raced off to school, conscious, for the first time in my life, really, that people could bury even their worst pain somewhere deep inside them—that they could carry it around and hide it in a way that no one else would ever even know it was there.

MRS. KNUDSEN TOOK a seat in a club chair in our living room.

“Can I get you something to drink?” my mother asked her. “Tea, perhaps?”

“Tea would be nice,” our neighbor said, her eyes oversized and dewy behind thick eyeglasses.

My mother moved to the kitchen, where she boiled water in a metal pot, using a dishtowel to grasp the handle as she poured the bubbling liquid into a cup. She brought the tea and a can of evaporated milk to Mrs. Knudsen, who waited in the living room, hands on her lap.

“You have a beautiful home,” she told my mother, accepting the tea.

“It’s not much, really.”

“Maybe not, but it feels like a real *home*,” Mrs. Knudsen said. “Some houses have a special quality, you know. You can feel it. They have a warmth to them, a light. There’s love inside.”

“Well, we’ve tried to make this a loving home,” my mother said.

“And you’ve done that, dear.”

“Thank you. We’ve always been very happy living in this house.”

“Yes,” Mrs. Knudsen said. “I’ve lived on Dahlgren Place many years myself.”

“How long has it been?”

"Fredrik and I moved here in 1920. He was a mason, you know. Built our house practically by himself. We had our Robbie here six years later, almost to the day."

Mrs. Knudsen blew gently on her tea and then took a sip.

"He was always a good boy," she said wistfully. "Very devoted. There was nothing Robbie wouldn't do for us."

"It sounds like he was a very good son," my mother said.

"Oh, we never had a single bad day with him. He was everything a mother could ask for—like your own son, uh ... "

"Nathan."

"Yes ... Nathan. Another good boy."

Mrs. Knudsen took another sip of tea.

"Robbie was very much like my husband, you know. He wanted to be a mason, too. Fredrik was teaching him ... " She stared past my mother, as if looking for something in the distance.

"We had thirteen wonderful years together in our house," she said. "We tried to make it a real *home*, like yours. A home suited for a family."

Mrs. Knudsen's hands, mottled with spots, shook as she sipped her tea.

"Robbie grew up on Dahlgren Place, just like Nathan," she said. "I can still see him running down the street, playing ball, climbing trees in our backyard. He was only nineteen, still just a boy when we lost him."

"I'm sorry," my mother said. "It must be painful. I can't even imagine."

"Oh, you should never know from it," said Mrs. Knudsen, dabbing her eyes with a tissue she pulled from beneath her watchband. "No mother should ever know what it's like to lose a child."

She gazed into the distance again, then back at my mother.

"I had him late in life, you know. I was almost forty."

"That's almost unheard of today," my mother replied.

"Yes. Fredrik and I called him our miracle baby. We'd tried for many years to have a child, with no luck. We'd almost given up. But our house on Dahlgren Place brought us luck."

"Houses can do that," my mother said. "They can bring people good things. Jewish people call it *mazel.*"

Mrs. Knudsen gazed about our living room.

"You have one of those houses," she smiled. "A lucky house."

"Yes, we've always felt lucky to have lived here. That's why it's so difficult that we have to move."

"Yes," Mrs. Knudsen sighed. "It's very difficult. And that's what I'm here to talk to you about."

Mrs. Knudsen raised her teacup to her mouth, then lowered it abruptly.

"Things haven't been easy for me," she said hesitantly. "To be perfectly honest ... Fredrik didn't leave me with much to speak of. He died, you know, in a construction accident shortly after I lost Robbie."

"I remember," my mother said. "He fell off a scaffold at a skyscraper they were building in Manhattan."

"That's right," Mrs. Knudsen said, staring off again. "Anyway, there was nothing in the bank. No insurance. Nothing much at all. When he died, it was very difficult for me. I couldn't find work. I had no worthwhile skills. No one wanted to hire an older woman."

My mother offered more tea, which Mrs. Knudsen declined with a wave.

"I don't want to add to your burden," she said. "I know you're facing difficulty, having to move and all. But I've come to ask for your help."

"How can I help?"

"It's everything that's going on. The bridge. The road coming through Bay Ridge. Suddenly, I'm being forced to move from the only home I've ever really known and ... "

Mrs. Knudsen paused to collect herself, her eyes welling with tears.

"It's all right," my mother assured her, as Mrs. Knudsen again removed the tissue tucked in her watchband and blew her nose.

"You see ... I love this neighborhood," she continued. "My entire life has been here, all my fondest memories. Fredrik and I often said we'd live the rest of our lives on Dahlgren Place."

"I understand."

"And now ... well, to be honest, I just ... don't know *where* to go." She gazed earnestly at my mother. "If I'm forced to move from here, where will I live? You see, I really have nowhere to go. Nowhere."

"Maybe the city can find you another place," my mother suggested.

"I heard there's not much available for someone with limited means," Mrs. Knudsen replied.

"What about family? Are there relatives you could possibly live with?"

"The only one who's still alive is my sister-in-law. She lives in Florida. She's alone, too."

"Well, perhaps the two of you could share a place."

"I don't think so. You see, she's been sick lately. Living with her is not really possible."

"And friends?"

"Not really. Most have passed away. Some have moved. I've kept pretty much to myself the past few years."

Mrs. Knudsen dropped her gaze, tucking her tissue back under her watchband.

"I'm alone now, Lily," she said. "All alone."

At a loss, my mother said nothing.

"Oh, I suppose God will determine my fate," Mrs. Knudsen said finally. "Let's face it, a couple of years from now I'll be nothing but a ghost."

"Don't say that, Mrs. Knudsen—please."

"Why not, dear? It's true." Mrs. Knudsen sipped her tea. "We live and die, Lily. That's the way life is. And my life is ending. I know that. My time is past. I'm seventy-two years old and everything I've ever lived for is gone. The only place I find comfort and peace in is my home. And now I'm losing that, too. There's nothing left for me, dear. Nothing, really."

Mrs. Knudsen reached out and cupped my mother's hands between her own, cold and quaking like the heartbeat of a sparrow.

"I know this is hard for you to understand, Lily, being young and having such a wonderful family," she said. "But death will be a comfort to me. It truly will."

My mother didn't know what to say. Mrs. Knudsen squeezed her hands tightly, as if to assure her it was all right.

"I'm at peace with the thought of dying, of seeing my husband and son again," she said. "But until the day God calls me, I'll need another place to live."

Mrs. Knudsen's lips flattened in a faint smile. "What I've come to ask, Lily, is if you could please help me try to find something—if you could come with me to the city's Relocation Bureau. I don't know what else to do. I don't know how to handle matters like this on my own, and I don't know who else to turn to for help."

Mrs. Knudsen stroked my mother's hand. "Please ... help me."

"Of course I'll help you, Mrs. Knudsen," my mother said, this time without hesitation. "We'll go there together. I'll do whatever I can."

"God bless you, Lily," our neighbor said, dabbing her eyes with her tissue. "God bless your soul."

"Thank you, but that's not necessary," my mother replied. "You've been a wonderful neighbor for many years. Helping you find another place to live is the least I can do."

Chapter 33

A series of eviction notices arrived in rapid succession after that. Printed to appear like official court documents, each sounded more ominous than the last. First came a letter from the Triborough Bridge and Tunnel Authority informing us that our house was required for the immediate purposes of demolition, and that our failure to vacate would result in stern legal action. Then we were informed that if we didn't notify officials within twenty-four hours of our intent to relocate, the city would rescind its pledge to provide a moving allowance. A third notice informed us that work on the expressway was commencing imminently, and that if we didn't vacate within ninety days we'd face instant eviction.

"Throw 'em in the trash," Stephen Calico, advised my father when he called the attorney to ask for advice. "The letters are meaningless, simply a scare tactic."

"A scare tactic?" my father said.

"Absolutely," Calico said. "There's no question you'll have to move at some point, unless you're willing to fight eviction in court. But the city is trying to get you to move *sooner* rather than later, by provoking fear."

"Well, they're certainly doing a good job of that," my father said.

"No surprise—they're highly practiced," Calico said. "Their tactic is to panic people into bailing out immediately so they can snap properties up quickly. The fewer people who prolong moving or resist eviction, the fewer headaches they'll have. In reality, you have a lot more time to vacate than they're letting on."

"How much more?"

"Based on where your house is located, at the far end of Bay Ridge, I'd say you'd be among the last people forced out. You're probably looking at a year, maybe even eighteen months, before you'll truly be forced to vacate."

My parents seemed relieved to learn that. Those twelve to eighteen months would be a gift. Unlike hundreds of other Bay Ridge families, we wouldn't have to face the immense hardship of immediate relocation. Instead, we'd be able to search for another home in a more reasonable time frame.

There'd be a price to pay for the extra time, however. We'd have to watch Bay Ridge slowly and agonizingly unravel. Witness friends and neighbors depart under extreme duress. Live through the dismemberment of Dahlgren Place and a slow death to life as we'd known it in Brooklyn.

Signs of that were already cropping up throughout Bay Ridge.

Resigned to their fate, many residents were accepting the city's settlement offer without protest, often for a fraction of what their properties were worth, and abandoning the neighborhood in droves.

As city officials forged ahead with rights-of-way purchases, Bay Ridge took on the look of a mass-evacuation scene. Red-lettered CONDEMNED signs sprouted in front yards. Moving vans and utility trucks sat curbside as crews loaded furniture, clothing, and other personal belongings. Household goods and memorabilia lay strewn across sidewalks. Garage sales drew hordes of buyers. Trash cans overflowed with unwanted items.

An even more poignant ritual—that of the farewell—was also being played out on many streets, as evictees gathered with their neighbors to offer good-byes. People shook hands, hugged, and kissed, exchanging addresses and phone numbers. Some, dazed and weeping, walked down streets they'd lived on their entire lives. Others wandered one final time through their former homes, as if to cling for a moment to the remnants of lives that now seemed damaged and lost.

Seventh Avenue merchants were doing the same. Even worse, most found themselves facing grave financial hardship. Offered relocation sites too far from Bay Ridge to be profitable, and unable to sell their businesses, the vast majority had little choice but to accept the city's settlement and close their doors for good. Many stores were abandoned outright. Inventory was dumped for pennies on the dollar. Shop owners bid farewell at going-out-of-business sales up and down the avenue.

Facing similar hardship were elderly residents—old-timers rooted in Brooklyn since the days of its earliest enclaves—many of whom subsisted on Social Security, pensions, or meager fixed incomes. In most cases, the prices they were offered for their homes fell far below the cost for a comparable dwelling anywhere in New York. And with the city's vacancy rate at an all-time low, housing was especially difficult to find, particularly in neighborhoods like Bay Ridge or the rent-controlled apartments in which many lived. For those people, choices were few. And they were far from enviable.

My parents, however, faced a different dilemma.

"What do you think?" I overheard my father ask my mother when a second offer for our house arrived, two weeks after my mother's meeting with the two city officials.

My mother studied the offer, which had been increased from the original eleven thousand to twelve thousand, five hundred dollars.

"I still think they're trying to shortchange us," she said. "Our house is worth more than twelve-five, Artie. It's a game they're playing. We shouldn't have to accept a lowball offer just because the city believes we're going to panic in the face of their threats."

My father mulled it over.

"Didn't you tell me once that the architect who designed our house was a pretty well-known guy?" he asked.

"Yes. A disciple of Frank Lloyd Wright."

"Well, that ought to make our house even more valuable, I'd think."

"That's my feeling, too."

"Then let's write back," my father said, smiling, "and tell the city what they can do with their latest offer."

And my mother sat down at her typewriter and, in a polite but firm response, did exactly that.

CHAPTER 34

In the midst of all this, groundbreaking for the bridge took place far from the tumult in Bay Ridge—at Fort Wadsworth, a military base on the Staten Island shoreline.

The ceremony, befitting its significance, was marked by pomp and circumstance. Bands played. City and state officials offered glowing testimonials about the virtues of the bridge. Then, donning construction hardhats and wielding specially engraved, chrome-plated spades, they stood shoulder to shoulder and turned the earth behind their feet. Cameramen captured the historic moment. Champagne glasses were raised in celebration. And construction of the bridge was officially underway.

"Today is not just a groundbreaking, it's a *heartbreaking* to many people in Brooklyn," lamented Councilman Sherman, standing in John Paul Jones Park, where the mood was far from festive.

"The bridge may be many things to many people," Sherman said, "but it should never cease to be identified with the cruelty that's been inflicted on Bay Ridge and its people in the name of progress."

Sherman and the small group with him then gazed skyward, following the path of a biplane trailing a large, fluttering banner.

NAME IT THE STATEN ISLAND BRIDGE! the banner read.

By now, the name of the bridge was seemingly the only matter still open to debate. And even that was sparking controversy.

Staten Island civic leaders were pushing for the name on the banner. Names like the Gateway Bridge, the Freedom Bridge, the Neptune Bridge, and the Narrows Bridge had also been proposed. Ethnic overtones colored the debate, as well. The Scandinavian community wanted the bridge named after the Norse explorer Leif Ericson. The Italian Historical Society campaigned to name it after Giovanni da Verrazzano, a Florentine explorer who'd been the first European to enter New York Harbor. Irish groups opposed the bridge being named after an Italian. Others protested they'd never even heard of Verrazzano.

Within days of the groundbreaking, however, a compromise would be struck. The bridge would indeed be named after Verrazzano. City officials would drop the double-z used in the accepted Italian spelling, however, and officially name the span the Verrazano-Narrows Bridge.

"I got another name for it," Mr. Mangini told our neighbors. "I'm Italian, so I can say this about another Italian."

"What's that?"

"I think they ought to call it the Guinea Gangplank."

Everyone laughed.

"Or maybe," Mr. Sandusky quipped, "it should just be called the Kiss of Death."

No one laughed at that, however. No one thought it was funny in the least.

Chapter 35

The bulldozers arrived the very next day, rolling into Bay Ridge atop a procession of flatbed trailers that wheezed to a stop at Seventh Avenue and MacArthur Street, the farthest intersection in the neighborhood from the Narrows shoreline.

No sooner had the procession halted than a team of helmeted construction workers disembarked from the trailers, assuming positions along MacArthur Street. Wooden sawhorses were erected to cordon off the thoroughfare.

As news about the bulldozers spread, people emerged from homes and stores to gather at the intersection. Pooch, Tommy Lowery, and I raced the fifteen blocks from Dahlgren Place to join the growing throng.

"I can't believe this," Pooch said. "They're gonna tear down them homes."

"Whaddaya mean?" Lumpy Lowery asked.

"Can't you see, knucklehead? They're gonna demolish MacArthur Street."

The words were barely out of Pooch's mouth when the bulldozers were unshackled from heavy metal chains, then inched their way down steel ramps and began churning up MacArthur Street, leaving deep tread marks in the doughy asphalt. The equipment halted in front of several condemned homes, where construction workers gathered to converse.

"You think those bulldozers can take down those houses?" Lowery asked.

"They'll tear 'em to pieces," Pooch said.

And that they did.

Plowing effortlessly through a row of hedges, the lead bulldozer traversed the front yard of a house and tore into its entryway, collapsing the dwelling's screened-in porch and bearing down on the flimsy wooden structure. Instantly, the walls of the tiny Cape Cod leaned sharply backward and came crashing down in a heap. The bulldozer, belching fumes, then climbed over the debris, crushing everything beneath its churning treads.

A collective gasp arose from the onlookers, who instinctively recoiled as the house crumbled to the ground. Few, if any, had ever witnessed anything like this. Some people let out anguished groans.

An elderly woman wailed like a newborn baby. "Oh, my God! *My dear God!"* she shrieked, dropping to her knees, arms raised to the heavens.

A few people knelt next to her, crossing themselves, gazing skyward, begging their God for mercy. A woman flew into the arms of her husband, her body going limp as he lowered her gently to the sidewalk. Other people, sobbing or watching in disbelief, walked aimlessly about, dazed and weeping. A man, blinded by anguish and grief, wandered into oncoming traffic and was nearly struck by a screeching car.

"Holy shit!" Pooch exclaimed. "I can't believe what I'm seein'."

None of us could.

The homes on MacArthur Street were old—some dating to the Civil War—and they crumbled instantly under the bulldozers' assault. Thick, angry clouds of red-yellow demolition dust erupted from the earth as the dwellings collapsed and tumbled to the ground. The entire street rumbled with the groan of machinery, the clamor of glass shattering, bricks splintering, wooden walls crashing to the ground. Children cried. Dogs yelped. Even the houses themselves seemed to emit anguished groans, guttural and humanlike, as they creaked and fell in giant, dusty heaps.

Then, suddenly, the bulldozers stopped dead in their tracks as Joey Palumbo and his two grown sons emerged from behind their house.

"You wanna tear down *my* house?" the newly evicted Palumbo shouted at the demolition workers. "Well, I'm not going to give you bastards the satisfaction!"

The workers, like everyone, stood cemented in place, eyeing the Palumbos in stunned, uneasy disbelief.

"The only ones gonna tear our house down are me and my boys!" Joey Palumbo raged. "I'll kill the first sonovabitch who comes near it."

Then Palumbo's sons, strapping longshoremen like their father, rolled out a wheelbarrow filled with bricks and began hurling them at the modest clapboard cottage, shattering its picture window and puncturing a plastic awning over the entrance.

Joey Palumbo, armed with a sledge hammer, raced up the tiny brick stoop and swung the hammer at the front-porch wall, splintering the structure with a powerful blow. Then his sons—one armed with an axe, the other with a crowbar—followed him up the steps and the three of them attacked the house with a savage, relentless fury.

Muscles bulging, veins popping, sweat pouring from their faces, they pummeled the dwelling, tearing through siding, chopping out sections of walls, smashing holes in the ceilings, and ripping out an interior staircase.

Palumbo, wild-eyed and bleeding, hammered through a wall, then climbed atop the roof and tore off shingles, tossing them about like playing cards. One of his sons, wielding a CONDEMNED sign like a baseball bat, punched through the windows of a bedroom. Palumbo's other son, grunting and howling, his body convulsing, battered the walls of the house with his axe and then his fists.

For nearly twenty minutes, Joey Palumbo and his sons carried out their violent act of protest and catharsis, alternately raging and laughing, working savagely and then pausing to gather themselves. All of us, including the demolition workers, gathered in clumps, some standing, others taking curbside seats, and just watched. Cops stood in open-mouthed disbelief, content to let the drama play out.

Eventually it did.

Palumbo and his sons worked to a point of sweaty exhaustion before abandoning what would have been a hopelessly prolonged task. Putting their tools to the ground, they emerged from the partially demolished house, huddling like football players in the middle of the street. Then, heads bowed, they drew closer together and began to cry, their muscular bodies quaking, their piercing sobs echoing up and down MacArthur Street.

The crowd, shooed away by cops, disbanded soon after that. And the bulldozers resumed their work.

Within hours, a block-long section of MacArthur Street had been leveled and surveyors were planting stakes in the ground to site the expressway's two-hundred-foot-wide right-of-way.

There'd be months of demolition to follow, with similar acts of heartache playing out on the neighborhood's soon-to-be-battered streets. But nothing would ever approach what happened on that first day of demolition—the reaction of the Palumbos, the shock of those first few homes coming down, the emptiness and chaos and disbelief we all felt.

No one could be sure precisely what the neighborhood's fate would be. But Bay Ridge, it was clear, had been violated in some elemental way, its skin punctured, its fragile chemistry altered, the neighborhood set to bleed from a grave and gaping wound.

And we'd been wounded right along with it. Wounded grievously. Wounded in a way that made us wonder whether the blow we'd just been struck could ever possibly stop hurting.

Chapter 36

The speed of dismemberment after that day was staggering. All through fall and early winter, demolition continued, unrelenting, as if city officials were unleashing a pent-up fury on Bay Ridge, punishment for its months of resistance to the bridge plan.

Nothing was immune to the assault. Block after block of homes and businesses was snapped up, vacated and then demolished by equipment that tore effortlessly through the neighborhood's dense tissue. Wrecker's balls, swinging from massive cranes, slammed into apartment-building walls, sending brick, glass shards, and roof tiles flying. Workmen hacked through wreckage, tossing it onto massive piles that were scooped up by backhoes. Dump trucks carted away tons of soil, rock, and other debris. Trees were chain-sawed and torn from the earth, their soil-encrusted roots sprouting like lifeless tentacles from boles and trunks.

By year's end, what had once been a quiet, orderly neighborhood had been transformed into a landscape of devastation and loss. Mountains of rubble rose from where homes once stood. Telephone poles, lampposts, and traffic-light stanchions lay scattered. Discarded possessions littered the ground. Abandoned dwellings stood shuttered and empty.

All the while, scores of evictees continued to flee, forced from their homes the instant they signed the city's acquisition papers. In some cases, demolition on apartment buildings began on their rooftops while tenants still resided on lower floors. Building superintendents abandoned their buildings outright, leaving remaining residents bereft of heat, hot water, and electricity. Trash overflowed from incinerators, rotting in hallways and cellars. Lobbies were littered with chunks of plaster, glass, and splintered furniture. Vandals snuck into vacated buildings, shattering windows, tearing plumbing fixtures from the walls, and defacing the buildings with graffiti.

And it wasn't only evictees who were fleeing Bay Ridge now. People living *near* demolition sites were leaving, as well—running to escape the cloud of condemnation spreading over the scarred neighborhood. Landlords and homeowners ceased making repairs to their dwellings. Lawns lay neglected. Homes seemed pallid, moribund. Many of them, neither saleable nor seized by the city, were simply left to rot, like pumpkins on the vine.

Then Pooch moved.

It was shortly after Christmas, in the middle of our ten-day holiday break, when the city acquired and condemned his family's six-story apartment building. In its place, a huge, snakelike ramp would enable traffic to flow from the nearby Belt Parkway onto the new bridge.

"Some Christmas present we're gettin' from the city, huh?" Mr. Pucci said wryly when I arrived to help Pooch pack—and to say good-bye.

Mr. Pucci thrust his arm up at the elbow, symbolic of how the city was shafting his family. "Goddamned bridge," he muttered.

"I'm really sorry," I said.

"Me too, kid," Mr. Pucci said and shrugged. "Me too."

With dozens of families moving all at once, the scene in Pooch's building was utter chaos. Residents angled their way in and out of apartments, carrying boxes of household goods. Children raced through narrow hallways, climbing over furniture and moving crates. Moving men toted couches, appliances, mattresses, and other bulky items down twisting stairwells. Elevators, their doors ajar and alarms ringing shrilly, were jammed with people and possessions.

Pooch's family had yet to find another place to live. But, like others, they were being forced out anyway. Most of their possessions would have to be placed in storage while they doubled up with Pooch's grandparents in a cramped Queens apartment.

"We're gonna miss you, Nathan," said Mrs. Pucci, a kindly, waiflike woman who seemed about to cry. "You've been like another son to us."

"I'll miss you, too," I said, uncomfortable for the first time in my best friend's apartment.

"I can't believe we gotta move," Pooch groused, as he removed belongings from his closet and placed them in a large moving crate.

I'd never seen him this down in the dumps before. Usually, he was adept at masking his emotions behind the streetwise bravado he'd mastered even at age fourteen.

No one knew what to say. Nick Pappas sat on Pooch's bed and stared into space. Tommy Lowery stood stiffly, looking completely bewildered. I kept busy by trying to peel a poster of Duke Snider off a wall near Pooch's bed.

"This picture must've been taken the year Snider led the National League in homers," I said, trying to lighten the mood. "He's a lot younger in the picture than he is now."

"*The Duke of Flatbush*," said Lumpy Lowery, mimicking the Southern twang of Red Barber, the old Dodgers announcer. "I still think, in his prime, he was better'n Mantle. Maybe not as good as Mays—but better'n Mantle, for sure."

"His swing sure was perfect for poppin' them home runs onto Bedford Avenue," chirped Nick Pappas, mimicking Snider's batting stance—bent slightly at the knees, left elbow pointing up.

"Mantle was great, but he got hurt too much," Pappas said. "Always one thing or another. Missed the seventh game of the Fifty-five Series with a bum leg."

"That's the reason the Dodgers won," Lowery said.

"That—and Johnny Podres pitched a helluva game," I reminded him.

"And Sandy Amoros made that catch off Yogi Berra," Pappas added.

"Maybe fifty-five was just our time to finally win one," I said, echoing my father's sentiment. "No one can be losers forever. Not even the Dodgers."

I remembered the day my father had said that, too—the day the Dodgers had won the World Series, five years earlier: the streets of Bay Ridge exploding in celebration; people singing and dancing on Dahlgren Place; radio reports about the victory pouring from taverns; the *Daily News* headline screaming, "Who's a Bum?"

I was nine years old and I'd never see anything like it again: flags and banners streaming from telephone poles and traffic lights. Effigies of Yankee manager Casey Stengel dangling from lampposts. The entire borough of Brooklyn shedding its image of perennial losers, emerging finally from the enormous shadow of Manhattan and the mighty Bronx Bombers.

I couldn't believe how much had changed in those five short years—the Dodgers long gone and Bay Ridge getting chewed up by demolition and the Narrows bridge forcing people to move. All of it going or gone, and all so quickly.

Pooch continued to empty his closet, shaking his head glumly.

"Hey, you'll be only, what—maybe twenty minutes away by bus, right?" Nick Pappas asked, putting a positive spin on things.

"Half an hour," Pooch sighed. "And *two* buses, not one."

"Doesn't matter," I said. "We'll still get together. We can see each other on weekends. Pooch can come to Bay Ridge. We can go to Queens."

"Yeah, and what happens when you guys gotta move, too?" Pooch said. "Who knows where you'll all be livin' then."

No one wanted to think about that, and no one said a word. Instead, we helped Pooch pack his belongings: stacks of rubber-banded Topps baseball cards; Monopoly and Parcheesi board games; a pock-mocked Louisville slugger; comic and stamp books; a Schafer Beer 3-D popup of the 1955 Dodgers, and several dog-eared *Playboy* magazines, which we spent nearly half an hour drooling over.

"Lookit this!" Nick Pappas unfurled a *Playboy* centerfold.

My mind immediately melted, turning from joyous Dodger celebrations and the sad specter of moving to something infinitely more stirring now: a woman's half-naked body.

"Can you believe the tits on her?" Pappas said. "Boy, I'd love to get my hands on those."

"You wouldn't have a clue what to do with 'em," Pooch said, smiling for the first time all day.

"The hell I wouldn't," Pappas countered.

"You'd take one look at her naked and come all over yourself," Pooch said. "You'd lose complete control of your hard-on."

We cracked up and then leafed through the magazines, debating who was more appealing—the French sexpot Brigitte Bardot or buxom American beauties Marilyn Monroe, Jayne Mansfield, and Mamie Van Doren. We settled on one of the anonymous *Playboy* centerfolds.

"You guys can have 'em," Pooch said about the magazines. "It's my good-bye gift to you losers. Somethin' to remember me by."

"Yeah, I bet you're *done* with them anyway." Nick Pappas snickered, balling his fist and shaking it back and forth. "Some of these pages are all stuck together and *skeevy*."

We laughed again and then spent several minutes wrangling over who'd get what magazine, contemplating how we'd sneak them into our homes.

"This is for you, Wolfman," Pooch told me later, off to the side.

Then he handed me his favorite Swiss Army pocket knife, one we'd spent hours playing Territory with in the grassy turf of Owl's Head Park.

I didn't know how to respond, feeling gagged in a lengthy, awkward silence. The knife, after all, was one of Pooch's prized possessions.

"You'll probably need it now that I won't be around to protect your ass anymore," he joked.

And then, in the only overt gesture of affection he'd ever shown me, he put his arms around me and pulled me tightly toward him.

"Take it easy, Nathan," he whispered. "And don't take shit from no one. Hear me?"

"Yeah," I promised.

"Good," he said. "I'll see ya around."

Then he was off, squinting through the rear window of his father's Packard as it pulled from the curb. He gave one final wave as Mr. Pucci's big green sedan, at the heels of the family's moving van, turned and disappeared around the corner.

And just like that, the best friend I'd ever had was gone.

Gone along with him, I knew, was a big part of my childhood, a time I'd cling to forever, but one I knew I could never reprise, even in my wildest teenage fantasies.

Chapter 37

Not everyone was leaving Bay Ridge as peacefully as Pooch's family, however.

Bitter and angry, unwilling to bend to the city's will, many people continued to resist eviction, dwindling in number by the week but remaining steadfast in their defiance. Protestors, in symbolic displays of resistance, tossed eviction notices in trash cans and set them ablaze. Lawsuits contesting the city's acquisition offers clogged the court system. Some evictees snuck back into their former homes under the cover of night. Others, following Joey Palumbo's lead, committed arson on their own properties, satisfied to watch their condemned houses ravaged by fire rather than demolition crews.

At times, the civil disobedience teetered on the brink of outright insurrection. Skirmishes erupted with police, as evictees handcuffed themselves to their homes, resisting efforts to move them away. Rifle-toting sentinels threatened to shoot appraisers and relocation officials. Helmeted Tactical Patrol Force officers and uniformed Parks Department personnel stood vigil over construction equipment targeted for sabotage.

But even those precautions couldn't contain the smoldering firestorm.

As they made their way around the neighborhood late one afternoon, Harlan Fitzhugh and Joseph Short, the city's top two relocation officials, were ambushed by a gang of hooded toughs who beat the pair with broomsticks and fists, leaving them bloodied and unconscious on a snow-swept street.

Taped to the men's clothing were crudely scrawled messages: LEAVE BAY RIDGE ALONE! OUR HOMES ARE NOT FOR SALE!

The incident drew busloads of police, as well as pledges from the city that similar acts would reap swift punishment. But cops didn't wait for another incident. Two days after the violence, half a dozen men were arrested in connection with the beating of Fitzhugh and Short. Among them were Joey Palumbo and several mob-related goons from the Brooklyn docks. Defiant to the end, Palumbo was booked on assault and sentenced to four years in jail.

"Those hoodlums *should* go to jail," my father said that night. "It was wrong, what they did. I don't care how angry they are. They have no right to hurt innocent people who were only doing their job."

"Your father's right," my mother said. "God knows, I fought against the bridge as hard as anyone. But the fight's over now. I feel terrible for people being forced to move, especially the ones facing the greatest hardships. But it's time for everyone to move past their anger and get on with their lives."

Maybe so. But many Bay Ridge residents continued to make it resoundingly clear that they were far from ready to simply let go.

Protests assumed myriad forms. In one incident, a group stood defiantly in the path of a bulldozer, halting demolition until cops gently coaxed the demonstrators away. In another instance, saboteurs sliced the fuel lines of several bulldozers, rendering the equipment immobile. And each day, local residents bore witness to the sight of parishioners, led by Monsignor Terrence Dougherty, marching peacefully outside All Saints Episcopal Church in resistance to the planned demolition of the tiny religious landmark.

"We will not abandon a parish that's the heart of our community," the pastor told reporters. "The city cannot have our church. It's not theirs to have. Our parish belongs to its parishioners. And we'll do everything in our power—and God's power—to preserve it."

Then he and about a hundred parishioners took their protest one step further. In quiet defiance, they slipped inside the church, barricaded the doors, and vowed to stay there until the city and Archdiocese reconsidered their plan to bring the beloved parish to the ground.

Chapter 38

Our attention turned almost fully now to the task of finding another place to live.

Although we still had months to go before expressway construction would force us from Dahlgren Place, my parents agreed it made little sense to delay our search for a new home until the final, frantic moment of eviction. Besides, the longer we waited, we knew, the more difficult the search would be. Even now, the options for nearby housing were growing more limited by the day. The mass evictions had sent hundreds of desperate families scurrying for the few available residences left in Bay Ridge. And prospects in other desirable neighborhoods nearby weren't much better.

To compound matters, my parents had yet to receive an acceptable offer for our current home. They had no idea if and when any such offer would arrive—and, if it did, how much money they'd have at their disposal. Still, we had no choice but to begin our search.

The burden of that job, as did most household matters, fell entirely to my mother—whose initial search, through classifieds and realtors, proved fruitless.

"Oh, I don't know about that," she replied when my father suggested we take advantage of the city's pledge to assist with relocation.

"Do you think the city's really going to help?" she asked.

"I don't know," my father replied. "They said they would."

"What they said and what they'll do, I'm sure, are completely different things. Do you know how many families they must be dealing with?"

"Thousands, I suppose."

"Do you really think they're going to show me something as nice as the house we're living in now?"

"Probably not. But you've got nothing to lose by trying."

"Except valuable time."

"Maybe. But didn't you promise Mrs. Knudsen you'd go with her to the Relocation Bureau?"

"Uh-huh."

"Well, you've got to take her there anyway, don't you? You might as well keep your eyes open for us, too. Who knows? Something suitable may pop up."

"I suppose."

And so she did. Reluctantly, my mother went to the city in search of the relocation assistance officials had pledged.

THE NEW YORK City Relocation Bureau was housed on the fifth floor of a century-old office building on the Upper West Side of Manhattan. There, city officials were meeting with about twenty displaced Bay Ridge residents a day. Since the office was open only four hours at a time, meetings were restricted to no longer than fifteen minutes in duration.

My mother and Mrs. Knudsen made the ninety-minute trek to the Relocation Bureau by subway. Mrs. Knudsen was silent for most of the ride, staring out the window as the train climbed over the rooftops of Brooklyn and plunged into the tunnel leading to Manhattan.

"Things'll be all right, Mrs. Knudsen," my mother assured her. "You'll see. We'll find you another place to live."

When they arrived for their scheduled 10 AM meeting, however, prospects seemed dim. The Relocation Bureau was dark and shuttered. A gaggle of women stood in the hallway outside.

"No one has any idea when they'll open," one of them said. "I've been coming here for three days, and every day the office opens at a different time."

"But ... we have an appointment," my mother sputtered.

"Lots of luck," the woman said, laughing.

"If you think this is bad, try *calling* sometime," another woman lamented. "There's only one phone line into the office. Yesterday, I called every ten minutes for the entire day. All I got was a busy signal. If you're lucky enough to get through and leave a message, you never get a return call."

The group of women milled about for nearly an hour before two men arrived, unlocked the office door, and switched on the lights. Several minutes later, the first appointee was summoned inside.

My mother and Mrs. Knudsen waited another two hours, as one woman after another was shuttled into the office, emerging eventually with a slip of paper and a frown. Scrawled on the paper were several addresses, denoting the locations of dwellings the women were to inspect as possible residences. Their sullen expressions mirrored how they felt about where they were being sent.

Then, precisely at noon, the door to the office swung open and the two men emerged, clad in trench coats and fedoras.

"We'll reopen in an hour," one of them muttered.

"But we've already been waiting more than two hours," my mother said.

"We'll be back at one o'clock," the man said, deadpan.

And the two of them left for lunch.

BY THE TIME my mother and Mrs. Knudsen were shown into the office, it was literally minutes before closing. Several women, still waiting, were instructed to return the following day. They left, grumbling in protest.

There wasn't much to the Relocation Bureau—just a row of metal filing cabinets and several desks cluttered with paperwork. One of the desks, it was clear from a nameplate, belonged to Harlan Fitzhugh, who remained hospitalized after his vicious beating in Bay Ridge. The other desks were occupied by shirtsleeved men who robotically did paperwork or chatted on the phone.

My mother introduced herself and Mrs. Knudsen to a man whose nameplate identified him as Louis J. Boudreau.

Boudreau looked tired, his puffy, red-rimmed eyes resembling little more than slits. He dragged on a Camel, exhaling as he combed through a rolodex stuffed with business cards and slips of paper.

"We're only obligated to show you two apartments," he said impassively.

"That's it?" my mother asked. "Just two?"

"That's all the law requires. And if you turn those down, you either have to find a residence on your own or the city will have no choice but to evict you."

"Are you saying you'll just put us on the street?"

"All I'm telling you is what we're *required* to do by law."

Mrs. Knudsen, her eyes hollow, glanced at my mother. Boudreau pushed two pieces of paper across the desk and requested that each woman sign one.

"What's this?" my mother inquired suspiciously.

"It simply details the terms of what the city is obligated to do."

Reluctantly, my mother and Mrs. Knudsen signed.

"If we find you an apartment, we'll reimburse you three hundred dollars for moving expenses," said Boudreau, expressionless.

"But moving expenses will run a lot more than that," my mother protested.

"That's all we're authorized to offer," Boudreau said. Then he collected the signed agreements, stuffed them into a drawer, and took a long pull on his cigarette.

"We can provide you with an incentive, however," he said.

"An incentive?" my mother asked.

"Yes. An incentive for you to find living quarters on your own."

"What's that?"

Boudreau stuffed his cigarette butt into an overflowing ashtray.

"If you find another place to live without our involvement," he said, "we're prepared to offer you more than simply moving expenses."

"How much more?"

"We can offer you two hundred dollars for each room in your current home. And if you find new living quarters within the next ninety days, we'll double that amount and cover your moving expenses, too."

Boudreau shuffled through a sheath of papers bound by large metal rings. The papers contained listings for every known vacancy in the city.

"What about something in Bay Ridge?" my mother inquired.

"I'm afraid we don't have any listings there," Boudreau replied. "The city's vacancy rate is extremely low these days, only about one percent."

"What does that mean?" Mrs. Knudsen inquired sheepishly.

"It means," Boudreau explained, "that there's not many options available."

Mrs. Knudsen seemed even more frightened now. Boudreau continued to peruse his listings.

"But maybe," he said, "we can find you something nearby."

"What do you mean by nearby?" my mother asked.

"There are a couple of listings in North Gowanus, about two miles from where you live now," said Boudreau, scribbling the addresses on a notepad, then tearing off the sheet and offering it to my mother.

"That's it? For the *both* of us?"

"That's all I have anywhere near Bay Ridge," Boudreau said. "There are several listings in other neighborhoods in Brooklyn, but why don't you try these first? Maybe you'll find one of them suitable."

"But … "

"I'm sorry," said Boudreau, glancing at his watch, "but it's already past closing time."

Then, standing and moving from behind his desk, he said, "Call and make another appointment if the addresses I gave you don't work out."

Then he escorted my mother and Mrs. Knudsen to the door and closed it behind them, as if he could hardly wait to send them packing and put an end to another draining day.

EARLY THE NEXT morning, my mother accompanied Mrs. Knudsen to the first of the addresses, on President Street in the North Gowanus section of Brooklyn. She discovered that her earlier pessimism has been well-founded.

A grimy neighborhood that hugged the Gowanus Canal, North Gowanus was one of Brooklyn's oldest enclaves, consisting largely of vast stretches of aging industrial architecture. Scrap-metal yards, concrete coal bunkers, and an assortment of foundries, tanneries, and warehouses edged the neighborhood's winding industrial canal. Boarding houses, unsavory taverns, and cheap railroad flats lined cramped, gloomy streets. Wispy streaks of coal smoke rose from chimneys and factory smokestacks.

A narrow thoroughfare lined with tightly packed wood-frame houses, President Street was nearly devoid of greenery, except for several craggy ailanthus trees that poked through cellar gratings. High masonry stoops with wrought-iron handrails jutted onto sidewalks speckled with pigeon droppings. The air reeked from the stench of nearby sewage-treatment plants.

The apartment my mother and Mrs. Knudsen had been directed to was on the fourth floor of a dingy, turn-of-the-century brownstone framed by rooftop water towers, pigeon coops, garish company signs, and an onion-domed church, home to Brooklyn's Russian Orthodox community.

My mother and Mrs. Knudsen climbed a creaky, winding staircase to reach the apartment, one of three on a dimly lit landing. Their ascent ended at a queue of nearly twenty women waiting in the hallway. All had been sent to inspect the very same apartment.

"I can't believe this," my mother mumbled.

Mrs. Knudsen gasped to catch her breath from the four-story climb.

Just then, two women emerged from the apartment, accompanied by an agent from the Triborough Bridge and Tunnel Authority.

"Are you telling me this is considered *comparable* to what I live in now?" one of the women asked incredulously. "If that wasn't so horrifying, it'd be funny."

The TBTA agent, grim-faced, offered no response.

"I'm paying seventy-two dollars a month for a five-bedroom apartment with hot water and utilities in a beautiful building in Bay Ridge, and you're offering me this rat trap in the middle of a slum for two-fifty a month?" the woman asked. "You know, maybe what I have in Bay Ridge isn't much, but at least it's *something*. Here, I'd have *nothing*."

The TBTA agent nudged his way past the line of women in the hallway.

"The apartments we're being shown are not only unfit for our families, they're unfit for *rats*," the angry woman snarled. "They're triple what we pay now and so small that they'll force my family to split up. And you call them *decent*?"

"I'm only here to drive you around, lady," the TBTA agent said, starting down the stairwell.

"Well, you ought to be ashamed of yourself!" the woman said. Then she followed him out of the building, along with several others—apparently abandoning their search on the spot.

My mother and Mrs. Knudsen were shown the apartment by the building's superintendent who, word had it, had been offered a hefty finder's fee for any apartment he helped rent. He didn't have much to support his sales pitch, however. The apartment reeked of urine. Roaches scurried across the kitchen counter. There were holes in the living room floor, and the bedroom ceiling was cracked from an overhead leak.

"Pretty nice, huh?" the super asked, as my mother and Mrs. Knudsen both quietly cringed. "Whaddaya think?"

"I think we'll pass," my mother replied, and Mrs. Knudsen nodded in concurrence.

"Someone'll take it," the super smiled.

"Just not either of us," my mother said.

"*Dreck*," she whispered to Mrs. Knudsen, using the Yiddish word for crap.

Then the two of them left the building. Even a broken and battered Bay Ridge, they agreed, was infinitely better than what they'd just been shown.

Chapter 39

Construction of the bridge and expressway proceeded side by side with demolition—and just as rapidly.

As 1960 drew to a close, much of Bay Ridge resembled a construction zone. Offshore, giant cranes pumped tons of sand, muck, and gravel from beneath the surface of the Narrows. Alongside them, floating derrick boats drove steel pilings into the underwater surface and then poured the thousands of yards of reinforced concrete needed for the bridge's foundations. Two hundred feet under water, oblivious to shifting tides and treacherous currents, hundreds of workmen in airtight enclosures labored to build the span's pier footings. Simultaneously under construction were the two gigantic anchorages designed to support the bridge's approaches, anchor its cables, and house electrical controls for lights, signs, and traffic signals.

The expressway, by now, was assuming an even more tangible shape. Already, a deep gash, two hundred feet across, had been carved through the heart of Bay Ridge, with steep, jagged crags buttressed on either side by tightly spaced walls of timber.

The gaping, quarter-mile excavation created a huge moat that split the neighborhood in two. Cross streets were closed off, lined with steam shovels, cranes, bulldozers, and other equipment. Side streets and service roads were clogged with detoured traffic. The entire neighborhood seemed shocked into paralysis by the clamor of construction and demolition. And the noise was as endless as it was earsplitting. All day long, bulldozers roared, wrecker's balls thudded, and jackhammers assaulted the air. Convoys of trucks, coughing up dust and fumes, rumbled through the streets. Pile drivers thrust reinforcing shafts through solid bedrock, the air reverberating with the incessant pounding of steel on steel.

Then, as if it were possible, the noise got worse. Since portions of Bay Ridge were built on rolling hills, work crews had no choice but to use dynamite to tear through the solid rock in an effort to keep the expressway level. And so they began blasting.

Soon, dozens of explosions a day rocked Bay Ridge to its core. Chunks of brick were jarred from homes. Tiles flew from rooftops. Gaping fissures opened in the ceilings of buildings as the ground below them heaved with the powerful blasts.

The blasting wreaked other forms of havoc, as well. Electrical power was curtailed when a dynamite charge set a gas line ablaze. Another explosion ruptured a water main, sending sheets of water skyward. Subway service was halted when a massive sinkhole opened on Fourth Avenue, throwing mud and debris onto the underground tracks. Several homes not even earmarked for demolition had to be leveled anyway, when their foundations were damaged by explosions.

Worse than the noise, though, was the dust. With each blast, foul clouds of gritty rock dust erupted from the ground, seeping from beneath the steel-mesh mats used to contain the explosions and settling on streets, lawns, and homes. Trees, plants and shrubbery were enveloped by the red-yellow fallout. Children, covered head to toe, retreated from streets and playgrounds. Windows were shuttered. Door jambs were lined with towels. People donned gauze masks and shielded their eyes from irritating dust particles when daring to venture outside.

Nothing helped, however. Like the noise and chaos, the dust crept insidiously into every part of our lives, sifting into our house, clinging to our clothing. We could taste it, coarse and gritty, in our food. We could see it dribble from our bodies when we bathed. We could feel it in our bedding as we tried to sleep. We could sense it, toxic and heavy, in our lungs. Each day we tried to purge it from our lives. My father lined our window sills with rags. My mother raced frantically through her garden, using water cans and hoses to flush the vile powder from her wildflower beds.

But nothing helped. The dust was everywhere. And we couldn't help but feel soiled by its presence. Poisoned. Damaged. Ruined.

Just like Bay Ridge.

That, by now, had been damaged irreparably, too.

Split in half by the huge gash in its fabric, Bay Ridge had become, in effect, two separate neighborhoods. Dahlgren Place and the other streets on our side of the gaping trench now lay separated from nearly all of our resources. Stores that had been within easy reach were now accessible only by walking blocks out of our way and crossing a makeshift overpass. We could no longer get to school without being driven. Going to Owl's Head Park and other playgrounds was nearly out of the question.

We hadn't moved yet, of course, but a great physical divide existed now in our world. It was as if we'd been isolated, quarantined, as if Bay Ridge itself had somehow been tipped from its axis, its delicate day-to-day balance thrown jarringly out of kilter. The neighborhood seemed far less livable now. No longer vital. No longer whole.

Nor did we. Even as a teenager, I could sense that, like our neighborhood, we were being reshaped in some irrevocable way by the disintegration of our world, the wrenching impact of loss. Everything that had always seemed substantive seemed fragile now. Everything familiar and safe was being wrestled from our grasp.

The entire world seemed alien now, forbidding. And what we were losing was all too clear. We were losing a place that had defined and anchored us. We were losing neighbors and friends, the web of connections that had nurtured and sustained us. We were losing our way of life.

Maybe things would be all right once all this passed. Then again, maybe they wouldn't. For the time being, though, we were not unlike the trees being bowled over in much of our wounded neighborhood: uprooted, in shock, and deprived of all nourishment. Living in some transient place between life and death, heaven and hell.

CHAPTER 40

When school resumed after winter break, I learned that I'd been recommended to take part in a special honors program connected, of all things, to the construction of the bridge.

The program, extraordinary as it was, in many ways was a natural. Hamilton High's location on the high bluff overlooking the Narrows provided it with a unique vantage point from which to witness construction of the landmark bridge. The fact that the project would take shape literally outside the windows of the school's westernmost classrooms had inspired several teachers to develop an intriguing eighteen-month curriculum focused entirely on the bridge.

Sanctioned by the Board of Education, the curriculum included courses in physics, math, social studies, and civics. No program of its kind had ever been offered in New York. Only the most qualified math and science students, twenty-two in all, were invited to participate on a voluntary basis.

"I'm not sure it's such a good idea to focus whatever time you have left here to study a bridge that's causing people such heartache," my mother said. "The bridge, you know, is not exactly a wondrous thing to a lot of people, including your own family."

"What do you think?" I asked my father later.

"Is it something you really want to do?"

"I guess I have mixed feelings because of everything that's happening. I can understand mom's feelings, but ... "

"But *what*?"

"But it sounds kind of interesting, to tell you the truth. And it feels good to be asked."

"You *should* feel good," my father said. "They're apparently letting only the brightest students take part."

Still, I was reluctant.

"I don't want to do anything that would hurt mom or you," I said.

"The only thing that would hurt us is if you turned this opportunity down because you were afraid of how we'd feel," my father replied. "Do you really want to give it a try?"

"I think so, yes."

"Then let me talk to your mother."

By the next morning, I had gotten my parents' approval to enroll.

And the following day I was seated in the classroom of a teacher who'd change the course of my life as surely as would the bridge itself.

RAISED ON A tiny sod farm in Iowa, Edwin Urbansky had gotten a degree in physics from Iowa State before enlisting in the Merchant Marines at the outset of World War II. He was first mate on an oil tanker when the ship, sailing through enemy-infested waters near Gibraltar, was torpedoed by a German U-boat. The explosion tore the tanker apart, killing most of the crew.

In the midst of the fiery chaos, Mr. Urbansky and four shipmates somehow managed to scramble into a lifeboat and lower themselves into the Atlantic. The only thing that would wind up saving them was Mr. Urbansky's knowledge of science.

Subsisting on rainwater, the offal of fish, and decapods extracted from seaweed, the shipmates drifted for nearly two weeks, ingeniously managing to survive. They sent distress signals by reflecting sunlight off their belt buckles. They dampened their clothing during intense daylight to keep their body temperatures cool and stable. At night, they sat back to back for warmth, rotating their arms and necks to remain limber, navigating by the stars and drawing maps on each others' backs with oil slicks pulled from the shark-infested waters. Eventually, they were rescued three hundred miles from the shipwreck.

Mr. Urbansky's story of survival had made the rounds for years at Hamilton High. So had stories about his innovative, engaging approach to teaching physics.

Now fifty-two, Mr. Urbansky had been teaching at Hamilton fifteen years, having arrived after the war to join a cadre of dedicated teachers lured to the city's public school system during the Great Depression, when private-sector jobs all but evaporated. Hands down, he was considered the school's most popular teacher. From the very first day in his class, I could understand why.

"Over the next few years, one of the most extraordinary engineering achievements of the twentieth century will take shape right before our eyes in Bay Ridge," Mr. Urbansky began.

He gestured toward the bank of windows that ran the length of our classroom, revealing a panoramic view of the Narrows.

"The greatest suspension bridge in history will be built right outside our classroom—and we'll have the privilege of bearing witness to it," our teacher gushed. "We'll get to learn about it, too."

A fair-skinned man with flaxen hair and corn-fed features, Mr. Urbansky wore a loosely knotted tie, rumpled white shirt open at the collar, and sleeves rolled midway up his arms—making him appear ready to literally plunge into his lessons.

His classroom looked equally ready. The entire front wall above the blackboard was plastered with photos of bridges, blueprints, and engineering drawings. Math calculations were scrawled on the chalkboard. Several bridge models, fashioned from balsa wood, were perched on a table adjoining his desk.

Mr. Urbansky selected one of the models and approached the class. It was a handmade replica of the Verrazano-Narrows Bridge. "This bridge," he told the class, "will be a magnificent creation—a true marriage of technology, art, and inspiration."

He held the model aloft, as if christening a child.

"From the standpoint of physics, there's a lot to learn simply from what we'll observe," he said. "We'll learn about the science of bridge design, the challenges that engineers and workmen face, and how those challenges will be addressed. But mostly, I hope, you'll get an understanding about what an incredible achievement the bridge represents."

Mr. Urbansky all but lit up when he spoke. His enthusiasm was contagious, his smile alone able to forge an immediate bond with the students, who were quiet and rapt. I was instantly intrigued, drawn to both my teacher and the possibilities of his class.

"Make no mistake, this class will challenge you," Mr. Urbansky said. "But it'll also enable you to understand why men aspire to build the things they do, and what it takes to build them."

Then he smiled.

"Get ready to learn," he said. "By the end of this program, I hope you'll see the physical world in a whole new way."

I left school that day more excited by the prospects of that class than at any other time I could remember. Sophomore physics, I suspected, wasn't going to be just another course I'd sleepwalk through, daydreaming until the bell rang, acing the tests but then forgetting the lesson as soon as I walked out the door. No, I thought. This just might be a class where I could really *learn*, where something inside me could be awakened, where a fire could be kindled from embers I never even realized were there.

"What do you think?" my father asked that evening.

"I think I'm gonna like it," I said, trying to low-key my enthusiasm in my mother's presence.

"Good," he said and winked. "There's nothing more exciting than learning about something you feel passionate about. Go for it, Nathan. Go for it and see what happens."

BY THE SECOND day of class, Mr. Urbansky had launched headlong into his initial lesson plan. And I was totally hooked.

"There are more than two thousand bridges in New York City," he began, dimming the lights for a slide show. "Some are simple pedestrian walkways. Others are breathtaking, architectural treasures built by the greatest minds in engineering, masterpieces that reflect the limits of what man is capable of achieving."

Mr. Urbansky's slides ran the gamut, including bridges created from the crudest materials—jungle vines and tree limbs—to modern concrete-and-steel structures with great swooping suspension cables and portals that reached gracefully to the sky.

"Bridges like the one to be built across the Narrows are necessary for the prosperity of cities like New York," Mr. Urbansky said. "But all of them do more than simply carry people and vehicles over land and water. They're about *much more* than just facilitating travel, transporting goods, and helping cities function."

Mr. Urbansky ran through his slides, his silhouette barely visible in the darkened classroom, his hands slicing the air enthusiastically as he spoke.

"New York," he said, "is one of the world's great cities. But it exists as an *archipelago*. Does anyone know what that is?"

"A group of islands," said Mitchell Weiner, the smartest kid in our class.

"That's right," Mr. Urbansky nodded. "Of the city's five boroughs, only one—the Bronx—is actually connected to mainland America. And because New York is an archipelago—a city of deep harbors, wide rivers and navigable waterways—its people are separated by bodies of water."

Then he paused, his smile visible even in the flickering projector light.

"Our bridges draw us together as a people," he said. "They *connect* and bind us. Not only are they crucial to our social and economic survival, they embody the idea that we can overcome the physical barriers that separate us, that we can span wide expanses of space and join together."

His slide show ended, Mr. Urbansky flicked on the lights.

"The bridge across the Narrows will make a powerful statement about who we are as a people," he said. "It'll be a way of saying there's no challenge we're unwilling to face, no problem we're unwilling to tackle, no limits to what we can achieve."

He smiled broadly. He did that whenever he wanted to make a special point.

"Does everyone understand?"

The class nodded as one. After the way Mr. Urbansky had explained it, we not only understood what he was saying, we couldn't help but believe it, too.

Chapter 41

That winter dumped a heavy blanket of snow on Bay Ridge. Outside, kids built igloos on the streets, belly-flopped down the hills of Owl's Head Park, and tossed snowballs at steel-chained buses fishtailing past construction zones along Seventh Avenue. At demolition sites, construction equipment moved around and through snow-covered mountains of rubble. Out on the Narrows, jagged ice floes drifted past the bridge construction site, as workers labored in crosswinds that set cranes swaying and huge icicles dropping like spears into the freezing water below.

But while the inclement weather did little to slow demolition and construction, it managed to hamstring the efforts of anti-bridge protestors, whose ranks had thinned by now to only a determined handful. By mid-February, the most demonstrative protests had, for the most part, ceased.

Except for one.

The sit-in by parishioners at All Saints Episcopal Church was now nearly a month old and far from resolved, as demonstrators remained steadfast and officials pondered ways to end the sensitive stalemate.

Wary of appearing heavy-handed, both church and city officials mulled their options: evict the protestors and proceed with the existing expressway plan or re-route the roadway so it would bypass the church. A third option, considered far more vexing, was to literally raise the church from its foundation and relocate it intact onto a tract of city-owned land nearby.

While those options were considered, parishioners remained barricaded inside the church, led by Monsignor Terrence Dougherty in contemplation and prayer. Despite their outward resolve, most of the hundred or so protestors were deeply conflicted over their actions. Other than several retired labor union members, most had never participated in any kind of formal protest, let alone one that involved such an open display of defiance against the city and Archdiocese. Deeply religious and steeped in traditional values, most lived lives governed by respect for all forms of authority, especially church and state. Now, however, they'd spent nearly thirty days inside a church they were trying to save—praying, singing hymns, sleeping on pews, and receiving food, toiletries, and other supplies from supporters permitted to shuttle past the police lines outside.

Monsignor Dougherty reassured them that their actions were noble, that God would look favorably upon them for trying to save His church.

"This is a *church*—not just another building," he told them, as a row of votive candles cast wavy shadows across the pulpit.

"It's wrong for the city to treat our church as if it's something to be simply swept aside. We cannot allow a hallowed place of worship to be violated like that. We must stand for what's right and save our church."

He read from the Bible, quoting key verses and psalms. And, together, the parishioners sang, their voices wafting from the church as gently as the softly falling snow, their prayers broken only by the sound of dynamite exploding in the gaping trench that once was Seventh Avenue.

BEYOND ALL PRAYER, however, were the ill-fated businesses along Seventh Avenue, most of which were out of either time or luck.

Doomed to demolition, many merchants had already been forced from Bay Ridge, left to fend for themselves. Despite their past success, the vast majority would find it impossible to reestablish themselves in other neighborhoods, where even longtime reputations in Bay

Ridge carried little weight. Possessing few alternate skills, most would be forced to retire or drift into unfamiliar lines of work. More than a few would return to their ancestral homeland, abandoning not only Brooklyn but their bright and hopeful American Dreams.

The impact of their departure was as real as the excavation being carved through Bay Ridge. Once a thriving thoroughfare, Seventh Avenue was now a virtual dead zone. Buildings stood behind makeshift plywood walls, condemned or in ruin. Remaining merchants, needing to deplete their inventories, conducted near-giveaways, with bargain-seeking shoppers descending on stores like hungry scavengers. Others simply took whatever settlement the city offered and left, their shelves still stocked with remnant merchandise, their trash bins overflowing with the bits and pieces of their former businesses.

"It's a crying shame, what's happening to these people," my father said, as the two of us walked one Saturday to get our final haircuts at Caruso's Barber Shop. "Not only are they being forced out of business, they're getting compensated for only a fraction of what they're losing."

"Why?"

"Under eminent domain, the government is not actually acquiring a business—only the premises," my father explained. "The city pays only for the physical structure and the land."

"So?"

"So, someone could literally buy a business for, say, twenty thousand dollars, but if the building it occupies is valued only at five thousand dollars, that's all the owner will be offered. On top of that, owners receive nothing for the business they're losing, or for their fixed assets—the things inside their business. They also get nothing for the value of their good will."

"What's that?"

"It's the reputation a business has established," my father said. "A business' reputation has value, too, you know. In many cases, the most valuable asset a business has is its good name, the fact that people like doing business there. How some appraiser can decide that a business is worth nothing more than the value of its building and land is beyond me."

"It doesn't seem fair."

"It isn't. In a lot of cases, their business is all these people have. They're losing everything they've poured their heart and soul into for years."

I thought about that as we crossed a temporary footbridge over the massive trench that now split Bay Ridge in two. With work halted for the weekend, the partially built expressway resembled a desolate, snow-capped canyon. Kids sledded down the walls of the crevice, climbed on idle earth-moving equipment, and slid across frozen ponds formed by melted snow. It was a far cry from the makeshift playground Bay Ridge once was to me and my friends.

"Kids'll play anywhere," my father said, laughing. "They don't have to worry about anything—they're just kids."

For the first time in my life, I didn't feel like a kid anymore. There was no way I could escape what was happening around me by simply immersing myself in innocent play. Those days were over. There was no way I could ever see Bay Ridge through the same set of eyes, no way I could ever feel that young again.

Acquired by the city for pennies on the dollar, Caruso's Barber Shop was earmarked for demolition and had been rented to its former owner, Sal Caruso, who was offering haircuts at half-price as a good-bye gesture to customers.

Outside the shop, Sal's barber pole stood glinting in the sunlight, its red, white, and blue stripes rotating upward across the pole. Inside, the shop was jammed, each of the five barber chairs occupied by men getting haircuts and shaves. Behind them, facing a mirrored wall, nearly a dozen others sat awaiting their turn. Some chatted. Others picked through tattered newspapers or back issues of *Popular Mechanics, Sports Afield,* and the *Police Gazette*.

My father and I settled into seats under the mounted head of a deer buck. In front of us, beneath a wall-length mirror, we could see a shelf full of powders, combs, hair brushes, witch hazel, and hair tonics. Electric razors hung from metal hooks. On a wall were a Burma Shave sign and posters of Miss New York Subways and Miss Rheingold.

Sal Caruso removed the barber's gown from a customer's chest and cleaned his neck with a whisk brush.

"Next!" he called, and one of the waiting customers ambled over.

Six men later, it was my father's turn.

"The usual, Mr. Wolf?" asked Sal, sloe-eyed, with receding black hair and eyebrows bushy enough to warrant a trim of their own.

"The usual is fine."

"Sure thing." Sal smiled, snapped the barber's gown clean, and placed it across my father's chest. "The usual it is."

The conversation in the shop, not surprisingly, was the usual, too: local gossip, politics, and sports. The introspective, reclusive Floyd Patterson had won the heavyweight title from Archie Moore in 1956, but had surrendered it to the Swedish fighter Ingemar Johansson three years later. A rematch was scheduled in several months. Talk centered on the upcoming fight.

"I dunno 'bout dis Patterson," said Sal, a comb in one hand, a pair of scissors in the other, his accent thick with the Old Country.

"What's your problem wit' him, Sal?" another barber clucked.

"Ah," Sal said. "He's too much of a gentleman to be a fighter."

He snipped at my father's hair, hardly missing a beat as he yapped.

"Ya know, Patterson once helped a guy pick his mouthpiece off da canvas when he knocked it outta his mouth," Sal groused. "Now, what kinda fighter does dat?"

"I can't see Marciano doin' it," said the other barber. "Or Joe Louis."

"Dat's what I mean," Sal agreed. "You can't be *helpin'* guys when you're in da ring tryin' to beat their brains out."

Both barbers chuckled, along with my father and several other men. I laughed, too. I loved hearing talk like that. I couldn't wait to grow up so I could talk about fighters and ballplayers and politicians with grown men who'd take my opinions seriously. The only opinion I could offer at the moment was about how my hair should be cut.

"How ya doin', kid?" Sal smiled when my turn came. "Whaddaya gettin' dis week?"

I told Sal not to cut it too short. He glanced at my father, who nodded his okay.

"Kids are wearin' their hair longer these days," Sal said. "Soon, they won't need barbers at all."

"That'll never happen, Sal," said my father, picking up a *Saturday Evening Post* and taking a seat.

Ten minutes later, my scalp thick with Brylcreem, my haircut was complete.

"Sal, it's been good." My father exhaled, slipping a ten-dollar bill into a jar stuffed with tips. "You gave the best haircuts in Brooklyn. I don't know what I'm gonna do for a haircut once you're gone."

"Well, Mr. Wolf, you'll just find yourself another barber," Sal said and laughed.

"I guess I'll have to. But it won't be easy."

Then he shook Sal's hand.

"We'll miss you, Sal," my father said. "It won't be the same without you."

"Thanks," Sal nodded, pursing his lips. "It's been a long time here in Bay Ridge."

"Whaddaya gonna do?"

"Go home, I guess. Back to Sicily. There's nuthin' left for me anymore in Brooklyn."

"I'm not sure there's anything left for *any* of us anymore," my father said. "A lot of things are ending now that the bridge is coming in. It was good while it lasted, but I guess it's over now."

Sal shook his head. "What can ya do? Ya know what dey say. All good things gotta come to an end."

"I'm sorry, Sal," my father said. "It stinks—what the city's doing to you."

"Yeah," Sal agreed. "Nuthin' much I can do 'bout it, though."

"Nah," my father said, shrugging. "Nothing much *anyone* can do."

And, with that, we left Caruso's Barber Shop for the final time and made our way back to Dahlgren Place. Past blackened snow drifts and the slushy ruins of Seventh Avenue. Past demolition equipment poised outside boarded-up stores. Past merchants standing amid groups of former customers, bidding them good-bye.

Past all that.

Past the wreckage of Hessemann's Grocery, where we'd shopped for as long as I could remember. Past Thumann's Candy Store, where we'd go, sweaty from play, to buy salted pretzels, comic books, Bazooka bubble gum, packs of baseball cards, and strips of candy dots. Past Hinch's Ice Cream Shop, where we quashed down lime rickeys, egg creams, ice cream sodas, and frosty malteds from chilled metal containers. Past Pete's Hardware, where my father bought his tools, and Giorgio's Shoe Shop, where we had our shoes repaired, and the GM dealership where we bought our Plymouth, and all the other businesses that had been part of our lives for so long.

Some of them gone already. Others soon to leave.

Gone: targets of demolition.

Gone: victims of progress, consigned to the memory.

Gone: like so many other things that defined the Brooklyn we'd grown up in, the Brooklyn we were losing.

"Well, I guess it's good-bye to all that," my father said, as we traversed the mammoth trench on our return trip home.

"We're saying good-bye not just to these shops, Nathan," he sighed. "We're saying good-bye to an era—a whole way of life."

At fourteen, I hadn't lived long enough to fully understand what he was saying. But I was old enough to see something in my father's eyes fade, as if a tiny glow, like that of a distant star, had gone forever dark.

Chapter 42

But there was a whole different way to look at things. That's what Mr. Urbansky told us. We could see what was happening in Bay Ridge through a prism of our own creation, he said. We were young; we had that choice. We could view events in terms of gain, not loss—birth, not death. We could embrace the dawn of a bright new age as readily as we could lament the end of an era. We could look eagerly ahead as easily as we could see sadly behind.

We could see the bridge in a special way, too, Mr. Urbansky said. Through the lens of science and technology. Free of politics, absent of coloration, beyond spontaneous, raw emotion. Not as an object of derision and fear, but as a work of soaring imagination and beauty. A treasure to study, a wonder to behold.

"There it is," our physics teacher gushed, pointing to the first visible sign of the bridge—the arched pedestals of its massive twin towers poking through the fog-shrouded Narrows like fingertips reaching for the sky.

And there it was. The most ambitious engineering endeavor of the past half-century. A physical embodiment of what men could achieve if they possessed the vision, the ambition, the passion; a symbol of what each of us could achieve if we, too, were bold enough to dream, if we, too, aspired to reach for the sky.

That's what Mr. Urbansky said.

That's what he said as he forged ahead with our curriculum amid the demolition and construction in Bay Ridge, Brooklyn's past receding, a new reality emerging, the gleam in my teacher's eyes a stark counterpoint to the sadness in the eyes of my father.

THE WEEKS THAT followed saw us immersed in a series of skillfully conceived lessons delivered by a teaching team light years ahead of its time. And soon we, too, were seeing the bridge in a whole new light.

In physics, we learned the rudiments of bridge design and studied the major breakthroughs in bridge-building through the centuries. We learned how the earliest bridges were little more than organic constructions fashioned from fallen trees, plaited vines, and woven nets. We learned how simple stone arch bridges allowed the Romans to move armies and maintain their empire; how advances in surveying, draftsmanship, and metallurgy enabled engineers to conquer geographical challenges previously thought insurmountable; how advances in technology allowed the construction of long spans capable of withstanding seismic movements; how modern bridges were the product of high-strength steel and the revolutionary techniques pioneered a century earlier by John Roebling, the mastermind behind the Brooklyn Bridge.

Two weeks into the curriculum, we shifted our focus to the bridges of New York, the earliest of which, we learned, had been built as part of the Croton Aqueduct System, which transported water through giant mains from northern reservoirs into Manhattan. Other spans, Mr. Urbansky explained—drawbridges, lift bridges, arches, cantilevers and cable suspension spans—had sprung up as the city expanded, mirroring, at first, the stark ornamental ironwork of Europe, but later reflecting a modernity unique to America.

We spent a week studying the Brooklyn Bridge, an aesthetic masterpiece that Mr. Urbansky likened to the Great Pyramids of Egypt and the Hanging Gardens of Babylon. We spent another week on the George Washington Bridge, a Depression-era marvel that many people considered the world's most beautiful span. We studied New York's utilitarian crossings, too: the Triborough Bridge, an immense structure that connected three distinct land masses via a network of viaducts and overwater spans; the Manhattan Bridge, the first span to employ the principle of two-dimensional tower construction, enabling it to expand and contract as needed; the Hell Gate Bridge, the immense steel arch that carried passenger and freight trains in and out of the city; the Marine Parkway Bridge, whose sleekly angled stone and curving steelwork opened to the beaches of the Rockaways.

Mostly, though, we focused on the landmark bridge rising outside our classroom window.

"Because of its tremendous size, the type of geography it spans, and the enormous load it will carry, the Verrazano-Narrows Bridge presented engineers with a series of complex challenges never before faced," Mr. Urbansky said.

He explained how engineers had to deal with a mind-numbing array of considerations: the sheer magnitude of the structure, the location of its towers and anchorages, navigational requirements, weather conditions and water depths, tides and currents, the varying geologic conditions of the earth, sand, mud and solid rock beneath the water.

The mere design of the bridge, he told us, involved years of exhaustive study, meticulous calculations, and thousands of detailed drawings. Literally millions of components had to be considered: tens of thousands of plates, angles and beams; hundreds of thousands of bolts, rivets, wires, and pins; more than ten million holes, which had to be precisely plotted to line up with others.

"Literally every detail of this bridge needed to be carefully thought out," Mr. Urbansky said. "The diameter of the cables. The size, weight, and location of the towers, foundations, and decks. How many traffic lanes are required. How long the bridge will take to build. How much money it'll cost … "

In fact, Mr. Urbansky said, the Verrazano-Narrows Bridge needed to be designed with such precision that it was necessary to locate the span's six-hundred-and-eighty-foot towers perpendicular to the earth's surface, but precisely one and five-eighths inches farther apart at their summits than at their bases, to account for the curvature of the earth over the Narrows. Four-hundred-ton roadway components had to be planned down to the millimeter. And because the soil on the Brooklyn side was not as firm as on the Staten Island side, the Brooklyn foundations had to be built larger and set deeper.

To assure this precision, Mr. Urbansky explained, planners had to take extraordinary precautions. Measurements needed to be cross-checked repeatedly. Surveyors on both sides of the Narrows, using tellurometers—instruments that measured distances with reflected radio beams—had to make multiple observations and then switch sides and repeat the exercise from the opposite shore. Allowances had to be made for shifting tides and currents. Measuring tapes had to be set at specific tensions, with readings adjusted to allow for expansion or contraction resulting from even subtle changes in temperature. Many measurements had to be taken after midnight, when bridge components were uniformly cool. Materials needed to be tested repeatedly for tensile strength, metallic content, size, and finish.

The Verrazano's design, Mr. Urbansky explained, also needed to account for the bridge being elastic, capable of expanding and contracting with the seasons, and undulating from the effects of wind and traffic.

We learned that sunlight could warp the structure on one side while the other side remained in shade. We learned how the two anchorages—the massive concrete blocks anchoring the steel cables supporting the suspended roadway—used special roller-mounted saddles capable of moving as the cables changed in length, depending upon the weight on the bridge. We learned that the road deck contained steel expansion joints that interlocked like fingers as the bridge changed size and shape.

"Flexibility is critical when it comes to bridge design," Mr. Urbansky said, showing us a film about America's most famous bridge collapse—that of the Tacoma-Narrows Bridge over Puget Sound in Washington State.

"Engineers have learned how to reduce this kind of aerodynamic instability," he said as we watched, awestruck, the ill-fated bridge known as "Galloping Gertie" oscillating wildly and then tumbling into a deep gorge.

Picking up a bridge model, Mr. Urbansky demonstrated how, when a well-designed bridge contracted during cold weather, its roadway could actually curl up in an arch, then flatten out with heat, rising and falling as much as twelve feet depending on the temperature.

"It's almost as if the bridge is alive, reacting to changes in its environment," Mr. Urbansky said. "A well-made bridge will bend and move, but never break. Sometimes, you can actually feel it move. But it's designed to do that, and it's perfectly safe."

But there was far more to the Verrazano than even its precision design.

"The coordination of the project alone is mind-boggling," Mr. Urbansky explained. "Just look at scheduling and logistics. Materials need to be produced in mines and quarries, and then fabricated in factories, foundries, and steel mills. Components need to be assembled to assure there are no mistakes, then disassembled and shipped to storage facilities, rail yards, and docks, eventually arriving in the correct sequence for re-assembly and erection."

Someone snickered at the word *erection.* But Mr. Urbansky just smiled. He could be cool that way.

"Not *that* kind of erection," he said, and the all-male class chuckled.

"What I mean," he continued, "is that every part needs to be delivered to the right place at exactly the right time or the entire job comes to a halt. And what happens then?"

"People get angry," someone answered.

"That's right," Mr. Urbansky said. "More importantly, money gets lost."

It was clear, from the way he spoke, that Mr. Urbansky saw bridges through far more sophisticated eyes than ours. We saw them as mundane structures, everyday pieces of New York's landscape, worth little more than a passing glance. He saw them as architectural monuments that married science and art. Harmonious combinations of masonry and steel. Structures worthy of appreciation and study. Each with its own unique story to tell. Each capable of teaching us something new.

He wanted us to see them that way, too. More than anything, he made it clear, he wanted us to look beyond the surface of the physical world and discover an element of magic and wonder we otherwise would miss.

"Think about it," he smiled. "That's all I ask."

Think about it.

Think about how a magnificent work of architecture like the Verrazano-Narrows Bridge could somehow come together from concept to reality, piece by piece, emerging as something tangible, assuming a life every bit as real as our own. Think about how something so complex, beyond the scope of any single individual, could become the product of decades of meticulous planning, a sturdy, well-conceived assemblage of millions of parts, a coordinated effort of thousands of people. Think about the bridge not just as a work of utter brilliance, not just an engineering achievement to be appreciated, not just a work of beauty to be marveled at—but as a *reminder*.

"The bridge," Mr. Urbansky said, "reminds us that nothing within the realm of our imagination should ever be considered out of our reach."

He paused, gesturing toward the Narrows.

"I want you to remember that," he said. "If nothing else, I want you to remember that, while none of us may ever build anything as awe-inspiring as the bridge, we should never stop *aspiring* to do it. We should never stop imagining. We should never stop daring to dream."

Chapter 43

But while some dreams were taking shape in the Narrows, and even in our classroom, others continued to crumble with the clamor of demolition.

Five weeks into the sit-in by protesting parishioners, city officials decided they couldn't—or wouldn't—alter their plans for the demolition of All Saints Episcopal Church. The Brooklyn Archdiocese concurred. There'd be no rerouting of the expressway, no relocation of the tiny religious landmark, no compromise whatsoever. Church officials announced they'd move ahead with plans to combine the parish with a church in Sunset Park. City officials announced that the church would be razed.

Both the city and Archdiocese stressed how difficult their decision had been. Demolition, they said, would be undertaken with the utmost sensitivity. However, they noted, in the end they really had no choice—and neither did the protesting parishioners. Protestors had forty-eight hours to abandon the church. If they didn't, the city warned, they'd face eviction and arrest.

"I cannot believe the city would cast this important religious landmark aside so callously," Monsignor Terrence Dougherty lamented. "I cannot believe that God himself has abandoned this, his church."

Clasping his hands before him, Monsignor Dougherty knelt at the altar. Forming a circle around him, distraught parishioners embraced one another as they joined in prayer, their sobs filling the church with anguish and grief.

Monsignor Dougherty issued a desperate plea to Archdiocese officials to reconsider. He appealed directly to the Vatican to intervene, then to federal authorities to spare the Civil War-era church on the basis of its historical significance. But neither church nor government was moved. Their decision, they said, was final.

As the countdown to the eviction deadline proceeded, police officers mobilized in front of All Saints Episcopal Church, prepared to carry out the city's edict. Hundreds of onlookers gathered behind wooden police barricades.

Several officers, their religious convictions in conflict with their civic duty, asked to be relieved of their assignment. Their requests granted, they slipped into patrol cars and drove off. Most of the cops, however, stood firm, saddened by their obligatory task but duty-bound to carry out their orders. At the deadline, several of them slipped through the church's rear windows, removed the entryway barricade, and escorted the protestors outside.

The onlookers, once again, seemed stunned beyond reaction. Catcalls were hurled at the unnerved officers, several of whom, bodies taut, eyes darting about, seemed on the verge of tears themselves.

"Shame on you!" a woman shouted at one of them. "Why don't you go and arrest a *real* criminal?"

Head bowed, the cop moved ahead silently, placing his handcuffed prisoner in the rear seat of a patrol car. Other protestors, squinting in the bright sunlight, were led out one at a time. Some were heralded with applause that melded with the jeers at cops.

Finally, Monsignor Dougherty, his brown robe brushing the ground, a gold crucifix in his grasp, was marched from the church, a police officer at each elbow.

"God bless you, Monsignor!" a woman shouted, as the crowd's applause heightened. "We love you, Father. We love you!"

"God bless you, too!" Monsignor Dougherty said, as onlookers inched forward and police tensed for trouble.

There was no trouble, however. Only anguish. Only bitterness. Only a sense of impotence. Only a sense of grief and a feeling that everything we once cherished was unraveling before our eyes.

Over the next week, workers carefully removed the contents of the church. Pews, pulpits, lecterns, and altarware were disassembled and carried away. Liturgical artwork, baptisteries, window mosaics, bibles, crosses, and vestments were boxed and trucked to Archdiocese headquarters. Disciplined for his actions, Monsignor Dougherty was reassigned to an obscure parish in Staten Island, his days as a pastor numbered.

And soon after that the bulldozers moved in and took All Saints Episcopal Church to the ground. Relegating it to its long, eventful past. Reducing it, like so much of Bay Ridge, to little more than a memory.

Chapter 44

As the weeks unfolded, the Hamilton High School bridge curriculum forged ahead—unique in its focus, innovative in its approach, branching out beyond physics to nearly all my other subjects.

In math, we learned the bridge's vital statistics. We learned that the foundations for its two twenty-seven-thousand-ton towers would be dug seventeen stories below the surface of the Narrows and assembled to a height of six hundred and ninety feet above the water, higher than most Manhattan skyscrapers. We learned that a hundred and sixty thousand tons of structural steel, three times the amount used for the Empire State Building, would be used for the span. We learned that the main road deck would have a suspended length of six hundred and seventy feet, and that the total length of the bridge, including ramps and approaches, would be more than three full miles.

"By understanding the bridge in mathematical terms, we can get a better appreciation for the enormity of this undertaking," said our math teacher, Martin Hendricks, who, before long, had us comprehending concepts tied to the geometry of concrete and steel.

We learned that the bridge's main deck, on either side of mid-span, was built on a four-percent grade, rising and descending in a graceful curve that saw it rise four feet for every hundred feet of pavement, so that a clearance of two hundred and thirty-seven feet could be achieved at the center of the Narrows, allowing for the passage of naval and commercial shipping, including the world's largest ocean liner, the Queen Mary. We learned that each of the four cables from which the overwater roadway would be suspended measured seventy-two-hundred feet in length and thirty-six inches in diameter; that each could withstand a pull of a quarter-billion pounds; and that each consisted of sixty-one strands of four hundred and twenty-eight pencil-thin wires that, if laid end to end, would reach halfway from Times Square to the moon.

But the curriculum didn't stop with only physics and math.

In civics, we delved into the process for political and administrative approval of public works projects like the bridge. We learned how plans were developed; how federal, state and city agencies functioned; how funds and subsidies were allocated. We learned about the government's power of eminent domain, and about the complex, sometimes testy negotiations that took place with the U.S. military to obtain the land for the bridge and its approaches.

In art class, we copied renderings of the Verrazano and other bridges—seeing them for the first time as dazzling, brawny works of sculpture; studying concepts such as line, shape, form, proportion, symmetry, and scale.

In social studies, we learned about the transportation systems that had shaped modern-day America: how hand-dug canals had provided early means of commerce; how the transcontinental railroad had transformed the West; how an entire new industry, centered around commercial flight, was taking shape at New York's two main airports, LaGuardia and Idlewild. We learned how key advances in transportation had helped Brooklyn evolve from its agrarian roots into a modern urban environment. We learned how bridges, tunnels, and other forms of arterial construction were intertwined with the economic, political, and cultural life of cities like New York. We learned how the colossal road-building effort underway as part of the Eisenhower-inspired National Defense Highways Act was reshaping the American landscape.

"America is building a network of roads that's nothing less than extraordinary," said Miss Greene, our social studies teacher. "People living generations from now will not be able to even *imagine* America without them."

Tall and statuesque, Miss Greene was the most attractive female teacher at Hamilton High. Barely in her thirties, she wore colorful blouses and pleated, pastel skirts that swayed gracefully as she moved. Her auburn hair, pinned atop her head, seemed iridescent in the hanging, bowl-like lights of our classroom.

But Miss Greene had everyone's attention for more than her striking looks. Like Mr. Urbansky and Mr. Hendricks, she had a passion for her subject that was not only captivating, but contagious and enlightening.

"America's new Interstate Highway System is a social triumph unmatched in history, the largest peacetime construction project ever," she said. "But it's not just about the technological achievement these roads represent, or even that they'll be a mainstay of commerce for centuries. What's important to understand is how they're changing our nation in a way that reflects new patterns of American life."

America, Miss Greene told us, was a nation in the midst of sweeping transformation. Cities like New York were changing. Rural life was disappearing. The line between the city and the countryside was blurring. Our nation had become an automobile-centered society. The car was front and center in American life.

"The roads and bridges we're building now are nothing less than a passport to a whole new way of life," Miss Greene said. "They'll allow people to escape the shadows of their offices and factories, to live and work wherever they want, to enjoy a mobility that previous generations only dreamt about. Because of these roads, people will be able to come and go as they please. They'll no longer be prisoners in their homes."

In many ways, Miss Greene said, the nation's new roads were an expression of how Americans saw themselves—who we were as a people.

"America," she said, "has always held a fascination for the open road. We migrate, explore, cherish our ability to feel unrestrained by boundaries and barriers. Our roads and bridges reflect that. They express our desire to celebrate our mobility and freedom, conquer the distances between us, leave our footprint on our landscape, move forever forward."

Miss Greene also touched bravely on topics that hit uncomfortably close to home.

"Sometimes the public works projects we build, beneficial as they may be, are also painful to people," she said one day. "We've certainly seen that in Bay Ridge."

Miss Greene studied the class, carefully measuring her words.

"It's unfortunate," she said, "what happens sometimes in the name of progress, when past and future collide head-on. Entire towns bypassed by the Interstates have withered. People have been dispossessed. Families have been separated from each other by freeways. Cultures, languages, and social bonds have been destroyed. Look at the ghost towns of the Old West, once-thriving communities relegated to the past."

Brooklyn, in many ways, was no different, Miss Greene said.

"Brooklyn's story has always been one of settlement, development, resettlement, and change. Right here in Bay Ridge, Indians once hunted, fished, and farmed until they were dispossessed by Dutch settlers, who in turn had *their* farms destroyed, their fields torched, and their livestock seized by the British, who were eventually displaced by waves of other immigrants."

Miss Greene explained how, decades earlier, people lamented the loss of Brooklyn's pristine countryside to urban development. She told us how the construction of the Brooklyn Bridge, something we took for granted, once spelled the end to an entire way of life, just like the Narrows bridge was doing now.

"Change often wreaks havoc and spells death to an older, more comfortable way of life," she said. "But it can also bring rebirth. Places like Brooklyn have always thrived, then withered, and then been revived. It's part of a natural, healthy cycle."

Miss Greene paused, her eyes conveying sincerity.

"What I want you to understand is that the world's great cities are constantly remaking themselves, redefining what they are, tearing themselves down and rebuilding," she said. "We're seeing that now in New York. Our city is shedding old skin—changing to accommodate the car, the same way it changed once to accommodate trolleys and subways. In many ways, it's transforming itself into what it's destined to become."

Then she smiled.

"Just like *all of us*," she said. "You are being transformed, too."

I'd never thought of things that way before. I'd never thought of the world around me, or myself, as an entity that was unfinished, evolving, being transformed into something different than it was at just that moment—something unpredictable, with greater depth than what was obvious to the naked eye.

But I began to see myself that way now. Not only was my view of the physical world changing through my studies about the bridge. My view of myself was changing, as well.

BUT NOT EVERYONE at school saw magic in the bridge. Not everyone was as stirred as I was by the special curriculum. At the outset of the semester, in fact, Hamilton High had assigned a guidance counselor the sole task of assisting students with emotional difficulties caused by the traumatic events in Bay Ridge. Our principal, Maxwell Livingston, also addressed the subject during a school assembly.

"The building of the Narrows bridge is obviously a very emotionally charged topic for many of you," said Principal Livingston, a kindly man who'd spent his entire thirty-year career at Hamilton High.

"There are many emotions stirring—anger, fear, uncertainty, and disorientation, to name just a few—because of what's taking place. All of them are normal, understandable, human."

Principal Livingston gazed out over the sea of students before him, separated in some cases by empty seats formerly occupied by departed classmates.

"I want to assure you that Hamilton High is a place you can find help in sorting through your emotions," he said. "Please don't hesitate to contact our teachers, administrators, and guidance counselors. You have my word that any such contacts will be confidential. No one but you will know."

No one could be sure how many students sought that kind of help. Nobody spoke about it. Within a week of Mr. Urbansky's initial class, however, six of the original twenty-two students had abandoned the special bridge curriculum, either transferring to traditional courses or because their families had moved from Bay Ridge. There was even talk that the program, despite its merits, might be scrapped in the face of growing parental protests.

That never happened. But one day, we did witness the conflicting views about the program play out right in class.

"This is bullshit," Mitchell Weiner blurted out, halting Mr. Urbansky in mid-sentence.

"Excuse me?" Mr. Urbansky said. No one back then used words like bullshit in school. Few students openly challenged a teacher.

The entire class swiveled to the rear of the room, where the kids whose last names started with the final letters in the alphabet sat. Mitchell rose unsteadily to his feet.

"Did you say something, Mitchell?" Mr. Urbansky asked.

Having qualified for a program called the S.P., and bright enough to have skipped a grade, Mitchell was the smallest kid in class, with oily black hair and a pockmarked face. Normally shy, his sudden bravado stunned everyone into a nervous, curious silence.

"The whole bridge," he sputtered. "All the stuff you're teaching us … "

"Yes?"

"It's nothing … but bullshit."

Mr. Urbansky studied Mitchell for an instant, his expression mirroring a mixture of curiosity and concern.

"I know the Narrows bridge project has been painful to many people," he said tentatively. "We can talk about that if you'd like."

"*Can* we?" asked Mitchell, his voice high-pitched and quavering.

"Sure."

Mitchell rose to his full height, as if summoning every ounce of courage that was present in his delicate frame.

"You're telling us how incredible the bridge is—a work of science and art, a symbol of progress and technology," he said, sniffing. "But you never talk about what it's done to Bay Ridge, how it's destroying our neighborhood."

Mr. Urbansky seemed far less confident on this turf than with his physics lessons. He simply stared at Mitchell, whose hands trembled at his sides.

"There's a whole other side to the bridge, Mr. Urbansky," Mitchell said. "We never talk about that—only physics, as if that's all that matters."

Then Mitchell pointed toward the windows, which opened to a broad view of the bridge construction site.

"What's happening out there is not just about physics, you know," he mumbled. "There's a lot more going on than that."

Mitchell sniffed again.

"I'm sorry, Mitchell," Mr. Urbansky said. "I'm—"

"No," Mitchell interrupted. *"I'm* the one who's sorry. My mother and father are sorry. My whole family is sorry. Our lives are being ruined by the bridge. Destroyed! Can't you see that? Doesn't it matter?"

"Mitchell—"

"No. I hate the bridge! I don't want to learn about it anymore! I don't see the beauty or wonder you talk about. The whole thing is nothing but an ugly piece of concrete and steel. A curse! I wish it was never being built. I wish it would fall into the Narrows!"

Then Mitchell began to weep—silently at first, but soon, despite his efforts to suppress it, loud enough for everyone in class to hear.

"Mitchell—" Mr. Urbansky started.

"No," Mitchell stammered. "Leave me alone. I have to leave!"

Then he stormed past Mr. Urbansky and out the door. And everyone sat there in silence, as Mr. Urbansky, shoulders slumped, stared forlornly at the bridge models on his desk.

Class was dismissed early that day. Mr. Urbansky never said a word about the incident. As for Mitchell Weiner, none of us ever saw him again. His family, we were told, moved the very next week somewhere out west, far from Bay Ridge and Brooklyn, far as they could possibly get from the source of their pain.

THERE WERE DAYS like that. Lots of them. Days when I saw what the bridge was doing to the lives of people like Mitchell Weiner, my parents, our neighbors, my friends. Days when I didn't know what to think or how to feel.

I was trying to see the bridge like my teachers encouraged us to, I really was. I was trying to see beyond the tempest on the streets, beyond the chaos and heartache, beyond the dislocation and grief. I was trying to view things with an open mind, as though they had an upside, as though they were part of an inevitable process of progress and change; the product of creation, not destruction; the product of a conscious choice man was compelled to make—to forge boldly ahead or remain anchored permanently in place.

And yet … I could never be quite sure.

There were days I was ashamed of thinking of the bridge, for even an instant, as anything positive at all, as anything other than a symbol of unwelcome disruption, uncertainty, and emptiness. There were days I was bewildered by the conflict raging within me. How could something have so many different meanings to so many people? How could I possibly feel uplifted and inspired about something that made so many people fearful, frustrated, bitter? How could I love something one moment and hate it the next? Why did progress have to come at the price of such pain?

I struggled to reconcile my feelings. But, instead, all I was left with were more questions. More uncertainty. More confusion. More doubt.

I'd embarked on a journey of self-discovery—that much I could tell. But what that was awakening in me was every bit as perplexing and disturbing as it was eye-opening and exciting. It was a journey with two distinct sides. And it was a journey whose destination, at the moment, was not even remotely in sight.

Chapter 45

With the clock ticking on Dahlgren Place, my mother resumed the city-assisted search to find us another place to live. She wasn't optimistic, but refused to renege on her pledge to assist Mrs. Knudsen in our neighbor's own search for a new residence.

"I know I'm just going through the motions with the city," she said. "But I can't allow Mrs. Knudsen to simply fend for herself. I promised I'd help, and I will."

But this time when my mother and Mrs. Knudsen arrived at the Relocation Bureau, the prospects for assistance seemed more remote than ever. And the line of women awaiting appointments was even longer than before.

"We come back here day after day," one woman grumbled. "We stand around like beggars, and we're just bounced from one person to the next. We're shown apartments we like, but can't afford. Then we're shown places we can afford, but that are unlivable. It's a joke."

Several women nodded.

"Actually, you're lucky," one said, rolling her eyes. "At least you got to *see* apartments. Some of us have been sent to look at places and there's no one there to even show us in. Apartments they told us were vacant were actually occupied. Some addresses they've sent us to don't even exist. Like you say, it's a joke. Only it's not funny."

My mother and Mrs. Knudsen joined the waiting line.

"I'm convinced the city's true aim is to frustrate and demoralize us to a point where we'll just disappear," a woman exclaimed. "Honestly, I think they'd rather see us dead. That'd certainly make things a lot easier for them."

"Oh, dear," whispered Mrs. Knudsen, glancing at my mother for even the tiniest expression of hope.

My mother, however, could offer little on that front. She felt the same suffocating sense of futility as the others. It was fruitless to work with the city, she'd concluded. Nothing constructive would come from a bureaucracy so seemingly tied in knots, from a process so apparently designed to drive people into maddening rage.

"The city keeps promising it'll help," a woman said. "But I don't know."

"Face it," someone told her. "All their talk is just empty words. In the end, you gotta take care of yourself. In the end, you're on your own."

She was right, my mother thought. Nothing of substance was coming in the way of help from the city. The only people who'd help us, in reality, were ourselves.

AFTER A LENGTHY wait, about a dozen women, including my mother and Mrs. Knudsen, were escorted into the Relocation Bureau, where they were greeted by Louis Boudreau, the official who'd met with them during their previous visit. Boudreau set up folding chairs in front of his desk, so he could address the group *en masse*.

"I must tell you," said Boudreau, his fleshy cheeks sagging, "our agency has been working extremely hard to assist people in finding a new home. But we've been thwarted in fulfilling our role."

"How's that?" someone asked.

"To be perfectly candid, I think many of you are being too picky."

"Picky?" the woman asked.

"Yes," Boudreau said. "We feel that many people are purposely balking at the city's attempts to help—resisting out of spite. People aren't happy they're being evicted from their homes, so they're taking their anger out on us by being as difficult as possible."

"That's a crock."

"Well, clearly we're experiencing a difference of opinion," Boudreau continued. "Apartments we consider affordable, you consider too expensive. Apartments we consider suitable, you find inadequate."

"But they *are* inadequate," the woman said. "They're either too small, more than we can afford, or located in lousy neighborhoods. They're nothing like the places we live in now, nothing like Bay Ridge."

"I'm afraid the city disagrees," Boudreau retorted. "The apartments you're being shown, in our view, are at least equivalent to—if not better than—the places you live in now. Keep in mind, many of you have lived in your current residences for years. Rents and home prices aren't what they once were."

"But the city promised it'd relocate us into suitable, equivalent residences," the woman said, clearly frustrated. "It promised us no one would be forced from their homes with no place to live."

Boudreau stared at her, his own frustration evident, too.

"And we're trying to adhere to that promise," he retorted. "Believe me, we're doing all we can. But there are limits. We certainly can't give everyone, and in some cases their lawyers, everything they want."

"I think what you're saying is that you're washing your hands of this, aren't you?" another woman said.

Boudreau started to speak, but was interrupted in mid-sentence.

"You don't really want to help us, do you?" the angry woman cackled. "You just want us to go away. In reality, there's no help coming from you, is there? Just the *pretense* of help."

And with that, three of the women abruptly rose and exited the office. One, looking over her shoulder, made a spitting sound and gave Boudreau the finger.

THE REMAINING GROUP of women, my mother and Mrs. Knudsen among them, sat restlessly as Boudreau excused himself to enter a private cubicle. He emerged moments later with a man he introduced as Howard Seabright.

A tall, dour man with high-cut nostrils and a sparse, uneven mustache, Seabright, Boudreau said, represented the New York City Housing Authority.

"The NYCHA is America's premier public housing authority," Boudreau said. "Its mission is to provide decent, affordable housing in a safe, secure environment for moderate-income New Yorkers."

"Public housing?" one woman blurted. "Now you wanna stick us in the *projects*?"

"I'd rather be dead," another woman said, "than live in any projects."

Boudreau, it was obvious, had hit a raw nerve. White, middle-class Brooklynites, for the most part, wanted nothing to do with public housing. The stigma was that such housing was exclusively for a lower-class social stratum, specifically poor minorities.

"At least give Mr. Seabright a chance to talk," Boudreau scolded. "For God's sake, we're trying to *help* you."

"Help us? By plopping us in Title I? No way!"

Indeed, Title I was an especially dirty word in places like Bay Ridge.

A model for the newest form of residential life in New York, Title I was a federal housing program that had seen billions of dollars earmarked to address America's crumbling inner cities. The program, overseen by none other than Robert Moses, was literally transforming the face of New York's outlying boroughs. Hundreds of blocks in areas deemed blighted were being condemned and bulldozed. In their place, the city was building dozens of slab-like, high-rise housing developments.

The urban renewal effort, however, was creating as many problems as it was supposedly solving. Bleak and monotonous, the city's Title I projects were models of dullness and regimentation, far more ominous-looking than the six-story apartment buildings that had historically housed Brooklyn's middle class. Repetitive brick towers designed without ornamentation, they were widely seen as cold and alienating, symptoms of a flawed social-engineering scheme that dispossessed the poor, devastating neighborhoods and lives.

"There's no way I'm subjecting my family to Title I," a woman said.

"Please," said Boudreau. "Mr. Seabright is *not* here to talk about Title I."

The group stirred in their seats, but grew attentive.

"What he *is* here to talk about, if you'll just give him a chance," Boudreau said, "is a new housing program aimed not at the poor, but at people like *you.*"

Seabright offered a tepid smile. "That's correct. What I'm here to tell you about is public housing for the non-poor—housing for families whose earnings are above income limits for low-rent projects, but perhaps too low for new privately built homes."

Seabright explained that New York had recently launched a landmark housing program using city money rather than federal funds. Rents, he said, were kept low by using the city's borrowing power to finance the developments, which were administered by the NYCHA.

"What do the apartments cost?" a woman asked.

"The city charges sixteen dollars per room per month," Seabright said. "Title I projects go for seven dollars a room. See the difference? And private developments will run you upwards of twenty-five dollars a room."

"So we can get a three-bedroom apartment in these developments … for how much?"

"Three bedrooms with living room, kitchen and bath—six rooms in all—costs ninety-six dollars a month," Seabright replied. "Gas and electric is included."

The women edged forward, but remained silent.

"The apartments," Seabright continued, "are brand new, freshly painted and ready to move in. The rooms are also a lot larger than the ones in Title I. The bathrooms have showers. The toilets come with seat covers. The closets have wooden doors. Each apartment is equipped with a refrigerator and stove."

"People like these apartments," Boudreau interjected, "because they're nice, inexpensive, and don't have the stigma of low-income projects."

"Yeah, but what's the wait like?" a woman asked. "I heard it's two years before anyone can get in … that all we can do is put our name on a waiting list."

"Frankly, that's true in most cases," Boudreau said. "There are only a limited number of apartments available, and eleven thousand applications are already on file."

Several women groaned.

"Based on your hardship, however, the city is making all vacant apartments available to you on a first-come, first-served basis," Seabright said, smiling. "You'll go right to the top of the waiting list."

Several women stirred again in their seats. My mother gently grasped Mrs. Knudsen's hand. Expressionless, our neighbor simply stared ahead.

"Where are these apartments?" someone asked.

Seabright told the group there were several vacancies at the Farragut Houses, a project in downtown Brooklyn, as well as at the Marlboro Houses, a development near the city's sprawling subway repair shop in Coney Island. There were also a few apartments available, he said, at the Fort Greene Houses, a complex that once housed navy yard workers. That complex, which had fallen into disrepair after World War II, had been recently renovated and divided into a pair of developments known as the Walt Whitman Houses and the Raymond V. Ingersoll Houses.

"All are *prime* locations, I'm sure," a woman said, snickering.

"Actually, Fort Greene *is* a good location," Seabright countered. "It's close to subway and bus lines. There's plenty of shopping. Good schools. The Walt Whitman Houses are named after the poet Walt Whitman, who worked as editor of *The Brooklyn Eagle* and actually lived in Fort Greene. So did another famous poet, Marianne Moore—a big Dodgers fan, I might add."

"Like we're supposed to give a shit?" a woman whispered. "What do a couple of poets we never heard of have to do with us?"

"Like I said," Seabright continued, "Fort Greene is nice."

But he was stretching the point, at least in the view of his audience.

The Fort Greene section was bordered on one side by the Brooklyn Navy Yard, and on the other by a several-acre park. In between, rows of brownstone and brick houses lined narrow, tree-lined streets crisscrossed by the busy thoroughfares of Fulton Street and DeKalb, Flatbush, and Atlantic avenues, whose intersection was marked by the thirty-four-story clock tower of the Williamsburgh Savings Bank, the tallest building in Brooklyn.

The problem with Fort Greene, however, had far less to do with its location than with its changing racial composition. Like several other Brooklyn neighborhoods, the community had begun to attract a growing number of poor blacks, migrating to New York from the Deep South. That, of course, was anathema to most whites in Brooklyn.

"Why don't you just put us in that development they're talking about building in Crown Heights, where Ebbets Field used to be?" a woman asked. "That could be the city's final slap in the face. Take away everything we ever loved about Brooklyn and then stick us in the cesspool of what remains."

"Those kinds of remarks," Boudreau said, "are simply not necessary."

"Why not? They're *true*."

And, with that, the woman rose and—like the others before her—left in a huff.

Only eight of the original dozen women remained.

"Can we get to see these apartments?" one of them asked.

"We're prepared to take you there today," Seabright said.

"There's one provision, however," Boudreau interjected.

"What's that?"

"If you're interested, we'll need a commitment immediately."

"*Today*?"

"Yes. Today."

"We wouldn't even have time to think about it—talk it over with our families?"

"I'm afraid not," Boudreau replied. "If you like what you see, our requirement is that you sign a two-year lease right on the spot."

"And if we don't like it?"

"Then the city has fulfilled its obligation to show you two alternative living quarters."

"But that's unreasonable," a woman argued. "It's not fair."

"As I said," Boudreau responded, "the demand for these apartments is enormous, and the apartments need to be rented immediately. We need to know today what your intentions are. We have no choice."

Two of the women rose angrily, knocking over a row of chairs as they stormed off. Seabright and Boudreau remained impassive.

"We have a bus outside, ready to take you there," Boudreau said.

"What do you think?" my mother asked Mrs. Knudsen.

"Oh, I don't know," our neighbor replied. "What about you?"

"Our family, I've decided, will look elsewhere, on our own," my mother said. "But please don't let that affect your decision."

Mrs. Knudsen, her eyes moist and rheumy, smiled weakly.

"I don't think any of these places is for me, Lily," she said. "My entire life has been on Dahlgren Place. To be honest with you, I don't think there'll ever be another place for me to live."

And the two of them, once again, returned to Bay Ridge with nothing to show for their time but additional frustration and heartache.

Chapter 46

It was a blessing in disguise, Selma Klein said. It truly was. We may not see it that way just yet, she told my mother, but one day we would. We'd realize that, difficult as it was, it was really a stroke of luck that we were being forced by the city from our home, forced to find another place to live.

"You're fortunate," said Selma Klein, her bleached red hair coiffed atop her head as she held court at my mother's Friday night mahjong game.

"I mean that, Lily, I really do. The city's doing you a favor."

She drew a cup of coffee to her mouth and took a sip. Seated around her was the usual gathering of women, chatting as they played, the sound of their ivory mahjong tiles slapping against the Formica top of our kitchen table. Even through my half-closed bedroom door, I could make out their words.

Eight crack.

"Getting forced from your home is the best thing that could've happened to you," Selma Klein reiterated.

Seven bam.

"I don't understand," my mother said. "How is being forced from a home we love a good thing?"

Through a haze of cigarette smoke outside my bedroom door, I could see Selma at the far end of the kitchen table, peering over the top of eyeglasses flared at the tips like butterfly wings, a filtered Pall Mall between her manicured fingertips.

Six dot.

"It's a good thing," she said, "because it forces you to leave Bay Ridge. It forces you to think, once and for all, about getting out of Brooklyn."

The women were silent as their mahjong tiles cracked on the tabletop.

Flower.

Soap.

Three crack.

"Can't you see it?" Selma asked. "Brooklyn is falling apart."

East.

"It's dying."

Green.

"It's only gonna go downhill fast."

Six bam.

"Better to get out sooner rather than later."

Mahjong!

"Better to get out … while the getting is good."

WHO COULD ARGUE, really? After all, there were lots of people like Selma Klein around these days. More than ever. And they all seemed to have a valid point: Brooklyn was unraveling at the seams, falling apart, threatening to crash and burn. Everything we'd grown up with was disappearing before our eyes. Everything we'd cherished about Brooklyn was becoming lost in a painful, permanent way.

The Narrows bridge? The expressway through Bay Ridge? Those were only part of a far bigger picture. Symbols. Evidence. Painful reminders that Brooklyn was changing, that nothing about it would ever be the same.

"Look around, girls," Selma said, exhaling a trail of cigarette smoke. "Brooklyn's *gone*. It's nothing but a memory now."

Who could argue? The case was open and shut. The handwriting was on the wall.

The Dodgers were gone for good—that we knew only too well. So were the trolleys, the ferries, the *Daily Eagle,* and so many other familiar totems, ingrained for decades as part of Brooklyn's unique persona. Downtown Brooklyn, overhauled by new development, had already faded as an entertainment and shopping district. Steeplechase Park and Ebbets Field were earmarked for demolition. The navy yard was being decommissioned after more than a century of service. The Brooklyn Academy of Music had slipped into bankruptcy. The Paramount Theater had been converted into a college gymnasium. Just like a modern new city was emerging in Manhattan, a whole new borough was superseding the Brooklyn we'd grown up in.

There was one big difference, however.

Without the tourist attractions or corporate resources of Manhattan, Brooklyn seemed like the aging ballplayers my father talked about: hopelessly past its prime. Tired and damaged. Lost forever amid a swirling sea of change.

And more jarring than the change itself was the sheer speed of it all. Change of this magnitude had never swept across the local landscape so swiftly. But now? Now it seemed as if the slow, steady process of evolution that had shaped Brooklyn across two-plus centuries had been fast-forwarded. Decades of relative constancy had given way to dizzying transformation. The familiar, comfortable texture of everyday life was disappearing literally overnight.

And it was happening not just in Brooklyn, but all over New York.

The entire city, it seemed, was being transformed at lightning speed. Historic structures were being razed. Old-time, European-styled buildings were being replaced by monoliths of glass and steel. Established neighborhoods were being bulldozed. Thousands of people were being displaced by highway construction and urban renewal.

But there was more to what was happening to Brooklyn than merely a swiftly changing landscape. The borough was changing at its very core. Right before our eyes, its great industrial base was fragmenting, its musculature withering like that of someone growing old.

Congested and crowded, its infrastructure crumbling and obsolete, Brooklyn could no longer compete for the industry that once made it a manufacturing powerhouse. Cheap labor and abundant land, the very qualities that once lured industry to the borough, were now driving it away. Manufacturing costs were skyrocketing. Factories couldn't expand. Companies were being chased away by militant labor unions. By moving to modern industrial parks outside the city, they could cut costs, achieve generous tax incentives, gain access to road, water, and rail links. They could grow. Adapt. Survive.

And so they'd begun to leave. A steady stream at first. Growing more pronounced by the year. Fleeing Brooklyn for greener pastures elsewhere. Draining the borough of key resources, its tax base, its energy, its powerful working class.

Sperry Gyroscope, a major force in Brooklyn for decades, relocated to Long Island, along with Eberhard Faber, the pencil factory where my mother once worked. Pharmaceutical giant E.R. Squibb shifted operations to New Jersey after a century in Brooklyn. American Safety Razor Company, which employed fourteen hundred workers, abandoned Brooklyn for Virginia. American Manufacturing Company, once Brooklyn's second largest employer, moved its rope and bagging production out of state.

And it wasn't just the large, well-known companies that were fleeing. Smaller businesses that had flourished in Brooklyn for decades were shipping out, too. Department stores like Namm's and Frederick Loeser's pulled up stakes. Landmark restaurants like Lundy's closed. Even longtime breweries were bidding good-bye. The era of small-batch beers had ended by now. Large, mass-market brewers were invading the city. Transportable cans made it cheaper to produce beer elsewhere and ship it to the city. Brands like Schlitz, Rheingold, Schaefer, and Piels were fast becoming little more than memories.

So was the Brooklyn waterfront.

The shipping industry, for decades a symbol of Brooklyn's booming economy, had undergone monumental changes in recent years. Trucks had replaced ships as America's primary movers of goods. Incoming cargo was no longer being packed in burlap bags and wooden crates, then being offloaded one piece at a time. Brooklyn's traditional break-bulk handling of cargo had become passé. Modern shipping companies were transporting cargo in reinforced-steel containers that doubled as railcars and truck bodies, with cranes hoisting the containers in far less time than it took longshoremen to handle the same volume.

Unequipped to accommodate the new generation of container ships, and lacking land to build new facilities, Brooklyn's waterfront had become outmoded almost overnight. Shippers had no choice now but to set their sights on New Jersey, where massive container ports were being built near convenient forms of transportation. Warehouses, docks, and other port facilities in Brooklyn were no longer needed. Neither were longshoremen and other dock employees. Maritime unions collapsed. Businesses were shuttered.

Within the space of several short years, waterfront activity in Brooklyn had all but vanished, a far cry from the days when the bustling docks had given the borough much of its big-shouldered, take-no-shit identity. In contrast, much of Brooklyn's waterfront now lay abandoned. Shipyards sat idle. Warehouses lay empty. Former factories, their windows broken, stood like barren, eyeless hulks. Wharves and piers were converted to parking lots, bus barns, sanitation garages, and sundecks. Some rotted. Others burned. On some nights from Bay Ridge, we could look north and see dock fires light up the horizon in a dull orange cast, as though the sun was setting somewhere over the far edge of Brooklyn.

In many ways, it was.

SELMA KLEIN TIPPED her mahjong rack to its side, flipped the tiles, and shuffled them across our kitchen table.

"It's all over for Brooklyn, girls," she said. "I know it. You know it, too. The Old Brooklyn is history. What we're getting in its place—God only knows."

The mahjong players selected their tiles and aligned them on their racks. My mother cut several pieces of Danish and served them with a fresh pot of coffee.

"Know what else?" Selma Klein said. "No one in the city gives a damn."

"Why not?" someone asked.

"That's the way the big boys want it. Brooklyn's changing, but that's okay with the people in power. What they're getting now is exactly what they want."

Who could argue with that, too?

Selma Klein, after all, was right.

Like other aging industrial giants across America, time had snuck up on Brooklyn. And time was mandating much of the change.

Most New York power brokers, in truth, were pushing for large sections of Brooklyn to be transformed, backing the conversion of industrial zones into office and residential districts. Property values, they reasoned, would skyrocket if grimy, smog-producing factories were replaced by modern new office towers, civic buildings, housing developments, and parks. Jobs lost in the manufacturing sector would be more than offset by growth in other industries.

And they weren't alone in their thinking. To many civic leaders, New York's destiny no longer lay in industry, but in transforming the city from a manufacturing hub to a consumer's market. A whole new era had dawned—a major turning point in the city's endless, churning evolution. Even as manufacturing firms were fleeing, service industries were flocking to the city. Banking, insurance, real estate, health care, and retail firms were putting down roots. Commodity brokers and the Stock Exchange were asserting their authority. Financial institutions, law firms, advertising agencies, and multi-national corporations were gaining strength. Politicians and business leaders were lauding the shift in focus.

On the bandwagon, too, were most New Yorkers. The city's shift from a blue- to a white-collar economy was widely viewed as positive. Office jobs were seen as cleaner, better-paying, and less grueling than jobs in factories and shops. Manual labor, after all, was for the old generation—or those unable to achieve the social benefits of college. Sure, you could still land a job as a civil servant or teacher, or work in construction. But it was even better to pursue work that had more of a *future*. Administrative, technical, and professional positions allowed people to feel like they were *moving up*, doing better than the previous generation had. Jobs like that allowed people to dress in a suit and tie instead of in overalls and work boots. They allowed people to feel more like human beings and less like machines, more like individuals and less like cogs in a squeaky old wheel.

And so the changes continued unabated—along with the meltdown of Brooklyn.

Much of this, as kids, we hadn't paid attention to. Nor could we have truly understood what was happening. Lost in childhood, oblivious to the changes creeping like a shadow across New York, we were too busy playing, going to school, watching TV, forging friendships, building memories, having fun. Life was simple that way. Problems were something for adults to worry about.

Some changes, however, even *we* couldn't ignore. We couldn't ignore, for example, that Coney Island was beginning to adopt a rundown, delinquent quality, its reputation as a carefree fantasyland starting to erode, its lights growing dimmer in the nighttime sky. We couldn't ignore that kids from Brooklyn were hitchhiking to the cleaner, quieter beaches at Neponset and Riis Park in the Rockaways. We couldn't ignore that more and more people were driving to Jones Beach or to Robert Moses' pristine state parks on Long Island; some were even flying to Florida, the Caribbean, and out West for their vacations.

And we couldn't ignore what was happening to Flatbush Avenue.

Almost overnight, it seemed, the palatial movie theaters along the avenue had gone into a palpable decline. Doomed by their size, victimized by TV, independently owned neighborhood movie houses had lost their communal appeal. People were no longer wowed by large single-screen theaters and ornate trappings. Attendance was down. Film companies were diversifying into other forms of entertainment. Hollywood studios were divesting their holdings, turning to theme parks, selling off their back lots to make way for condominiums and shopping centers. Maintenance costs on the old independents were climbing, leading to neglect. Chain-owned multiplex cinemas were growing in popularity.

All of this had had a chain-reaction effect. The old movie palaces—the places we'd spent our childhood Saturdays in—were fading. Some were being padlocked. Others were being converted to banks, churches, and bargain retail outlets. Without the draw of its weekend movie matinees, Flatbush Avenue no longer held its longtime allure. In recent years, we'd stopped going there almost entirely. So had most other kids in Brooklyn.

And there was yet another thing I couldn't ignore—something even closer to home. It now appeared that the corrosive changes creeping across our lives might also affect my father's company. Like other Brooklyn businesses, Mergenthaler Linotype was rife with whispers about a possible relocation, even closure. It was no secret that business was off markedly from that in the company's heyday. Demand for linotype machines had waned. With the growing popularity of TV, Mergenthaler's largest customers—newspapers—were no longer an indispensable part of people's daily lives. Folios and ad pages were dwindling, along with readership. Suburban commuters, forced to drive instead of taking subways, had turned from evening papers to network news shows. Suburban weeklies were on the rise. Labor conflicts had forced the closure of most of New York's major dailies. The city's vast Yiddish- and Italian-speaking generation was also dying off and, with it, the need for ethnic newspapers. To make matters worse, the hot-type systems that relied on Mergenthaler linotypes were being phased out, replaced by the first wave of offset printing and cold-type photocomposition, the precursor to computers.

"What's the talk at Mergenthaler?" I overheard my mother ask one night.

"You always hear things," my father said. "People talk."

"What are they saying?"

My father paused, apparently anxious not to fuel a growing fire.

"There's talk," he said, "about the company possibly leaving Brooklyn."

"You mean *relocating*?"

"Uh-huh."

"Where to?"

"Long Island. Pennsylvania. Nobody's really sure."

"When?"

"No one knows."

"Why?"

"I suppose they have their reasons."

"Will they be letting people go?"

"That, I can't tell you."

There was a lengthy silence. Then my mother resumed, sounding worried.

"What'll we do, Artie? I mean, if the company moves?"

"We'll make that decision when the time comes, Lily. Right now, it's only a rumor. Nothing but smoke."

Perhaps.

But what *wasn't* a rumor was the fact that Brooklyn was changing in another elemental way: new arrivals were flooding in, longtime residents were abandoning the borough just as quickly, and the population churn was having a dramatic effect.

Neighborhoods that once teemed with first-generation European immigrants, almost entirely white, were filling now with minorities. Blacks, fleeing the Jim Crow South, were settling in Crown Heights, Brownsville, East Flatbush, and Bedford Stuyvesant, joining immigrants from the Caribbean, Africa, and Latin America. Chinese, Koreans, and other Asians were taking up residence on Flatbush Avenue. Soviet émigrés were flocking to Brighton Beach. Haitians, West Indians, Dominicans, Pakistanis, and Indians were forming enclaves along Eastern Parkway.

It hardly mattered that the prospects for Brooklyn's new arrivals were far less glowing than for kids like us, college-bound and reaching for the sky. Many—saddled with the burdens of language and discrimination, poverty and education—were capable of only the most menial jobs. They bused tables and scrubbed pots in the sweaty kitchens of the city's greasy spoons. They pushed racks of clothing through the garment center. They worked as hospital orderlies, drove cabs, emptied trash in the nighttime shadows of Manhattan's office towers.

But still they came, pulled into New York's powerful orbit, melding into the city's alloy of cultures, drawn to Brooklyn for the old, familiar reason: seeing it, like previous waves of immigrants, as an entry point to New York's melting pot. As a staging area. As a place where they could get their feet on the ground, assimilate, consolidate their gains, learn to become American, chase their dreams of a better life.

But more than dreams were arriving in Brooklyn now. Arriving with the newcomers were different complexions. Unfamiliar tongues. Strange new names. Foreign customs. And fear. All forms of it: Fear of crime. Fear of decay. Fear borne of prejudice. Fear unlike anything the borough had ever seen. And it was spreading like an unchecked epidemic. Destructive, hysterical, and irrational—but palpable. And real.

People in Brooklyn no longer walked anywhere they wanted at any hour of the day or night, as they'd done for years. Windows were closed and doors were bolted once darkness fell. Racial tension was rising. In Bensonhurst, a black teen was attacked by a gang of whites simply for wandering into the neighborhood. In seeming retaliation, a white youth was clubbed to death by a group of blacks in Crown Heights. And things, it seemed, were going downhill fast.

Brooklyn, the popular wisdom had it, was in grave peril. People like Selma Klein were talking, and being taken at their word. Neighborhoods, it was said, would fall like dominoes. Already, banks were refusing to approve mortgages in some neighborhoods, driving property values down and feeding the panic. Unscrupulous speculators were exploiting the fear through "blockbusting" and other illegal practices. Landlords were turning their back on real estate improvements.

There was no doubt about it anymore. The greatest mass migration in American history was underway.

As new minorities arrived, more and more middle-class whites fled, as if a powerful tide was washing over Brooklyn, eroding its substrate like sand on a beach. Neighborhood by neighborhood, the working-class families who'd once defined the borough were following the siren call out of town, leaving traditional neighborhoods behind. Off they were going, on the same upward path of past generations. For the same reason their grandparents had escaped the pogroms and *shtetls* of Europe. For the same reasons their parents had fled the squalid tenements of Manhattan. Off to somewhere they thought they could find a better life. Gravitating from the crowded center toward wide open spaces. Heading to greener pastures. Ascending from darkness into light.

EIGHT CRACK.

Two bam.

Seven dot.

I could still hear the mahjong players, chatting as their game wore on.

"I heard the MacDougals are moving," Selma Klein said.

"Really?" someone asked.

"Yep. And the Schmidts are going, too."

"Where to?"

"Long Island."

The mahjong tiles cracked against the kitchen tabletop, like punctuation marks to the nonstop chatter.

Five crack.

"A lot of people are getting out, believe me," Selma said.

Flower.

"They may not admit it but, trust me, if they're not already moving they're thinking about it. They're *looking."*

East.

"They want to get out of Brooklyn … before the colored move in."

There was a long pause, broken only by the calling out of mahjong tiles.

Four dot.

Six bam.

Two crack.

"Face it," Selma said. "No one wants to be around when the *schvartzers* take over."

Eight bam.

"No one wants to be left behind when Brooklyn turns to *dreck.*"

That couldn't be argued, either.

Everyone, it seemed, wanted out now. Along with everything else, people's *views* about Brooklyn had changed. Their mindset was different than ever—far different than during the earliest postwar exodus, when returning servicemen, their pockets flush with combat pay, first began chasing their dreams to the suburban frontier.

Back then, the feeling was that battle-weary GIs had earned a ticket to a better life, an escape from the old ethnic enclaves. They'd earned the right not to have to face a housing crunch that saw them doubling up with parents and in-laws in cramped, stifling city apartments. They'd earned the right not to have to live in converted attics and basements, barns and tool sheds, chicken coops and summer bungalows. They'd earned the right to leave Brooklyn, if that's what they wanted.

But now it was different. People were frightened, pure and simple. Frightened by business closures, by rumors of mass unemployment, by Brooklyn's ethnic changes, by the borough's apparent fate.

Selma Klein had hit the nail on the head.

Brooklyn's Golden Era was history. The innocence and optimism of the early postwar years had dimmed. People were giving up on the tired, old borough, giving up on New York altogether. The entire city, they reasoned, was spiraling into hopeless decline. Its tax base was starting to wither. Its subways were starting to deteriorate. Its crime rate was rising. Its school system was beginning to slip. And on top of everything, it seemed, all of them had *lost their voice*.

Once so powerful, Brooklyn's working populace had somehow grown impotent. Once such a proud part of New York, people like my parents now seemed powerless. Their rallies to keep the Dodgers in Brooklyn had failed. Their bus caravans to keep the navy yard open had been for naught. Their strikes to halt corporate relocations had proven fruitless. Whatever social weight they'd carried once had evaporated. The bridge over the Narrows was being built whether they liked it or not. The expressway through Bay Ridge was being rammed down their throats whether they were in the way or not.

Besides, more and more of their neighbors and friends were moving away. Retirees were leaving for burgeoning new communities in Florida and other warm-weather states. Families were following jobs out of state. People in neighborhoods like Bay Ridge were being forced out. Everywhere you looked, people were leaving. Hell, even the Goldbergs, the fictional Jewish family my parents watched on TV, had moved to Long Island after years in the city.

Brooklyn had been great for a lot of years, people reasoned. It had been great for their childhoods, for most of their lives. But it wasn't great anymore. Brooklyn was for the Old Way, for their parents and grandparents. But the Old Way was fading, and their grandparents were dying off, and they were sure as hell not their parents.

It was time to go with the flow. Time to cut bait and run.

"Can I let you girls in on a little secret?" Selma Klein asked.

"Sure," a woman said.

"*We're* looking, too."

"You are? Where?"

"All over. Long Island. Jersey. Rockland County."

"Where's that?"

"North. Near that Tappan Zee Bridge they just built. Homes are going up all over. These new subdivisions—that's where everyone wants to go now. People want to move up. They want something better. Tell me, what's wrong with that?"

Nothing, the mahjong players agreed.

"What are the houses like?" one of them said.

"They're beautiful. Brand new. There's nothing like them anywhere in the city."

"And the prices?"

"They're not bad. The Schmidts paid eighteen thousand for a three-bedroom in Levittown. No money down. Two-fifty a month for a mortgage, plus gas and electric."

"That's still a lot of money."

"Not to own a brand new house, it isn't."

I heard the mahjong tiles being shuffled so another game could begin.

"To me, if it's a choice between old and overcrowded housing in Brooklyn—living on top of Negroes—or a nice, new home on Long Island, it's no choice at all," Selma declared.

"What about Harry? How'll he get to work?"

"We got a car. He'll drive."

"He doesn't mind?"

"*Mind*—why should he? Believe me, Harry won't mind driving an hour to work for what we're gonna get in return. And I won't mind driving to one of these new shopping malls out there, either. You girls ever see those?"

"No."

"Well, they're nice, believe me. All the shopping you need, right in one location."

I heard the women chuckle, as a new mahjong game began.

Eight dot.

"All this is great," someone asked, "but what about our mahjong game?"

Seven bam.

"Are you kidding?" Selma Klein laughed.

Two crack.

"That's the *least* of your problems."

Six bam.

Seven dot.

Flower.

"With all the people leaving Brooklyn," she said, "you'll be able to find a good mahjong game wherever you go."

Chapter 47

All through that spring, expressway construction inched westward toward the Narrows, continuing the jagged swath through Bay Ridge. Work crews labored through unseasonable heat and drenching rains that pelted the channel and formed swiftly moving rivulets in the cavernous trench. Dump trucks hauled construction materials and debris along traffic-clogged streets. Jackhammers assaulted the ground. Cranes hoisted giant concrete stanchions, setting them on both sides of the carved-out terrain so that the bridge approach could be raised and joined to the body of the span.

Dynamite blasting continued, as well.

By now, the blasting was close enough to Dahlgren Place that photographs and artwork were jarred from our furniture and walls. Kitchen cabinets and hutches were emptied of glassware and dishes. Shelves were stripped of breakables. In our backyard, my mother's wildflowers, choked by rock dust, dangled like stillborn children from their stems and vines.

Similarly lifeless was most of Seventh Avenue. Retail and commercial landmarks that had defined the avenue for decades had long since crumbled under the steel treads of the city's bulldozers. Buildings and walkup apartments along the avenue had been leveled. Intersecting streets had also been obliterated, replaced by rubble-filled lots in which kids played King of the Hill.

Streets nearest the construction zone had also been impacted. Homes seemed somehow withdrawn, almost in shock. Blinds were drawn and doors closed. Stoops, sidewalks, and fire escapes were empty. People rarely ventured out, content to remain indoors with the new wave of color TVs and window-mounted air conditioners sweeping through middle-class Brooklyn.

Proceeding just as methodically was bridge construction. Each day, barges hauled components and equipment to the Narrows construction site, where they were hoisted by derrick boats and met by teams of workers on the partially built span. With the span's underwater foundations and anchorages now in place, the early vestiges of the superstructure had begun to take shape. Just offshore, the Brooklyn tower rose like a gigantic, rust-colored tuning fork. So did its sixty-story, twin-legged counterpart near the Staten Island shoreline. Draped over the tops of both towers, the bridge's four partially completed cables rose and fell across nearly the entire breadth of the Narrows, plunging into the anchorages near each shoreline. Dangling from the massive cables were dozens of vertical suspenders, designed to support the bridge's two road decks. Soon, the deck components would be floated in pre-assembled sections to the job site, raised, and connected to form the overwater portion of the span.

All of this had transformed not just the Narrows, but the entire Bay Ridge shoreline. Formerly occupied by picnickers, walkers, and fishermen, the area was now the scene of construction field offices, work shanties, storage sheds, dumpsters, and rows of portable toilets. Makeshift mixers churned out concrete. Workers and their equipment moved in a beehive of activity.

And all of it was clearly visible from our classroom.

"What a beautiful day for bridge-building," Mr. Urbansky would often say, beaming and gesturing toward the slate-gray waters of the Narrows, where the early-morning fog lifted like a curtain on the construction site.

Mr. Urbansky seemed more enthusiastic than ever. Now he had something other than photos and drawings to illustrate his lessons. Now he had something tangible to show us.

We learned about each of the bridge's key components: how the anchorages were giant structures that literally anchored the bridge to the earth; how the towers were designed to support the bridge's cables and transfer the weight of the suspended structure through their foundations to the earth below; how the vertical hanger cables carried the weight of the road decks; how the bridge's four load-bearing cables were each the product of thousands of miles of wire carried from anchorage to anchorage by bicycle-like spinning wheels mounted on diesel-powered pulleys.

But for all its complexity, Mr. Urbansky told us, the Verrazano-Narrows Bridge would be a classic example of pure, functional architecture—a triumph of simplicity and restraint, possessed of a form that was almost serene.

"This bridge," he explained, "will be sleek and absent of ornamentation. In many ways, it'll be the most beautiful form of architecture man is capable of."

He smiled, seeming satisfied that his words were hitting home.

"And it's the creation," he said, "of a man whose vision and talents soar like the majestic structures he builds."

He pronounced the man's name for us as he spelled it on the blackboard.

"Ahh-mann," he said. "Othmar Ammann. The foremost bridge designer of the twentieth century. Some say the greatest ever."

Mr. Urbansky taught us about the visionary bridge-builders who'd helped shape modern-day New York, referring to them as gifted renaissance men with talents not only in engineering, but in music, language, art, sociology, and philosophy. He taught us about John Roebling, whose century-old Brooklyn Bridge stood as a hallmark of structural integrity and exquisite beauty. He taught us about Gustav Lindethal, a turn-of-the-century master driven by his pursuit for perfection. He taught us about David Steinman, who'd built bridges he equated to symphonies of stone and steel.

But Othmar Ammann, Mr. Urbansky said, was his favorite of all.

Then in his eighties, the Swiss-born Ammann had designed or consulted on dozens of America's greatest bridges, including no less than seven of New York's major spans.

Describing Amman's talents as if he were speaking of a legendary painter or musician, Mr. Urbansky explained how the great bridge-builder had brought a true aesthetic quality to the science of structural design, and how his bridges were not simply soaring marvels of creativity, but enduring monuments to ingenuity and beauty. He praised Ammann's loyalty to simple, elegant lines and classic forms, extolling the engineer's ability to create stark, modern steel towers that were very different from the granite towers and Gothic-style arches of the fabled Brooklyn Bridge but, in their own way, just as beautiful. He told us how the unassuming, studious Ammann was meticulous in his calculations and redundant in his safety measures, yet counted himself merely lucky that none of his bridges had ever collapsed. Ammann, Mr. Urbansky said, was also almost *sentimental* about his creations, once referring to his George Washington Bridge as something akin to a beautiful daughter.

Each day, we were told, Ammann sat at the window of his suite on the thirty-second floor of Manhattan's Carlyle Hotel, twelve miles away, peering through a telescope to monitor the progress of the Verrazano-Narrows Bridge.

"This bridge," Mr. Urbansky said, "will no doubt be the final creation of this aging master. The world will be poorer when he passes on, but the physical monuments he created will live on for centuries."

Mr. Urbansky smiled one of his special smiles.

"It would be nice to leave a legacy like that, wouldn't it? Wouldn't it be nice to make a lasting and meaningful difference in the world?"

Most of the class nodded.

"Well," Mr. Urbansky winked, "maybe some day one of you will."

Even before he'd said it, I'd begun to think it could even be me, believing it more and more with each passing week.

I found myself literally transfixed by what Mr. Urbansky was teaching, passing his tests with flying colors. With the class genius, Mitchell Weiner, having moved, I'd finish the school year with the top grades in the program.

But something even more important was happening. Mr. Urbansky's physics class was proving to be nothing short of a revelation to me, an awakening to things about myself that, until then, had been dormant. It was as if, in the midst of the chaos in Bay Ridge, a bright light had suddenly been cast on what had formerly been darkness. Something was building inside me now, as surely as the bridge being built outside our classroom. A direction. A goal. A course for my life.

Mr. Urbansky had been right all along. I could see that now. Our ability to bear witness to the construction of the bridge was nothing short of a gift.

And so, in his own way, was my teacher. Through his lessons, Mr. Urbansky was transforming a mundane physical structure into something infinitely more wondrous and magical than my teenaged mind might otherwise have grasped. Through his eyes I was seeing the bridge as more than the sum of its cables and beams, arches and cantilevers, angles and curves; more than even the engineering masterpiece touted by planners—or the metal behemoth cursed by protestors. I was seeing how a brilliant idea, abetted by the principles of science and math, could be transformed into something lasting, something that could evoke emotion, something that could lift people to a higher place and allow them to dream.

Unexpectedly, miraculously almost, the same bridge that was destroying the neighborhood I loved had somehow set me to dream. My imagination fired, the dream growing by the day, I began to believe that maybe one day I, too, could build bridges like the one rising in the Narrows, bridges that could make other people feel everything I was feeling, bridges that could move people to create other great things.

I was feeling something else now, too.

The bridge and expressway were leading me to wonder where they *really went*—what they led to, what lay beyond the safe, provincial borders of Brooklyn. I wondered what it would be like to cross the bridge and venture far beyond the confines of Bay Ridge to cities like Boston and Miami, regions like the Midwest and Sunbelt, landmarks like the Rocky Mountains and the Grand Canyon, even to Los Angeles, where the Dodgers now played.

Maybe there really was a wider world out there to explore, I thought. Maybe the world didn't begin and end with my bicycle rides through Brooklyn. Maybe the bridge could really *take me places*.

Stirred by my growing sense of self-discovery, I wanted to share what I was feeling with someone. But I couldn't imagine who—and I couldn't imagine *how*. The few remaining friends I had in Bay Ridge? No way. They'd laugh me to kingdom come. My parents? Perhaps, but not quite yet. No. What I was feeling about the bridge—what I was dreaming I could do with my life—couldn't be shared with anyone, at least for the moment. Besides, it was only just assuming a tangible form. The words needed to explain it were far beyond my teenaged grasp.

No. I'd keep quiet for now, keep my thoughts and feelings locked up inside—allowing them, like the bridge itself, to assume a distinct shape and transport me to wherever I was destined to go.

I found myself wondering if my father could remember when he was my age, inspired by the Depression-era marvels reshaping New York—the kind of architectural treasures inspiring me now. I wondered if it was possible that I'd get to live the dream he'd been forced to abandon, if I'd get to build the things he never could. I remembered how he'd told me that, no matter what I did, I should always take the time to dream—how he'd said that even though everyone lived to have regrets, there were also surprises that came along in life, things that made the regrets easier to take.

I regretted being forced to give up the life we'd known in Brooklyn. I regretted the pain the bridge had caused so many people, including my own family. But I knew I'd also blindly stumbled upon one of those surprises my father had told me about. I'd discovered it in Mr. Urbansky's classroom. I'd found it in the bridge.

Chapter 48

The city's third offer on our house arrived weeks before the end of school. Stamped URGENT, the offer, we were informed, was the final one—in essence, a notice to take it or leave it. Our only recourse to prevent outright seizure of our home, the letter stated, would be a protracted and potentially costly legal challenge.

"What are they offering this time?" my father asked.

"Thirteen-two," my mother said.

"Okay," my father nodded. "At least they upped it a bit."

"I still don't know," my mother said. "Our home is worth more than thirteen thousand, two hundred dollars. We've lived a lifetime here, Artie. Our memories alone are worth more than that."

"The city's not gonna pay us for our memories, Lily," he replied. "You know that and so do I. They'll never be able to pay what our home is truly worth to us. All they're paying for is the least they can for the four walls, the roof, and the land. That's a fact of life we have to accept."

My mother squinted thoughtfully. "I know. But maybe we should hold out for more—fight the offer."

"You mean take the city to court?"

"If that's what it takes—yes."

My father paused. He didn't want to risk another confrontation, it was clear. They'd gotten too far past that point to return to it now.

"Can we really afford a legal fight?" he asked.

"Probably not. But some people in Bay Ridge have served as their own lawyer in cases against the city. Or they've found lawyers willing to take their case for free."

My father contemplated that possibility. "There's no guarantee we'd win if we went to court, is there?"

"No," my mother said. "And the odds are we'd probably lose."

He hesitated again. "You sure you really want to fight this?"

"No, Artie, I'm not." My mother shook her head glumly. "To tell you the truth," she admitted, "I'm tired of fighting now, too."

"All of us are, Lily," my father agreed. "I don't think fighting anymore is gonna get us much further, and I'm not sure it's worth either the money or the heartache. As much as we love and value this house, maybe it's time we faced reality and just accepted the city's offer."

My mother said nothing.

"How much do we still owe on our mortgage?" my father asked.

"About seven thousand."

"Okay," he reasoned, "so we take the thirteen-two they're offering, pay off the seven, and that leaves us with what—sixty-two hundred dollars, right?"

"Round it off to an even six thousand after expenses," my mother said.

"Okay. Well, that could be enough for a down payment on another house."

My mother, once again, was pensive and silent. "Where?"

"I'm not sure. We need to look around."

"We already *saw* what the city was showing us," my mother said. "That got us a big nothing."

"I know. But that was public housing. There's an awful lot of private construction going on these days. There may be more options available than we think. We can look anywhere we want."

"In Brooklyn?"

"In or out of Brooklyn."

My father was certainly right about that. There were, indeed, plenty of options to consider. Aside from the burgeoning suburban communities in Long Island, New Jersey, and north of the city, New

York City itself was in the midst of the greatest building boom in decades, with new homes and apartments sprouting up in nearly all five boroughs. Two- and three-story garden apartment complexes were being built in Queens. Co-op housing projects were rising on vacant lots in the Bronx. Single-family suburban-style homes were going up in Staten Island, in anticipation of the bridge. And large subdivisions of attached and semi-attached townhouses, along with single-family units, were cropping up at the eastern end of Brooklyn—in neighborhoods like Mill Basin and Canarsie.

"I'd start looking right there," my father suggested. "In Canarsie."

"But that's just vacant land. Nothing but landfills and swamps."

"Not anymore, Lily. It's being built up pretty quickly, from what I hear. Homes, schools, roads, you name it."

"What kind of homes?"

"Nice, from what people are saying. New. Lots of amenities. More of a suburban feel than older neighborhoods like Bay Ridge. Far enough away to give us a new start, but not so far that it'd feel like a foreign country. We'd still be close to family and friends. I'd still be able to get to work easily. It would still be Brooklyn—just a different part."

My mother thought it over.

"All right, Artie," she conceded. "I'll notify the city that we'll accept their offer. Thirteen-two may not be all that our house is worth, and God knows we'll need every penny of it for a new place, but it's more money than we ever had at one time before."

"By a long shot," my father chuckled. "It'll sure feel good, while it lasts."

Then the two of them laughed and shared a kiss.

Our search for a new home, months after it actually began, was now underway in earnest.

Chapter 49

To people growing up in the heart of 1950s Brooklyn, Canarsie seemed at the very edge of the earth, an undeveloped wilderness adjacent to Jamaica Bay in the low-lying Flatlands section, near Brooklyn's eastern border with Queens.

Founded decades earlier as a fishing village, the area had once served as a honky-tonk resort, with speakeasies, vaudeville houses, beer gardens, and amusement rides drawing throngs of summertime visitors. But while most of Brooklyn had been transformed across decades of development, little about Canarsie had truly changed. Even now, the area consisted largely of vast stretches of undeveloped marshland, dusty roads, tiny truck farms, and acres of cattails, scrub brush, and wild horse grass.

Canarsie, for years, had also been the butt of Borscht Belt jokes—derided as an aboriginal, foul-smelling backwater—and with good reason. Large tracts of land were used by the city for garbage dumping. Mountainous landfills lured swarming flocks of seagulls. Clamming and fishing operations had been halted by the pollution of Jamaica Bay.

But Canarsie wasn't a joke to many people anymore. Easily accessible via the Belt Parkway—the six-lane road built as a circumferential route around Brooklyn—the area was in the midst of a dramatic transformation. City officials and private developers had targeted Canarsie as Brooklyn's new housing frontier, an attraction for middle-class residents looking to flee the borough's older neighborhoods in search of suburban amenities close to home. Much of the area's former swampland was being drained and filled in. Several NYCHA-run apartment buildings overlooking Jamaica Bay had been built. Newer developments were cropping up as well. A complex of single- and two-family suburban-style homes, known as Seaview Village, was under construction.

"Let's take a ride there and see what the fuss is about," my father said one Sunday, and we piled into his Plymouth for the half-hour drive.

Running along Brooklyn's western perimeter, the Belt Parkway carried us past Coney Island, Brighton Beach, and a string of other shoreline neighborhoods, including Sheepshead Bay, where the city's fleet of commercial fishing boats lay moored to a long stretch of docks.

"That's where your mother and I took our ferry ride from on our first date," my father said.

"Out to Breezy Point," my mother reminisced.

"And the rest," my father said, "is history."

They laughed at their own special memories, the sum of their life together, the kinds of things only long-time married couples could share. It was good to see them like that, the weight of the past year having lifted a bit, their bond no longer seeming so threatened by the trauma in Bay Ridge.

Bobby Darin was on the car radio singing "Mack the Knife," and then Elvis with his number-one hit "It's Now or Never."

My mother hummed to the music. My father opened his window and the cool, sea-scented air rushed into the car.

As we drove, the brick-and-concrete backdrop of Brooklyn fell away, opening to a cloudless sky that seemed to touch the glistening waters of Gravesend and Jamaica Bays. We drove past miles of marshy shoreline and craggy beach dunes; past inlets, streams, creeks, and estuaries fed by the daily sweep of the ocean tide. Visible through lush, high vegetation were a string of telephone poles, tiny stilted houses, and the ruins of abandoned Quonset huts and wooden shanties. Cabin cruisers in dry dock sat alongside newer homes and marinas on Mill and Paerdegat Basins. To the west, Swinburne and

Hoffman islands, slips of land used once to quarantine immigrants with infectious diseases, sat low in the water. Beyond them, the Staten Island shoreline gave way to Sandy Hook, a barrier peninsula in New Jersey, and then to the Atlantic Ocean, stretching to the horizon.

"I can't believe this is still Brooklyn," my sister said.

"It's still a wilderness in some ways, but the area is changing," my father said. "We come from the *old* Brooklyn. What you're seeing now is the *new* Brooklyn. And it's all happening very fast."

All around us was evidence he was right. Once we exited the parkway, we could see that the transformation of Canarsie was nearly frenetic in its pace. Construction equipment was strewn everywhere. Bulldozers scooped and cleared large mounds of earth. Crews unloaded appliances and plumbing fixtures from tractor-trailers. Workmen scurried about, building concrete forms for sidewalks, climbing across the wooden frames of partially built houses, wielding hammers, cutting pipe, laying brick, setting roof tiles.

It was a familiar sight, similar to what we witnessed each day in Bay Ridge. But here, houses were being built; nothing was being demolished. Everything was new. Even the way of life.

We drove on newly paved roads through one of the subdivisions—a mini-community consisting of block after block of two-story brick townhouses with concrete porches and narrow driveways that sloped down toward single-car garages. Those homes, selling for twenty-five thousand dollars, were being snapped up even before ground was broken on construction. In other sections of the neighborhood, split-levels and ranches were rising on quarter-acre lots—more expensive at about forty thousand dollars, but selling just as fast.

New streets and sidewalks were also under construction, tying sections of the community together. Several low-slung, suburban-style schools had already been built, a sharp departure from the red-brick, turn-of-the-century schools sprinkled through most of Brooklyn. Asphalt-covered schoolyards with handball courts, softball diamonds, and basketball hoops were being completed.

There was even a park with grass-and-clay ball fields, just like the ones at Owl's Head Park.

"Hey, this is pretty exciting," said my father, his enthusiasm genuine. "Maybe Bay Ridge isn't the only place to live, after all."

"Maybe not," my mother agreed tentatively, still aching for the unique character of our existing home and the look of older, established Bay Ridge, but willing, out of necessity, to make concessions.

"It sure has a lot to say for it," my father said.

Even my sister, slumped sullenly in the rear seat next to me, couldn't help but agree.

"It's okay, I guess," she admitted.

"What do *you* think, Nathan?" my father asked.

"I like it," I responded, sincere in my answer.

"Think you could live here?"

"Yeah, I think so," I said, trying to envision moving to Canarsie and starting a new life—but not quite ready to let on yet that an entirely different scenario, something far more improbable, was also taking shape in a quiet corner of my mind.

Chapter 50

By late spring, some days were warm enough for Mr. Urbansky to move his classes to a grassy knoll outside our school, a hillside perch that afforded us an unobstructed view of the bridge construction site.

We were hardly alone in our interest. Joining us outdoors were dozens of observers, many of them retired construction workers who sat bundled on lawn chairs along the shoreline, shading their eyes from the sun or peering through binoculars as they carried on a non-stop commentary about the project.

There was certainly enough going on to hold their attention. Up on the bridge, hundreds of men were busy at work. Steelworkers, tethered to the superstructure by safety belts, treaded across beams and girders, positioning and securing steel components. Concrete workers, electricians, and carpenters moved along flimsy catwalks supported by guy wires and rigged with sections of chain-link fence to prevent them from falling over the edge. Ironworkers straddled the bridge's thick, swooping cables, checking connections and tightening bolts. Others baked rivets in coal-burning forges, tong-tossing the red-hot bolts to workmen who caught them in metal pails, then positioned them while riveters used pneumatic hammers to drive them into place.

As amazing as anything to me was the fact that the workmen labored with no safety nets beneath them, nothing to prevent them from plunging, with the slightest misstep, hundreds of feet into the water.

"I've taught you about the major components of the bridge and the key principles involved in design and construction," said Mr. Urbansky, raising his voice over a stiff inland breeze. "What I haven't told you about is how none of it would be possible—*none of it*—without the men up there on that bridge."

Mr. Urbansky handed us a pair of binoculars, which we passed around for a closer look.

"The workmen on that bridge are fearless," said Mr. Urbansky, making what we were seeing sound like a daring form of aerial artistry. "Imagine working six hundred feet above the water, balancing on beams, being battered by wind gusts that constantly change direction. One wrong step and you're dead."

There were upward of a thousand workmen on the bridge at any given time, Mr. Urbansky told us. Twelve thousand in all would be needed to handle the project from start to finish, mostly ironworkers and bridge-builders from unions in Brooklyn and Manhattan, as well as itinerant workers known as boomers because they moved from city to city, job to job, following the building boom around America.

Then there were the Caughnawagas.

"*Indians*," Jimmy Franklin, a classmate, whispered in a way that conjured the images of Native Americans that we'd grown up with—savages who roamed the prairies of the Wild West.

"Those guys are famous," Franklin said. "They built most of the buildings in the city."

Indeed, that wasn't far from the truth. A tribe of mixed-blood Mohawks, the Caughnawagas maintained a permanent home four hundred miles north on a reservation near the U.S.-Canada border. Their impact on New York, however, had been considerable since before the turn of the century.

Before that time, the Caughnawagas had established a quiet, peaceful life on their reservation, farming, making snowshoes, and working in the timber-rafting industry. Some peddled medicines brewed from native plants. Others roamed the United States and Canada, dancing and war-whooping for circus crowds.

But life for the tribe changed dramatically in the late-nineteenth century. It was then that the Dominion Bridge Company began building a cantilevered railroad bridge across the St. Lawrence River, crossing at a point near the reservation. Caughnawagas were hired as day laborers for the project, unloading boxcars and performing other menial tasks. Quickly, however, they demonstrated a far different aptitude: oblivious to heights, unnerved by the clamor of work around them, blessed with a unique blend of agility and balance, they were natural-born bridge-builders.

Drawn instinctively to the work, Caughnawagas were soon climbing all over the partially built bridge, balancing calmly on steel platforms, scrambling across beams and girders, functioning in small, well-coordinated teams, and earning the nickname "skywalkers."

And, thus, a tradition was born.

High-steel work was tough and unforgiving, but it paid well and quickly became a source of enormous pride. No longer were the Caughnawagas considered trivial. No longer were they relegated to a sad, irrelevant future. Of the two thousand men on the reservation, seventeen hundred became ironworkers, redefining who the Caughnawagas were, adding strength to tribal bonds, and forging a legacy.

Caughnawaga ironworkers basked in a glory uniquely their own. Ironworkers held a special place in the tribal heart. Their achievements were heralded. They earned the respect of elders, the admiration of children, the affection of women in the tribe. The graves of men who perished on construction jobs occupied a sacred place in the tribe's burial ground, marked forever by crosses cut from iron and steel.

Their legend spreading, Caughnawaga work crews were soon involved in all types of high steel. Seeing themselves as mountain builders, they flocked to the sites of the man-made mountains reshaping North America, helping erect the buildings, bridges, and other structures that formed the skylines of modern cities. Their gypsy-like work took them to Cleveland, Buffalo, Pittsburgh, Detroit.

And, of course, to New York.

By the time work began on the Verrazano-Narrows Bridge, Caughnawagas had already left an indelible mark on America's greatest city, having helped build many of Manhattan's most famous skyscrapers and virtually all of New York's bridges.

Most maintained weekday residences a short distance from Bay Ridge, in furnished rooms, rental flats, and hotels near the ironworkers union hall in North Gowanus. Known as Downtown Caughnawaga, the enclave, like others in Brooklyn, was a product of companionship and familiarity. Local groceries and restaurants catered to Caughnawaga dietary needs. A church conducted services in the tribe's native language. On weeknights, in smoke-filled bars with names like The Wigwam and The Reservation, Caughnawaga ironworkers drank, raised a ruckus, and spent a good part of their five-hundred-dollar weekly paychecks. On Friday nights, their pockets flush with cash, they piled into cars and sped up the New York State Thruway on whiskey-fueled jaunts to their reservation, arriving to joyous receptions. Then, early each Monday, they'd return to Brooklyn.

The Caughnawagas fascinated me as much as the bridge itself. I saw them as tough and fearless beyond anything I could ever be: cocky, strong, hard-living, their complexions ruddy from the wind, sun and heat, their bodies marred by the blisters, burns, and scars of their work. I envisioned them in their bars, their tool belts and hard hats slung on racks, quashing down whiskey and beer chasers, arm-wrestling, cursing, shooting dice, boasting about who could lift the most steel, drive the most rivets, spin the most cable.

"Those guys have balls of steel," Jimmy Franklin said.

I agreed, peering through the binoculars so I could see them at work in the distance, looking like spiders building an enormous web.

"You think you could work up there, Wolf?" Franklin asked.

"I don't know."

"Well, I do." Franklin laughed. "You'd shit in your pants, I'd bet. All of us would. They'd have to carry us off the bridge on a stretcher."

I had little doubt he was right.

But I saw the Caughnawagas in a different way, beyond the macho qualities I was sorely lacking. I saw them as unlike anyone I'd ever met in Brooklyn—born to a different culture, holding different values, adhering to different traditions, possessing a different view of the world, prideful and courageous in a way I never could be. I saw them as legitimate legends come to life, coming from far away yet leaving an indelible mark on my city.

I wanted to know more about them, hear their stories, roam the country like they did. I wanted to know what it felt like to work high up on the bridge, girders clanging, sparks flying, the Manhattan skyline aglow in the early morning sunrise, the wind whining like music through the cables. I wanted to know what it felt like to be up there in the clouds, high above the waters of New York Bay, walking in the sky. And then driving to a place where old men cheered my arrival, young children gathered in awe, and women welcomed me to their beds.

I wanted to know all that. Just like I wanted to know for the first time what lay beyond Bay Ridge. Just like I wanted to know if a boy like me could one day be carried far from home, far from Brooklyn, by his great and growing dreams.

Chapter 51

Searching for another home became a new kind of ritual for my parents, as ingrained in their weekly routine as attending to their jobs, doing housework, or socializing with friends.

Early each Sunday, the two of them embarked on daylong excursions to various parts of Greater New York, checking out the housing developments cropping up around the region. Canarsie and adjacent new neighborhoods were still possibilities, but my parents' search soon broadened well beyond Brooklyn—beyond even the borders of New York City itself. Before long, they were looking at homes north of the city, in Westchester and Rockland Counties, as well as east, in Long Island, and west, in New Jersey.

The choices, they discovered, were eye-opening. Fueled by the forces reshaping New York, including the mass exodus from Brooklyn and the newly built highways circumventing the city, a sweeping new vision was reshaping the entire metropolitan region. The suburbs were hotter than ever. Developers were gobbling up vast expanses of open land all around the expanding fringes of the city. Thousands of homes a week were being built on former cornfields, orchards, and potato farms. Entire new communities were being stitched together virtually overnight.

And the demand was intense. Builders and real estate developers knew precisely how to market and sell the suburban way of life. In some new communities, people were sleeping in line to sign up for a chance to buy a house.

"There's no doubt anymore that we should buy *new*," my father said one day, ticking off the advantages of a newly-built house rather than an older, pre-existing dwelling.

"Think about it," he reasoned. "It'd be like buying a new car instead of a used one. We'd be the first people to live there. Everything—appliances, electrical, plumbing, windows, roof—would be new, guaranteed to function. There'd be no surprises. You wouldn't be inheriting someone else's headaches. You never know what you're really getting when you buy an older house."

"But what would you do with all your free time, Artie?" my mother joked.

"Whaddaya mean?"

"I mean, what would you do with yourself if you didn't have things to fix around the house?"

"Maybe I'd take you out more often." My father winked, and the two of them laughed.

They were doing far more of that lately, laughing like they used to before the hubbub over the bridge nearly tore our lives apart.

"We've never really owned anything *new*, have we?" my mother asked.

"Not in this life," my father replied. "But maybe it's time we did."

The two of them laughed again.

"You're right, Artie," my mother said. "Maybe we've finally earned something new to call our own."

NEW YORK'S BURGEONING new suburbs were a far cry from anything the region had ever seen—and, unlike in the past, they were being targeted not at the city's elite populace but at the expansive, restless middle class looking to flee traditional, changing neighborhoods like Bay Ridge.

Streamlined construction techniques, adopted from World War II production methods, had dramatically reduced the cost of building, bringing homes within the reach of most working families. New types of construction material—plywood, gypsum board, copper tubing—were available in abundance. Cheap, boxlike houses using pre-cut, pre-assembled, standardized components set on concrete slabs could be mass-produced by work crews with highly specialized skills. Those cookie-cutter homes started at about nine thousand dollars, topping out at just under twenty thousand.

And the homes were selling like hotcakes, too. Financing options made them highly attractive, particularly to veterans like my father, who could purchase government-approved homes with no money down, using federally guaranteed, low-interest mortgages. Property tax incentives made the deals even sweeter.

Suburban living, it was clear, was no longer strictly the province of college-educated, white-collar workers. Now, just about anyone with a decent, steady job could handle the monthly nut. Even average blue-collar stiffs from Brooklyn. Even people like my parents.

Equally appealing to the suburbs' affordability was their accessibility; they were easier than ever to get to. Built on empty tracts of land instead of around existing infrastructure, like earlier suburban outposts, the new communities no longer needed to be located strictly along commuter rail and bus lines; now they could be plopped down literally *anywhere.* The modern parkway system that now looped New York—thanks, ironically, to Robert Moses—had made that possible. Not only had Moses' roads, tunnels, and bridges opened up whole new areas to development, they'd tied the region together in a whole new way. Homes no longer needed to be built in the shadows of the city. Businesses could be located virtually anywhere. Everything anyone needed—shopping, schools, parks, places of worship—could be reached in minutes. Theaters, restaurants, museums, sporting events, and other attractions were just a short drive away. All you needed was a car. And everyone, these days, had a car.

My parents, in truth, had never viewed the suburbs as a viable option until now. They'd always loved Brooklyn, wanted to remain tied to the life they'd had, even though things there weren't always easy, even though the city was changing. They didn't want to give up on New York, didn't want to surrender.

But the suburban dream was seductive. There was a romance to it. Status, too. To most people like my parents, moving *out* meant moving *up*. It was a statement that you'd *arrived*, reached another plateau in the American Dream, worked your way up and moved to greener pastures. Sure, their years in Brooklyn had been special. Sure, they had great memories of a childhood spent playing on streets, playgrounds, and schoolyards, surrounded by family and friends. But Brooklyn was for their childhood. And besides, like Selma Klein said, Brooklyn was history. It was old and tired. Chaotic and crumbling. Dying.

But there was more to the great suburban exodus than simply the widespread belief that Brooklyn's best days were behind it: people *liked* what they saw in the new towns outside New York City. Suburbia, to most people, was everything that Brooklyn wasn't anymore. It spoke of a different spectrum of values and emotions: optimism and prosperity in contrast to decline and despair; a bright new future instead of a tired old past. The suburbs had everything people wanted to run *toward* instead of *from*: a brand new home with modern conveniences. Fresh air. Open space. An escape from cramped, sweltering apartments and the tumult of the city. An escape from the minorities transforming Brooklyn.

You could live differently in the suburbs. That's what people were saying. You could grab your own little piece of heaven. No longer living like the Kramdens, in their two-by-nothing flat on Chauncey Street, with hand-me-down furniture and desperate dreams of escape. No longer like Chester Riley, commuting with his lunch pail on crowded subways to a sweaty Brooklyn factory.

Different.

More in line with the postwar American Dream. More like Ozzie and Harriet Nelson, in fictional Hillsdale. More like the Cleavers, in their tidy little house in Mayfield. More like the Andersons in *Father Knows Best*. More like TV and Madison Avenue were telling everyone it could be. In gracious, cozy homes. On safe and quiet streets. In towns where kids could go to clean, modern schools instead of antiquated, densely packed ones. Where they could play on manicured grass fields instead of in concrete playgrounds or on heavily trafficked streets. Where they could join the Cub Scouts and Little League instead of succumbing to the growing scourge of juvenile delinquency. Where they could grow up sheltered. Be safe. Be happy.

AS THE WEEKS passed and their search continued, I saw my parents gradually succumbing to the whole suburban notion.

"Maybe Long Island is the answer for us, after all," my father suggested one night, pronouncing the area *Lawn Giland*—like most people from Brooklyn did. "It's got a lot going for it, you know?"

"Oh, I don't know," my mother said. "All the houses they're building out there kind of look the same. They're so … "

"So … *what*?"

"So vanilla. Bland. The whole area seems so sterile, nothing like Brooklyn."

"That's the whole idea, Lily. People don't *want* Brooklyn anymore. You hear what they're saying: they'd rather live in a vanilla suburb than a chocolate city."

"You feel that way, Artie?"

"Not really."

"Me neither."

"But we're not leaving Brooklyn out of choice, like a lot of people. We're being forced out, remember? Why turn our backs on the option of having something new in the suburbs?"

"Yeah, but those homes—I mean, they're nice in a way, but they just don't have the character, the details, the uniqueness of our house here. They sure don't have the memories."

Even my father had to agree.

"I see your point," he said. "But, that's the reality today, Lily. Everything's changing. So are homes. They're not being built the way they once were. That's another fact of life we've gotta accept."

"I suppose."

"And as far as memories go—yes, we have some wonderful memories in Brooklyn. But maybe we can create some new ones out there. Maybe we can be just as happy on Long Island as we've been on Dahlgren Place."

My mother mulled the thought.

"Can we afford it, Artie?"

"Why not? What do you think it'll cost, when you break it all down?"

"Oh, I don't know. A decent house out there will probably run three, four hundred dollars a month."

"Well, lots of people seem to be finding a way to handle it," my father said. "Just look how fast the Island is growing."

My mother was silent.

"Let's put a pencil to paper and figure it out," my father suggested. "I'm in line for a raise soon. That'll help."

"What about a VA mortgage? Would we qualify for that?"

"I don't see why not. I did my four years of service."

My mother thought it over.

"I suppose I could always help out more, too," she volunteered. "Now that the kids are older, I could go back to work full time. I'm sure I could find something on the island."

"A lot of businesses are moving there, that's for sure," my father agreed.

My mother shook her head affirmatively, the idea seeming to take hold.

"Okay," she said finally. "Let's try and figure out a way."

WITHIN WEEKS, MY parents' search had led them to a tiny suburban town on Long Island known as Valley Stream.

"We want you to come and take a look," my father told my sister and me the night they returned. "We think we may have found something all of us will like."

By now, my sister had reluctantly accepted the idea that we were really moving and that there was little she could do about it. Of course, I also had my own ideas about the impending move, but was still keeping them close to the vest.

"Is it another house?" my sister asked.

"A whole new community," my mother replied.

"Actually," my father said, "a whole new way of life."

Lying east of Queens, in Nassau County, Valley Stream was the closest town to the borderline between Long Island and New York

City. To reach it we drove on the Belt Parkway, well past Canarsie this time, out of Brooklyn, and then through Queens.

Soon we were passing through a park-like area of open land, groves of trees, and wildflowers reminiscent of those that had once grown in my mother's garden. Azaleas burst from roadside bushes. Colonial- and Tudor-style homes lined both sides of the parkway. A pristine lake glistened in the sunlight. Through the trees, I could see the wooden backstops of softball fields set alongside rows of picnic tables. The air felt lighter and cleaner than anything in the city.

"That's because this is not the city anymore," my father said. "We're in the country now."

"The *country*?" I asked, having always defined that as the mountains, woodlands, and winding roads of the Catskills.

"It's not the same as being in the mountains," my father said. "But compared to where we're coming from, it sure feels like the country."

It looked a lot different than where we were coming from, too. Like the other new suburban communities on Long Island, Valley Stream was laid out far differently than the compact, older neighborhoods of Brooklyn. Rather than conforming to the city's rectangular block-and-grid template, clusters of homes were arrayed along a spaghetti-like maze of curvilinear drives and cul-de-sacs with names like Blueberry Lane, Morning Glory Road, and Marigold Run.

"Are all the streets out here named after flowers?" my sister asked.

"Seems like it," my father said.

"Well, mom should like that," I offered.

In the rearview mirror, I could see my mother smile.

We drove past a library, a synagogue, a pair of churches, and a sprawling, low-rise high school shared by several nearby towns. Farther down the road were a bowling alley, a dinner-theater, a multiplex movie complex, and a community recreation center that resembled the Brighton Beach Cabana Club.

"I told you there was a lot going on out here," my father said. "Isn't it nice?"

"It's nice as long as you have a car," my sister grumbled.

"*Two* cars," my father laughed.

"How long would it take you to get to work from here?" I asked.

"Forty minutes. Same as it takes me by subway now. Only I'd be driving."

"Can this old jalopy handle it?" I said.

"That, we'll have to see."

What we were seeing right then, however, was far from unappealing.

Constructed around a large village green, the heart of Valley Stream consisted of stores similar to those in Bay Ridge, but far more modern. There was nothing resembling Thumann's Candy Store, Phelps Pharmacy, Hessemann's Grocery or the older stores and produce stands along Seventh Avenue. But there was a bakery, several banks, a newsstand, a delicatessen, and other retail stores. Also nearby were F. W. Woolworth, W. T. Grant, and Sears department stores, as well as Arnold Constable, an upscale retail outlet.

"Plenty of clothes shopping out here," my father said, clearly aiming his remark squarely at my sister, whose interest was certainly piquing.

We drove about a mile from the center of town—past a Long Island Railroad station, the mammoth Green Acres shopping plaza, and several strip malls—to a subdivision where a trio of model homes was positioned around a trailer that served as a sales office. Inside, a salesman showed us a diorama of the subdivision, with push pins denoting home sites that had already been sold.

"This is a lot different than Brooklyn," he said, smiling. He was a pleasant enough fellow, possessed of the straightest set of white teeth I'd ever seen, and dressed in a neatly pressed tan suit.

"Why don't you take a gander at our models?" he suggested.

The model homes were small and set on tiny lots, but attractive by comparison to most older homes and apartments in Brooklyn. Compact enough to easily maintain, they were nevertheless large and expandable enough to accommodate most families.

The house my parents gravitated to contained three cozy bedrooms and an unfinished attic. The downstairs was centered around a family room with a fireplace-and-TV wall niche. A large picture window opened to a front lawn landscaped with shrubs and matching rows of dahlias. An unfenced yard spilled from the rear of the house to form a wide, common swatch of land that ran along the backyards of newly-constructed homes on the adjacent street. The kitchen was equipped with an electric stove, refrigerator, and laundry alcove containing a washer and dryer. And the house, like every other one we'd seen in Long Island, had a driveway and carport.

"What do you think?" the salesman asked when we were done looking.

"Well, we have some questions," my mother replied.

Then, turning to my sister and me, she said, "Your father and I would like to discuss things with this gentleman. Why don't the two of you wait in the car?"

A half-hour later we were on our way back to Brooklyn—driving, for the most part, in silence.

"I'd be fine there, Lily," my father finally said. "I really would. As long as I can get to work and a handball court on weekends, I'd be fine. You?"

"Well, it's not Dahlgren Place," my mother said flatly.

"No—and nothing ever will be. I think we all recognize that."

My mother said nothing for awhile.

"What do you kids think?" my father asked.

"It's not bad," my sister said, a glimmer of enthusiasm in her voice.

"Nathan—you?"

"We'll have to get used to it, but I think it's nice," I said. "Just very different."

"There's nothing wrong with different," my father said. "The whole world now is different."

We all fell silent again. Outside, the fading sunshine glinted off the open expanse of Lower New York Bay, as the garden apartments of Queens, and then the homes and apartment buildings of Brooklyn, lined both sides of the Belt Parkway. Before long, we were back in Bay Ridge, the work site at the Narrows looming ahead as we exited onto chewed-up streets lined by idle cement trucks, cranes and other construction equipment.

"You know, I think I'd be okay there, too, Artie," my mother finally admitted.

My father shot her a sideways glance.

"Really?"

"Uh-huh."

"You're not just compromising to accommodate me, are you?"

"No. I think it'd be kind of nice, I really do. As long as the four of us are together and there's a place for me to garden, I'll be fine."

And, with that singular remark, I knew we had found a new home.

The very next night, my parents returned to Valley Stream and left a five-hundred-dollar binder. The target date for our move, the salesman told them, would be in five months, just before Thanksgiving.

It was the right time for us, my parents said later, as we feasted on a celebratory Chinese dinner at the New Toyson Restaurant. A time to look ahead and start anew. A time to leave Brooklyn behind and move ahead. A time for a fresh new start.

"I only hope our new house brings us the same kind of luck as our old one did," my mother said. "I only hope Valley Stream is as good to us as Brooklyn was, and that we're as happy there as we've always been on Dahlgren Place."

The next day she started to pack. For the first time in months, I heard her humming an aria as she moved about the house.

Chapter 52

By the start of summer, large sections of Bay Ridge were as much a memory as they'd once been real, reminiscent of the dusty ghost towns Miss Greene talked about in social studies class. The expressway being carved across the wasted terrain of Seventh Avenue had done to our neighborhood what the railroads had done a century earlier to the boomtowns of the Old West. Like them, Bay Ridge seemed little more than a scarred collection of washed-out landmarks and severed connections. Abandoned. Crumbled. Lost to us forever, like a childhood we'd outgrown, something we'd imagined, a dream.

Lost, too, were the people who'd populated our lives: neighbors, friends, familiar faces, people we'd grown up and grown old with, people whose lives had intersected our own. Like much of Bay Ridge, they were already fading into the growing distance between present and past. Still part of who we were, but even more so part of our memory.

Dahlgren Place felt just as lost. Most of its former residents had long since moved, leaving homes deserted and mangled. Trees, felled at the roots, lay across broken sidewalks, alongside toppled stop signs, telephone poles, and piles of debris. The only homes remaining in our cul-de-sac—ours and Mrs. Knudsen's—seemed lifeless, drained of color, as if suffocating gradually in the fetid air of condemnation.

Most of our neighbors were gone, as well. Mr. Sandusky had left to open another TV-repair shop in the Bronx. Mr. Pappas had moved his family to Arizona. Mrs. Pedersen had relocated to a Trump-built apartment complex near Coney Island. Aside from us, the only people left were Mr. Mangini, Edith and Leo Banion, and Mrs. Knudsen, who seemed to have retreated permanently into her home. No one had seen or heard from her in days.

Still, as a way of lifting people's spirits, my parents pushed for one final welcome-summer block party. It was only fitting, they said, that we celebrated together one last time before saying good-bye; it was only right that we created one final happy memory on Dahlgren Place.

The half-dozen people who gathered for the party tried hard to make the most of it. Everyone brought their usual foods and set them out on a bridge table in front of our house. Mr. Mangini strummed his mandolin. Edith and Leo Banion sang. My sister and I picked at a stack of my mother's potato blintzes.

"This is hard," Leo Banion said. "I can't believe we really have to say good-bye."

"Me, either," said his wife, blowing her nose into a ragged handkerchief.

"C'mon," Mr. Mangini said. "It's not the end of the world."

"No," said Mrs. Banion, "just the end of some very good times."

"Yes," my mother agreed. "It *has* been good, hasn't it?"

Then she turned to me. "Why don't you run over and see if Mrs. Knudsen can join us? No one should be all alone at a time like this."

"Doesn't she know we're having a party?" I asked.

"Yes, but perhaps she forgot," said my mother, who'd recently helped Mrs. Knudsen secure an apartment in Starrett City, a high-rise project in Canarsie.

I walked the pathway to Mrs. Knudsen's house and climbed the stoop that our elderly neighbor had spent so many mornings scrubbing clean. Unwashed for months, it was caked with dirt, overrun by insects and uncut grass. Weeds poked through the seams between the bricks.

I rang the doorbell.

No answer. All I could hear was the chatter from a TV in Mrs. Knudsen's darkened living room.

I rang the bell again.

Still nothing. Just the echo of the doorbell chime and the television show.

I peeked through the window where Mrs. Knudsen's faded Gold Star, peeling at the edges, was pasted to the glass. All I could see, though, was our neighbor's living room and the glare from the TV reflecting off the walls. There were no signs of packing. No cartons or boxes piled high, like in our house. No signs at all of an impending move.

I rapped on the window as hard as I could without breaking the pane.

"Mrs. Knudsen. Mrs. Knudsen."

Then I saw my father, trailed closely by my mother and our neighbors, walking briskly toward the house, concern etched on their faces. Then I saw them running.

"Mrs. Knudsen!" I yelled. "Mrs. Knudsen!"

It didn't take long for the police to arrive, jimmy the front lock, and break into the house. And there they found Mrs. Knudsen, clad in a housecoat and slippers, slumped in a living room chair, lifeless as the furniture around her. An empty vial of sleeping pills lay at her feet. In her lap was a photo of her son Robbie, the hero soldier whose death had left her so broken and alone.

Mrs. Knudsen had probably been dead several days, police said. There was no way anyone could've known. She'd kept to herself so much near the end.

"The poor, sweet dear," my mother said, weeping as my father moved to nudge Beth and me out of the house.

"I can't believe she killed herself," I muttered.

"I only hope it wasn't painful," my mother said.

"A lot less painful, I'm sure, than her life was at the end," my father said, making it sound like Mrs. Knudsen was better off now, freed forever from her prison of loneliness and grief, hopelessness and fear.

"She always said she never knew where she could live if she had to leave her home here," my mother lamented. "Maybe she sensed all along that her life was over, that the bridge would wind up killing her."

We walked back to our house, the final block party on Dahlgren place at a premature end.

"We'll move on with our lives, but maybe Mrs. Knudsen just couldn't do that with hers," my father said. "Maybe there was nowhere else but Dahlgren Place where she could ever really feel at home."

Chapter 53

The rest of the summer flew by, with packing or discarding fifteen years of accumulated belongings keeping us fully occupied, the days passing in a blur.

For my mother, preparations for our move became virtually a round-the-clock activity. Each day, she busied herself boxing dishes, utensils, cooking implements, photos, and bedding. Odd pieces of furniture, old clothing, used toys, and other unwanted bric-a-brac were donated to the Salvation Army or sold at a garage sale she organized. The rest of her time—what there was of it—she used to help my sister prepare for her freshman year at Cortland State, an upstate college that Beth would enter in the fall.

My father was busy, too. Although overtime at Mergenthaler had all but dried up due to slowing business, his workday remained a daily eight-to-five proposition. And cleaning out his cellar workshop alone was nearly another full-time job. Literally hundreds of tools, machine parts, and other implements were organized and boxed. The linotype machine he'd been rebuilding was disassembled and carted off by co-workers. Paperback and hardcover books were donated to the local public library. Stacks of old newspapers and magazines were bound and placed at the curb, where city sanitation workers, liberally tipped, willingly hauled them away.

Despite the grueling work, though, things were looking up. For all the hardships connected to leaving Bay Ridge, there was a lot to look forward to: a new house, an opportunity to experience the ballyhooed amenities of the suburbs, a chance to start a fresh new chapter in our lives. All of that was having a positive effect. A growing sense of excitement and anticipation had replaced our former feelings of emptiness and displacement.

"I'm actually looking forward to this," my mother said one evening. "I'd probably be enjoying it, if it weren't such hard work."

"You set down deep roots when you've lived somewhere as long as we have here," my father said. "It keeps you plenty busy, getting ready to move."

I was busy, too—but in a different kind of way.

I had landed a summer job as an assistant athletic director at the Brighton Beach Cabana Club, where I spent most days signing out basketballs, volleyballs, knock-hockey sets, and ping pong paddles while eyeing bikini-clad girls practicing the latest dances—the Bristol Stomp, the Twist, the Watusi, and the Mashed Potato—at a jukebox near the BBCC athletic hut.

Nights, however, were different. Most of my closest friends—Pooch, Lumpy Lowery, Nick Pappas—were no longer there to pal around with. Watching television was nearly impossible, our reception clouded now with ghostlike images cast by the steel skeleton of the bridge rising in the Narrows.

Besides, TV didn't interest me as much as before. Shows like *Abbott and Costello*, *The Andy Griffith Show, The Real McCoys,* even *Bonanza,* seemed trivial in light of everything that had happened to us in the past year. There were rumors about a National League baseball team being formed to supplant the Dodgers and Giants in New York, but the Mets were still a year away. With no team to pull for, baseball was nowhere near as absorbing as the girls at the BBCC, or the lusty photos of naked women in the *Playboy* magazines Pooch had bequeathed me on his departure.

On top of that, my interests had shifted elsewhere. Stirred even during summer vacation by Mr. Urbansky's bridge curriculum, I found myself borrowing books about engineering and architecture from the public library, devouring them the way I'd once absorbed *Classic Comic Books* and the sports pages of the *Daily News*.

I pored through architecture magazines I found in the dusty alcoves of a newsstand on Eighty-sixth Street. I read several books on bridge-building that Mr. Urbansky had recommended. I consumed biographies of Frank Lloyd Wright and other great architects. I read about the great architectural treasures of New York: the buildings, bridges and monuments of Manhattan; the classic houses sprinkled throughout Brooklyn; the other landmarks that made the city world-famous.

But there was more to my nighttime activities than reading. Locked in my bedroom, I ceased imitating the batting styles of my favorite ballplayers and instead practiced drawing—tracing images of well-known structures around the world, sketching crude renderings of monumental creations I might one day design myself. Idols, I found, had evolved from comic superheroes, G-men, celebrities, and sports stars to men celebrated not solely for their looks or physical prowess, but for their brilliance and creativity; men whose work left a lasting and meaningful mark; men like Othmar Ammann, whose beautifully crafted engineering marvel was rising just yards from where I lived.

My interest growing like a windswept flame, I began to believe that, one day, I, too, could build things like the Narrows bridge. Majestic spans that swooped gracefully across mountainous ravines. Towering buildings that rose like concrete scepters over the skylines of great cities. Breathtaking monuments that stood as lasting symbols of ideals like freedom, justice, social progress, hope.

Architecture was something, I'd begun to believe, that I, too, could do with my life. Something real. Something important. Something far more within my grasp than playing baseball for the Dodgers, a team I no longer rooted for, at Ebbets Field, a ballpark that no longer existed.

For the first time, I was excited by the possibilities my life could hold beyond the confines of childhood, beyond the limits of Brooklyn. I couldn't wait to see where the journey I was on would take me as it continued to beckon and unfold.

Chapter 54

Our move just weeks away, I finally mustered the courage to approach my parents with the idea I'd been secretly harboring for months.

Until now, I'd been reluctant to broach the topic, fearful my suggestion would be met with instant rejection, dismissed as nothing more than the immature reasoning of a fifteen-year-old. But immersed again in school, fired anew by the bridge curriculum at Hamilton High, figuring I had nothing to lose, I decided it was time to open up. It was now or never.

"I think I'd like to stay in Bay Ridge through the end of the school year," I told them.

"*What*?" my mother blurted, nearly dropping the dish she was drying.

My father, who'd been reaching into a cabinet to retrieve some glassware, descended from his stepstool.

"I'd like to finish my junior year at Hamilton instead of at the new school in Valley Stream," I said.

"I don't understand," my mother replied. "You mean you don't want to leave Bay Ridge? You don't want to move with us?"

"No, that's not it at all. I have no problem moving, no problem with Valley Stream or the high school there."

"Then what is it?"

I hesitated, groping for the words I wanted.

"What I'm trying to say," I stammered, "is that, when we move, I'll be in the middle of my first semester as a junior, right?"

"Yes. And *so*?"

"So I've been thinking it'd make more sense for me to finish the full year at Hamilton and start at my new school as a senior next September."

My parents stood in disbelief, staring first at each other and then at me.

"Well, that's certainly a novel idea," my mother said. "And how do you propose to do that, Nathan? For example, where will you live?"

"I've been giving that some thought, too."

"And?"

"I could live with Aunt Sylvia and Uncle Murray."

My mother's older sister Sylvia and her husband Murray lived several blocks away, in an apartment building untouched by the construction in Bay Ridge.

"I could live with them until the end of the school year in June," I reasoned. "They have the space now that cousin Mark is away at college. I could stay in his room."

"Oh, I don't know about this," my mother replied.

"Why not? It'd just be for a couple of months."

"A *couple*? No, it would be for *seven months*, Nathan. From December through June. That's a long time—quite an imposition on your aunt and uncle, don't you think?"

"To be honest with you, I don't think they'd mind at all."

"Let's slow down here, champ," my father interjected. "I don't understand this completely. There's something I'm missing, right?"

"Not really."

"Are you afraid of the move?"

"No."

"Is it that you don't want to leave your friends?"

"No. Most of them have moved already."

"What is it then? Is there some kind of unfinished business you need to tend to?"

Again, I hesitated, unsure of how to convey my thoughts, the words sitting on a shelf I couldn't quite reach.

"I guess you can say that."

"Say what?"

"I guess you can say I have unfinished business."

"I still don't understand."

"It's hard to explain."

"Try."

I wasn't sure how, but I gave it my best shot. Staring at my father, I said, "Remember how you used to talk about growing up in New York—you know, during the Great Depression and all?"

"Yeah. What about it?"

"You talked about how, when you were my age, you were fascinated by things you saw being built—buildings, monuments, bridges, things like that?"

My father squinted, as if trying to recall something that took place a lifetime ago.

"You talked about how the things being built … *inspired* you. About how just looking at those things made you want to learn about them, build things like that yourself one day. Remember that?"

My father nodded assuredly now.

"Well, I think I feel the same way," I admitted. "I think those kinds of things mean the same to me as they did once to you."

There—it was finally out. Everything I'd harbored for the past few months. Everything that was on my mind almost around the clock now.

My father said nothing. He just stared as if he were looking through me.

"What do you mean?" my mother asked.

"I think I found what I might want to do with my life," I said. "Study architecture. Build things."

I pointed toward the Narrows. "Like the bridge out there."

"The *bridge*?" my mother asked.

"Yeah," I said, "the bridge."

My parents looked at each other wordlessly, utterly perplexed. And I went for broke.

"Mr. Urbansky's class is very important to me," I said, finding the words and pushing them out. "It's given me something to think about, a new direction—maybe for the rest of my life."

I pushed on, opening up fully now, figuring I had nothing left to lose, that maybe they'd understand how important this was to me by the tone of my voice, the look in my eyes.

"I've never had a class like this before. I doubt if I ever will again, not at this point in my life. Other high schools aren't even teaching the things we're learning, including the high school in Valley Stream."

I looked at my father, always easier to reason with.

"Remember you told me once to always find the time to dream—that you didn't have the time yourself to dream anymore, but I should *make* the time?"

He nodded and blinked.

"Well, I think architecture has become my dream," I said. "I just want to hang around longer and find out if it's true. I want to finish Mr. Urbansky's bridge program. Please."

My parents seemed dumbstruck.

"Well, you've certainly caught us off guard with this, Nathan," my mother said. "I don't know what to say."

"Just promise me you'll give it some thought."

More hesitation. More bewilderment. More skepticism. But then—at last—a vague smile, a subtle nod, a ray of light.

"All right," my father agreed. "I promise you we'll give it some thought."

"*Serious* thought?"

"Yes."

"And you'll talk it over with Aunt Sylvia and Uncle Murray?"

"Yes. You have our word about that, too."

"Just tell me what I've suggested is at least a *possibility*."

My parents hesitated again.

"Yes," my father said tentatively. "I'd say it needs more thought, but I'd consider it at least a possibility."

I wanted to jump for joy. But instead, I simply thanked them matter-of-factly, retreated to my room, and took a seat among the boxes containing the contents of my childhood, convinced there was a whole new part of my life about to begin. Something intriguing. Something exciting. Something bolder than any fantasy I'd ever harbored.

There was nothing more I wanted at that moment, nothing more I needed, than for my parents to simply say yes.

Chapter 55

There wasn't much drama to our move. No curbside prayers for God to spare our house. No tortured lamentations about the sad demise of Brooklyn. No anguished cries when the bulldozers arrived to do their work. None of that.

Unlike other streets in Bay Ridge, Dahlgren Place died a quiet death— unattended by witnesses, devoid of outpourings, as obscure in its demise as it was throughout its existence. No one lived there anymore when the demolition crews brought the last of its homes to the ground. No one was around to cry or rage or spill forth their bitterness and regrets. Those emotions were absent, packed up and carted away by everyone who'd once lived on the quiet, little street.

"I don't want to be anywhere near here when they tear down this house," my mother said the morning we moved, days before our house was leveled. "I don't want my final memory of our home to be a pile of rubble."

None of us wanted that, but my mother put it best. She wanted to remember our house, she said, exactly the way she'd seen it that first time—when she and my father were beginning their life together, and Brooklyn was still in its glorious postwar heyday, and everything about their lives seemed to stretch out before them, full of possibilities that were limitless and bold. She wanted to remember the house the way she'd seen it every moment since then, too. Intact.

In bloom. Full of music and laughter and celebration and the simple daily acts that made us a family.

"I want to remember it," she said, "as a place that made me feel alive and whole."

And that's pretty much how all of us decided to remember it. And how we always would.

THE SALE ITSELF went off without a hitch.

At the downtown office of a city-retained law firm shortly after Thanksgiving, my parents signed the city's acquisition papers, handed over the title to our house, and received a check for the agreed-upon amount of thirteen thousand, two hundred dollars. The entire transaction, sandwiched between four similar closings, took less than twenty minutes.

An hour later, four of my father's co-workers finished helping us load our possessions onto a rented truck and, following them in my father's Plymouth, we drove away. Past the heavy machinery and the workmen with the jackhammers carving out the expressway. Past the construction crews at the Narrows bridge site. Past the clouds of dust and the noise and the places that would always be memories. Out of Bay Ridge. Out of Brooklyn. Out of the only life I'd ever known.

We were silent for most of the ride, but somewhere on the Belt Parkway, about halfway to Long Island, my mother swiveled around, gazing first at my sister and then at me.

"Everything's going to be fine." She smiled. "You'll see. Things might've been tough on us for awhile, but this move is going to be good for all of us. Our old life was wonderful. Our new life will be wonderful, too."

Somehow I believed her. Somehow it wasn't so bad leaving Brooklyn for the final time. After all, we had our memories. We had each other. We had a whole new life to look forward to.

On top of that, my parents had granted me the singular wish that, for the moment at least, made our move entirely acceptable to me. Much to my surprise, they'd agreed to let me stay in Bay Ridge through the balance of the school year. I'd live for the next seven months with my Aunt Sylvia and Uncle Murray, joining my parents on weekends at our new home in Valley Stream.

In the meantime, I'd remain in Mr. Urbansky's physics class at Hamilton High, soaking up the curriculum that had opened up a whole new world to me. I'd hang around long enough to see if building things like the bridge was really something that was in my blood. I'd hang around to see if it was really something I might want to do with my life.

Chapter 56

Flagg Court, where my Aunt Sylvia and Uncle Murray lived, was nothing like Dahlgren Place. But it was still in Bay Ridge, still in Brooklyn, still close enough to our former street to feel a lot like home.

A luxury apartment complex similar to those in Brooklyn's most exclusive neighborhoods, Flagg Court had been designed by Ernest Flagg, a renowned architect whose projects included Manhattan's Singer Tower, a Beaux Arts structure that headquartered the famed sewing machine manufacturer and had once been the world's tallest building.

Set behind neatly trimmed, imposing hedges, Flagg Court was the most elegant example of communal living anywhere outside of Manhattan, consisting of a castle-like building wrapped around a swimming pool, arcade, bowling alleys, and playhouse. At the canopied entrance, a uniformed doorman announced arrivals by intercom before buzzing them in through steel-reinforced glass doors leading to a well-appointed lobby. Upstairs, cavernous apartments costing upwards of a thousand dollars per month featured ten-foot-high ceilings, ornate plasterwork, candelabra-like light fixtures, and a stunning view of the Narrows.

Aunt Sylvia was an elementary school teacher in the Flatbush section of Brooklyn. Shaped by her years of work with young students, she had a kindly face, calm demeanor, and soft-spoken, pedantic pattern of speech. Her resemblance to my mother was striking, and I felt completely at ease in her presence.

That was far from the case with Uncle Murray. An executive in New York's garment center, Uncle Murray had thinning hair and a chalky, pitted face. Stiff and formal, heavy with the scent of Old Spice cologne, he was nothing at all like my father. For one thing, he wore a suit to work, instead of work clothes, and carried an attaché case instead of a toolbox. His hands, unlike my father's, were soft and fleshy, his nails trimmed as neatly as Flagg Court's hedges. Unlike my father, who read the *Daily News* and *New York Post* back to front, Uncle Murray read the *New York Times* from front to back, even tackled its complex crossword puzzles. Most of all, Uncle Murray didn't give a hoot about baseball. He had no opinions about the pennant races, couldn't argue whether Duke Snider was better than Mickey Mantle or Willie Mays, and couldn't even name the eight teams in the American and National leagues, let alone recite their lineups.

Needless to say, we didn't have much to talk about. In truth, though, that hardly mattered. Flagg Court may have been different than Dahlgren Place, but it was far from difficult to live there. Pleased with my decision to remain in Bay Ridge, I settled into the bedroom previously occupied by my college-bound cousin Mark.

The spacious, light-splashed room was more than suitable. Sports posters were plastered on the walls. Trophies from Mark's achievements as a champion swimmer gleamed from atop a mirrored dresser. A comfortable, twin-sized bed was set between a pair of windows opposite a well-lit desk lined with a full set of the *Encyclopedia Britannica.* A seventeen-inch color TV broadcast crystal-clear images unimpeded by the steel towers of the bridge.

I made myself at home immediately—and kept busy. Most afternoons, I stayed after school working on bridge-related projects assigned by Mr. Urbansky. At night, behind closed doors, I studied, hoisted a pair of barbells, watched TV, and worked on drawings of bridges, skyscrapers and monuments I was sure would one day make me as celebrated as Othmar Ammann. On weekends, I shuttled between Brooklyn and our family's new home in Valley Stream.

As fall passed, then winter, I took to swimming laps in Flagg Court's pristine heated pool, emerging to show off my growing biceps and flirt with the teenaged girls stretched across poolside lounge chairs. I also graduated to the basketball courts and touch football games at Owl's Head Park, where the action drew hordes of high school and college kids, and was more rough-and-tumble than anything at P.S. 104.

Most of the time, though, I was fully absorbed with school. Caught up in the challenging puzzles of mathematics and physics. Inspired by the passion of Mr. Urbansky and the glittering promise that architecture now held for my life. Fascinated by the bridge that had displaced our family, but was now, I was discovering, transforming my entire being.

By late spring, just days before the end of school, Mr. Urbansky took our class down the steep bluff to within yards of the bridge construction site—this time to witness what he said would be a landmark event in the construction of the span.

The attendance in our physics class had dwindled to a mere dozen students by then. That, however, hardly dampened Mr. Urbansky's enthusiasm—or my own. He taught each day with the passion of a maestro at the top of his game. I soaked up his every word.

"This is a special day in the building of the bridge, and I wanted you to see it close up," Mr. Urbansky shouted through cupped hands as we stood amidst a crowd of observers on the Brooklyn shoreline, the waters of the Narrows choppy and white-capped, the bridge's towers obscured by low-hanging banks of fog.

The air buzzed with anticipation. Helmeted engineers in suits and ties mingled with contractors and bridge officials. On either end of the channel, Coast Guard cutters sat positioned to block the movement of vessels through New York Harbor. At the midpoint of the waterway, directly under the partially built superstructure, derrick boats loaded with massive lifting struts bobbed gently in the Narrows, as if awaiting the arrival of a special guest.

"There's still a lot of work to be done, but by the end of today what you're seeing will finally take on the look of a real bridge," Mr.

Urbansky told us. "What we're here to see is the first phase in the construction of the bridge's road deck—the lifting of the keystone piece."

On virtually every suspension bridge ever built, Mr. Urbansky explained, construction of the overwater roadway began at the towers and proceeded toward the middle. Because of the immense size of the Verrazano, however, workmen would need to hoist the first deck piece at the precise center of the span and then work outward, adding the sixty other deck components. This technique was necessary, he said, to prevent distortion of the bridge's cables and enable its towers to remain erect throughout construction.

Fabricated in factories all across America, each of the four-hundred-ton deck components had been transported by specially built freight cars for assembly in Jersey City, five miles away. One by one, Mr. Urbansky explained, the huge, reinforced-steel components would be floated to the bridge site, then raised, swung into position, and connected to the vertical suspenders dangling from the bridge's four cables. Simultaneously, he said, workers would raise the materials needed to erect "second-pass" steel—roadway deck grid, fillers, center barriers, and the stiffening trusses, struts, and braces needed for stability. They would then connect the deck pieces together, in sequence, readying them to receive the tons of concrete that would comprise the roadway.

"Here comes the keystone piece!" shouted Mr. Urbansky, gesturing toward a tugboat towing a barge up-channel. Atop the mammoth keystone piece, an ironworker stood barking commands into a battery-powered bullhorn. High above, on the bridge, a signal man with a walkie-talkie relayed the commands to hoisting machine operators.

We passed around a pair of binoculars as we watched the barge slowly position itself midway across the Narrows. Then we saw workers attach huge chains to the keystone piece. And soon the hoisting cranes, their diesel engines roaring, began raising the enormous steel block.

Ten feet the keystone piece rose, swaying in the crosswinds. Then twenty. A hundred. Two hundred. Up nearly to the point where the vertical suspenders dangled four hundred feet above the water.

"This," said Mr. Urbansky, "is a very difficult operation. Extremely dangerous."

And no sooner had he said that than the nearly unthinkable happened.

A Caughnawaga workman fell from the bridge.

It happened so suddenly that we didn't realize immediately what had occurred. Not until we heard the retired ironworkers near us let out a collective gasp. Not until we heard Mr. Urbansky mutter something and drop his binoculars. Not until the falling workman, appearing as a tiny speck against the immense backdrop of the harbor, slipped through a narrow crevice in the skeletal superstructure, dangled by his arms for a split-second, and then plunged from a catwalk, striking the channel with a nearly imperceptible splash.

Instantly, all work ceased. Bridge workers shouted frantically into bullhorns. Foghorns and alarms sounded. Bridge officials raced to the shoreline. Coast Guard cutters and fire rescue vessels plowed through the water, converging at the spot where the workman's lifeless body floated face down, bobbing like a tiny harbor buoy.

We stood, silent, staring in stunned disbelief as rescue workers dove headlong into the frigid channel and swam frantically toward the fallen worker.

Before we could see much more, however, Mr. Urbansky hustled us back to school. And there we sat glumly for the remainder of the morning, quietly contemplating what we'd just witnessed. Several students, granted permission, were dismissed for the day. On the shoreline, grief-stricken Caughnawaga tribesmen gathered to console one another and pray. Work was suspended. Bridge workers were sent home.

"I'm very sorry you had to witness that," said Mr. Urbansky, reaching for some way to console us. "But accidents are unfortunate realities when people undertake ambitious projects like the bridge."

He walked around the classroom, seeming anxious and troubled.

"You need to understand that nothing of this magnitude can be built without tremendous sacrifice and gut-wrenching work," he said. "Tragedies are sometimes part of the price we pay when we endeavor to build great things."

The tragedy evoked more, however, than merely momentary reflection and work stoppage. The very next day, structural steelworkers staged a full-blown strike, protesting what they charged was a lack of safety at the job site. Union demands for safety nets were rejected, since the proposed nets, management claimed, would prevent materials from being lifted onto the structure from the water. Negotiations dragged on for days. Finally, as a compromise, makeshift nets, similar to those used by circus aerialists, were rigged to steel poles and positioned in some spots on the bridge.

Only then did the bridge-builders return. And so did the Caughnawagas, having laid their fallen comrade to rest at the sacred burial site at the tribe's upstate reservation, his grave marked by a cross fashioned from steel beams taken off the job site.

"It's a hard life—up there on the bridge," Mr. Urbansky told us. "But, regardless of what happens, work must go on. It always does. It always must."

And it did.

It went on, in fact, for another two years. Well after the bridge curriculum concluded with the end of the school year. Well after I'd left Bay Ridge, joining my parents full time in Valley Stream. Well after I'd graduated from a regional high school near our new Long Island home.

I missed the final stages of construction on the Verrazano-Narrows Bridge: the workmen finishing off the main and secondary road decks; the concrete mixers moving in to pave the roads; the painters applying finishing coats of shiny silver to the span's rust-colored steel; the electricians stringing lights along the span's towers and cables.

I missed the expressway being finished off, too: the bulldozers and road graders leveling the roadway's surface; the gravel contractors trucking in fill; the compactors smoothing the materials; the welders laying down reinforcing steel; the masons pouring concrete and placing rubber expansion buffers between the sections of pavement.

I missed it when the culverts and drainage lines were set in place; when the traffic lanes were painted; when the dividing barriers and traffic signs were erected; when the mercury vapor lamps were installed; when the landscapers planted grass and rows of tiny young trees.

I missed it, too, when work crews paved over Dahlgren Place and finished building the giant, curving bridge approach that soared over what once was our street, casting a giant shadow over what once was our home.

What I wouldn't miss, however, I swore to myself, was the day they opened the bridge. I wouldn't let myself miss that for anything in the world.

CHAPTER 57

Opening Day for the Verrazano-Narrows Bridge took place in November of 1964, five full years after construction had begun and nearly a year after the assassination of President John F. Kennedy.

New York, over the course of that half-decade, had become a vastly different city. America had become a different country. And we, it was clear, had moved far beyond the carefree childhood that stretched across Brooklyn's postwar era of innocence and prosperity, the borough's Golden Years. We were well past childhood now. And the Brooklyn we'd grown up in was gone now, too. Gone for good.

All of that was there to see the day they opened the bridge.

Marked by a gala celebration, the bridge dedication was the most festive occasion Brooklyn had seen since the Dodgers had won the World Series nearly a decade earlier. Wracked by sweeping change, the borough hadn't had much to cheer about since then. Opening Day gave at least some people a reason to celebrate.

Nearly ten thousand of those celebrants gathered under a bright, cloudless sky near the Brooklyn and Staten Island approaches to the magnificent new span, which arched the Narrows like a glittering rainbow of concrete and steel. Cars, parked bumper to bumper, lined both shorelines and the shoulders of the newly built expressway. High school and military bands played. Colorful bunting hung from nearby buildings. A huge American flag, affixed to the vertical bridge suspenders, flapped wildly in the chilly gusts. A flotilla of vessels clogged the sun-splashed Narrows.

Present along with the onlookers were scores of politicians, civic leaders, military brass, highway officials, and other dignitaries. Absent, in contrast, were the thousands of Bay Ridge residents who'd protested the project, as well as those who'd been displaced. Their failed protests were merely faded echoes now, the people themselves as much a part of the past as the way of life they'd battled to preserve.

Absent, too, was the army of workers who'd built the bridge—the ironworkers and bridgemen who'd pieced the mammoth structure together with their courage and skill. Most had already followed the siren call to work elsewhere, to construction projects throughout the world. Others, uninvited to the ceremony, boycotted it entirely, gathering instead at a private mass in honor of the three men who'd died while building the span.

I was there, though. I was there on Opening Day.

By then I was making the daily trek from Valley Stream to The City College of New York, whose campus in Harlem was nestled amid elegant brownstones and stately apartment buildings reminiscent of those in Brooklyn.

CCNY's School of Engineering didn't have quite the reputation of the Pratt Institute, the college my father had longed to attend, but it was top-notch nevertheless. Moreover, it was affording me the opportunity my father never had a chance to embrace. I was living the dream he'd seen aborted by the harsh realities of his youth. I was studying to become an architect.

And so I came to Opening Day for the bridge: the architectural monument that served as an inspiration for everything I was studying at college; the engineering marvel that had chased my family so painfully from our home, but had unexpectedly inspired me to chase a dream of my own; the structure that had risen from the chaos and ruins of Bay Ridge to become a symbol of twentieth-century achievement, the powerful changes reshaping New York, the passing of the Brooklyn we had known.

I also came to see my old friends. We had chosen the day for a reunion of sorts. It would be the first time any of us had seen each other since we'd left Bay Ridge, the first time I'd be back to the neighborhood in two years.

I wasn't sure what I'd see when I got there—or how I'd feel. But I couldn't wait to find out.

WE MET ON the Brooklyn shoreline, at John Paul Jones Park, where throngs of people stood huddled in the November chill, awaiting the ribbon-cutting ceremony on the Staten Island side.

Above us, the steel underbelly of the bridge loomed gray and immense, the Brooklyn tower rising high over the rooftops of Bay Ridge. News helicopters hovered overhead. The ocean liner *United States*, returning from its annual dry-docking in Virginia, stood at anchor, waiting to complete its journey to Manhattan. Fireboats, Coast Guard vessels, and other small craft bobbed in the choppy waters.

"Holy shit, lookit who's here!" gasped Tommy Lowery when he saw me.

Lowery was taller now, no longer toting the baby fat that once earned him the nickname Lumpy. With him were Nick Pappas and another friend, Marty Friedman, both looking older and more mature. The four of us shook hands and embraced.

Then, bounding toward us with long, swaggering strides, was none other than Pooch. Wordlessly, he pulled Lowery into a viselike headlock and immediately brought Tommy to his knees. Everyone laughed. Just as quickly, he released his grip, helped Lowery to his feet, and pumped everyone's hands.

Pooch, too, was more mature now, thicker in the chest and shoulders, filling out a black muscle shirt and Navy pea coat. His hair, like everyone's, was longer now too, jet black and parted down the middle.

"How ya been, Wolfman?" he asked.

"Good. You?"

Pooch flashed a thumbs-up and toothy smile.

He had graduated from Grover Cleveland High School in Brooklyn's Greenpoint section, but had decided, wisely, that college wasn't for him. Instead, he'd enrolled in an apprentice program run by the International Association of Bridge, Structural & Ornamental Ironworkers, the same union tied to the construction of the bridge.

It was strange, I said, how we'd both been drawn to a similar line of work—construction—although from different sides of the business. Pooch, like the ironworkers who'd built the Verrazano, would work with his hands. I, as my father had always hoped, would work with my head.

"Yeah, that's really somethin'," he said. "*Ironic*, huh?"

"I'm surprised you even know what that means," I said, hoping he'd take it as a joke.

"Whoa," Lowery said, trying to egg Pooch on. "Rank out! *Rank out!*"

Pooch simply smiled.

"Well, you always were the one with the brains," he said.

"Who says?" I smirked.

"*This* says." He smiled, flexing and pointing to a bicep the size of a softball.

We all laughed and then tried to catch up. Nick Pappas was attending St. John's, the Jesuit university in Queens. Marty Friedman was going to college somewhere in Pennsylvania. Tommy Lowery was finishing his senior year at Stuyvesant, one of the city's elite high schools. With a military draft and lottery now in effect, and hostilities heating up in Vietnam, Pooch said he'd likely be doing a two-year hitch in the army before coming home to Brooklyn. The rest of us were shielded from military obligations by our student exemptions.

"Don't worry," Pooch said. "I'm gonna go over there and keep all you college pussies safe."

Our laughter at his comment was strained, however. There was nothing funny about what was going on in Vietnam these days. Nothing funny at all.

THE FIVE OF us meandered along the shoreline, joining a crowd of onlookers at the old Sixty-ninth Street ferry slip, where we used to embark on all-day jaunts across the mouth of New York Harbor to the beach at St. George, Staten Island.

Not anymore. After decades of operation, the ferry service had been terminated the day before, its fleet dispersed for service in Central America. The ferry office was closed now, its entrance and windows boarded. Water lapped against the empty ferry slips. Gulls perched idly on old wooden pilings.

"I can't believe there'll be no more ferries running from Brooklyn to Staten Island," Nick Pappas said.

"No one needs 'em," Tommy Lowery said, "now that they have a bridge."

"People won't know what they missed."

"People won't care."

Overhead, a jetliner followed the Belt Parkway on its flight path to Idlewild Airport, where a rash of new terminals was being built to serve Pan Am, Eastern, TWA, and other major airlines. With commercial aviation booming, hundreds of flights took off and landed each day at Idlewild, soon to be renamed for the slain president, and the skies over Brooklyn were filled with the unfamiliar sound of airplanes.

"I still can't get used to all these planes," Pooch said over the screech of the passing jetliner.

"Better learn to," Nick Pappas retorted. "They're here to stay."

"I dunno," said Pooch, shaking his head. "The bridge is opening. Steeplechase is closing. Ebbets Field is an apartment building. They're talkin' about tearing down the Parachute Jump. Shit, the whole freakin' world is changin'."

He was right about that.

And it wasn't only Brooklyn that was changing, either. Or only New York. Even more ominous changes were in play now—some of them far from home.

War was spreading in Southeast Asia, sending uneasy tremors through Bay Ridge and most of New York. The army processing center at Fort Hamilton was busier than ever, with scores of inductees taking physicals, getting sworn in and shipped out for basic training. Troops and supplies were being airlifted overseas from Floyd Bennett Field and other nearby military bases. Even more ominously, a stream of U.S. Army and Red Cross ambulances, growing steadier by the week, could be seen winding their way through Bay Ridge, transporting wounded GIs from Idlewild to a newly built VA hospital on the grounds of Fort Hamilton.

It was still too early to understand how the war would impact the country, but early signs were in the air. American flags were being unfurled throughout Bay Ridge, with support for the war voiced by patriotic and civic groups. Signs of discord were brewing, as well. At Brooklyn College, a militant group of students had recently staged a sit-in, shutting down the campus when the navy set up a recruitment table. Similar protests at NYU, Columbia University, and CCNY were headlining nightly newscasts.

So were other budding forms of unrest.

In downtown Brooklyn, Woolworth's Department Store was being boycotted by protestors who charged the retail outlet with racial bias in the South. At Board of Education headquarters, parents were protesting plans for the busing of black students into all-white neighborhoods throughout New York. At rallies in midtown, members of the National Organization of Women were demanding equality for females in the workplace.

The 1950s, it was clear, were over now, along with the decade's steadfast adherence to uniformity and conservatism. Rocked by the Kennedy assassination, the war, and the growing Civil Rights movement, the country seemed on the precipice of something turbulent and powerful. People were restless. Values were shifting. Traditional rules and conventions were being questioned. Hints of a cultural and social revolution were in the air.

Everything, it seemed, was changing—and more quickly than ever: television, movies, literature, art, even clothing. The clean-cut look of the past decade—bobby socks, saddle shoes, penny loafers, poodle skirts, and cardigans—was being shed. Hair was getting longer. Hemlines were getting shorter. Accessories were gaudier. On Eighty-sixth Street, a boutique selling tie-dyed T-shirts with bold colors, snappy slogans and psychedelic imagery opened at the former location of a Nedicks hot dog stand. Bands of young rebels, called beatniks, were congregating in Owl's Head Park. An emerging counterculture was on the rise at Hamilton and other city high schools, where whispers about marijuana were more than simply rumors.

Music was changing, too. New FM channels were rendering AM radio obsolete. The doo-wop and saxophone sounds of the past decade were fading. Artists like Elvis Presley, Chuck Berry, Bo Diddley, and Jerry Lee Lewis were taking a back seat to folk rock, blues, and radical protest songs. British bands were nudging American groups off the charts. Payola, the play-for-pay scandal, had just driven disc jockey Alan Freed off the New York airwaves. Freed's popular rock 'n' roll shows were gone now, too, no longer drawing lines of screaming teenagers like my sister to the Brooklyn Paramount, which itself was earmarked for closure.

"I wonder where all of this is gonna lead," Tommy Lowery pondered.

"Who knows?" Pooch said. "All I can tell you is that things are a lot different now than when we were growing up."

His gaze faraway, Pooch seemed to contemplate his own remark.

"The fifties were a lot calmer," he said. "Things seemed much simpler."

"Ah, there was plenty of shit going on in the fifties, too," I said, echoing something my father once said about the Cold War, the Communist witch hunts and the other social problems swept under the rug during the fifties—all because people were weary of radicalism and conflict, because they needed a respite from the past thirty years.

"A lot of stuff was happening under the surface when we were growing up," I said. "We just didn't have a clue about it."

"That's right," Pooch laughed. "We were too busy with other things."

Yes, we all agreed. We were too busy having fun to see what was happening around us. We were too busy being kids.

WE WALKED TO the edge of the ferry slip, gazing toward Coney Island and, to the north, past the Brooklyn Heights promenade to the tip of Manhattan. In the distance, the Statue of Liberty jutted from the waters of the harbor, blurry in the afternoon haze. Up on the bridge, a motorcade of shiny black limousines stopped at a checkpoint near the Brooklyn approach and then, cleared to pass, streamed past teams of contractors conducting last-minute safety checks.

"You gotta admit, it's a beautiful bridge," said Tommy Lowery, nodding toward the Verrazano, illuminated by the midday sunlight.

To myself, I agreed.

"Shit, I wonder what it's like up there," Lowery said.

"Well, I'm gonna give you jerk-offs a chance to find out first-hand," Pooch said, informing us he'd just used three months of paychecks to buy himself a Mustang, a sporty convertible recently introduced by Ford.

"As soon as they open that sucker," Pooch said, "the five of us are gonna ride across it in style."

Then I saw the person I'd hoped to see more than anyone—even more than Pooch. Dressed in a long, tweed overcoat and battered gray fedora, nearly inconspicuous among the throngs, Edwin Urbansky stood chatting with a group of fellow teachers, shielding his eyes from the glare and gesturing up at the bridge. Standing near him were Miss Greene, my former social studies teacher, and Mr. Hendricks, whose math classes I'd taken during my sophomore and junior years at Hamilton High.

"Mr. Urbansky," I called out, approaching the trio.

He stared at me for a moment, as if trying to place my face.

"Nathan? Nathan Wolf?"

"Yep. One and the same."

"Wow." He smiled, extending a hand. "You've sure grown up since the last time I saw you. I hardly recognized you."

I greeted Miss Greene who, even bundled in an overcoat and scarf, looked as fetching as always. Mr. Hendricks smiled in recognition, too.

"Where are you living these days?" Mr. Urbansky asked.

"Out on the Island. In Valley Stream."

"How do you like it?"

"It's okay."

"Very different than in Brooklyn, I'll bet."

"Like night and day."

"It must be strange coming back after, what, two years?"

"It sure looks a lot different around here, with the bridge and all."

"Yeah," Mr. Urbansky said. "A lot has changed in a very short time."

"That's for sure."

Miss Greene inquired about my family. I told the teachers my mother was fine, busy as ever with her gardening and a new part-time job; that my sister was away at college; that my father drove to work every day in Brooklyn and still played handball on Sundays at Coney Island.

"And you?" she asked.

I told them I was enrolled at CCNY—studying architecture.

"Really?" Mr. Urbansky said. "That's terrific. How do you like it so far?"

"It's not easy, but I really do like it."

"Are you doing all right with the subjects?"

"I'm holding my own."

I wanted to tell Mr. Urbansky how much his curriculum had meant to me. How his passion had inspired me. How his classes had enabled me to see the physical world in an entirely new way and, so doing, had turned my life in an exciting new direction. As usual, though, the words were well beyond my grasp.

"I just want you to know … " I sputtered.

"Yes?"

"Well, that your class … meant a lot to me."

I looked at the other teachers.

"*All* your classes did."

"Thank you, Nathan," Mr. Urbansky said. "That's the best thing teachers can ever hear. Reaching students like you is the reason we teach."

Miss Greene and Mr. Hendricks nodded in agreement.

"Stay in touch." Mr. Urbansky smiled, extending a hand. "Drop by some time. I always like to see how former students move on with their lives."

"Sure thing," I said, shaking his hand.

But I'd never see Mr. Urbansky again. I'd return to Hamilton High only once in the next twenty years, for a formal class reunion. By then, however, Mr. Urbansky was long gone, having retired and returned to his Midwestern roots. Another memory. Another part of

Brooklyn I'd carry around with me, like childhood itself, for the rest of my life.

AT THE RIBBON-CUTTING for the bridge, Robert Moses, dressed to the hilt, gazed proudly at New York's newest landmark, arching triumphantly across the sun-splattered expanse of the Narrows. In reviewing stands on either side of him, swarms of dignitaries sat huddled in mufflers and gloves, woolen blankets warming them from the stiff breeze whipping across the channel.

Moses read a congratulatory message from President Lyndon Johnson, who hailed the bridge for its breathtaking beauty and superlative engineering. Then he paid tribute to select people in the assembled crowd. City officials, including the mayor and members of the Board of Estimate, were singled out for their contributions. State and federal officials—among them the governors of New York and New Jersey—were lauded. So was the bridge's brilliant designer, Othmar Ammann, who sat in a black overcoat and high-starched collar, largely unnoticed by the people around him.

Still modest and unassuming at eight-five, Ammann was witnessing the opening of his final bridge, the closing curtain on an extraordinary career. Within several years, his legacy cemented for all time, he'd be gone.

So, in many ways, would Moses. The target of increasing criticism and eroding power, the Master Builder, too, would gradually disappear from New York's public stage, his projects linked to the declining fortunes of the city, his impact on New York a subject of debate, his place in history left in the hands of scholars.

But now he stood at the Staten Island approach to the Verrazano-Narrows Bridge, the crowning achievement to his lifetime of public works, presiding over the event he'd awaited for nearly half of his forty-year career: the opening of New York's final and grandest bridge, its long-awaited link to America.

"This soaring steel span, with its powerful towers and fine-spun cables, is a vivid reminder that skill and scientific planning are the keynote of all great achievements," Moses gushed. "This magnificent new colossus ushers in a new era for New York and brings a new dimension to the greatest seaport in the world. It's what people *should* see when they visit our great city."

Then Moses and the assembled dignitaries posed for photos, an oversized pair of ceremonial shears poised to cut an enormous red ribbon stretched across the bridge's toll plaza. Photographers jockeyed for position. Flashbulbs popped. The dignitaries smiled, the ribbon falling limply when they spliced it, then flying off in the gusts, alighting in the water below.

The Verrazano-Narrows Bridge was officially open.

Cannon blasts from Fort Wadsworth and Fort Hamilton boomed across the harbor. Vessels in the channel sounded their foghorns. Fireboats shot spray high into the air. The crowds on both shorelines erupted in a rousing cheer. Then the dignitaries retreated to several large tents, where they feasted on champagne and mounds of food until the biting chill sent them scurrying for cover.

A procession of antique cars was first across the bridge, followed by a string of limousines and official vehicles. Private cars queued up to pay the fifty-cent toll, some carrying passengers who'd camped around the clock for nearly a week so they'd be among the first to cross the majestic new span. Hundreds of other cars, many with American flags affixed to their fenders, streamed across in a motorcade stretching for miles.

Soon after, we took our turn.

Piling into Pooch's Mustang, we inched our way in bumper-to-bumper traffic along the steep, sharply curved Belt Parkway approach, Pooch and I in the front seat, the others behind us. No one said a word—we couldn't. We just took in the spectacle. On the radio, the Beach Boys sang about the way the girls looked on the sun-splashed beaches of California. Then the Four Seasons came on, and the Supremes and Smoky Robinson. And then that new British band, the Beatles, the biggest thing since Elvis, the group that DJs Cousin Bruce Morrow, Murray "the K," and the WMCA Good Guys said could change the entire world.

And right then, it felt like that was surely possible, like *anything* was possible.

We sang along with the music, slowly ascending the bridge's access ramp, moving past the span's mammoth anchorage and beneath its grid-like steel underbelly, climbing above the rooftops of Bay Ridge, upward until the traffic opened up and Pooch punched the accelerator and we flowed onto the Verrazano's upper deck, moving swiftly across the bridge, the wind in our faces, the top of the convertible open to an azure sky that looked close enough to touch.

It was sheer exhilaration.

Horns blared. People waved from their car windows. We whooped and laughed and flung our arms about, more carefree than we'd been in even the sweetest moments of childhood. Never had I felt so alive, so free, so pulsing with excitement.

And never had I seen New York in quite the same way.

Through the vertical suspenders on the north side of the bridge, the vast sweep of Manhattan and New Jersey stretched as far as the eye could see. On the south side, beyond the mouth of Lower New York Bay, tankers and other ships sailed toward the open waters of the Atlantic. Below us, sailboats, tugs, and cabin cruisers sliced through the Narrows, past cargo vessels and passenger liners anchored in the harbor. Before us, like monumental archways, loomed the gigantic towers of the bridge, its arching roadway swallowed up by the treetops of Staten Island. To our rear, the panorama of Brooklyn spread out like a collage of buildings, streets, and elevated train lines receding in the distance.

And as we moved across, slowing as traffic bunched and halted, I could feel the bridge swaying gently, just like Mr. Urbansky said it would. Moving as if it were alive. As if it, too, pulsed with excitement. As if it were a newborn child, opening its eyes for the first time to a bright new world.

Chapter 58

All that day we remained in Bay Ridge. Walking its streets. Looking for familiar faces. Surveying our old stomping grounds. Searching for lost terrain. Trying to slip back, even for only a few hours, into the special magic of childhood.

But that was over.

We could see that now. Childhood was gone. Gone along with the homes we'd lived in and the lives we'd led. Stripped away, once and for all, with the building of the bridge.

Our old neighborhood, in many ways, was gone, as well. Bay Ridge had changed dramatically since we'd last seen it, as if layered over on an artist's canvas. Eight hundred structures had been demolished by the city. Former streets, once lined with private homes and apartment buildings, had been paved over by the expressway, a swath of gray-white concrete that spliced the heart of the neighborhood. Swallowed up, too, was all of Seventh Avenue, along with the structures that once housed shops, offices, and apartments. The once-bustling thoroughfare was nothing more than a memory now. Like our childhood, part of the past.

So were legions of people. In all, some seven thousand residents had been displaced by the expressway, scattered like leaves in a sudden gust. In truth, not all had been distraught about leaving. Many, pleased with their settlements from the city, were more than willing to abandon Bay Ridge, resettling in other parts of the city, relocating to the suburbs, or severing their New York ties entirely. For those people, life went on. Many migrated seamlessly to new realities, finding new jobs, making new friends, putting down other roots, making themselves anew, carrying on.

Others, however, weren't as lucky. For many, especially the elderly, displacement was wrenching. Shocked like uprooted trees, many old-timers would wander through the remains of their life as if trying to navigate a dense fog—disoriented, shattered by the disintegration of their world, consumed by their loss, unable to restore their equilibrium.

Years later, some could be found residing in neighborhoods that still felt like foreign countries, living in places that fit like poorly-made clothing, blaming their failing health or loved one's death on the bridge, bitter to the end. Some would embark on regular pilgrimages to Bay Ridge, longing for the safe haven of the old neighborhood, pausing at the site of their former homes as if visiting shrines. Reminiscing. Mourning. Fading off in time with the rest of the old Brooklyn landscape. Victims of time. As much a part of the past as everything they'd struggled vainly to cling to.

"Holy shit, lookit this," Pooch said as we surveyed the neighborhood, trying to reconcile the old with the new, struck by the odd mix of fond memories and jarring revelations.

"It's hard to believe this is where we grew up," Tommy Lowery said, gesturing toward the expressway, which was already accommodating a steady stream of traffic heading toward the bridge and, in the opposite direction, the East River crossings into Manhattan.

"It's hard to believe there were houses here once," Lowery said.

"And stores," Marty Friedman said. "Remember all those stores. Thumann's Candy Store. Caruso's Barber Shop. Phelps Pharmacy. Hessemann's Grocery."

We took turns rattling off others: Ming's Chinese Laundry, where the owner used an abacus to calculate change; Max's Texaco Station, where my parents obtained our dinnerware; the Staziak Funeral Home, whose owner had led the anti-bridge fight; the office of Councilman Alan Sherman, whose political career had all but ended with the Battle of Bay Ridge.

All of them were part of the Lost Brooklyn now, all simply memories.

"And what about the *people*?" Pooch asked, ticking off the names of former neighbors and shopkeepers. They were gone now, too.

We walked to Pooch's former street, Narrows Drive. But the apartment building he'd lived in had been leveled, replaced by an elevated approach merging onto the upper roadway of the bridge.

Tommy Lowery's street was gone, too. So was Marty Friedman's. And so, to my amazement, was Dahlgren Place.

Our entire cul-de-sac and the five-block street that emptied into it had been reduced to nothing more than an empty lot, paved with concrete, cast forever in the shadow of the overhead expressway and its snake-like bridge approach. There wasn't the slightest hint that homes once stood there, that people once lived there. It was as if I'd grown up on a street that existed solely in my imagination.

"I can't believe we used to play punchball and stickball here," Pooch said, standing in what would've been the center of the cul-de-sac.

"I can't believe I once *lived* here," I said, stunned by everything I was seeing, everything that was *missing*.

Pooch and the others walked in circles, trying to reconstruct the makeshift baseball diamond we'd played on for years, searching for signs of home plate, the bases, the foul lines. I wandered about, too, trying to pinpoint where our house once stood, where I'd lived the first fifteen years of my life.

But nothing remained of our street. Not our house or those of former neighbors. None of the landmarks that had defined my childhood world. None of it. Disoriented and bewildered, all I could do was offer guesses of where things once were, wandering around as if in darkness, groping for something familiar.

Nothing was familiar, though. Nothing. It was as if I were a stranger in a new land, as if I'd been disconnected from something uniquely personal—the sense of place that had been encoded in my muscles and bones, that had defined who I was, that had anchored me to my emotions.

At one time, standing on this same spot, I knew exactly where everything important to me could be found, how long it took me to move about my world, how all of it made me feel. I knew how the sun cast shadows on the street at different times of the day, how the rhythm of Dahlgren Place changed subtly as nightfall descended, how the trees cycled with the seasons and riffled with the bay breezes as I drifted off to sleep. I knew the precise spot where I'd learned to ride a two-wheeler and where I'd hit my first home run in stickball. I knew how I felt when my father rounded the corner on his way home from work and my mother called me in for supper. I knew how it felt to be nestled inside the comforting walls of our home.

None of that existed anymore. None of the landmarks. None of the sights or sounds. None of the emotions. Now, I was like a ghost. On the outside looking in. Trying vainly to find my way back home. Feeling frightened in the very place I'd once felt most secure, lost in the very place where everything had once been most familiar.

And yet, the strangest thing of all was that, even with all that was gone, much of Bay Ridge still felt familiar. Despite its changes, much of the neighborhood remained remarkably intact, as if it had somehow escaped a grievous wound.

Fort Hamilton was still there, just beyond a remnant tree line. So was the Narrows, stretching like a sparkling ribbon north and south into Upper and Lower New York Bays. The schoolyard at P.S. 104 was still there, too. So were Owl's Head Park, the RKO Dyker movie theater, and other familiar sights. Hamilton High still stood atop the bluff overlooking the Narrows. Eighty-sixth Street still bustled with cars and pedestrians. Children played in the streets. People engaged in the rituals of family and home. The scent of salt air still wafted across streets that looked like Dahlgren Place once did.

And somehow, Bay Ridge still felt like *home*. So did Brooklyn.

In many ways, I realized just then, it always would. Brooklyn would live inside us always, just as it had when we were there. It would always be part of us—always be, in some important way, *home*.

Decades later, part of us would still be out on its streets, grimy from play, racing through alleyways, jumping rope, riding two-wheelers, rumbling about on roller skates, smacking spaldeens over the rooftops. Decades later, part of us would still be in elementary school practicing our penmanship, reading comic books, flipping baseball cards, sitting in the movie houses of Flatbush Avenue, losing ourselves in our dreams and fantasies.

In Brooklyn, we'd still be children, surrounded by things that were familiar and comforting, things we could count on, things we loved. Our parents and relatives would still be alive. Our friends would be close. Our world would be innocent and manageable. Our lives would be out there in front of us, ready to live, stretching to the horizon, swelling with big, bold dreams. And anything would be possible—love, family, wealth, power, contentment. Anything and everything.

Brooklyn would live inside us that way, always, because we'd want it to, *need* it to. We'd need that part of our life to stay as we remembered it. Simple, special, orderly, predictable. Washed clean of imperfections. Viewed through the prism of childhood. There for us to reminisce about. There for us to cling to. Part of who we were. Even though we'd moved on. Even if that Brooklyn—that childhood—was forever gone, forever beyond our reach.

WE PLAYED ONE final stickball game in the P.S. 104 schoolyard, and afterwards we sat, legs tucked to our chests, against the wall of the school, the strike zones for the stickball court chalked on the brick behind us.

Pooch had gotten his hands on a six-pack of Ballantine, and he used his belt buckle to pop open a high-top, foam fizzling from its mouth as he placed it in a brown paper bag and took a long, thirsty swig. Then he passed it around.

It was the first beer I'd ever drunk, and it was good—icy cold from sitting for hours in the trunk of Pooch's Mustang, made even tastier by the fact that I was drinking for the first time with my oldest and closest friends.

We sat against the schoolyard wall, trading wisecracks, stories, and reminiscences, engaging in the same bittersweet nostalgia of every Brooklyn expatriate we'd ever meet. Pining, like all of them, for the Brooklyn of our youth. Basking, like all of them, in the conviction that we'd lived in a special place at a special time—and that we were lucky for having lived it. Aware of the lasting bond between us. Knowing we'd venture back periodically, in search of the Brooklyn lost to us now, the Brooklyn that once was home. Aware of the pitfalls of sentimentality, but convinced that things would never be simpler or easier than they'd been back then.

Pooch recalled the day we'd tossed water balloons from the rooftop of his apartment building, howling as they exploded at the feet of unsuspecting passersby. Tommy Lowery remembered when he'd been on TV from Ebbets Field, shagging fungoes from Gil Hodges as part of Happy Felton's Knothole Gang. I recounted the details of an unforgettable punchball game, when we'd routed a bunch of kids from Gelston Avenue.

"We sure had some great times growing up," Lowery said.

"I'll never forget it," I agreed. "Brooklyn was the greatest place on *oith*."

"Shit yeah." Pooch laughed. "Great memories. Lotta good times. Something that'll be part of us forever. Shit, I guess sometimes you don't know how good things are till they're gone."

He popped open another high-top and raised it in a toast.

"Ain't no better place to grow up in than Brooklyn," he said, and then downed a gulp.

"At least *back then*, there wasn't," Nick Pappas intoned.

"Amen to that," Pooch said, taking another swig.

We killed off the six-pack, watching as two kids, trying to retrieve a spaldeen, scaled the chain-link fence separating the schoolyard from the backyard of an adjacent house. Other kids played Chinese handball against a rutted wall, and basketball on a rim that dangled precariously from a metal backboard. Down the street, a deliveryman toted a case of soda up a stoop and a sanitation truck sprayed jets of water across the asphalt, sweeping it clean with its huge rotating brushes.

And I was struck by another thought: Somehow, all of it would survive.

The bridge and expressway may have reshaped Bay Ridge, changed thousands of lives, and altered New York forever. It may have signaled an abrupt, unwelcome end to an entire way of life, to innocence and childhood itself.

But Bay Ridge would go on.

And so would Brooklyn.

Maybe it would no longer be the Brooklyn we'd grown up in. Maybe it would be changed in some elemental, intractable way. Maybe it would be *someone else's* Brooklyn. But it would survive. Continuing on its evolutionary path. Moving on like the rest of us.

Just like the borough's orchards and truck farms had given way to development, just like the early settlers had been supplanted by waves of immigrants, Brooklyn would continue to change. The old ethnic enclaves that teemed once with European immigrants would be inhabited by émigrés from different lands. The neighborhoods abandoned by white middle-class families would be alive with new sights and sounds, colors and textures, languages and lifestyles. Bodegas would occupy the sites where Irish taverns once stood. Movie theaters would be transformed into supermarkets, drugstores, and discothèques. Synagogues would become churches. Old landmarks would be replaced by new ones. New generations of children would grow up playing on the streets. There might even be a renaissance, a time when Brooklyn would come full circle, rise from its ashes.

I could see that, too.

I could see the floodtide of decline ceasing one day, people returning, money flowing back, new businesses taking hold, historic structures being restored, neighborhoods being reborn, a new layer of paint being added to the borough's age-old canvas, a new Brooklyn rising on the foundation of the old. Changing yet remaining, in its own unique way, what it *always* had been: vibrant, bustling and dynamic. A great bubbling cauldron of people engaged in the endless cycle of arriving, assimilating, co-existing, working, playing, celebrating, praying, mourning, dreaming, rising, and then departing.

Just like we did.

It was, I could see, just like Miss Greene told us in social studies: A story as old as Brooklyn itself. A story of relentless transformation, cycles of disappearance and resurgence, neighborhoods falling and rising again, a city as fluid as our lives. Forever being reshaped, reformed, redefined. Forever luring people—hopeful, optimistic, eager, calling Brooklyn home, and then moving on with their lives.

And now it was time for me to move on, too.

I said my good-byes to Pooch and the others, and hopped in my father's Plymouth for the drive to Valley Stream, heading to my new home past the spot where my old home once stood, past the barren tract that had once been Dahlgren Place.

The Verrazano-Narrows Bridge was lit up for the first time now, its mercury vapor lamps streaming up the span's towers and cables, its graceful form glowing like a low-slung necklace across the ink-black waters of the Narrows. On the shoreline, hundreds of spectators remained huddled against the chill as fireworks burst across the nighttime sky—just as they used to during the old Tuesday night spectaculars at Coney Island.

It felt good seeing the bridge that way. Majestic and serene. Bathed in a clean white light. Absent of heartache and discord.

It had been many things to many people. A metaphor for the New Brooklyn. The physical embodiment of dislocation and fear. The final link between New York and the rest of America. A symbol of the future. A monument to everything we'd lost.

But now I saw it in yet another light, in a way that neither Robert Moses, the visionary behind it, nor Othmar Ammann, the architect who'd designed it—or even Mr. Urbansky, the teacher who'd opened my eyes to its beauty—could ever have seen. Not simply as an architectural marvel. Not merely as something either frightful or inspiring. I saw it, instead, as something deeply personal. A crossing of sorts. A pivotal part of a journey I was on. Something at the heart of a young man's dream.

Driving past the bridge, I recognized, once and for all, that childhood was over. Brooklyn was behind me. Everything else was out there. Everything else was ahead.

Author's Note

The Death of Dahlgren Place is a work of fiction, inspired by events that took place between 1959 and 1964 in Brooklyn, NY—and pieced together from historical accounts, as well as from the recollections of the author and others who lived in Brooklyn during construction of the Verrazano-Narrows Bridge. Although based on real-life occurrences, many of the story's landmarks and place names are fictional, as are all its characters, with the singular exception of Robert Moses, and any resemblance to real people, living or dead, is unintended and coincidental.

Born in Brooklyn, New York, Eliot Sefrin graduated from The City College of New York and has worked as a newspaper and magazine reporter, editor, and publisher. *The Death of Dahlgren Place* is his second novel. His first *Under A Cloud*, was an award-winning story about a controversial police shooting in a poverty-stricken, minority neighborhood in New York. The author can be contacted through his web site, www.eliotsefrin.com. Graphic artist and cover designer Stephen Shub can be reached at www.frontiernet.net/~sshub.